I Am Having So Much Fun Here Without You

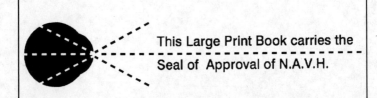

This Large Print Book carries the
Seal of Approval of N.A.V.H.

I Am Having So Much Fun Here Without You

Courtney Maum

THORNDIKE PRESS
A part of Gale, Cengage Learning

GALE
CENGAGE Learning·

Farmington Hills, Mich • San Francisco • New York • Waterville, Maine
Meriden, Conn • Mason, Ohio • Chicago

GALE
CENGAGE Learning®

LIBRARY OF CONGRESS CATALOGING-IN-PUBLICATION DATA

Maum, Courtney, 1978–
    I am having so much fun here without you / by Courtney Maum. — Large print edition.
        pages ; cm. — (Thorndike Press large print basic)
        ISBN 978-1-4104-7207-6 (hardcover) — ISBN 1-4104-7207-8 (hardcover)
        1. Families—Fiction. 2. Large type books. 3. Domestic fiction. I. Title.
    PS3613.A87396I26 2014b
    813'.6—dc23   2014021318

Published in 2014 by arrangement with Touchstone, a division of Simon & Schuster, Inc.

Printed in Mexico
2 3 4 5 6 7 18 17 16 15 14

THIS ONE'S FOR MY DOMO.

The river coursing
through us is dirty and deep.

— C. D. WRIGHT

1

Moments of great import are often tinged with darkness because perversely we yearn to be let down. And so it was that I found myself in late September 2002 at my first solo show in Paris feeling neither proud nor encouraged by the crowds of people who had come out to support my paintings, but saddened. Disappointed. If you had told me ten years ago that I'd be building my artistic reputation on a series of realistic oil paintings of rooms viewed through a keyhole, I would have pointed to my mixed-media collages of driftwood and saw blades and melted plastic ramen packets, the miniature green plastic soldiers I had implanted inside of Bubble Wrap, I would have jacked up the bass on the electronic musician Peaches' *Fancypants Hoodlum* album and told you I would never sell out.

And yet here I was, surrounded by thirteen narrative paintings that depicted rooms I had lived in, or in some way experienced with various women over the course of my life, all of these executed with barely visible brushstrokes in a palette of oil colors that would look good on any wall, in any context, in any country. They weren't contentious, they certainly weren't political, and they were selling like mad.

Now, my impression that I'd sold out was a private one, shared neither by my gallerist, Julien, happily traipsing about the room affixing red dots to the drywall, nor by the swell of brightly dressed expatriates pushing their way through conversations to knock their plastic glasses of Chablis against mine. There was nothing to be grim about; I was relatively young and this was Paris, and this night was a night that I'd been working toward for some time. But from the minute I'd seen Julien place a red sticker underneath the first painting I'd done in the series, *The Blue Bear,* I'd been plagued by the feeling that I'd done something irreversible, that I wasn't where I was supposed to be, that I hadn't been for months. Worse yet, I had no anchor, no one to set me back on course. My wife of seven years, a no-nonsense French lawyer who had stuck by my side in grad school as I showcased found sculptures constructed from other people's rubbish and dollhouses made out of Barbie Doll packaging, was a meter of my creative decline. Anne-Laure de Bourigeaud was not going to lie and tell me that I'd made it. The person who would have, the one person who I wanted to comfort and reboost me, was across the Channel with a man who was more reliable, easygoing, more *available* than me. And so it fell to the red stickers and the handshakes of would-be patrons to fuel me with self-worth. But halfway through the evening, with my own wife brightly sparkling in front of everyone but me, I was unmoored and drifting, tempted to sink.

In the car after the opening, Anne thrust the Peugeot into first gear. Driving stick in Paris is cathartic when she's anxious. I often let her drive.

Anne strained against her seat belt, reaching out to verify that our daughter was wearing hers.

"You all right, princess?" I asked, turning around also.

Camille smoothed out the billowing layers of the ruffled pink tube skirt she'd picked out for Dad's big night.

"Non . . ." she said, yawning.

"You didn't take the last Yop, right?" This

11

was asked of me, by my wife.

The streetlight cut into the car, illuminating the steering wheel, the dusty dashboard, the humming, buzzing electroland of our interior mobile world. Anne had had her hair done. I knew better than to ask, but I recognized the scent of the hairspray that made its metallic strawberry way, twice a month, into our lives.

I looked into her eyes that she had lined beautifully in the nonchalant and yet studied manner of the French. I forced a smile.

"No, I didn't."

"Good," she said, edging the car out of the parking spot. "Cam-Cam, we'll have a little snack when we get home."

Paris. Paris at night. Paris at night is a street show of a hundred moments you might have lived. You might have been the couple beneath the streetlamp by the Place de la Concorde, holding out a camera directed at themselves. You might have been the old man on the bridge, staring at the houseboats. You might have been the person that girl was smiling in response to as she crossed that same bridge on her cell phone. Or you might be a man in a shitty French export engaged in a discussion about liquid yogurt with his wife. Paris is a city of a hundred million lights, and sometimes they flicker. Sometimes they go out.

Anne pushed on the radio, set it to the news. The molten contralto of the female announcer filled the silence of our car. *"At an opening of a meeting at Camp David, British Prime Minister Tony Blair fully endorsed President Bush's intention to find and destroy the weapons of mass destruction purportedly hidden in Iraq."* And then the reedy liltings of my once-proud prime minister: *"The policy of inaction is not a policy we can responsibly subscribe to."*

"Right," said Anne. "Inaction."

"It's madness," I said, ignoring her pointed phrasing. "People getting scared because they're told to be. Without asking why."

Anne flicked on the blinker.

"It's mostly displacement, I think. *Verschiebung.*" She tilted her chin up, proud of her arsenal of comp lit terms stored from undergrad. "The big questions are too frightening. You know, where to actually place blame. So they've picked an easy target."

"You think France will go along with it?"

Her eyes darkened. "Never."

I looked out the window at the endless river below us, dividing the right bank from the left bank, the rich from the richer. "It's

13

a bad sign, though, Blair joining up," I added. "I mean, the British? We used to question things to death."

Anne nodded and fell silent. The announcer went on to summarize the fiscal situation across the Eurozone since the introduction of the euro in January of 2002.

Anne turned down the volume and looked in the rearview mirror. "Cam, honey. Did you have a good time?"

"Um, it was okay," our daughter, Camille, said, fiddling with her dress. "My favorite is the one with all the bicycles and then the, um, the one in the kitchen, and then the one with the blue bear that used to be in my room."

I closed my eyes at all the women, even the small ones, who wield words like wands; their phrases sugary and innocuous one minute, corrosive the next.

Aesthetically, *The Blue Bear* was one of the largest and thus most expensive paintings in the show, but because I had originally painted it as a gift for Anne, it was also the most barbed.

At 117 × 140 cm, *The Blue Bear* is an oil painting of the guest room in a friend's rickety, draft-ridden house in Centerville, Cape Cod, where we'd planned to spend the summer after grad school riding out the what-now crests of our midtwenties and to consider baby-making, which — if it wouldn't answer the "what now?" question — would certainly answer "what next?"

The first among our group of friends to get married, it felt rebellious and artistic to consider having a child while we were still young and thin of limb and riotously in love. We also thought, however, that we were scheming in dreamland, safe beneath the mantra that has been the downfall of so many privileged white people: *an unplanned pregnancy can't happen to us.*

Color us surprised, then, when a mere five weeks after having her IUD removed, Anne missed her period and started to notice a distinct throbbing in her breasts. We thought it was funny — so symbiotic were we in our tastes and desires that a mere discussion could push a possibility into being. We were delighted — amused, even. We felt blessed.

During those first few weeks on the Cape, I was still making sculptures out of found objects, and Anne, a gifted illustrator, was interspersing her studies for the European bar with new installments of a zine she'd started while studying abroad in Boston. A play on words with "Anne" (her name) and *âne* (the French word for "donkey"), *Âne in America* depicted the missteps of a shy, pes-

15

simistic Parisian indoctrinated into the boisterous world of cotton-candy-hearted, light-beer-guzzling Americans who relied on their inexhaustible optimism to see them through all things.

But as the summer inched on and I watched her caress her growing belly as she read laminated hardcovers from the town library, a curious change came over this Englishman who up until that point had been the enemy of sap. I became a sentimentalist, a tenderheart, an easy-listening sop. Much like how the lack of oxygen in planes makes us tear up at the most improbable of romantic comedies, as that child grew within Anne into a living, true-blue thing instead of a discussed possibility, I lost interest in the sea glass and the battered plastic cans and the porous wood I'd been using all summer and was filled with the urge to paint something lovely for her. For them both.

The idea of painting a scene viewed through a keyhole came to me when I happened upon Anne in the bedroom one morning pondering a stuffed teddy bear that our friends, the house's owners, had left for us on a chair as an early baby gift. They were, at that point, our closest friends and the first people we had told about the

16

pregnancy, but there was something about that stuffed animal that was both touching and foreboding. Would the baby play with it? Would the baby live? I could see the mix of trepidation and excitement playing over Anne's face as she turned the stuffed brown thing over in her hands, and it comforted me to know that I wasn't alone with my roller-coaster rides between pridefulness and fear.

And still — Anne is a woman, and I, rather evidently, am not. There was a great difference between what was happening to her and what was potentially happening — going to happen — to us. Which is how I got the idea to approach the scene from a distance, as an outsider, a voyeur.

Except for the tattered rug and the rocking chair beside a window with a view of the gray sea, I left the room uninhabited save for the stuffed bear that I painted seated on the rocking chair, a bit larger than it was in real life, and not at all brown. I painted the bear blue, and not a dim pastel color that might have been a trick of the light and sea, but a vibrating cerulean that lent to the otherwise staid atmosphere a pulsating point of interest. Unsettling in some lights, calming in others — the blue stood for the thrill of the unknown.

When I gave the painting to Anne, she never asked why the bear was blue. She knew why, inherently, and in the giving of the painting, I felt doubly convinced that I loved her, that I *truly* loved her, that I would love her for all time. What other woman could wordlessly accept such a confession? A tangible depiction of both happiness and fear?

In the fall, that painting traveled with our belongings in a ship across the Atlantic, and it waited in a Parisian storage center until the birth of our daughter, when we finally had a home. We hung it in the nursery, ignoring the comments from certain friends and in-laws that the bear would have been a lot less off-putting and child *appropriate* if it hadn't been blue. The very fact that other people didn't seem to "get it" convinced us that we had a shared sensibility, something truly special, making the painting more important than a private joke.

We continued feeling that way until Camille turned three and started plastering her walls with her own drawings and paper cutouts and origami birds, and we began to feel like we'd enforced something upon her that only meant something to us. So we put it in the basement, intending to scout for a new bookshelf system so that we would have enough wall space to hang the painting in our bedroom. But then I met Lisa, and too much time had passed, and when *The Blue Bear* was brought up, the discussions were accusatory, spiteful. And so it stayed in the basement, hidden out of sight, not so much forgotten as disdained.

Months later, when I started gathering the paintings for the exhibition, my gallerist said he still remembered the first key painting I'd ever shown him, and that he'd been impressed by it. Might I consider including it in the show? The suspicion that *The Blue Bear* didn't mean what it used to mean was confirmed when I told Anne about Julien's proposition and she said if he thought it made the show more complete somehow, what did she care. Go ahead and listen to him. Sell.

After finding a parking spot outside of our house in the fourteenth, we moved automatically into our pit-crew positions to execute the life-sustaining gestures of our domestic life. While Anne gave Camille the aforementioned liquid yogurt, I went upstairs to draw her a bath, adding a peach bath ball that she liked. Anne came in to supervise her splashing while I tidied up the kitchen. Then I tucked her in bed and kissed her, and her mother read her a story before lights-out.

In our bathroom, I brushed my teeth quickly and splashed water on my face. Without it ever being stated, I knew well enough to be out before Anne came in so that she could take care of her own needs without having to look up and see the reflection of my face next to hers.

I slipped into bed and waited for the distant sound of singsong reading to fade. When I heard my wife's footsteps in the hallway, I picked up the book on my nightstand and started to read *Poor Fellow My Country,* the longest Australian novel of all time.

Anne went into the bathroom, shut me out with a closed door. When she came to bed, she did so smelling of rosemary with her dark hair in a high bun, hair I had been besotted with back in grad school, but now no longer touched. She said good night without looking at me, and I said good night back.

It has been seven months and sixteen days since I last had sex with my wife. I loved her, and I lost sight of her, and I took up with someone else. And although she never asked who it was or when it started or exactly what it was — sex, flirtation, lust —

she said she didn't want to know, she wanted it to be *done.* She wanted me as a husband and a father again, but no longer as a friend. And I made a promise to her that I would end it, although the relationship had already reached its final chapter. By the time Anne confronted me, certain I had a mistress, my mistress had left me to *marry* someone else. I told Lisa that I loved her, and she didn't care.

And so I find myself in a kind of love lock: pining for the wrong person, grieving beside a woman whose body I can't touch, being given a second chance I can't find the clarity to take.

Once upon a time, I was very in love with Anne-Laure, and — incredibly — she was in love with me. And sometimes, it still comes at me, the sight of her, my dark-haired, sea-eyed beauty, a woman I have built a life with that I don't deserve. And I will think, Deserve her. Get back to the way you were in your apartment in Rhode Island, class-skipping together naked under a duvet, laughing about how many pillows Americans like on a bed; back to the woody Barolos she brown-bagged to BYOB dives; get back to her intelligence, her daringness. Get back to the French in her, timeless, free, and subtle. Get back to the person faking sleep beside you. Reach over, beg, get back.

Impossible as it is, I know that Anne still loves me. And when I catch myself looking at her across a room, atop a staircase, coming home from work with a shopping bag full of carefully chosen things, everything comes flooding back and it makes me fucking ache because I can no longer connect these memories that feel so warm when I think about them to what we're currently living. Somewhere down the line, it got hard to just be kind, and I don't know why, and I don't know when, and when I see all of the reasons to be back in love with her again, I want more than anything to be swept up in the tide of before. Somewhere in the losing of my love for Anne, I lost a little bit of my love for everything else. And I don't know what I'm waiting for to get those feelings back. Nor how long I — we — can wait.

2

Near the end of September, Julien called to tell me that he had mail for me, and news. After walking Camille to school as I did each morning, I bought an elephant ear at a neighboring bakery and ate it standing behind a news kiosk, biding my time for whatever awaited me in a scented envelope.

When Lisa said she was leaving me, she asked if she could write. The paradox of her request always makes me think of the Serge Gainsbourg song "I Love You, Me Neither." Lisa Bishop even looks like Jane Birkin, the little minx. In any case, because I'm an idiot slash glutton for punishment, I said yes. I said write me at the gallery. I said never at my home.

When I tried to imagine what these letters would be like, I had visions of me clue-searching for evidence that Lisa missed me, that she felt she'd made a mistake. I expected that when she finally did get married and was thus exposed to the libido-numbing administrations of conjugal life, that the letters might increase in volume and in temperature, that they'd be lurid, sexy things. In my fantasy world, I wrote her back, keeping a message-in-a-bottle thing going at the gallery, keeping my (now only intellectual) dalliances far away from home. *I miss you back. I'm empty. But you're right, it had to end.*

In reality, however, Lisa's letters have been so disheartening, I haven't responded. I've thought about writing her to ask her to stop writing, but there's something so terribly childish about that, so very "sticks and stones," I haven't done that either. Besides, sticks and stones *have* broken my bones, and words have also hurt me.

I don't mean to be churlish about it, but you spend seven years on top-notch behavior only to finally give in, falter, seriously fuck things up, the least your accomplice can do is have the decency to love you back.

I always assumed that Lisa wanted me to leave my wife. I spent a lot of time wondering why else would she be with me, and not enough time asking her why she actually was. And why was she? For the sex, she finally said. The novelty. The *fun.* And this from an American, a *journalist,* a woman endowed with neither the prudishness of her countrywomen nor the ethics of her trade. This isn't how things are supposed to *work* when you're a cheater. Lisa was supposed to go all fatal attraction for me. She was supposed to want to meet my kid and dream about being a fab stepmum who was a taller, brighter, *wilder* version of Anne. What she wasn't supposed to do was casually drop over a light lunch of nigiri sushi that she was leaving me for a cutlery designer from London, a prissy toff named Dave.

"Good Lord, he doesn't go by 'David'?" I remember asking with a cough.

"No." She stuck her chopsticks into the center of the wasabi, two stakes through the heart. "He's very nice."

"Oh, I'm sure he is, with a name like that."

"Please," she said. "You're not winning any originality awards with 'Richard.' " She sighed and pushed away her sushi. "Are you seriously going to say that you're surprised?"

My jaw dropped, answering her question. "When did you even meet this person? When did you have time?"

"You're married, Richard. I have lots of time."

She got the check and we took a walk around the Seine while she prattled on about how she'd done a piece on him for the *Herald Tribune* lifestyle section. Purportedly, he was the first culinary arts designer to introduce the plastic spork to take-out restaurants in England, although the validity of this claim was currently being challenged by a Norwegian upstart named Lars.

"It's a pretty stressful time for him," she said, fussing with her scarf.

When a woman you have cried against postcoitus tells you she's leaving you for a man whose claim to fame is the conjoining of a soup spoon and a fork, you wait for the ringer, you wait for the joke. What you don't wait for is a second revelation that she's leaving you to get *married*.

By this time we were seated on a concrete bench by the Seine, its gritty surface speckled with broken green glass, accompanied by the acrid smell of urine.

"I thought you didn't *like* marriage," I said. "I thought you didn't believe in it."

"It's funny," she said, flicking a piece of glass onto the ground. "Everyone says when you know, you know. And it's true. Something just clicked. It's all very calming, really. It's not half as dramatic as it was with you."

I looked at her incredulously to see if she hadn't gone and sprouted a demonic windup key between her shoulder blades.

"Are you mad at me?" she asked, pulling my hand against her face. "You know it wasn't going to last with us, even if it's been great." She kissed the inside of my palm with her nasty mouth half open, so her kiss was wet. "And it *has* been great." She started kissing my fingers. I pulled my hand away.

"You're serious."

Her hazel eyes got big. "I am," she said. "I'm leaving. I'm moving to London in two months."

I stared at my sneakers. I stared at the Seine.

"I'm crazy about you," she continued. "You know that. But this has to stop. If I waited any longer, it would probably ruin your life."

Twenty-nine years old to my thirty-four with no idea that I'd been having to sleep in the guest bedroom of my own house because the energy she'd filled me with, this fucking yen for life, the desire at every hour of every single day to be inside her, had made me a walking dead man in my home life, that I had entire days where I couldn't remember what I said to my own daughter on our walk to school; that at gunpoint I couldn't recall my wife's outfits from the past week — from the past *night* — that I drank more than I used to and I ate less than I used to and I never, ever dreamed that we were done.

There wasn't much more to it — I saw Lisa four more times before she left for London and we never had sex again. After double-timing me for I don't know how long, she felt self-righteous, almost evangelical, about being engaged. She said she'd gotten it out of her system, the cheating, and that she was truly looking forward to being a good and dutiful wife as if she was embarking on some kind of vision quest, my God.

And then she left me. Left me unsure whether to want her back or hate her, left me with the missive that I shouldn't try to win her back, but could she keep in touch with me — from time to time, could she write. Left me with the mother of my child demanding that I put an end to whatever was numbing my insides, and the fact that I didn't get to do that, that I didn't get to choose, that I wasn't the one who finally manned up and said "end this," has made it that much more difficult to find my way back into my life.

As I was wiping a deluge of pastry flecks off of my pullover, getting ready to head to the gallery, a man in purple high-tops and a yellow helmet pulled up next to the news kiosk on a beat-up scooter.

"Richard!" he yelled, flipping up his face shield. "I *thought* that was you!"

Just when I thought my spirits couldn't get any lower, my submarine heart took a dive. I wiped my buttery fingers on my jeans and stretched my hand out to greet his in an amalgamation of a fist bump and a punch.

"Patrick," I said. "How's it going?"

"Good, good! I was just on my way to my new studio, in Bercy? And at the red light I was like, is it or isn't it? I haven't seen you in years!"

"I know, man," I managed, with a "whatever" shrug. "Offspring."

"Oh, yeah? Me, too." He took off his helmet. "It's good to see you! I kept thinking I'd run into you somewhere, but . . . I don't know. Have you been traveling?"

"Not much. You?" I said, preparing myself to resent every answer to every question I was about to ask. "I thought you moved back to Denmark?"

"I did. For a year. But once you've been in the States, everything feels kind of rigid, don't you think? I just finished a residency in Texas, actually, at the Ballroom Marfa?

29

Brought the wife. The kid . . . oh, here!" he said, reaching into his back pocket. "I just came from the printers actually, so . . ." He waited as I examined the flyer in my hand. "I've got a show coming up at the Musée Bourdelle. Performance art, if you can believe it."

"Oh, yeah?" I said, my stomach tightening.

"Yeah, it's pretty . . ." He shifted his weight on the scooter. "Have you ever read *The Interrogative Mood* by Padgett Powell?

"It's just a book of questions," he continued, after my "no." "A novel of them, really. Question after question. For example." He adjusted his helmet under his arm. " 'Should a tree be pruned? Is having collected Coke bottles for deposit money part of the fond stuff of your childhood?' "

"You've memorized them?"

"No," he said, with a laugh. "Just a couple here and there. They've got me set up in Bourdelle's old studio, where I'll be in residence for a week, sitting there with the book. Each person can come in one by one and sit with me, and I'll just pick up with the questions from where I left off with the last person. Anyway," he said, nodding toward the flyer. "You should come! I'm really excited about it."

30

"Yeah," I said, running my thumb across the heading. "I might."

"Well, I've gotta run, but it would be really great to catch up some more, hear what you've been up to? Hell, our kids could have a playdate!"

I smiled at him weakly. "Seriously?"

" 'If someone approached you saying, "Lead me to the music," how would you respond?' "

I blinked. He blinked back at me. He shrugged. "It's from my show."

"Oh," I said, pushing a laugh out. "Cool."

He eased his scooter back to the pavement with his purple high-tops, repeating that he really, really meant it. Coffee. Soon.

And off he went. Goddamn Patrick Madsen, who was so generous and wholehearted I couldn't even hate him and his rip-off show. Back at RISD, he'd majored in kinetic animation — for his sophomore evaluation, he'd outfitted the heads of four taxidermied boars with recordings from the film version of *Roe v. Wade* that were only activated when a woman walked past. For his thesis show, he wired and grooved a series of his German grandfather's photographs from the Second World War so that they could actually be played on a record player. The sounds that came out of the photographs were terrifying; high-pitched and scratched. He won a grant for that, which he used to study robotics and engineering in Osaka, Japan. And now he was doing performance art. If I hadn't felt like enough of a hack for making a sell-out show of accessible oil paintings (scenes viewed through doorways? *Jesus*) I certainly did now.

When I finally arrived at the gallery, I found Julien *comme d'habitude,* his desk littered with single-use espresso cups, his ear glued to the phone. I tossed the paper bag with a croissant I'd brought him onto his desk and waited for him to finish up his conversation. *"Tout à fait, tout à fait."* He nodded while simultaneously throwing me a thumbs-up for the croissant. "It *is* a lot of yellow. Do you have good windows? It'll look more sage-colored in natural light."

He flicked a ten-centime piece my way so that I could get an instant coffee from the machine in the back. By the time I returned, he was done with his phone call and had started in on his croissant.

"People are weird about yellow. Too much yellow, they freak. These idiots want to put a five-meter painting in their kitchen be-cause they've got this new table that — anyway." He reached into a drawer. "Here."

I had two letters. From the manic script on the outside of the envelope, I knew the first was from my mum. The second was from Lisa Bishop, evil colonizer of Englishmen's hearts.

"Humph," I said, sitting down to start with the envelope from my fellow Haddon. She'd never given me an explanation for it, but my mother had been sending weird news snippets and recipes to me at the gallery for years. She sent postcards to our house on the Rue de la Tombe-Issoire, but the strange stuff she sent here. Whenever we saw her over the holidays, I considered asking her about it, but there was something beguiling about the irrationality of the arrangement that moved me to keep quiet.

The news snippets and recipes rarely came with a personal note, although once in a while she'd scrawl something beneath a heading. This particular post contained a double missive: a recipe for grape soup with the annotation *We've tried it!* and an article from that day's *Sun*.

BRITS 45 MINS FROM DOOM

by George Pascoe-Watson

British servicemen and tourists in Cyprus

could be annihilated by germ warfare missiles launched by Iraq, it was revealed yesterday.

They could thud into the Mediterranean island within 45 minutes of tyrant Saddam Hussein ordering an attack.

And they could spread death and destruction through warheads carrying anthrax, mustard gas, sarin, or ricin.

The 50-page report, drawn up by British Intelligence chiefs, says the dictator has defied a United Nations ban by retaining up to 20 Al-Hussein missiles with a maximum range of 400 miles.

It adds: They could be used with conventional, chemical, or biological warheads and are capable of reaching a number of countries in the region including Cyprus.

I tossed the clippings to Julien, a big fan of my mum's taste.

"Have you been following this?" I asked.

"You can make soup out of *grapes*?"

"No, the *conflict,* you idiot. What do you think?"

"Makes me glad to be French, actually."

I grabbed the paper back and searched for a new topic.

"I ran into an old friend of mine, from art school, earlier," I volunteered, watching

34

Julien open his checkbook. "Kind of an activist. But he's doing performance art now."

"Hmm," he said, continuing to multitask. "Does that sell?"

"Performance art?" He signed the check and slipped it into an orange-and-white envelope bearing the logo of France's only telecommunications company. "Nope."

"His will."

"Why so glum, Haddon? Did you want my croissant?"

"No." I sighed, pushing back from the table. "It was just that I was thinking. I need to shake things up."

"What, like *that*?" Indicating the article in my hands. "Death and destruction? Something *performative*?"

I crossed my arms. "Well . . . yeah."

"Can we do one thing at a time here?" He reached behind him for a manila envelope perched within risky distance of a vase. "I called you with good news, and you've brought me *this*." He made an all-encompassing gesture in the direction of my face. "*The Blue Bear* went. Ten thou."

I felt my heart slide down my ribs like something ill-digested. There was a faint ringing in my ears and my eye sockets felt punched. I'd managed to convince myself that no one would want that painting, that just like the well-intentioned visitors during the months after Camille's birth, no one would "get it," and that it would find its way back home.

"Rich?" Julien said, handing me the envelope. "It sold?"

"Right," I said, startled. "That's good. Great."

"Curious thing, actually, as it went to a countryman of yours — someone in London. He was at the show, apparently. Bit of a strange bird. You know, blah blah blah, it's a gift for his fiancée, blah blah blah, their house. These people, they tell you everything. I hear about their floor layouts, their children, the chevron carpet in the —"

I ripped the envelope open while Julien dribbled on. The contract stipulated the sale of *The Blue Bear* to one Dave Lacey from London, England.

"He specifically said it's for his *fiancée*?" I said, looking up.

"Or his partner. Why?"

My heart clenched. "*Lisa* moved to London. *Lisa* has a fiancé."

Julien rolled his eyes. "Well, his name isn't Lisa." He pointed at the contract. "It's Dave."

"But that's just it," I said, tracing my

finger around the postmark on Lisa's latest letter. "That's his name. Did you *invite* her to the show?"

"Did I invite her — Richard. Come back to us on Earth. No, I didn't *invite* her to your opening, I figured you'd be coming with your *wife.* Now, it's a coincidence, I'll grant you that, but I had a protracted conversation with this fellow and I'm pretty sure his 'fiancée' isn't going to be walking down the aisle in a gown."

"But same-sex marriage isn't legal in England," I protested, my head reeling with the reasons Lisa would have bought a painting of mine, and this one in particular.

"He talked to me about throw pillows. I don't think this guy's your man. And even if he was, it's sold, darling. Can we be happy? Can we move on? This was a great show for you. Are you going to read that or not?"

I looked down at Lisa's letter. I shook my head, not.

"Suit yourself, you flagellator. It's over, but not done. Ah, another thing. I'm getting an intern." He liberated a blue folder from beneath a slew of paperwork and handed it to me. "Which one? I was thinking about that Bérénice girl. Look, she's from Toulouse." He pointed at the printout with a pencil.

"She included a photo? That's legal?"

"My thinking," he said, ignoring me, "is that with a name like that, she'll be very manageable. Girls from the southwest, they're a bit dull, you know, but studious. They don't get uppity about things like the Parisians. Like she's not going to have a crying fit if I ask her to send a fax."

"I can't talk about this," I said, standing with my mail. "I need to think."

"Yes, well, there's not much to think about. The painting was for sale, it sold. That's the way these things work, Richard."

"Yeah, thanks."

He stood to embrace me with a peck on both cheeks.

"Take Anne out to dinner. Celebrate." He took one look at my face before rescinding this suggestion. "Or rather, wait for the next one. You'll see. They're all going to go. Be happy about it, will you? Live in the now." He walked me to the tall glass doors at the entrance. On the pavement, just to the right of the gallery, a small, untended Chihuahua was squeezing out a crap.

"And let me know if you try that recipe," he said, pulling the door open. "I love anything with grapes."

■ ■ ■ ■

I had a place near the Premier Regard where I liked to read Lisa's letters. Far from my house, but close to the gallery, I could trick myself into thinking I was reading business correspondence; a letter from a fan. In front of the Église Saint-Sulpice, there was a little square around a fountain that hadn't worked in years. There were these mechanized cement columns surrounding the northern side of the square that slid below the pavement when an emergency vehicle had to come through, or when there was a funeral — in which case the emergency vehicle was a hearse. Reading them in the open, surrounded by nannies and panhandlers and nuns, allowed me to soften the signification of their existence. I was just a man on a conical structure opening up a letter. No harm in reading mail! But the truth was that as long as Lisa kept writing me, Julien was right about it: our relationship was over, but it wasn't done.

Usually, I approached these reading sessions with the excited energy of a child, but today I felt anxious. Running into Patrick had extinguished the embers of my artistic self-worth, *The Blue Bear* had sold — an unretractable mistake — and it had possibly sold to my ex-mistress, leaving me feeling like I was at the end of both my creative and my domestic life.

Lisa had never been jealous of Anne-Laure. Selfish, yes, and flighty, but vindictive, she was not. There was no reason for her to do something as manipulative as buy a painting that I'd done for my pregnant wife, but at the same time the coincidences seemed too outlandish. A buyer from London. A buyer named Dave.

Lisa and I had still been seeing each other when I was finishing the paintings for the Premier Regard show — she loved the whole idea of it, assigning more meaning to keys as objects than I did. While Anne more or less turned a blind eye to my two-year dip into the commercial art pool, tolerating it as you would the "let me do a play for you!" phase in a young child, Lisa genuinely liked the key paintings. She helped me feel like I wasn't selling out so much as providing the public with a set of experiences they could connect to. More than a piece of metal to be inserted into a lock, she got me thinking about the passage keys grant to places that can't be reached with the aid of a locksmith, or by a letter with a stamp, and how the taking away of keys sometimes denies access to the truly physical: bellies, buttocks, closed eyelids, toes. Mind you, she gave me this little pep talk six weeks before asking for the key to her apartment back because she was getting married, she was moving, just like that. Sitting there on the cold concrete, I reconsidered her character. Maybe she *was* calculating enough to have orchestrated the purchase of the bear.

Lisa's stationery was petal yellow with her name letter-pressed in green. This stationery always struck me as out-of-characterly plutocratic. Even my own wife didn't have monogrammed stationery, and she had a flipping *de* in her maiden name.

September 18, 2002

Dear Richard,

The letter started, as most letters addressed to me did.

It's been seven weeks now since I've arrived in London. Isn't that nuts? I haven't even unpacked all of my bags yet, I've mostly been concentrating on the bedroom and the kitchen, which Dave is letting me redo. I'm going to use

41

a lot of white tile, even for the walls, like that restaurant I told you about in Stockholm. Remember?

I think of you often and I wonder if you are okay. You were in very bad shape when I left Paris. So panicked. So urgent. I guess you're still mad at me for leaving, but one day you'll realize what a useless emotion anger really is. Honestly, what you were trying to hold on to with us would have perished in the holding. Don't turn into one of those expats who thinks that artists need to suffer in order to be creative! There's so many of them in Paris. They all have thinning hair and navy boat sweaters and, now that I think of it, a lot of them are named Greg.

Anyway. Back in college, I had a writing teacher who told me that writing should be fun. Back then, I didn't believe him (I was reading lots of Plath), but it's true that once I started working, I had so little time for my own writing. When I did sit down to do it, I often thought, What a shame that this isn't fun! Until I changed my tone a bit. Which reminds me! It looks like the *Independent* is going to run the design column that I pitched. Can you believe they took an American? It's curiously well paid!

I've been trying to work on my own stuff twice a week, and on weekends, I go in town and take photographs. Or I go out in the countryside and take photographs. Dave is so organized, he's inspiring me to get organized myself. Every morning he wakes up, has a cup of black coffee, reads one or two articles, and then shuts himself in his office until five o'clock, when he comes down and has a tea. He keeps on working for an hour or two until he's done for the day. Got goose bumps yet? I know how much you hate routine. His creative process is an organized one. But does that mean it's boring? I don't know, it's up for argument; but I'll tell you something, Richard, stability — when tossed in with the right amount of love, respect, passion (and a little bit of sex!) — is better than you think. I hope, for your sake, that you've learned how to live your life a little better. Maybe you should try giving up alcohol for a while. Maybe you should try being <u>faithful</u>!! :) I'm happy, Richard. Are you?

Always thinking of you,
Lisa

Like always with Lisa's letters, once I

finished reading them, I was left with a seasickness of conflicting emotions. Pleasure, because she'd written, and disappointment, because her letters never amounted to what I really wanted: a confession that she missed me, that she'd made a mistake in leaving, that she wanted me back.

With that figurative letter in hand, I could recoup some dignity and control. I could write back "no." But what happened with *these* letters, these catalogs of her coffee *and* tea-drinking fiancé, the white tiles of her new life, was that they left me jealous and distracted. It was calculating of her really: because the letters left me wanting more from them than I was getting, I still wanted her.

I had to ask Lisa to stop writing me, but I lacked the courage to ask. What would a future be like without the occasional proof that she'd existed? That, for a bottled moment, she'd adored me back? I owed it to Anne-Laure to cut off communication with Lisa. I'd promised her that. But I needed it — I really needed it — this secret line to something private. One day soon, I'd get in touch with Lisa and tell her to stop writing. But in the meantime, along with other home improvements to my marriage, I had to find the decency to tell my wife that *The Blue Bear* had sold.

3

I certainly can't blame the French education system for the problems in my marriage. In fact, I'd say that the French make it almost too easy to have a life when you're a parent. State-subsidized spaces in the neighborhood nursery are every citizen's right, and the public school system is gratis. The cafeteria serves a cheese course, classes run till 4:30 p.m. (and that's without extracurriculars), and most schools run on a six-day program, with half days on Wednesdays for elementary school students and Saturdays also, once your kid's in middle school. That's right, in four short years, my daughter will have school on Saturdays, from 9 a.m. to lunch. Now, in theory, yes, that means one can't go running off on a weekend getaway if one can't get a sitter, but it also means that one can start doing something outrageous on a Friday like knock back a bit o' port.

Sometimes I think that I wouldn't live in France if I hadn't married a native, but it probably isn't true. I spent two years at the École des Beaux-Arts exchange program in Paris and two more years in the graduate painting program at RISD in Providence, and although I had more fun in America, I never could have afforded to have a broken wrist set, and I sure as hell would never have coughed up what those people pay for their childrens' higher education. If Anne and I already have rows over our vacation and recreation fund on her fancy lawyer salary and my less fancy artist one with a daughter in a free school that serves her duck casserole and Reblochon before naptime, I can only imagine what would happen if we had to dole out fifty grand a year so that Cam could get felt up on a pool table littered with plastic Solo Cups by some imbecile named Chuck.

And yet. And yet. Sometimes I feel that Anne and I lost something that was essential about us — to us, even — when we left the States. We were foreigners studying in what was admittedly a strange land where the customs and mores never ceased to provide us with fodder for private jokes. Everything delighted us. We were insouciant and pompous. Anne started taking hip-hop ballet classes and wearing linen trench coats. She stocked canned snails in my pantry and empty shells in my freezer "just in case." On weekends in Boston, she'd make me stand in crowded places and report back on whether I agreed with her about how *clean* people smelled. "Like mangoes," she said. "American girls always smell like fruit."

And she was my best critic. As talented as — if not more talented than — I as an illustrator, she had a built-in bullshit detector that served as a barometer for my graduate thesis show: an interactive series of pop-culture Russian dolls that depicted the rise or fall of cultural figures. For instance, in one set, the largest doll showed a painting of American women working on a factory floor during World War II. Under that, an image of a two-car garage, followed by a milk carton, then a stalk of corn. The smallest doll represented Martha Stewart. In another set, I'd shellacked newspaper clips of union protesters throughout Britain, and underneath that, an illustration of a British-made Gloster aircraft and so on and so forth with icons of the former British manufacturing industry until you came to a small doll representing Margaret Thatcher.

When we first moved back to Paris, I was still doing pop-culture politico work like this

— or rather, I was *trying* to in between changing nappies and running out to Franprix for overripe bananas. But sometimes, you just get really tired of keeping up the pretenses. It's like making small talk with the stranger seated next to you during dinner at a wedding. You're firing through the appetizers and first round of drinks, no problem, but by the time the chicken Marsala arrives — gelatinous and tepid — you think, Lord help me, I've got nothing left to say. Without realizing I was doing so, I slipped into time-out mode. With my art. My wife.

To her credit, Anne never asked that I start working on more conventional projects. I put the pressure on myself. Or rather, I felt pressure coming from Anne's family and transformed this into pressure upon myself. At that point, Anne was still studying for the requisite exams that would allow her to practice law in Europe. Aside from small amounts I made selling paintings in group shows and a laughable hourly rate I got from a translating job Monsieur de Bourigeaud found me in his firm, we weren't really making money. Oh, we *would* be, soon enough, or rather, Anne would be, but in the beginning, Anne's parents took care of us, even providing the down payment on our house.

Now, as a lower-middle-class lad from Hemel Hempstead, this kind of silver-spooning shouldn't have sat well with me at all. And at first, it didn't. Anne and I saw ourselves as comrades-in-arms, well educated and levelheaded, yes, but still intrepid. We wanted to do things *our* way. We hadn't needed anyone's help before this, and we didn't see why we needed it then.

That changed when we started visiting the flats that our paltry savings could afford us: heartless, one-room studios on the sixth floors of charmless buildings in neighborhoods where you wouldn't want to walk alone at night, and all this while Anne was seven months pregnant. In such a place, I wouldn't have been able to store my art equipment, let alone do any painting, and Anne began to have nightmares in which she found herself welded not just to the baby, but to the walls of the apartment, terrified that she'd be a homebound mum forever, with no way back out.

And then one Sunday, after lunch at their home in the wooded suburbs of Le Vésinet, her parents took us to visit a small town house in the fourteenth arrondissement of Paris: three stories with a tidy plot of land in the back, just big enough for a garden, and an unfinished work space on the second floor that could function as a studio. As I walked through the light-filled area of the largest private work area I might potentially ever have, I found myself hoping that Anne would swallow her pride and accept the blue blood coursing through her like a prodigal daughter coming home.

And she did. She caved. We both did. We accepted the Bourigeauds' financial help and started our new life. Due to a mind that is more pragmatic than mine, Anne never felt guilty about accepting her parents' cash. Instead, she repaid their generosity by being the very best mother, daughter, and lawyer that she could be, while I let the shame of such a handout build inside of me until it made me feel like less of a man, less of an artist, less than everything I had one day hoped to be.

It was around this time that I started looking for representation in Paris. Although I'd had several pieces from my thesis work along with some of my former installations exhibited in group shows around Europe, I couldn't find a gallerist willing to give me my own show. Apparently, I wasn't coming at the political-pop angle in the right way. My work wasn't loud enough, it wasn't flashy, it wasn't neon pink. Others told me that there wasn't enough cohesion among my various pieces, or that there was too much of it, to come back and visit when I was "known." Of course, you couldn't "be" someone without getting your own show, and you couldn't get your own show if you were a nobody. Feeling despondent, I nevertheless forced myself to visit the last three galleries on my list, one of which was the Premier Regard run by Julien Lagrange.

When he looked through my portfolio, he fixated on a photograph I'd slid near the back, a section most people never got to because they'd already decided that I didn't have that "thing" that they were looking for. But Julien was interested in *The Blue Bear,* the one painting that had nothing to do with all my other work, the one painting that was schmaltzy.

"Do you have other ones like this?" he asked.

"What," I said, "like, awful?"

He laughed. "No, depictive. Accessible. From the same point of view?"

I said I'd messed about with other scenes viewed through a keyhole, but it wasn't a direction I'd pursued because it was amateurish and sappy.

"Yeah," he said, drumming his fingers on the photo. "But this, I could sell."

He explained that due to the success of a British nautical painter he represented called Stephen Haslett, he had a solid clientele of British and American expats who liked to buy art that looked romantic in their new homes.

"They don't go for the modern stuff," he said. "These are the kind of people who come back from holiday with Provençal tablecloths and salt. Anyway, if you could put together a set of key paintings, I could give you a show."

I didn't believe him, but we stayed in touch. In fact, rather quickly we became friends, which is a hard thing to do in a country where people consider everyone they didn't go to elementary school with a stranger. Julien kept bringing up the key paintings, and I kept replying that I found his proposition beneath me. The problem was that I wasn't working on anything else. Aside from its joys and unparalleled weirdness, parenthood had me in a fathomless, sleep-deprived, creative rut. I could barely manage to squeeze oil paint onto a palette — I wasn't in any frame of mind to do cutting-edge art. Plus, I was keen to get out from underneath the Bourigeauds' golden thumb. I was ready — eager, even — to experience what it felt like to be commercially successful. *The Blue Bear* had been a nice experience for me, cathartic. Would it be so wrong to keep on painting tableaux seen through doors?

The creation of the key paintings was effortless. Meditative, even. Once I had a go at Julien's proposition, I found I couldn't stop. Having been corporally bound to one woman for so many years, exploring moments from my past relationships felt like a release. In hindsight, the nostalgic fugue state that catapulted my process was probably one of the reasons I was primed to meet Lisa when I did.

In addition to being a sentimental hat tip to ex-girlfriends, the show was also a salutation to my erstwhile twenties. The subject of *School Days,* for example, is a stall of lime-lined urinals in an abandoned elementary school that had been reappropriated as a squat.

R's Kitchen shows an overloaded sink that belonged to a New Zealand finger painter who liked communal nighttime Rollerblading and piercing people's ears. I am happy to say that I left that relationship with my distaste for both in-line skating and the smell of rubbing alcohol intact.

Pet Lover shows a mudroom back in Providence, and underneath the raincoats there's a kennel with no dog. But the real subject is an American girl named Elliott, the last woman I dated before meeting Anne.

And there were others, sixteen of them in total. But as much as they cast a glimpse into love's beginning, the paintings chosen for the Premier Regard show offer a still life of love's end. And the sale of *The Blue Bear* represents the saddest end of all.

By the time my wife got home that night, I had a pot of cream-and-cracked-pepper pasta bubbling on the stove along with a green salad with Roquefort and red pears, and an open bottle of Chinon breathing on the counter. My guilt over having received another of Lisa's letters coupled with the fact that I had to tell Anne about *The Blue Bear* had encouraged me to make two of my wife's favorite dishes. I'd even purchased pistachio éclairs.

I was sitting at the dining room table when Anne came in, working alongside Camille on the arts-and-crafts obsession that had consumed her the past year: origami animals. Perhaps due to her half-Breton heritage, she was inordinately fond of making origami crabs, but tonight, for a school project, she was folding monkeys.

Leather briefcase in hand, Anne bent down to kiss Camille while simultaneously running her finger across the flat nose of the paper primate that our daughter was hard at work on.

"That's beautiful, honey," Anne said, holding it up. "Is it a baboon?"

"It's a *lemur,*" Cam replied, grabbing her glitter glue stick.

"Obviously," I said, winking at my wife, who snubbed my chummy body language by drifting into the kitchen, returning with a wineglass to accompany the bottle on the table.

"And what about that, then?" She took off a high heel and massaged the ball of her foot through her pink stockings while inspecting my mess of koi paper and Scotch tape.

"It's a turducken. A chicken inside a duck inside a turkey."

Camille scrunched her nose at her mother. "Gross."

"So?" I asked, raising my wineglass to meet Anne's. "How go things in the world of Savda and Dern?"

"Ugh," she groaned, sinking into a chair behind Camille. "It looks like I've got a new case: these pregnant women in Lille. They've come together to file a lawsuit against wine label makers." She reached for the Chinon. "In America they have a warning saying women shouldn't drink during pregnancy because of birth defects. But we have nothing. People don't want to think about *defects* when they are drinking wine. But these women, they all had children born with fetal alcohol disorders. So they want a label. And a logo. Look." She reached for Camille's crayon and a piece of paper. I watched her long fingers push the stubby crayon across the page. "Like this."

What she was holding up was the image of a pregnant woman lifting a huge wineglass to her face with an interdictory red slash across her bulging belly.

"Vulgaire, non?"

I blinked.

"So you're defending pregnant drinkers?"

"Pfff," she said, slipping her scarf across the chair back. "I'll be defending the wine. You can imagine, there's a heritage to the label, it carries the image of the chateau, the name of the family, it has a date — an important year — and then, underneath this? A pregnant belly? We'll win."

With this, she drank more wine.

"And you, my little chicken, did you have fun in school?" She ran her hand through Camille's hair. "Are you not going to forgive me because I misidentified your lemur?"

Camille indicated that she was indeed holding a grudge about this by remaining hard at work on her zebra lemur tail.

Anne took the cap off of the glue stick, dreamily bringing it up to her nose. "Well, what about you, artist? What'd *you* do in school today?"

"Well, apparently my countrymen are forty-five minutes away from obliteration by mustard gas. And, um, I ran into Patrick Madsen."

It was undeniable. She brightened. "Oh, yeah? I remember him!"

I stood, then stomped my way into the open kitchen, hollering news of the Danish goldenboy over my shoulder as I did. "He's into plagiarism now. He's doing this show where he's just going to be sitting there, reading someone else's novel. An entire book of questions. They're not even his."

Anne followed me into the kitchen, leaning over the salad bowl to poke at the greens while I checked the pasta. *"The Interrogative Mood?"*

I closed my eyes. I had a sudden urge to shove my fist into the boiling water on the stove.

"I love that book," she continued, almost cooing. "Somewhere, I have it. I think it's in the — did I never make you read it? There's this one section in particular, it starts with a potato —"

"There's something else, actually," I said, my voice quieter. "*The Blue Bear* sold."

I regretted the way I'd announced it the second the phrase was out.

"It sold?" she said.

"It sold," I repeated. I couldn't bear to look at her face. I turned around and dumped the pasta into a strainer. "To a man in London, actually. He was at the show but no one met him. Odd, right?"

"It sold."

I finally turned around. My worst fears were confirmed: she was dragging her finger around the rim of her wineglass, distracted. Hurt.

"It actually went for ten thousand euros."

"Of which you'll get five."

I bit my lip. "Yeah."

"Well, I guess that's good news, then," she said, trying to cheer up. "A successful show."

"Anne." I flinched. "I'm sorry. I thought it wouldn't go."

"Well, that's a very curious way of going about it." She walked her jacket over to the coat tree in the corner, making a great fanfare out of the administrations of hanging it up. I followed and tried to embrace her, but she bristled at my touch.

"I thought that we agreed on it."

"You're right," she said. "We did. But I guess . . ." She looked over at Camille, at a loss for words. "Well, anyway, it's done now. The whole thing, it was a good show, Richard. I'm sure all the others will sell, too."

"Thank you for saying so."

"Of course," she said, pushing past me. "Let's just have dinner. It looks nice, by the way."

I said thank you, and she said you're welcome, and we continued about the evening too leaden with disappointment to be anything but polite.

Anne and I have been married over seven years now and I've cheated on her once. Depending how you look at it, this is either a very impressive or a highly repellent ratio. Either way, there is a façade around my indiscretion that is starting to fall apart. I said it happened one time. But it lasted seven months.

My father cheated on my mother once. My parents had been married for four years. For about three weeks, my mother had been complaining that she'd been receiving a series of phone calls in the evenings from a person she referred to as "the hang-upper."

She confronted my father about these phone calls, and, remarking that he turned the color of a squashed beet, began to suspect that he was having an affair. She found out with whom at a cocktail party in honor of a friend of my father's who had just been promoted to the board of directors of a prestigious university. My father, magnificently inebriated, left Mum by the punch bowl claiming he was going to "pop outside for a ciggy," but when a half hour passed with no sign of dear Dad, my mother went off in search of her Georgie and found him snogging Margaret Babcock from the Salisbury PTA in the cloakroom.

She left the party immediately and went to her mother's, where she stayed for three weeks straight without returning any of George's phone calls or opening the wrapped offerings he left in the mailbox. On the twenty-third day of her exile, she returned to the house with a large brown bag of groceries and began cooking dinner. When my father came home that evening, he was greeted with a pot roast and a stony demand from my mother that he sever his relations with Miss Babcock, apologize to their circle of friends about his lack of taste and conduct, and that if he ever dipped his hand into another person's proverbial basket again, he would rue the day he developed an X and a Y chromosome. And P.S., she was pregnant.

My mother loved my father, and my father couldn't live without my mother. My parents are a preposterous ensemble, but they're right together and my mum knew that and so she forgave him. I don't think that this is the case with Anne. I don't think that she will ever forgive me for my affair with Lisa. The fact that she refuses to talk about it and that I don't have the guts to force her to has made that kind of forgiveness unreachable — buried beneath an ever-rising wall of resentment and distrust.

And of course, there is the sex. Or full stop thereof. By the time we hit our wood anniversary at five years, we were down from making love maybe three times a week to three times a month, but that was still good, really — that was still great. Looking back, it was probably my physical distance that tipped her off to a disturbance in the natural order of things. In my mind, it felt unimaginably cruel to seek satisfaction from a body that had stood by me for so long, that had borne our child. The logic is preposterous, but I thought it was more respectful to avoid touching Anne until I was weaned off of my addiction to touching someone else.

For a long time, I was an idiot. We stopped making love the first night I slept with Lisa. In the weeks that followed, I remember thinking that the fact that Anne wasn't reaching for me was a godsend. I never asked myself *why* she wasn't asking for affection, why her normally electric libido had gone radio silent.

Things would have been different if she had stopped me at the start. If the night I had come home stinking of the orange-blossom oil Lisa used on the ends of her hair (an odor that I had previously expressed distaste for when it was squirted upon my head by a waiter in a Moroccan restaurant before the main course), if Anne had said end it, right now and here, end it before it's really started, I think I would have done so. I really think I would. Instead, she stayed silent while I prattled on about the couscous place I'd gone to with Julien with orange-blossom soap in the loo, and we both turned on our sides that night, away from each other, and feigned sleep.

How much did she know? Or think she knew? In her job defending total wankers, I knew how Anne approached them: *Tell me just enough.* And so it was with Lisa and me. From my behavior, my distance, the cease-fire of our sex, Anne knew just enough to suspect that I had met somebody else.

But this was Anne-Laure de Bourigeaud: a *fille de,* a lawyer, a citadel of pride. She didn't cry and she didn't scream, she didn't voice suspicion or flog me with barbed words. Instead, she deprived me of her Anne-ness: her humor, affection, love. And she took away her body, leaving only the physical interactions of a conjugal Robotron: her hand touching mine as she passed me a bag of groceries, my fingers sponging the inside of a wineglass that had touched her lips. In social situations, we still played the fine couple, but at home, and in our bedroom, each of us was just a body familiar with the other person's body, filling up the refrigerator with the requisite things each body needed, simply sharing space.

In my fuck-addled decision-making center, I saw Anne's war of silence against me as a sign of her reluctant acceptance of the situation. Her denial, the pride that kept her from confronting me, made it easy for me to pretend that nothing much had changed. After all, she was from the capital *B* of bourgeois families — sometimes I allowed myself to think that she was actually okay with the situation, that after seven years of marriage, this was just the way it was.

And just as it was characteristic of Anne to be too proud to confront me, it was also like her to reach a point of saturation, to say enough's enough. When Lisa broke up with me, I wasn't able to effectuate the clap-on, clap-off transition between home turf and mistress-land that I had been able to when I was oversexed and happy. I started to pine. I started to mope. I started to play a lot of kill-yourself-already music like Radiohead and Pulp while doing splattered-paint pieces like a third-rate Jackson Pollock. I wore sweatpants with dress shirts. This is Paris, where even the homeless circulate in proper pants.

And so it was one Friday, about three months ago, when Anne knocked on the door of my studio. It was early evening. I was drinking Guinness. Out of a *can.* I was thinking about Lisa. I was thinking, Why? I was thinking what could this toff Dave possibly have that I didn't. I was thinking about him fucking her. I was wondering how many times Lisa said she spent the past evenings alone, writing. How many times she'd lied.

Anne came into the center of the room and turned off the indulgent music eking from the speakers.

"I'm taking Camille with me to my parents'," she said. "I don't want you to come."

I was sitting on the floor with a paintbrush in my hand, my navy sweatpants splattered with the orange stuff I'd been flinging all afternoon. Anne looked at the painting, at the Guinness, and then she looked at me, huddled on the wooden floor like a pathetic beanbag. There weren't any sounds to distract us, the music cut off, the neighbors silent, the business hours for bird-singing long since over. It was the oddest feeling sitting there, wanting to cry and hold her and knowing that I couldn't. I wanted to apologize for everything I'd done, but at the same time I wanted to tell her what I'd been through with Lisa. She was my wife, after all. She was my best friend.

"Goddammit, Richard, look at me." Anne was glaring at me with something very close to hate. It cut me through the gut, and I started to whimper. Who am I fooling? I had seven hundred milliliters of stout in me. I started to *sob.*

"Don't you *dare* cry in front of me! You don't have the right!" Her chin was trembling and I had to hold my breath in to keep from crying harder.

"We'll be back by ten o'clock on Sunday," she said, speaking slowly. "And when we get

66

back, whatever this is" — she circled her hand through the air — "it's *over.*"

She held her fist to her lips to stop herself from crying. "I'm not going to forgive you. Don't you think for an *instant* that I'm going to forgive you. But you're going to forget this. You're going to forget this, and on Sunday night you're going to tuck Camille into bed and on Monday morning we're all going to sit down at the fucking breakfast table and she's going to tell you about her weekend and I swear to God, Richard, you better be in *shape.* You better fucking *be here,* all of you, and come down off of this —"

She reached down and grabbed the beer can by my feet and made as if to throw it in the direction of my painting, but something made her hesitate, and she stood there for a moment, her eyes filling up with the tears she had tried so hard to fight.

"You failed at being a husband," she said as she put the can back down beside me. "You better try and do a better fucking job at being a father."

My life had been illuminated by Lisa, made more vivid by her presence. I couldn't imagine letting go — really letting go of her — without losing a rekindled sense of self.

67

But I loved Anne-Laure. And I needed her. Everything, from the herd of midseason coats crowded in the mudroom to the glitter-pencil penguin drawings curling up beneath the magnets on our refrigerator door, every object in our household was part of our ongoing tale. And I couldn't have our story come to an end because of a woman who didn't want me. I had to make things right.

That entire weekend, I didn't leave the house. I stayed inside, tending a precious fire of nostalgia, surrounded by the smells and keepsakes of my safest home, forcing a promise that I would get over that godforsaken American. And that if I couldn't, I'd try even harder to make my wife and daughter believe I had.

4

I no longer love her. But oh, how I loved her.
That bald-headed Chilean minstrel sure had
it right. Current feelings of confusion put
temporarily aside, I can readily admit that
when I met Anne-Laure de Bourigeaud, she
was not only the most beautiful woman
south of College Hill that evening, she was
the most beautiful woman I had ever seen,
period. Anne-Laure was immaculate. She
wore underwear so delicate it could only be
hand-washed and she had perfect nails and
lustrous, onyx hair that she'd never tried to
highlight, a trend that she considers vulgar
and base. When I met her she was one of
those bourgeois girls you dream about tying
up and saying nasty things to. And she was
French. I had never been with a French girl
and I couldn't help fantasizing about her
whispering all sorts of nonsense in my ear
about rabbits and *cochons* and other farm
animals the French are fond of evoking in

the bedroom.

I met Anne in a predictably named martini bar called Olives in Providence. I had just started at the Rhode Island School of Design, where I was immersed in a short-lived love affair with the medium of bubble tape and Saran Wrap as a metaphor for the misguided conscience of the modern consumer. Anne was toiling as an office paralegal in a major Boston firm and was in Providence for the weekend visiting her cousin Esther, who was entering her second year as a grad student at Brown University.

Back then, I had a lot more confidence in both my artwork and my physique than I have now. Unlike Paris, the sun shines in America — I wasn't quite so pasty. I had American friends so wealthy, they'd grown up with more than one fridge. I was doing well in school: the teachers found my work provocative and the women (and some of the men, actually) adored my accent. I had a lot of just-so dress shirts — faded at the elbows, a little scuffed around the collar, "just so" in that they suggested breeding, but only up to a point — and the kind of floppy, untamed mass of sandy-brown hair that drives women with any kind of maternal instinct mad. They need to mess about in it, rumple you up. So this is what I was bringing to the table when I saw Anne at Olives.

Now, I do not hail from the island of the blind. I know what it looks like when two women are engaged in superficial conversation, leaving both physical and metaphorical room for interruption, and what it looks like when two women are actually enjoying each other's company, totally engaged. It was clear that I was dealing with the latter case at Olives. But a woman like Anne comes along once in a decade. Manners after miracles.

I watched the pair in conversation for a while: the cousin was a gesticulator and a fast drinker of appletinis. At one point, Esther stood and made the "watch this for me?" gesture at her behemoth of a purse (a girlfriend-to-girlfriend exchange that has always confused me, because it insinuates that your friend would have done otherwise — put it up for sale or something while you were in the loo), and I seized my chance.

I imposed myself grandly between Anne and the bar and offered to buy her a second round of whatever she was having.

"Actually," she said, "my third."

"Ah!" I grinned, thinking all was green-lit. "What'll it be, then?"

She stuck a toothpick through her last remaining olive and looked up — or rather, *squinted* — at my beverage upgrade offer.

"I'm fine, actually," she announced.

"Really?" Every bit of gray matter in my prefrontal cortex was telling me not to say anything about her melted-butter accent. Meanwhile, my downstairs soldier was rising to attention: *She's French, she's French, she's French.*

"Yes, well, I'm here with a friend, actually, and she's going to come back, so you'll probably have to buy her a drink also, and then we'll have to let you stay with us because you bought us drinks, and we'll have to make small talk, and at some point, my friend and I will pretend we have this 'thing,' but really, we'll just go across the street to another bar so that we don't have to continue talking to someone we don't know."

Oh, she was a tough one! But I was too far gone already, starboard to the wind. In my mind, she was already straddling me with her creamy, Frenchy thighs and I had my hand under the silk thong riding up between her ass and her ridiculous Tiffany bean necklace was slapping against my chest hair and I didn't give a fuck about her friend, I wanted Anne for mine.

"À l'aurore, armés d'une ardente patience, nous entrerons aux splendides Villes."

72

Now, I'm not one for spoken poetry, and my memorization skills have been compromised by a casual interest in pot, but it just so happened that I'd recently done a shadow-box piece for my mixed-media class in which I'd cut pyramid pictures out of Kahlil Gibran's *The Prophet,* filled the bottom of the box with sand, and Krazy Glued plastic G.I. Joe soldiers into place so that they were facing the pyramids, against which I'd silk-screened a line from the French poet Rimbaud: *In the dawn, armed with a burning patience, we shall enter the splendid Cities.*

It's an unparalleled feeling, the moment when you know without any doubt that you are going to come inside of a woman whom you haven't touched yet. Summoning up five years of advanced French into the delivery of a verse that was well timed felt impressive, but even better was the expression on Anne's face while she absorbed it, that irresistible mixture of befuddlement and desire that comes over a certain type of woman when she realizes she is in the process of being won over by a less attractive man. The energy was so electric, it was a miracle that we managed not to betray her cousin's earlier request and hightail it out of there, leaving Esther's bag untended.

When Esther did return, she found Anne drinking a martini that I had proudly purchased. Introductions were made, and Esther conveyed her dissatisfaction with my presence by rifling through her handbag with exaggerated exhales and muttered curses purportedly leveled at the hide-and-seek skills of her wallet.

"It's okay," said Anne, stilling her friend's flailing elbow with her hand. "I'll take care of it."

A classy way to say piss off, if you ask me. Esther looked up, reddened, and glowered at me.

"I see," she said. "Well, thank you. You'll make it to Pilates?"

"Of *course.*"

"Okay, well . . ." Esther buttoned up her coat, picked some lint off her collar, and generally indulged in the kind of busywork that signifies a girl's last chance.

"You'll call me if you need me?" she attempted.

Anne smiled. "Sure."

And the little dumpling left us to our stew. Anne wouldn't kiss me that night and she sure as hell made it clear she wasn't going to fuck me, even though she mentioned that she was staying in a hotel because she couldn't stand the alcoholic thicknecks running naked around Esther's dorm. This seemed particularly cruel of her, acknowledging that she was in possession of a prepaid, neutral space, but I had proclaimed myself in the possession of a "burning patience," and now needed to prove it.

Resigned to the fact that my evening was going to end with a slice of pizza and a solo wank, I asked Anne what she was doing the next day, and she said that she was leaving. She mentioned that she planned to return to Providence in three weeks' time to see Esther in some play. To my Glenfiddich-soaked mind, three weeks felt unfathomable, so I asked her if she was certain about not having me back to her room. She was. I suggested breakfast, and was impressed when she said she liked her mornings private. Out of options, I offered to drive her to the train the next day.

She replied that her hotel, the Biltmore, was approximately two blocks away from the train station. I pointed out that if we drove around the block three times, that would make a total of six blocks, which — if you took into account potential traffic or bad weather — could make for a bonus round of ten, maybe even twelve minutes together. Preempted, she agreed.

The next day, Anne kissed me when I

dropped her off. She said she thought it was a very intimate gesture, dropping someone off at a train station, that it made her feel old-fashioned. I agreed, and added that dropping someone off at a train station without ever having slept with them made it feel incredibly old-fashioned indeed. She said she found me arrestingly crude, but not inconsequential. We agreed to see each other again when she returned to Providence. I kissed her good-bye on the hand, just to spite her. It was November. By August, we were married.

If you were to succeed in prolonging the deliriously ecstatic puppy-dog love stage of the first months of courtship throughout the entire relationship itself — through marriage, unto death — would this same love, so celebrated, so sought after, break down in utter incredulity at the duration of its own existence?

I no longer love her. But oh, how I loved her. We were partners in crime when we met in America. We had accents. Tailored clothes. Anne wore nothing but stilettos for a year, and I took to wearing an American black-and-gold flag as a scarf. We drank heady red wine and threw Yorkshire pudding dinners on the weekends. We licked coke off of menthol cigarettes. We managed near penetration in the Absolute Quiet section of the Rockefeller Library. I made friends with lacrosse players at Brown University just to annoy her, and she did the same with select members of the crew team. Despite her physique, I made friends more easily than Anne did because my charm was more accessible. We spent a great deal of time apart, but, in our own way, remained inseparable.

I asked Anne to marry me five months into our relationship. I think I did it more for the drama of the gesture than for the appeal of marriage itself. I didn't want to reach a point in our relationship where we turned to each other, side by side in our usual places on some couch, and burped, "Don't you think it's about time we get married?" during the commercial break of our favorite program. Being a romantic, I have a certain respect for the idea of the old-fashioned, somewhat spontaneous (albeit highly awaited) marriage proposal, which I pulled off with finesse, if I do say so myself.

I took out a personal ad in the *Providence Phoenix,* an offbeat leftist publication published in the downtown warehouse district. It read thus: *Anne-Laure: Will you marry me? Richard H.*

Whether we were at my apartment or hers, Anne had a charming habit of reading the personal ads in any publication put before her. *The New Yorker,* the *New York Times, Cosmo, Glamour, Star* — no matter the quality of the periodical in question, she always read the personals before anything else.

I paid for and published the advert for the April 5 edition, 1995. Because she derives a certain pleasure from being withholding, to this day, Anne still hasn't told me when she saw it, but on May 21, I found an ad in the classifieds section that showed one of Anne's illustrated donkeys wearing a veiled tiara. Across the tiara was written the word *yes.*

We got married in Cape Cod at the same friend's house where we would spend the following summer with Anne skimming pregnancy books and me painting *The Blue Bear.* Anne wore the dress she'd bought for her debutante ball in Paris with sparkle jelly flats. We got drunk and had a barbecue. For dessert, we ate homemade Rice Krispies treats under blankets on the beach.

It was a lovely little party. Simple. Silly. Us. We went to bed at dawn in a room with white floorboards. I held Anne against my chest as she fell asleep. I ran my finger along the smooth gold band that had warmed from the heat of her own finger and traced circles around her knuckles and listened to her breathe. I fell asleep smiling, fully at ease with the ludicrous prospect of spending the rest of my life with this one, single person. It's not quite right what they say: love doesn't make you blind, it makes you optimistic.

I hadn't invited my parents to our wedding, or rather, I hadn't gone out of my way to insist that they be there. Edna and George Haddon had always taken a laissez-faire approach to my existence, and their way of showing their love for me was by trusting my life choices. We agreed that we'd have an informal celebration with family and friends in Hemel Hempstead whenever we got back, and in the meantime, they wanted postcards, phone calls, photographs.

I didn't find out that Anne had kept our marriage a secret from her own family until about ten days after our wedding when she broke down in tears over lunch. I thought she was upset because we'd had a dinner party the night before, and someone had smoked a cigarette in the bathroom, an indiscretion she considers adverse with good hygiene. She also dislikes eating leftovers (she finds them "disheartening"), and as our meal consisted of cold chicken from the previous night's dinner, I attributed her distressed conduct to the food. But no, it was because she had neglected to tell her family — a bastion of bourgeois refinement — that she'd up and married a man of modest means who aspired neither to be a banker nor a consultant (not even a *directeur marketing*!), but who simply wanted to be happy, live richly, drink well, and make love often to their precious, only child.

I was furious. For several months, Anne had led me to believe that she'd been carrying out a series of phone conversations acclimating her family to our approaching nuptials and her eternal union to a British commoner. In fact, these phone conversations had only taken place between herself and Esther, with whom she had concocted a complex plan that included a monthlong orientation period preceding my presentation as a serious suitor with respectable intentions, her father's subsequent acquiescence, and finally, our wedding, to be (re)carried out in their summer house in Brittany with all her friends and family in attendance.

Not only was I infuriated with Anne for keeping it a secret, I was disgusted by the bourgeois stench of the entire thing. I'd always found Anne's snobbery charming and sexy; it amused me to think of her filthy-rich family whose perfect little princess was living a double life in Boston: exemplary paralegal by day, whiskey-drinking *suceuse* by night. But this was different. This was geographical. This was going to touch upon our life. If we did move back to Paris as we'd been discussing, her parents would be something else entirely, no longer a foreign entity to be mocked over mimosas, but legal in-laws: phone-calling, Sunday-visiting, snooty, noisy in-laws with influence and authority over my new wife.

Initially, I loved the fact that we got married in a silo without giving the slightest thought to her family, my family, my country, hers. We were in love and we got married and the rest of the world could go shove it. But while I watched Anne sniffle over her untouched plate of chicken, I realized that our bubble was more fragile than I thought. We couldn't shut out the external factors forever. I started to wonder what would happen if and when we crossed the ocean. What side of Anne-Laure de Bourigeaud would greet me on her home turf?

After several tearful phone calls with her mother, two perforated round-trip plane tickets to Paris appeared, courtesy of the

Bourigeauds. It was time to meet the in-laws.

We planned our first official visit for a long weekend in October, and went straight from the Charles de Gaulle Airport to Anne's parents' place in Le Vésinet, thirty minutes outside of Paris. After a series of awkward cheek kisses and "nice to finally meet-you"s, we proceeded outside to the patio, where Madame had set up the aperitifs, skirting around the elephant in the garden by agreeing that it was, indeed, quite warm for October.

It quickly became clear to me that the Bourigeauds had spent the month before our arrival setting up a pros and cons list that must have looked a bit like this:

Pros (Regarding Richard)
- speaks fluent French (without too much of an accent, according to Anne)
- has an appreciation for culture and the arts
- is European
- is loved deeply by Anne
- appears to love Anne back
- well-enough traveled

Cons (Regarding Richard)
- will probably make no money in his chosen line of work
- comes from a modest family (probably with bad teeth)
- is a stranger (probably with bad teeth)
- is not French
- is not Catholic
- is not rich

I passed with flying colors through the first round of questions: the fact that my parents were on their fortieth year of marriage seemed to help my case a great deal, as did the fact that I spoke a rudimentary amount of Spanish, bringing my "spoken languages" tally up to three. But things got dicey when Alain de Bourigeaud inquired just what kind of artist I was.

"He's a *pop culturist,* Dad," Anne said, pushing her hair behind her ear. "Like Houellebecq, but for visual art."

I almost spit up my white Burgundy at the words *pop culturist.*

"Pop *politics,*" I ventured. "It's . . . I try to provoke thought."

Both Alain and his wife, Inès, stared at me blankly, clearly expecting some kind of follow-up. But I couldn't think of a single work of mine that didn't make me sound spastic.

"He's putting together his thesis show now, actually," went Anne. "About the rise and fall of popular figures? How one movement can lead to another movement, influence trends. Like, for example" — Anne put her hand on top of mine — "he has this series of Russian dolls that tracks the commoditization of the food industry all the way up to the cult of Martha Stewart?"

Her mother cocked her head. "How interesting. Who's that?"

Lunch passed without further incident, or rather, without any incidents at all, the mark of a successful luncheon in the Bourigeaud *maison*. When the final forkful of redfish was laid to rest on top of patterned china, Anne's mother suggested that Anne and she do the dishes before dessert. We'd had soup before the entrée, and a cheese and salad course after that — there were a *lot* of dishes to be done. I suspected that the time had come for me and Mr. B to have a little chat.

Sure enough, as the women began to clear the table, Monsieur asked if I wouldn't like to see their garden in more detail. ("Inès is simply a wizard with outdoor plants!") I accepted, catching Anne's eye as I walked toward the door. She gave me a thumbs-up, an out-of-character gesture that reminded me of my RISD roommate, Toby, who used to flip me the same hand signal after his morning visits to the loo.

Once outside, I realized I'd best not beat around the bush. In fact, I wouldn't even circle it. Just jump right in there, Richard. There's a good dog.

"Monsieur Bourigeaud," I began, in the rather dressed-up French I reserve for the old guard, "I'm sorry things turned out like this. I don't have as close a relationship with my family as Anne does, so I wasn't thinking, really, of other people. I know we acted hastily. It's just — they don't like to fly?"

Mr. B threw a weed over the hedge into the neighbor's yard. "If Anne cared so much about her family, I think she would have thought to introduce us to you beforehand. Or at least invite us to the wedding. That might have been nice."

I assured him that my own parents hadn't been invited either, an interruption he dismissed with a wave of his hand.

"Look, son, I don't know you well enough to decide whether I like you or not yet, but Anne certainly seems to, so I suppose that's good enough for now. But I want to get one thing straight: you need a job."

Deeply rattled, I explained as calmly as I

could that I didn't just sit around all day flinging paint upon the floor.

"I *sell* things, you know. In a proper gallery."

"I'm sure of it. Surely. But you're both young, still. Anne's going to be a great lawyer, but she's got a lot to learn." He reached down and tugged at another weed, treating me to a conciliatory view of his bald spot.

"If you do move back to Paris, we can help you get settled. I have lots of connections, friends who could be helpful, and I want Anne to be happy. I mean, that's all Inès and I want." He rubbed his chin, as if deciding whether or not to pursue this line of thought. "I'm an art lover myself, Richard, and I hold a great deal of respect for the work. But until you've got an established name in the business, I'd love to see you aim for something to rely on, a predictable income from a respectable source. I imagine that's not too much to ask in exchange for her hand?" He clapped me on the shoulder with his manicured paw. "What do you think?"

Knowing full well that disagreeing would lead either to an imposed divorce, forced exile in England, or the disinheritance of his only daughter, I agreed as, of course, I had to. Monsieur seemed genuinely pleased, and shouted out to the washerwomen inside that we'd be having digestifs with our café.

Upon our return, the changed energy between us was enough to signal that I had been accepted. Inès embraced me, and Anne smiled with weary gratitude. Inès launched immediately into the planning of our second wedding, insinuating that the first had simply been a rehearsal for what would certainly be the grandest, most unforgettable day of our lives.

"After all," Madame added as she put out the saucers for coffee and cake, "everyone likes seconds!"

That meeting with her parents was probably the first time I felt like there was someone other than Anne whom I couldn't disappoint. Nowadays, there are loads of people in my life to let down — my daughter, my gallerist, the baker at the *boulangerie* who looks absolutely crestfallen when I don't have exact change — but up until then, it had just been Anne and me. There were fewer expectations. There were so many fewer things to do *wrong*. We simply had to love each other and earn enough for an occasional dinner out. It was easy. Easy! Love was all there was.

But no one tells you what you start *doing* to each other when you wed. People talk about the stability and the comfort of knowing that you have someone who will always have your back; they speak of the convenience of pooled assets and tax benefits and the joy of raising children, but no one explains that six years into it, a simple request to *Pick up a half pound of ground turkey and maybe some organic leeks?* on your way home is going to send the free, blue sky crashing down like a pillory around your neck, see you clutching your paper number at the butcher's, ashamed to be just another sucker bringing white meat home.

And no one tells you what it's going to feel like when the mystery is gone, or about the roots of repugnance that will twitch and rise inside you when you realize that your spouse has met the actual person behind each name in your phone's repertoire, that she knows exactly how much wine you've drunk on any given evening, knows when you are constipated, that she has stooped over to pull your graying chest hair from the drain, and that the familiarity between you has transformed from something comforting into something corrosive. You can't believe that you used to spend entire afternoons with your tongues inside each other's mouth. Can't remember when it started: the tit for tat, the scorecards, the bonus points and penalties for things promised and not done. No one explains that the busier you become with your careers and house and children, the more time you'll find to disappoint each other; squirreling away indignities like domestic accountants. Tallying regrets.

And after years of emotional stockpiling, no one said how you would find your way into another woman's body like an infant finding his thumb, how it would unclog the years of muck and allow you, on your walk home now, to stand in line at the butcher shop with your joy for life intact, appreciative and optimistic and tolerant of the old woman in front of you who can't decide between veal or chicken because why should she rush? The world is full of choices, each more delightful than the last.

Why is it called "cheating"? Is it all that bad? I married my lover, time turned her into my sister. Truly, badly, I want my lover back. But we've twisted each other with our unspoken failures and our building scorn. A near decade later, we're warped. We are polluted. The well of love is black.

5

By the beginning of October, it was looking more and more likely that the British would join the United States in military action against Iraq. I was back at my favorite news kiosk, rifling through headlines inspired, apparently, by the lexicon of cowhands (HE'S GOT 'EM, GO GET 'EM!), trying to brainstorm ways I could develop an Iraq-themed project without coming across as a desperate opportunist, when I got a call from Julien that he needed to see me.

I found Julien in the gallery's storage closet, standing on his head. The watercooler next to him belched out a bubbly glug.

"Julien," I said, blinking. "What the fuck."

He bent one leg back and then the other, tucked his head against his kneecaps for several seconds before getting up.

"It's good for stress," he said, dusting off. "Did you meet Bérénice?"

I confirmed my observation of the Toulousian receptionist but did not share the fact that I found her reception skills somewhat lacking, as she had neither greeted me nor offered to take my coat. "How long has she been here?"

"She just started, but already . . . here." He pushed open the door for me so we could exit the closet. "Let's go to my desk."

Julien's desk was less cluttered than usual. Whether this was for the benefit of his new intern or accomplished by the intern herself, I have no idea, but I do know that Bérénice was one of those girls with a really severe bird look to her. Instead of making herself busy while we talked, she sat there across the room from us, peering over with her freaky eyes.

"Bérénice, dear, do you think you could pop across the street for a bit and bring us back some sandwiches? Ham and cheese? And get one for yourself."

Julien got up to deposit some euros on her desk, which she stared at for a while before unceremoniously stuffing them into the front pocket of her jacket.

"It's very strange," Julien whispered, as she headed for the door. "She doesn't have a purse."

Once she was gone, Julien shared with me

91

the shake-up of the morning.

"This British fellow," he said. "He wants you to bring the bear."

"Sorry?"

"They want you to hand-deliver it, the painting. It's Bérénice that talked to them this morning, so of course I called them back and said she was new here and that we don't do deliveries by the artist and so forth, but . . . they're incredibly persuasive."

"Wait, so you talked to this guy. A *guy.*"

"Yeah. The Dave fellow. They'll cover your travel expenses, plus a thousand euros."

I crossed my arms and tried to make sense of it. And couldn't.

"But, why?"

"Apparently, they practice this New Age form of art collecting. He said it was part of the process that you deliver the work yourself."

I got up and started pacing. "You have to agree, right, that this is a little too coincidental? Who else would want me to go all the way to *London* — and how am I going to do that, by the way, the thing's bloody gigantic — except for *her*?"

Julien picked something from his teeth. "I admit that it's unusual. It's definitely strange."

"What if it *is* her? What would that mean?"

"I guess it would mean that she wants to see you again. And that she has an inordinate amount of free time. I don't know what to say. Do you think you'll do it? The guy says they might not buy it if you won't."

I exhaled hugely and looked up at the ceiling that was yellowed from all the cigarettes that had been smoked beneath it.

"And when do they want me to do this?" I asked.

"I told them you had some time off coming up, over the Toussaint."

"You suggested my *vacation*?"

"You'll be in Brittany," he replied. "Just a ferry ride away. Bring your family with you. Visit your parents. Turn it into a vacay."

"Right, fantastic. A reunion between my ex-mistress and my wife."

"Well, you need to think about it. I told them we'd get back to them in two days."

"Do *you* think it's Lisa?" I asked, sitting.

"I don't know," he said. "I didn't. But now . . . I guess it might be."

We sat in silence for a while; I worked on biting the nail of my thumb off, and Julien stuck his into the rubber tunnel created by his telephone cord.

After a while Bérénice came back with the sandwiches. Faux crab for Julien and some kind of grilled vegetable concoction for me.

She claimed — preposterously — that they were out of ham.

As we sat there eating lunch, thoughts about conspiracies trampled through my head. Why would the U.S. government go to such transparent lengths to prove that weapons of mass destruction existed when even their men on the ground said that they didn't? Why would any self-respecting *boulangerie* be out of ham baguettes at noon? What would I do if Lisa was the buyer? Could I really deliver a painting to her doorstep and take off without delving back into the horizontal and upright and other corporal positions that had gotten me into so much trouble in the first place?

"I wanted to tell you," attempted Julien through a mouthful of baguette, "I have a potential buyer for that painting of the bikes. Which leaves me with, what's next? Do you have anything in mind?"

"Well, you're not going to like this," I said, scratching the back of my head. "But I was thinking — and it's just thinking — about maybe doing something on Iraq?"

"Politics?" He frowned. "I don't know, Rich. I don't really think of you as a political guy."

"But this is cops-and-robbers bullcrap," I

said. "It's a *farce*. Have you seen the head-lines?"

"So, what — you want to do some paint-ings of George Bush on a stick horse?"

I laughed. "That's good, actually. But no. I was thinking," I ran my hand down my pant leg, inventing an itch. "I was thinking that I might go back to installations."

"An installation." He grimaced. "About Iraq?"

I folded my arms across my chest. "I want to do something timely, you know? Some-thing that has meaning. Something that doesn't have anything to do with all of this." I swept my hand out to encompass the key paintings in the room.

"But *politics*?" Julien protested. "That's not really your thing."

"Well, it certainly *was* my thing before —"

"Or it's not your *clients'* thing. You've got a fan base now," he continued. "Collectors. Or, collectors of a certain sort. People like your work. It's nostalgic. It looks good next to curtains."

"Curtains," I said, darkening. "You're seri-ous."

Equally miffed, he went into the storage room and returned with two cups of instant coffee and some sugar packets. I was feeling disrespected. I took two packets instead of my regular one. "Listen," he continued, setting down the java, "you know I believe in you. But even the Damien Hirsts of the world understand that there is money in being consistent. His preserved sharks, his rotting cow heads, it's all coming from the same place of provocation and power. But he's not sentimental. You are. And you can't go from being sentimental and apolitical to being politically involved."

"So you're saying I can't do art with an opinion?"

"Art with an agenda, no." He drank his coffee in one shot. "Or rather, I'm saying you can't sell art with an agenda *here.* That's not what I rep you for. That's not why I took you. And that's not why most of the paintings in this show have sold."

"But this is who I *am,* Julien; the key paintings were a lark."

"They're a gift horse, Rich! You could do endless versions of them: former offices you've worked in, places you've vacationed, rooms in your childhood home. You've stumbled on a brand."

"I need to do this *now,*" I said, lowering my voice. "I want to feel like I'm a part of something. I'd like to be respected."

"Knowing that every painting here is going to sell doesn't make you feel that?"

I let my gaze drift down the hallway where *The Blue Bear* was hanging, massive and alone. Anne lied when she said she didn't care if I tried to sell it, and I knew that, and I included it in the show anyway. And it had sold.

"I don't know," I mumbled. "I just want Anne to like it."

And there it was. Despite the genre of work that *The Blue Bear* represents, Anne had been proud of it because it reflected a real sentiment. A vulnerability. A stated fear. Up until the other key paintings, I'd taken on real topics, maybe not a *war* per se, but I had opinions on world issues that stemmed beyond the domestic questions that plagued my mind of late: Is there anything more dispiriting than boneless chicken under plastic? Was Camille going to turn into the kind of child who uses eye rolls instead of words? Would my wife forgive me? Beneath my posturing around the Iraq conflict and my quest to find a smart idea, part of me just wanted Anne to respect my work again.

That night, Anne and I had a dinner party at the house of friends who had recently moved from Paris to Versailles. This was happening more and more now, the exodus of creative people in their thirties to suburbs they'd made vicious fun of ten years prior. The last time we'd been to Synneve and Thierry's, he'd dropped the word *wainscoting* into the conversation. Thierry might be a faithful husband, but he's started to think about decorative paneling in his spare time. By our midthirties, we're all fucked.

We'd gotten a babysitter for Camille, a once-in-a-blue-moon occurrence that had us both in noticeably improved moods. The prospect of an entire night to be enjoyed with people who were over four feet tall coupled with the uninterrupted flow of traffic on the normally gridlocked A13 made the atmosphere in the Peugeot register at "cordial" instead of its default "tense."

Anne had on her "special night" perfume, a heady mix of bergamot and neroli, along with a silk rose blouse and wide-legged, wool pants with heels. Nervous about sharing the news that now, not only had I sold *The Blue Bear,* but as further penance, I also had to deliver it to London, I opted for a warm-up topic that was safe and flattering. I said I liked her shoes.

"Humph," she scoffed. "They're old." She pushed into fifth gear.

The unexpected lack of traffic wasn't leaving me much time. I stared at the passing high-rises out the window, television satellites clinging perilously to the grids of narrow balconies.

"So I've got news," I said, my jaw tense. "About the *Bear.*"

"Oh?" she said, downshifting. I thought I detected a note of hopefulness in her voice.

"I went to see Julien the other day, and it turns out . . . it's really strange, actually." I fiddled with my seat belt. "They want me to deliver it. The buyers. They want me to bring it to London myself."

I watched Anne's face take on an expression of incredulity I'd seen her use when she was presented with evidence that wouldn't hold up in court.

"Julien said it has something to do with the way they go about art collecting. I don't know, it's spiritual or some such."

In reply, she sighed. "This doesn't sound right to me. In fact, it sounds absurd. Has he ever had a request like this before?"

"I don't think so," I said, staring at my hands. "I didn't ask."

"Well, what did you tell him?"

"Well, I told him — I told him . . . they're going to pay me, so I told him yes."

She turned to look at me. "How much?"

I stalled. "A thousand."

She laughed out loud. "That's ludicrous."

"Plus expenses."

"You can't be serious, Richard. Put things in perspective. You don't know these people, Julien doesn't either, you're going to have to trek across the Channel —"

"They've put a deposit down, I'm sure of it," I said, not actually sure of that at all. "I just feel like . . . I mean, it's pretty fascinating, right? The request itself? Maybe I could document the trip or something."

She rolled her eyes. "And when is this supposed to happen?"

"That's the thing, actually," I said, with a little cough. "Over the Toussaint?"

"Oh, perfect!" she cried. "Do these people even exist? Or is this some kind of elaborate plan to get out of seeing my family?"

"Julien's thinking was that I'd be just a ferry ride away."

"*Julien* thought this," she said. "Right."

"I don't know," I said, slumping deeper into the car seat. "I kind of feel like I don't have a choice. I wouldn't go for long — take the ferry over, stay with my parents, drop the painting off, come back. I mean, you could always come with?"

"Oh, God, no," she replied. "I want a real vacation. I don't want to spend sixteen hours on a *boat.*" She shook her head. "This is what happens when . . ."

She didn't need to finish her sentence. I knew that what she meant to say was that I never should have sold it.

"Do what you have to," she said, switching lanes.

As we drove, I pictured what would happen if the buyer *was* Lisa. What it would mean if she had actually bought the painting — the position it would put me in, a pawn wedged in the bosom of flattery and despair. But as much as a large part of me wanted to see her again, to test whether or not I was still susceptible to her pull, I knew that if I went over there and Lisa really was the buyer, it would be an irreparable betrayal of my wife. Again.

When we reached the commune of Saint-Cloud, the traffic slowed to the point where we couldn't distract ourselves with the outside scenery any longer. Our silence was too loud. I asked how things were going with her case, and she explained that she was going to pretrial in a month.

"It's looking like they're going all the way with this," Anne said, frowning. "They're getting the signature of every mother of a child born with a fetal alcohol spectrum disorder in the north of France."

"Don't pregnant women know not to drink?"

"It's different with wine," she said. "We grow up with it. My own doctor told me I could have two glasses a day. I mean, most women don't even want it. You just don't have that craving, or it isn't to your taste, but here's their argument — and that's what's so frustrating about it — these women are saying they didn't know. They didn't *know* that drinking alcohol was bad for their babies."

"So why aren't they blaming the doctors?"

"Exactly," she said, casting me a glance. "That will be a main part of our defense, that the fault lies in preventive education. They've always made a bigger deal about the side effects of drinking pregnant in America than they have in France. But then, the Americans make a bigger deal of everything. It's a bad sign, this trial. It shows very poor taste. It shows that French people are eager to place the blame elsewhere for their own choices. Between that and the arrival of Starbucks, you'll see."

"Après moi, le déluge."

She smiled. "Exactly."

"But Starbucks isn't here yet."

She shook her head. "It'll come. And supersized cereal packs. And strollers."

"The French have strollers."

"We don't have strollers," she said, her

eyes flashing. "We have *poussettes.*"

In between the commune of Saint-Cloud and the town of Versailles lies a fifteen-hundred-acre stretch of formal royal forest known as La forêt de Fausses-Reposes. This rather grim name ("The Forest of False Rests") refers to the refuge the hapless deer would take behind rocks and under trees in order to escape the droves of hunting royalty with their horses, and their bugles, and their yapping dogs.

"Can I ask you a question?" I said, watching the woods outside the window, thinking about how the poor, outnumbered deer were always found. "Do you think my work's . . . predictable?"

She looked over at me. "Where's this coming from?"

"Do you?"

"I need context."

"You're afraid to answer."

She ran her hand through her hair. "Well, what are you referring to? The key paintings? The entire body of your work? Your work isn't predictable. The show . . . I mean, it was almost a commission, wasn't it? It wasn't really coming from your heart."

"Thank you," I said, trying a hand on her thigh. I felt her leg stiffen. I hadn't touched her in so long.

"But in terms of the key paintings, yeah, I'd say that they're predictable."

I took my hand away.

"Why are you asking?" she persisted. "Is it because stuff sold?"

"No . . . I mean, you obviously want stuff to sell, right? But it's true that when it does . . ." I faltered, not sure how to continue. "Anyway, no. It's because of a talk I had with Julien. I was thinking, maybe, about doing something kind of political? Something about Iraq? An installation. Mixed media. Something like I used to do . . . before."

"Okay," she said, her lips pursed. "But Iraq?"

"I know. It's a little out there. But something's about to break."

"Right," she said, "but you can't just use Iraq for Iraq. What's your angle on it?"

I slumped against the window, knowing she was right.

"I'm not saying it's not a good idea, though," she said, turning to me. "I think it would be good — great, actually — to get back to that kind of stuff. It's just that you've been doing these key paintings for so long, it just surprised me."

My heart lifted. After all, doing something unexpected was the point.

"Plus, the show did well. It's the right time to take a chance."

"That's what *I* thought," I said, putting my hand back on her leg. "But Julien says I have a 'brand' now. He said — he pretty much came out and said that he wouldn't sell anything of mine that wasn't crap."

"So find another gallerist." She shrugged.

"I'd feel like a traitor."

I watched her wince. And my heart fell. As with so many things I'd said over the past couple of months, this word took on a threatening dimension once it was out of my mouth. *Traitor. Betrayal. Philanderer. Adulterer.* Every word had a second meaning, each sentence held a trap. When I tried to quiet the disparaging voices in my head and have a normal conversation, I just wrapped myself deeper into a sticky web of errors. My words were never right.

Anne reached for the volume knob on the radio. I'd lassoed myself into a corner. The sound of other voices filled the car.

By the time we reached the Raoults' house, we'd recouped our losses. Anne and I are good at parties. Parties are our thing. With a wineglass in her hand and one leg crossed over the other and her pillowy French lips painted with a smirk, Anne is at her most beautiful when she's being entertained.

Synneve Raoult was a Swedish stylist who was trying to start a mail-order sock company for men called TOOB. We spent the cocktail portion of the evening looking at her design samples while she bemoaned the state of creative entrepreneurship in France.

"I can't get a loan," she said. "From anyone. They just don't want you to start things here. They want you to follow."

"Not that different from Sweden," said her husband, Thierry, holding up a yellow-and-navy-striped sock.

"No," she said, "but at least there, when I was making clothing, the designers would put it in their store on consignment. Here, you need an LLC, a patent."

"And a thousand photocopies," said my lady on the couch.

The Swede and I burst out laughing. You can't know the Kafkaesque levels of ineptitude that the French government is capable of until you try to secure that holy grail of naturalization, *le titre de séjour.* There are support groups for immigrants who have lost their will to live because of the incompetence they were exposed to within the walls of the French prefecture. I myself once waited four hours in a communal lobby with the air quality of an underground bunker

only to be told that I had made the unfor-
givable error of showing up with four black-
and-white photocopies of my British passport instead of five. The prefecture's public
photocopier only took five-cent pieces, a
denomination that is never used in France,
and no, absolutely not, Madame would not
make change from my five-euro bill, nor
would she entertain my suggestion to use
the staff photocopier, even when I offered
to pay extra. No, I would have to exit the
building in order to make the fifth photocopy elsewhere and come back for the next
available appointment in four months. *Vive
la France!*

"I like this one," I said, holding up a white
pair covered in pastel-colored polka dots.

"I know," said Synneve, smiling. "If I ever
get this thing off the ground, I'm hoping to
introduce French businessmen to a sense of
humor. You Brits always have great socks."

Dinner was roasted salmon and boiled
beets and a chicory salad with walnuts and
blue cheese. The wine was Beaujolais,
mercifully, from a vintage that did not taste
like dried bananas. Thierry, a marketing
executive, regaled us with tales of his new
client, a German "eco" limo service trying
to conquer the French market with their
fleet of hybrid luxury vehicles that ran on

vegetable oil.

"The only problem," he said, "is that you arrive smelling like a vat of fries."

Anne countered with the recent updates on her pregnant alcoholics, and we passed the bottle of wine around, weighing the aesthetic ramifications of having a pregnant drinker icon on the back. By the cheese course, talk turned to my own projects, and Thierry apologized for not being able to make it to my show.

"It was a great turnout," said Synneve, passing me a block of Comté and a knife. "But, Anne, you're a better woman than I am!"

The temperature in the room went from mild to tropical. Or at least it rose significantly underneath my blazer.

"They're all about ex-lovers!" said Synneve, getting up to pour more wine. "They're all about . . . keys, right? Places you used to live?"

I avoided Anne's eyes, but I could feel them on me, like a crocodile resting in the water, sizing up its prey. "Not exactly," I said, handing off the cheese plate. "They're places I used to have keys to, yeah, but they're not all ex-girlfriends."

"They're mostly ex-girlfriends," said Anne, carving off a wedge.

108

"Well," said Synneve, "like I said, I'd be too jealous. A painting of another woman's bed!"

"Oh, yeah, no," said Thierry. "You'd go nuts."

"They're all women from the past," I repeated.

Synneve burst out laughing. "Well, obviously! I mean, you're not going to go and . . ." She reddened.

Anne drained her wineglass and filled it with water. She drained that, and filled it up again. No one else budged.

"Do you guys want to move into the living room?" Synneve attempted. "Have some fruit and cognac?"

Fruit and cognac are good for warming the throat and belly, but they can't heal a hurt heart. On the drive home, I took the driver's seat and Anne spent the entirety of the ride staring out the black windows of the car.

The only person I told about Lisa is Julien. I never talked about her to any of our friends, and while this was a good move for the integrity of our couplehood and Anne's pride, it also meant exposing ourselves to the verbal faux pas of people who weren't in the know about the leaky state of our union.

Once home, we liberated the babysitter and I waited in the bedroom while Anne checked on our sleeping daughter, kissed her dreaming face good night.

When Anne came in, I was sitting on the edge of our bed with my clothes still on.

She shut the door behind her and turned away to take off her necklace, to unbutton her blouse. On nights like this, after we'd been out in the adult world with good food and friends, I dreamed of going to her, running my hands up the back of her silk shirt, raising my hands under it to finally cup her breasts. I'd come close to trying, but every time I'd stop myself, convinced that she'd let me know when she was ready for physical reconciliation. That it would be disrespectful, violent even, to try to touch her first.

Anne took off her shirt and replaced it with a long-sleeved cotton top to sleep in. She used the bathroom. I used the bathroom. When she got into bed, after a short bout of reading, both of us fell into our ritual of feigned sleep, but that night the charade seemed to go on even longer than usual. My wife was right there next to me, a living, breathing bridge, and I could feel it in the space between us, the magnetic energy that might have been kindled through a single touch. But I didn't dare touch her, and she didn't move a limb. During the day, we were able to make small steps toward peace through our words and actions, but at night, there was no one there but us, no one to rely on or disappoint or use except each other, and the fact that we — that I — was incapable of physical communication made me feel like all our other efforts were in vain. On nights like these, I was a castaway on a vast and steel-blue ocean with no land in sight and no birds flying above, just the sound of thick, cold water slapping up against a boat.

6

That night, unable to sleep, I snuck into my studio and rifled through the place where I hide Lisa's letters under my dried-up watercolor paints. I pulled out the second one she had sent. A long-term fan of Kierkegaard, she wrote mostly about Regine Olsen, Kierkegaard's true love whom he deserted in order to devote his life to God.

On the other hand, by faith, says that marvelous knight, by faith you will get her by virtue of the absurd. But this movement I cannot make. As soon as I want to begin, everything reverses itself, and I take refuge in the pain of resignation. I am able to swim in life, but I am too heavy for this mystical hovering.

A wife in the bedroom, a lover's letter in hand. Mystical hovering, indeed. This letter was an entreaty to reimmerse myself in my life with Anne, to *move on,* as it were. But this request to forget her was undermined by the fact that she had taken the time to sit down and write me in the first place.

If I had not had my depression, marriage to her would have made me happier than I had ever dreamed of becoming. But being the person I unfortunately am; I must say that I could become happier in my unhappiness without her than with her.

That's how I feel about us. About you. I am happier missing you than if I hadn't left. What would have become of us if we'd really done it? Severed things with other people? Moved in with each other? Married? You think you could have handled the guilt, but I don't think so. I never saw a future with your little girl playing in some rented, second room. It would have killed us, ruined everything we had. I think we were meant to be exactly what we were. Lovers. It's a silly word, it's a supermarket romance term, a bodice-ripper placeholder, but it's true. People are goal-orientated, they like their efforts to turn into something: a promotion, a marriage proposal, a sold painting hanging on a buyer's wall. I liked our journey. I loved it. I

113

also loved that it didn't go where habit would have had it go.

You don't plan on adultery. Looking back, there might have been a certain availability about me when I met Lisa, but it wasn't something I *planned*. Things weren't even bad between Anne and me. I wasn't unhappy. I was lucky with my home life. But I was disconnected. Numb.

There was something that happened on the day that I met Lisa, but it's only in retrospect that it feels important: at the time, it was just another example of the physical negligence that had set in around year five of my marriage. I was in the bathroom with Camille, my shirt off, having just taken a shower myself, setting her up with a Noah's ark of floating animals for a morning bath. Anne was taking her on a girls' day, which meant I would get back to being a real guy just as soon as I bathed and powdered and dressed our little girl.

This shouldn't sound like it's going to, but I was looking at Cam's fanny. Just as a body part, mind you, an organ in the bath. I was thinking of the last time that Anne and I had bathed together — on a weekend trip, of course, the marital bathroom having long become a desexualized place of his and her toothpastes and roll-on deodorants. It had been years, literally, since we'd shared a bath at home. And this lack of physical connection with my own wife so contrasted with the multitude of times when I'd gotten down on my knees to cleanse my daughter's body that when Anne came in to remind me yet again about their estimated time of departure, I was filled with the urge to grab her with my soapy hands and toss her in the water, ruin her posh clothes.

But I didn't. Instead, I pushed a plastic sea lion toward a plastic floating iceberg while Camille forced a mermaid doll to dive up and down, and Anne grabbed a bottle of perfume and sprayed some behind each ear, and when she turned around again, freshly fragranced, I watched her eyes take us both in. I saw real love there for a moment, true warmth and affection, and I thought that it would happen, a spontaneous embrace, but then Camille's mermaid made a calamitous dive that sent sudsy bathwater all over the floor, some of which splashed onto Anne's suede boots and the moment was ruined. And when they left, I felt like a very small boy in a too-big house who just wanted to be loved. Touched. Kissed.

And it was that afternoon that I met her, January 12, 2002, at a photography exhibit called *The Devil's Playground* at the Pompidou.

The Nan Goldin exhibit was one of three different shows I'd planned to see that weekend to cleanse myself of the post-Christmas conspicuous-consumption blues. The highlight of the retrospective was a slide show of photographs Goldin had shot of her friends in intimate situations. A naked couple playing with their child on a couch, a man washing his boyfriend's hair in the bath, an attractive couple making out on the bed with all the windows open. It was exactly the kind of slide show that I needed at that moment: a proof that sexual intimacy exists.

Lisa had come into the dark screening room and sat beside me during a slide called *Simon and Jessica Kissing in My Shower.* I tried to think of something innocent, my daughter on a tricycle, Anne blowing on Cam's hot chocolate to cool it down. But I was powerless against my reaction to the person by my side. I hadn't even *seen* her and my entire body was alive. I could tell she was long-haired, long-legged, with restless hands and fingers. And she was alone.

When the slide show finished, I didn't get up from my seat right away, and neither did Lisa. I stalled for time by concentrating on

116

the credits as if they were crucial to my appreciation of the film. Who had done the lighting? Who was the key grip? What the hell's a key grip?

I wanted to say something, but I hadn't spontaneously said something to a female stranger in years. While I was going through a list of potential witticisms, she saved me from embarrassment by speaking up herself.

"Much more digestible than all her stuff on AIDS."

"It depends how you look at it," I blurted out in desperation, becoming even more anxious when she stood up from the bench. Before I had the chance to appreciate her genetic gifts in the light of the still-rolling credits, she said, "Why don't we get a drink?"

A drink. A drink is just a *drink*. And what would be the harm, really, of seeking refreshment with a fellow art lover? They had been provocative photographs. There was quite a bit to talk about. Better to discuss them with someone who had actually seen them than try to recap them for Anne.

We went up to the museum's sixth-floor restaurant, a pompous place called Georges that was famous for its egg-shaped eating compartments and the extra-long-stemmed roses jutting up from each table. There were nothing but windows all around. From our silver table, we had a spectacular view of the right bank.

Lisa ordered a cosmo, claiming that it was impossible to get a decent one in France.

"They've got something against red fruit here," she said, running her finger around the glass. "You have no idea what I had to go through to find cranberries for Thanksgiving."

"What'd you have to go through?" I beamed.

"Let's just say I shelled out a half hour's salary to get one pack. It's ridiculous." She dipped a finger in her drink. "Why don't the French like cranberries? It's such a useful fruit. I guess French women are too *ladylike* to get yeast infections."

I laughed into my manhattan, near dizzy with the free afternoon before me. If I wanted, I could have a second one. I could have a *third.*

"So, Lisa," I said, staring directly into her eyes, a tactic I had picked up from watching French men on the *métro.* "How about telling me the story of your life?"

"I don't know, Richard," she said, leaning closer. "How about telling me how badly an affair would fuck up your marriage?"

You can't get much past an American. But

118

then again, there was the ring. And the dead cell cast of seven years of marital fidelity on my skin. I was porous. Floundering. But we didn't sleep together right away.

At the end of our cocktail-a-thon, Lisa left me her address, inviting me to her house for dinner later that week, an invitation that I accepted with every intention to cancel once I was back safely in my house. But then the days went by in their parade of mundanity, me walking Cam to school and coming home to work on those stupid, stupid key paintings, having nothing new to say to my wife at dinner and her having nothing new to say to me, and on the eve in question, it felt like, what was the big deal, really? *It was just a meal!* I was a grown man. I could have female friends I didn't sleep with.

Until then, I'd never lied to Anne. I'd never had to. I got all of my weird shit out in my art. But on that Thursday, I heard myself tell her that I was going over to Julien's to watch a soccer match. That we'd probably grab dinner. And I died a little as my trusting partner simply nodded, and said, "That sounds like fun."

I don't know what I was expecting to happen as I set out for the Étienne Marcel quarter with a bottle of red wine. Or rather, I knew what was *supposed* to happen, but I was still operating in a whirlpool of denial where I was more focused on spending an evening with a beautiful woman I didn't know than the fact that with every step I took, I was making my way closer to having sex with someone else.

One seventy-seven Rue Montmartre was a five-story building with a large blue door and an inside courtyard with palm trees and two benches. There was no elevator. By the time I climbed the spiraling staircase to the fourth floor, I was winded, and as I'm not keen on audible panting by way of greeting, I waited several minutes before ringing Lisa's bell.

When she came to the door, aside from a decisive firming in my tallyhos, our exchange was cordial: she cheek-kissed me, thanked me for the wine, put away my coat.

Lisa's apartment was a two-level affair with an American-style kitchen and sitting room on the first floor and a staircase leading up to the bedroom, which gave out onto a little balcony with two folding chairs and three dirt-filled flower boxes. She never planted anything in those flower boxes the entire time I knew her. When I asked her why, she said that she didn't want to feel guilty when they died.

I sat down in the living room and Lisa emerged from the kitchen with a bottle of Sauvignon Blanc and a plate of oysters. Oysters, I thought. That's a bit much. Maybe she was one of these beautiful unhinged types who was going to stalk me and ruin my family life and career, like Dolores in Woody Allen's *Crimes and Misdemeanors.* But when she placed the oysters down, I reprioritized. What I really had to worry about was food poisoning.

"I know they look outrageous," she said, having caught the look I gave her shellfish. "And you don't have to eat them if you don't want to, but it's this special recipe I picked up from this Japanese place I like. You're not Jewish, are you?"

The creation in question involved warm oysters stuffed with sautéed shallots and buttered algae — *algae* — topped with sour cream. I was simultaneously apprehensive and intrigued.

"Take a sip of wine first," she suggested. So I did.

Her little concoction turned out to be so delicious, I slurped down four of the six oysters on the plate, a gluttonous faux pas I hoped she would attribute to her fine cooking rather than poor upbringing on my part.

After the oysters, she brought out a bowl of rocket tossed with large slivers of Parmesan cheese on black plates.

"I normally eat with chopsticks," she admitted, passing me a fork and knife. "But I didn't know if you'd be into that. I'm crazy about everything Japanese. It just seems more . . . intimate, you know?"

As I wasn't eager to eat my salad with a stick, I didn't say much by way of a response, but nodded as if she were expressing a fundamental truth that can't be disagreed with.

"Have you been to Japan, then?" A logical follow-up on my part.

"No . . ." She cut a sliver of Parmesan in half with her fork. "But I'd like to go. But not to Tokyo, to someplace in the countryside. Like Kyoto? Have you been?"

I shook my head, because I was chewing. "So," I said, after a forced swallow. "Shall we get the where-are-you-from and where-am-I-from thing out of the way?"

"Poughkeepsie," she said, laughing. "In upstate New York. Do you know it?"

I told her I did, which surprised her, and explained that although I was born in England, I'd spent two years at RISD — and one long weekend I went up and down the Hudson visiting the museums and small galleries with my then-girlfriend. I did not mention that this girlfriend was now my wife.

"So, is that what you do now? Art?" She put her plate back on the table and crossed her right leg over her left. Those legs. Those legs! She was built like a dancer, very long and lean with high, taut ballerina tits that did not appear to be restricted by a bra.

"Art is what I try to do, yes."

"Well, this is a good place for it." I knew that smile. That smile was an undecided one that said, *Your work could be total shite but I have no way of knowing, so I'll just go get the main course now.* Which is what she did.

While she fussed in the kitchen, I had a look about the room. I started with the stack of English magazines piled up in the defunct fireplace. The left side of the pile was almost entirely composed of *New Yorker*s. The right side was a rather eclectic mixture of old *AD* magazines, several *Elle*s, three or four *Marie Claire Cuisine*s, and a hefty stack of *Herald Tribune*s.

"Does it cost a lot to get these *New Yorker*s sent over?" I asked, kneeling down in front of her collection. The minute I said it, I realized I shouldn't be going all MI6 on her periodicals. Women can be touchy about personal space.

"Oh, no!" She laughed from the kitchen. "It's a job perk at the *Tribune.* The office gets them sent over and I smuggle them out."

Oh, God. A journalist. She'd tell everything to the press. Tomorrow I'd have my face splashed across the paper: MARRIED MAN CAUGHT IN CULINARY TRYST WITH SMALL-TITTED AMERICAN.

She appeared in a doorway with a recipe book in one hand and a whisk in the other, a whisk that appeared to be covered in a riot of cream cheese. "Could you come in here and open the wine you brought?" she asked, coquettishly. "My hands are . . . full?"

My stomach dropped. I still had time to get out of there, to choose flight over fight. An attractive woman had asked me to open up a bottle of wine. It was a simple request. A turn of a corkscrew. No one had actually screwed anyone. Yet.

I followed Lisa back into the kitchen, my guilt and fear dissipating with the bobbing demilunes of her spectacularly tight ass. She was wearing a cream-colored wrap dress that showed off her lithe figure in the most tantalizing of ways. She had cinched the dress with a brown leather belt, underneath which was a camisole of soft pink silk. On her feet, she wore brown Moroccan babouches of the same leather as her belt. Simple. Lovely. I realized I'd neglected to ask if she'd wanted me to take my shoes off when I came in. But fuck it. If I was going to make a life-changing error, I sure as hell wasn't going to do it in my socks.

Lisa showed me where the glasses were and leaned back against the counter to watch me get them. I put the glasses down and set about opening up the bottle, wondering if I should kiss her now, later, or never? She was leaning back on her elbows; it would be perfect — I'd heave her up onto the counter, I'd pull aside her panties, we'd make love right there in the kitchen with all the lights on and the shades up. Oh, Lisa. Beautiful Lisa with her long, auburn hair and mod bangs and the freckles on her cheeks. Lord, don't let me do this.

"Shall we?" she asked, nodding toward the wine. "I'll be out in a second."

I went back into the living room and poured us two large glasses. Lisa followed with the edible equivalent of interior decoration — she'd coordinated the main course with the living room. On matching square white plates sat two beds of black pasta with rather large dollops of white cheese and a ring of basil leaves and red pepper in a decorative circle around the plate rim.

"Chiaroscuro," she said happily. "Squid ink pasta with ricotta." I was beginning to think that she was playing a joke on my digestive system. Or maybe with my libido. I mean, we weren't actually going to fornicate after eating noodles soaked in the liquid escape mechanism of a squid?

During dinner, we talked about the safe stuff: films we'd seen, books we'd read, a new wine bar that just opened up in the area. Finally, I got around to asking her what had brought her to France in the first place.

"A man, of course." She shrugged. "I met him at Columbia. He taught poetry. It's okay," she said, smiling. "You can roll your eyes. You should. He was a Dadaist." She topped off my wineglass, then hers. "I'd just finished the grad program in journalism and I didn't have a job yet. Yves — that was his name — he got a job at the Sorbonne. So I decided to follow him over here. When I think back on it, he never really *asked* me to, I just assumed he'd wanted me to. I assumed wrong." Her lips shifted into a frown. "It turned out he *really* had a thing for students."

"But you stayed."

"Well," she said, "I stayed for a while. I

started at the *Tribune* as an intern, but it was shitty work. You know, stapling, making coffee. And it was impossible to move up. All the good jobs went to the staff of the *New York Times* who got transferred to Paris. I didn't know anyone, really. It's hard to make friends here. So I moved back to New York." She took off one of her moccasins, moved her foot in circles, and put her shoe back on.

"I spent a couple years freelancing for different publications until I finally got the same crummy job at the *Times* that I'd had at the *Tribune:* staple girl. But things move quicker in New York. I pitched a comeback column for the style section: the comeback of the shaving brush, the comeback of the flat. It was popular. You know, I moved up. And eventually there was an opening at the *Tribune* in Paris, and I thought, Hell, I'll try Paris again on my own terms. And I moved back."

"Still handy with the stapler?"

She laughed. "No, I do the culture page and once in a while I do the nightlife reviews for the Sunday issue. New bars, new clubs, what's in, what's out . . . of course, it's all geared toward wealthy expats, so what's in is actually quite out, if you know what I mean."

"And the professor?"

"Ugh," she groaned. "He's still at the Sorbonne. The last Dadaist in Paris."

She fell silent. I fell silent. I looked down at my plate in panic. If there was a cheese course, I had thirty, maybe forty minutes to decide whether or not I was going to make an unpardonable mockery out of my wedding vows.

"There's no dessert," said Lisa, looking straight at me. "Coffee?"

Oh, but I had much less time than that.

Lisa reappeared with a tray bearing two cups of espresso, a saucer of milk, and a cup of brown sugar. When she placed the tray down on the coffee table, a little bit of milk sloshed out of the saucer. All of the sudden I knew that this was it. Neither one of us was going to be drinking any coffee.

No one in my life has ever come on to me like Lisa Bishop. She walked over and sat down on me, just lowered herself on my lap like a naughty koala. Tossing her long hair behind her shoulders, she cocked her head and cupped her hands around my face.

"Richard," she said quietly. "I find you very attractive. It isn't good."

"No . . ." I answered, my heart engaged in somersaults. "It isn't."

Well, fuck it. Being there in the first place

128

was already a crime. I might as well make the bloody best of it. Clearing my mind of everything but lust, I pushed the rest of her hair behind her shoulders and slipped my hand behind her neck. I pulled her toward me and we started kissing, slowly. Her mouth tasted like vanilla, her tongue was soft and warm. She spread her legs farther apart and pushed herself against my erection. I moved my hands to her breasts, kneading them and stroking her nipple between my forefinger and my thumb. She let out a soft moan and pressed her cheek against my forehead. She began to stroke my hard-on from the outside of my clothing, which made me feel like a teenager again, getting me more excited still. I moved my right hand beneath her dress and teased my way toward her panties. They were silk, and they were loose. I moved them to one side just like I'd been dying to do in the kitchen, and put my fingers inside of her. She sucked in her breath and began kissing my ear and my neck with perverse abandon. Well, that was the end of it — I have a very sensitive neck that proved to be preposterously responsive to her hot, little tongue.

She pushed herself harder against me. I was touching her and kissing her and it felt so right and so fantastic, I moved straight from gobsmacked-level rapture to now-I-can-die.

There wasn't any music playing, the CD she'd had on had ended, and the sounds of us moving on the couch and of us touching each other were unbelievably intense. I had to have her. Immediately. I began to unzip my fly but she stopped my fingers. She licked her hand and stroked my cock with her wet palm. She started lowering herself down to suck me off but I eased her back up and kissed her.

"I can't wait," I whispered near her ear. She took me in her hand and eased herself on top of me again. She started sliding down, then up, teasing me brutally, the pleasure of her nakedness against mine too much. I put my hand on the small of her back and thrust myself inside of her: she gasped. We started moving together, and bloody hell, it was divine. I moved my left hand over her backside. I grabbed her naughty arse and pressed her down on me. She sucked in her breath and responded by kissing me fully with her tongue. With my right hand I was holding her panties to the side and touching her clitoris, and when I looked down I could see myself moving in and out of her.

"I'm gonna come, I can't . . ." I held her tighter.

"I want to come with you." She took me fully within her, grinding against me in a circular motion. She began to touch herself with her right hand. I could feel her touching herself there, and it felt like she was touching me each time I thrust inside of her. It was too much. Much too much.

"Lisa . . ." I sighed.

She moaned and held me tighter, pulling my head to her chest while she writhed her way through her enviably long orgasm. With me still inside of her, she lowered her head to my shoulder and kissed me softly on the neck.

"Hey," she whispered.

"Yeah?" I answered, floating.

She responded by kissing me on my nipple with a flash of her wicked tongue.

"Let's do it again, England," she whispered, slipping off her underwear.

Lisa made me happy. She made me feel capable and desired and potent and alive. She brought me back to my body: to the appreciation of my legs, my working hands, my strong back, my cock. She turned sex back into a play form, instead of the confusing, dark thing it had become with my wife.

A diversion. A confession. An action standing in for something else.

I didn't think I'd continue on with it. I thought that it would end with our symbiotic sex that one night. But no. That's a lie, actually. I knew once we were finished that it would happen again and again, and that I'd put as much energy into nurturing this new relationship as I would keeping it a secret from my wife.

And I was good at it, God help me. You don't put any thought into whether or not you will be until it happens, but I turned out to be a standout failed monogamist. Instead of feeling guilty, I felt grateful for my wife. Grateful for my daughter. Grateful that the one thing lacking from our perfect family circle was being supplied by someone else.

But now that Lisa has left me, the ease of what we had together hangs about like warm gunpowder after fireworks. Do I really want her back, or do I just want what we had? Our unchartered lovemaking. The absence of carved patterns and followed rules. The easy brightness of the new.

I put Lisa's letters back into the cabinet, no clearer on whether or not she was behind the situation with *The Blue Bear,* but certain that whatever she was doing, planning, or not planning, she finally missed me back. She would have spent enough time now in her posh house with her fancy spoon designer to learn that love wasn't as fun when it was predictable, when the game was fixed.

I've asked myself a hundred times since Anne confronted me in my studio whether, if I had it to do over, I would have gone up for that first drink with Lisa, accepted her invitation for dinner, allowed the whole thing to start. I don't know what this means for my future, but I don't regret my affair. I regret that Anne found out about it, and I regret that I hurt her, but to regret the entirety of the relationship itself would be to deny that I had real feelings for Lisa. Which I did.

I owe my wife much more than an apology: I owe her the difficult feat of falling back in love. But can we come back to love after an absence, or does it die from neglect?

It *does* die. It does wither. You can't even walk away from a meal on a table without it losing heat and changing, much less a plant, a pet, a marriage. I was an idiot to think that I could continue to see Lisa without it affecting my relationship with Anne. Is the damage irrevocable? Or is there a way back to our past where we can build around the dark places until our mistakes are far beneath us, dead for lack of sun?

Anne is giving me a chance, and I lack the courage to take it. There's no undoing what I've done.

7

The next day, after Anne went to work and I saw Camille off to school, I gathered up all of Lisa's letters and headed to the gallery, where Julien was in the middle of admonishing Bérénice over something she'd brought for lunch.

"She's got pickled cabbage in the storage room," he whispered, out of earshot of her desk. "She says it's good for *colds.*"

"It is, actually."

"Yeah, well, our printing paper smells like balls."

I announced that I would deliver *The Blue Bear* to London. That I'd do it next week, during my holiday.

"Great! We'll just settle on a day, then." He started flipping through his agenda.

"But there's one thing," I said, pulling out Lisa's letters and dropping them on his desk. "I spent all night going through these. You're probably right, that it isn't her, but I don't want to know until I have to. Until I'm there."

"Well, it wouldn't be hard," he said, reaching for one of the envelopes. "You've got the return address right there, and I can tell you where the painting's going —"

I slapped my hand down over the envelope to keep him from executing his intended task.

"Okay," he said, flinching. "Whatever you want."

"And can you hold on to those?" I nodded at Lisa's letters. "I don't want them in the house."

"Sure. But you've actually got more mail."

He went to the storage closet and came back with more contracts for sold paintings, another recipe from my mother, and a Halloween card from an expatriated American named Shelly Hampl who was both a client and a fan.

"She bought two key paintings, you know," he said, pointing at the oversize card that began to cackle when I opened it.

There's a certain kind of American woman — a little doughy, white, divorced — who comes to Paris to reinvent herself, a process that usually sees her emerging far higher on the extroverted scale than she's ever been before. Shelly Hampl is one of these women.

She's fond of saris, which she wears over ample jeans and pump-up Reeboks because, you know, in Paris *you just walk, and walk, and walk.* Not that there is anything wrong with her, per se. It's just that when you finally get a patron wearing pump-up high-tops, you hope they come accompanied by an entourage, a talent manager, and an Escalade.

After locating the tape measure from the rubble in Julien's desk, we went to measure *The Blue Bear* so that we could figure out how I could transport the damn thing to England. He promised me that his men would deliver it first thing in the morning, and after failing to convince me to purchase a ski rack for its transport, I gathered up my mail and the cackling Halloween card and kissed Julien good-bye. I was halfway home when I realized I'd swept up Lisa's letters along with everything else.

If I went back to the gallery now, it would be close to noon when I made it to the markets for the tsunami of errands Anne had entrusted me with before the next day's departure, which meant that they'd start to run out of the things we needed during the lunch rush, which meant that Anne would have my head. It really was a toss-up: confirmation of my infidelity in writing, or a dearth of car snacks. I decided to carry on.

Besides, I felt good about our vacation. We were good beside the sea. The weather would be balmy, not warm enough to swim yet, but mild enough to take beach walks with our shoes off, to watch Anne's parents' ancient Newfoundland root about for sticks. To help Camille gather seashells. To be a family again.

And Cam just loved her grandparents' house, and Brittany in general. The sharp wind off the ocean that pinkened all our cheeks, the deep sleep the sea air pushed us into. She loved the rambling stone house, the rickety staircases. She loved their rheumy dog. We would be fine. It would be healing. We just had to *get* there.

The rest of the day passed in a whirlwind of activity with me fetching and gathering and noting things we might forget on whatever scrap of paper I had near me when Anne called. The next day, a Wednesday, marked the start of a two-week vacation, but for the first week of it, Anne would be working remotely from her parents' home, getting ready for her pretrial. Accordingly, she was going to be at the office late that night, and was panicked that she wouldn't have time to pack. She dictated a preliminary list of must-haves to me from her office so that I could start packing for her.

"Bar soap," she said. "My parents only have lavender. And my black slacks that are hanging near my — Oh, and a one-piece, maybe? Do you think you'll swim?"

The truth was that we didn't need to be having the conversation. As I puttered around our bedroom, my hands moved automatically toward the things that formed her Anne-ness: a collection of poems by C. D. Wright that she always kept on the nightstand. A Chanel paperweight in the shape of a white rose. Her perfume, Rouge Hermès, which she only wore at night because she thought it vulgar to wear perfume during the day. A framed picture of Camille holding up a crayfish that she traveled with everywhere, even when Camille was with us. The black trousers she requested. Her favorite collared shirts. The rain boots she always took to Brittany for walks along the ocean. This awful, fleecy headband that she'd had since our time in Providence that she liked to wrap around her ears when we went walking. (French people have two great fears in life: drafts and wind. Drafts get you in the inside of your house, and wind gets you while you're out. Both are to be avoided at all costs.)

I put Anne's belongings on the bed so that she could review what I'd included, and then I stuffed my own bag with the dress shirts and the corduroys and the femmy socks that Anne's parents liked to see me in.

The next day saw me even more at odds and ends. Both my women had half days — Anne ran out at 8 a.m., a whirling dervish of reminders and don't-forget-to's, and I trotted Camille down the street to school so that she could be restless and excited and entirely unproductive somewhere other than in our house.

Julien's delivery guys showed up at 10 a.m. to deliver *The Blue Bear,* and the minute they left, I started transferring our luggage from the house into the car. You can't travel light with women. I've spent years now cohabitating with this species, and it's impossible, you can't. At some point in the evening, Anne had snuck off into the kitchen and added even more "emergency items" to the Haddon family tote bag: Yahtzee, sun hats, chocolate cookies, a head massager — for most of the year, Anne was the picture of economy and good taste, but a single trip to her parents could unleash the anxious urbanite within her who felt comforted by *things.*

A final round to ensure that the light switches were all facing downward and the stove burners turned off, and I had finally finished. It was just after eleven. I'd pick Camille up at school and make it to Anne's office on time by noon, which meant I'd score big points with Anne, which meant we'd have a pleasant drive to Brittany.

And we did. By some miracle of reverse congestion, all the traffic in Paris was heading south. Camille and I actually had to *idle* on the curb outside Anne's office, a blue-moon occurrence in the history of trips like this. Usually, Anne would already be waiting on the sidewalk, one high heel tapping, arms crossed, her face saying, *You're late.*

We got to Anne's parents' house a little before five. As was their custom, Mr. and Mrs. Bourigeaud were already outside when we arrived, waiting for us to get out of the car, kiss them, and be done with it so that they could get to the real prize: Camille.

I couldn't help it — every time I drove up to that stately beach house, I forgot how Mr. Bourigeaud had more or less forced me to take a translation job in the basement of the very law firm he and Anne toiled in so that I could "earn my keep," or how Anne cried the night he canceled a special dinner with her when she'd passed the European

141

bar because he had to work late. Screw it, I wanted him to like me. I wanted to be *in*.

"Anne, ma chérie! T'as l'air fatiguée!" Anne's mother, Inès, swept her up in the traditional French welcome composed of two cheek kisses and an observation of what is physically off about you. On this day, Anne looked "tired."

"And you, Richard!" she said, pulling me into her heavily scented embrace. "You look thin. He looks thin, *non?*"

Alain offered to help with our bags and then scoffed at how many of them there were.

"You could have hung this here, you know," he said, trying to undo the mess of bungee cords holding the bear down. "We have plenty of room."

"We were thinking he'd go on Tuesday, to deliver it," said Anne, ignoring her father's sudden possessiveness about a painting he'd never liked.

"It's a shame you have to go such a long way on your vacation," added Inès.

"Sounds very queer to me," said Alain, still fiddling with the cords. "You certainly do let people in the art world walk all over you!"

Not just in the art world, I thought, taking Camille's hand and starting for the house.

I will say this about the upper echelon in France: they know how to spend money. From what I saw living in America, wealth is dedicated to elevating the individual experience. If you're a well-off child, you get a car, or a horse. You go to summer camps that cost as much as college. And everything is monogrammed, personalized, and stamped, to make it that much easier for other people to recognize your net worth.

In France, great wealth is spent within the family, on the family. It's not shown off, but rather spread about to make the lucky feel comfortable, and safe. Consider the ways the two countries approach the practice of inheritance. In America, when you die, you can leave your money to whomever, or whatever, you want. You can leave millions — as has been done before — to your bichon frisé.

In France, the estate has to be passed down the bloodline in equal parts, and you can't leave anyone out — even the bad apples. If you have two children, say, and one of them is a drug addict who every three years shows up to say he's changed and then cooks heroin on your sterling silver and nicks all your cash, this sod's getting as much as the picture-perfect daughter who's been looking after you for years. It's an imperfect system, but it informs the way the wealthy live.

The French bourgeois don't pine for yachts or garages with multiple cars. They don't build homes with bowling alleys or spend their weekends trying to meet the quarterly food and beverage limit at their country clubs: they put their savings into a vacation home that all their family can enjoy, and usually it's in France. They buy nice food, they serve nice wine, and they wear the same cashmere sweaters over and over for years. I think the wealthy French feel comfortable with their money because they do not fear it. It's the fearful who put money into houses with seven bedrooms and fifteen baths. It's the fearful who drive around in yellow Hummers during high-gas-price months because if they're going to lose their money tomorrow, at least other people will know that they are rich today. The French, as with almost all things, privilege privacy and subtlety and they don't feel comfortable with excess. This is why one of their favorite admonishments is *tu t'es laissé aller.* You've lost control of yourself. You've let yourself go. Still, I'll always prefer an untamed British garden to a curated French one. I *like* letting myself go.

The Bourigeauds' house was at the end of a dirt road running on the west end of a public golf course. There were five houses on the road, each of them bordered on one side by maritime pines and conifers, and on the other side, the turquoise sea. Built upon a cliff, the stone house managed to be charming, despite its dramatic views. Nestled in the middle of two acres of oak and beech and hornbeam, there was an expanse of grass and reeds that effectively functioned as a front lawn, beyond which was a jagged cliff of porous rock dropping to the sea. In America, the border of the property would have been gated to keep children and sleepwalkers and drunkards from dropping to their deaths, but there was no division here between safety and stupidity: you had to draw those lines yourself.

Another custom of the Bourigeauds' was an arrival walk. They were big believers in moving the old legs after a journey — that the salty air would open your appetite and gift you with deep sleep. Today, however, Anne said she wanted to stay home and unpack. I knew what this meant, of course. It meant that she was going to hide away in the guest

145

bedroom and check her umbilical cord of a smartphone to see what was happening at work.

So I set out with Alain and Inès and Camille and their giant canine, Balfus, on the walking path that ran along the outskirts of the cliffs. Only five steps in, and I felt elated. Even through her cotton gloves, I could feel the warmth of my daughter's hand in mine, which I absorbed with her excited babbles about seahorses and kites. Ahead of us, her grandparents moved confidently up the sandy route they had taken hundreds, maybe thousands of times before, with Alain bending down from time to time to pluck a thistle from his pants and to pat his happy dog. The sea — immense and multicolored — I'd never tire of its beauty. High tide was coming in along the coast, the water moving in an orchestrated cascade of frothy, rolling waves. I swung Camille up onto my shoulders so that she could spot the stone lighthouse on Cap Fréhel.

The walk, if we'd done the whole loop, was a two-mile jaunt that wove up and down the cliffs before finishing in a set of woods near the entrance to the town of Saint-Briac, but we'd only gone halfway before deciding to turn back. We all agreed that it would be nice to have a cocktail, and to do the full walk in the morning, with Anne.

We were taking off our layers in the mudroom when Anne burst in, a chimera of tousled hair and red eyes and seriously pinched lips.

"Jesus," I said, slipping Camille's coat off. "What's wrong?"

Anne knelt down brusquely and put her hands on Camille's shoulders. "Did you have a good time, darling? Run up to your room, sweetie. I got everything unpacked."

Then she stood up and yanked me close to scream-whisper, "I have to fucking *talk* to you."

"Can you look after Camille for a little while, *maman?*" she asked, louder, loosening her grip on my wrist. "I just have to deal with a little thing at work."

And with that, she stomped out of the mudroom and pounded up the stairs.

I looked at her parents and shrugged. "She really needs this vacation."

Alain nodded his head, slowly. "So it appears."

I took my leave and started up the stairs after her, trying to guess what alarmist e-mail or phone call she had received. Some emergency at the office, an entreaty that there was no one, *no one* who could handle it but Anne. How quickly could she make it back to the capital?

But when she pushed the door open to our guest bedroom, my life fell through the floor. The bed was covered in mail. Petal-yellow envelopes. I'd forgotten Lisa's letters. I'd left them in my bag.

"What the *fuck* is this?" she asked, grabbing a stack off of the comforter. "You promised it was over! You said it was —" She started crying and sat down on the bed.

"How could you do this?" Her head was in her hands. "You can't even — and she's in London! This whole time . . . I've been so stupid. *They need me to deliver it.* You're a fucking monster."

I stared at the magazines, the contracts, her legal documents, the opened letters, the spread of evidence on the bed. She'd just been organizing, cleaning up, getting ready to start her vacation, unpacking my bag for me as she always did, and now I'd ruined everything.

"Anne," I said, standing like an idiot in the middle of the room. "It isn't what it looks like. I never wrote her back."

"Like hell you didn't!"

She started throwing mail at me: hurling one letter and then another, then sweeping all the mail onto the floor.

"Just stop it! I read them. All of them! You fucking *loved* her! And here I was thinking it wasn't . . . that it wasn't . . . I don't know. That maybe you were tempted, but —" I watched her swallow. "And I had — people said, seven years, it happens. Just wait. It'll pass." She broke down into sobs. Every muscle in my body went rigid. I couldn't breathe.

"You did this," she said, looking down. "For so long."

I was absolutely speechless. I couldn't apologize. I couldn't deny. All I could do was stand there as the weight of the pain that she was feeling moved throughout my body, pulled my organs toward the ground.

"You have to go," she said, wiping at her eyes. "You have to —" She almost started laughing. The sound was sick and sad. "We just fucking *got* here."

"Anne," I said, taking a step toward her.

"Anne?" she repeated. "Anne. Anne. What? What do you have to *say*, Richard? It's all here!" She kicked the letters on the floor. " 'You loved me too much, Richard. You were in very bad shape when I left!' She knew you pretty well, huh? She knows you better than us!"

"That's not true," I said, steadying my hand on the bed's cast-iron footboard. "She wasn't — it wasn't . . ." I couldn't get the words out. I couldn't talk.

"Oh, I know what it *was* now. I thought it was just a stupid fuck. But no, you had . . . you were having . . ." She bit her lip as a tear slid down her cheek. "You were going to leave us."

"I wasn't," I whispered.

"Bullshit," she said, sinking her head into her hands again. "It's still going on."

"It isn't," I said. "I swear."

She stood up abruptly and punched me in the chest. She punched me again, harder, and then slammed both of her fists against me, pushing me backward.

"Just fucking *stop* it," she shouted. "You fucking *stop*! I don't believe you and I don't trust you and I want you *out*!"

Tears sprang to my eyes as I grabbed one of her fists.

"I never wrote her back!"

"You just *go* to London. Go! I don't know how we're going to do this, I don't have any fucking idea, but I want you out of this house and I don't ever want to see you again!"

I held her wrist away from me and shouted, "I *never* wrote her back! I never even asked her to write me! And it's not her in London!"

"Bullshit!" she said, hitting me with her free hand. "I don't *believe* you anymore!"

All of a sudden there was a knock on the door.

"Everything all right?" Inès's voice called out meekly.

I watched Anne's face jerk into a mask.

"Everything's *fine,* Mother, it's just . . . a phone call. Can you take Camille outside?"

"You sure you're all right?"

"We're *fine!* Just take her outside!"

We both stood there fuming, literally expelling heat from our bodies, waiting until we heard Inès's steps retreat down the hall.

"I can't have this . . . with my parents."

"I'm not going to London."

"Well, you're sure as fuck not staying here." She walked away from me to gather up the paper shrapnel around the bed. "Go to her. Fuck your brains out. You still remember how?"

"I'm not going," I repeated.

"Yes, you fucking *are.*"

"It isn't *her,* Anne. Julien verified it."

"Oh, right, the keeper of the flame! I like how you've been outsourcing your philandering to the gallery, by the way. You certainly have a knack for multitasking when it involves your balls."

She stuffed letter after letter back into my

151

bag along with my magazines and the idiotic recipe my mother had sent, and then she walked to the window and stared out at the sea.

"Anne," I pleaded.

"You got a phone call," she said, turning around. "From your gallery. You have to go to London. The buyers, it's their schedule. And we fought about it, because we only just arrived. And you have to go right now."

"But there aren't any ferries."

She laughed out loud. "I don't give a royal shit about the ferry. You take the car, and you get *out.*"

"But, Anne," I said. "We can't. We need to talk. I have things I can explain."

"You don't need to *explain* anything. It's pretty goddamn clear."

"But we can't just stop like this. We're married."

"You've got some fucking nerve," she said, swallowing hard. "I'm going downstairs now, to tell them. In the meantime, pack your bag."

The Bourigeauds were distraught to hear that I had to leave so much earlier than planned. I also don't think they believed us. Camille whined and asked why I couldn't take her with me, and when would I be back. I said I had to spend a couple days at my parents', that Grandpa wasn't feeling well, and that I'd be back sometime next week. Anne was in earshot when I said this, and I watched her grip tighten around the salad bowl she was carrying to the table.

"You really shouldn't let your clients treat you like this," said Alain, sitting down. "You have to set some limits."

"It's his *gallerist* who needs limits. Why would you ask such a thing, on the first day of vacation?" asked his wife.

"It's a very important painting and we need it out of the house," Anne announced, slamming the salad bowl down.

"I thought it had been in the gallery?" said her mother.

"Same difference. Camille? Don't sit like that. Put your napkin on your lap. Mom, will you pass the wine?"

"And you *really* can't stay for dinner? I mean, this just seems a bit absurd."

"I really do have to get going. You know, traffic."

"Of course," said her father, staring at me curiously, no doubt wondering how much traffic there could be in the English Channel. "Of course."

I kissed everyone good-bye and apologized

profusely, gamely repeating that I'd be back in several days. Anne, in an award-winning show of solidarity, linked her arm through mine and said she was going to walk me to the door. But once we reached the mudroom, all pretensions fell.

"I don't want to talk about this or hear about this or even *think* about this right now."

"But I can't —" I said. "We need to."

"I need a fucking *break,* Richard," she said. "I'll have Camille call you. And then . . ." She shook her head. "And then, nothing."

Nothing wasn't something I could work with. Nothing didn't tell me if Anne was thinking of a separation, or considering a divorce. Nothing was worse than if she hadn't said anything at all.

Which was exactly what happened when she walked away, leaving me with only my mistakes to keep me company, and an entire sea to cross.

It was too late to catch a ferry and, with a national holiday upon us, all of the scenic places were filled, so I spent the night in a budget motel on the side of the interstate leading into Saint-Malo.

The first thing I wanted to do upon arriving was brush my teeth. Teeth brushing has always been a kind of ablution for me, an oral atonement to the gods. But when I opened up my Dopp kit, I saw that I'd forgotten to bring toothpaste. Or rather, it was in Anne's bag.

This oversight made me despondent. I literally felt like I wasn't going to be able to see my way out of the mess I'd created while having scuzzy teeth. Things were so bad that I actually went downstairs to the lobby to talk the befuddled night receptionist into squirting some of his own toothpaste onto my brush.

I think when you reach a moment of tremendous desperation, a point at which your worst imaginings have actually come true, you're protected by a force field of incredulity before reality sets in. As I sat there on the flimsy mattress across from a fleet of tent-cards promising an El Dorado of blockbusters just a credit-card swipe away, I couldn't believe that what had happened had actually *happened.* If I'd left the letters at Julien's, like I'd planned to. If I hadn't left them in my bag. It wasn't possible, it couldn't be, Anne couldn't have *read* them. It would be heartbreaking if she did. It would kill her. It, quite literally, would ruin everything we had.

But the proof that it had happened was right there in my suitcase, smothered between the letters I'd stuffed back in my bag. It was in the fact that I was sitting alone on the first night of vacation in a fifty-five-euro-a-night hovel with another man's Aquafresh lingering on my gums. And yet. And yet, despite this proof, I still refused to accept the fact that there might be no more us.

I know that I shouldn't have been able to, but that night I actually slept. In my dream, Anne and I were watching figure skaters in a competition. We were in a hotel room, but it wasn't the one that I was in now. It was an unrecognizable location, very late at night. We had plans to go somewhere, but when we saw the figure skating, we became fixated by it. Anne leaned her head against me and said she'd always wanted to wear one of the costumes with the feathers on the bustle that spun out so magnificently when you twirled. I said that I'd had ice-skating lessons when I was younger, which isn't true in real life, but it was true in my dream. And then Anne danced her fingers across my chest and suggested we order take-away, and the alarm clock on my phone rang, and I woke up, and I was still alone, and all the bad things were true.

8

If I'd gone to London from Paris, it would have taken me just over two hours on the Eurostar. But from my perch in Saint-Malo, I had to board a ferry that would take six hours — *six* — to get to Poole. Poole is a two-hour drive from my family home in Hemel Hempstead. Whether it was a good thing or a bad thing, I'd have plenty of time to think.

With the Peugeot and *The Blue Bear* safely parked in the boat's bowels, I made my way up to the public atrium, where a troupe of plum-and-navy chairs were flanked by a glass-encased duty-free center where one could watch the English splurge on tins of foie gras and macaroons.

I picked a rather dismal area under an air vent in hopes that no one else would sit in the two vacant seats beside me, but my aspirations were dashed by the appearance of a round and ruddy fellow sporting a felt hat.

He was wearing an orange raincoat and khaki pants with the utility pockets near the ankles, not a useful place for them at all. He had the excited energy of a man on an expedition, and I could tell the minute he performed the universal is-this-seat-taken gesture that he would want to chat.

"So where you heading to, then?" he asked, taking out a printing-press worth of newspapers from his bag.

"Well, Poole, obviously."

"Poole, obviously!" he roared, striking my arm. "And then?"

"Hemel Hempstead," I said. "That's where I'm from."

"Blimey!" he replied, nearly hitting me again. "I'm from Great Gaddesden myself."

"Is that right," I said, honestly surprised. "Were you on holiday?"

"Oh, no," he said. "I work for Xerox. Big presentation out in Rennes."

"Oh, yeah?" I said. "How's that?"

"Well, they just bought the Color Docu-Tech 60. Fastest full-color laser printer in the industry."

"You don't say."

"I do," he said, opening a paper. "People are really intimidated by color copiers, you know? So I'm their hand-holder. Harold Gadfrey," he said, holding out his hand.

I shook it. "Richard Haddon."

"Haddon," he said. "Mind if I read a spot of the paper here? You want one? They had a ton in my hotel. English or French?" he asked, showing me an assortment.

I pointed to the pink one, the *Figaro*'s financial section.

"Ah, good," he said, handing it to me. "I can't read French. You seen this, by the way?"

He shook the *Sun* in my direction. Above a photo of Saddam Hussein, the front headline read DOES HE OR DOESN'T HE? SKEPTICISM LOOMS.

I winced.

"I know," he said, shaking his head. "It's no good. So what do you think? Does he, or doesn't he?"

"I think he . . . doesn't?"

"I think he doesn't, too."

We stared down at our papers, relieved.

"It leaves you thinking, though, doesn't it?" he said, rustling the front page. "What can we do, really? I'm forty-two years old; I'm not going to fight." He sighed. "I'm not much of an activist, I guess. You?"

"I don't know," I said. "I'm an artist, so . . ."

159

He sat back and studied me, said he'd pegged me for a writer. "Well," he said finally, folding his paper open. "You should do something about Iraq."

"I'm thinking about it, actually."

"I'd think fast."

We spent the next hour reading, and then shared a light lunch together in the pub, talking about his work and my work, the various joys and responsibilities that made up our lives. Harold was a family man, two daughters, a wife of seventeen years, two-car detached garage — in his own words, "the whole bit." He was older than me by almost a decade, but he had the youthful air that accompanies people whose default mood is good.

When it came to discussing my family, the mood noticeably shifted. I told him my wife was a lawyer, that we lived in Paris, the basic facts. And then I pulled out a photo of Camille that I kept inside my wallet. She was on a tricycle in Brittany, with a ladybug helmet on.

"Ooooh," Harold cooed. "She's a sweetheart. Does she take after her mum?"

"Oh, yes," I said, ashamed that I didn't have any pictures of Anne on me. "My better-looking half."

"We've gotten a bit lax back in Great Gaddesden, I'm afraid," Harold said, pinching his waist. "Fat and happy! You should come by while you're in town, actually. My wife's a splendid cook!"

"Oh, that's very kind," I said, swallowing. "But I don't plan on being here very long. Just a couple days, you know, to go to London, and see my parents."

"Of course." He nodded. "Well, lunch, maybe? Or breakfast? I don't know a lot of artists," he said, shrugging. "In my line of work, Richard, you're an exotic plant."

After lunch, Harold rolled into the empty row of seats behind me for a snooze, and I read some more papers before dozing off myself. All in all, the time passed more pleasantly than it might have, and I found myself giving my parents' landline to Harold on our arrival in Poole.

"It's something, isn't it," I said, ripping off a piece of paper from my planner. "I haven't lived there since sixth form, but I still remember the number."

"It's nice they live in the same place," he said, passing me a slip of paper with his own cell-phone number written on it. "Not a lot of stability, otherwise, today."

I nodded. I was happy to have met him, this great pelican of a man. I was happy to see how glad he was to return home to his wife and daughters. His wife had called while we were in transit to tell him she'd made his favorite: steak-and-kidney pie.

When we docked, I got a coffee before calling my own family to let them know I was arriving early. I apologized for not calling earlier, a last-minute situation, I said, with the London buyer. My mother was crestfallen to hear that Anne and Camille weren't with me. I said I was, too.

My relationship with my parents is an odd one. Once they gave it to me, the Haddon seniors ceased taking an active interest in my life. In fact, the extent of independence I was given as a youngster could easily have been mistaken for negligence on my parents' part. It's not that my parents weren't affectionate — they were — it's just that they spent most of their time fundamentally distracted.

My father, a history teacher, would often come home after his classes and eat a bowl of cereal with his nose stuffed up the pages of the *Scientific Observer.* He used to balance the magazine against a vase we had on the kitchen table that my mother rotated once a month with various genera of plastic flowers. It never occurred to my father that most dads don't eat Weetabix for supper.

My mother worked at the local library to which she commuted on an ancient green bicycle with a makeshift wicker basket that she'd fashioned herself. On Saturdays, when most left-leaning women her age were at home breast-feeding and baking carob muffins, Mum taught an art class at the local community center for a group of middle-aged women who, in between watercolors and felt collages, delighted in exchanging recipes and trading their secrets for removing underarm stains from their husbands' shirts. My mother used to check out the latest self-help books from the library in order to find a theme for each class that would lend a certain "zest" to her students' artwork. Judging from the yellow legal pad that my mother left in the family den one day, "You Can't Love Your Husband Until You Love Yourself" and "Oral Sex: What If We Talked About It?" were just some of the creative catalysts for the Hempstead Women's Art League in the 1970s.

I sat in my car with the other cross-Channel commuters, waiting for the drawbridge to go down. I hadn't seen my parents since last Christmas, ten months earlier. It was inexcusable, really. Lamentable as a son, and as a father. How was it that Camille hadn't seen her grandparents in ten months? Where had Anne and I been, as a couple? But I knew the answer. We'd been in the dumps.

It was shocking driving through Hemel Hempstead. All of the villages around ours had been improved with fancy shopping centers and river walks, but the Bennett's End district still looked like total crap. Constructed after World War II as a "new town" development, Bennett's End was mostly made up of dreary public housing: two-story single-family homes with detached one-car garages. Street after street, the red brick, the white shutters. The homes with novelty mailboxes and neon-purple perennials and whimsical garden sculptures, the bikes overturned on the front lawns. It wasn't scenic, and it wasn't charming, but it was home, and I could feel it in my shoulders as the stress started unwinding. I was happy to be back.

I parked the car in the driveway and checked the sky for rain. I'd have to ask my dad to swap out his beloved Vauxhall Chevette for my Peugeot so that the *Bear* didn't get sopped.

Just outside the front door, I was stopped in my tracks by the smell of my mother's one-pot cooking. Red wine, sherry, tinned tomatoes, meat, the perversely comforting scent of burned carrots and singed garlic. My mum has always been a terrible cook. She's one of those people who doesn't care what food tastes like; she eats because she has to. This had been a problem during my own family's prior visits, until Anne finally invented a visit-salvaging tradition called "Duck in a Can." Each time we came over, we brought a massive (and I mean silo-size) can of duck confit that would last us through two dinners. I'd forgotten it this time. It didn't matter. Shitty food suited my shitty state of mind.

I rang the bell and immediately heard a scurry of footsteps behind the door. The little eye on the peephole slid open, then closed.

"Richy!" The door opened, and there was my mum, her dark curls frazzled, her hands in oven mitts. She threw her arms around me and I embraced her, running my hands along her birdy bones. Even when I was a teenager, she only came up to my shoulder.

"Oh, love, it's so good to have you here!"

"Hi, Mum," I said, pulling back to smile at her. "I brought you guys some treats."

"Ah, love, you shouldn't have." She accepted the plastic bag of wine and tinned

165

caramels I'd got from duty-free before nodding at my tiny suitcase. "Is that all you have?"

"That, and the painting," I said, looking toward the car. "I've got to get it in the garage."

"You've got to move the Vauxy, Georgie!" she yelled. "He's got that painting on the car!"

My dad popped out in a fuzzy yellow sweater and ancient brown trousers.

"My boy!" he said, pulling me to him.

"Aww, lovely," said my mother, watching us embrace. "What a shame that Anne and Camille couldn't make it."

"I know," I said, frowning. "I shouldn't be here either, actually. It's a unique situation. A very special client."

I put my stuff down in my childhood room, a robin's-egg-blue box with a desk beneath a window that looked out onto the small backyard. A weathered poster of Clint Eastwood in *Dirty Harry* still adorned the wall above the single bed I'd slept in as a child, along with an Arsenal football calendar from 1979.

"I love what you've done with the place," I said to my mother, standing in the shadow behind me. She hit me in the back, playfully, her oven mitts still on.

"You want noodles or rice with the stew?" she asked. She did both terribly. She used instant rice and tended to slow-cook instant noodles.

"Noodles would be great."

"Let's give them a call, first!" My mum tugged on my sweater. "Tell them you've arrived! I want to say hi to my grand-daughter!"

"All right," I said, trying to sound chipper. "Let me just get my things sorted, and I'll call."

Once she left the room, I shut the door and sat down on the bed. I checked my cell phone: no calls, no messages. Because I am a devious person, I called the Bourigeauds' landline.

"Allô?" said a voice that was definitely my spouse's.

"Anne?" I said. "It's me."

"Yes, well," she said. "You arrived."

"I have."

Silence.

"Listen," I said, "My mum really wants to speak to Camille. That's why I'm —"

"Yes," said Anne. "That's fine."

I listened to Anne call out for Camille and heard the phone drop, and then get picked up again by much smaller hands.

"Grand-maman?" went Camille.

167

"No, sweetheart, it's me."

"Oh, hi, Daddy! I caught sand eels!"

"Well done! Are you gonna eat them?"

"Yup. Mommy's frying them now. Did you take the ferry all the way to Grandma's?"

"No." I laughed. "The ocean doesn't go there. I had to drive."

"Oh," she said. "Okay."

I took advantage of the sudden pause to decode the noise I heard in the background, to try to visualize the stiffness of Anne's posture, to wonder if Inès was helping her or if she was cooking alone.

"How's Mommy doing, Cam?"

"She caught some fish, too. Can I talk to Grandma now?"

My heart sank. "Of course, darling. Just a second."

I opened up my bedroom door and found my mother standing in the hallway, wringing her now oven-mitt-free hands.

"Is that my little Cam-Cam?" she asked, all brightness, reaching for the phone.

I shut myself back inside the bedroom, listening to the cadences of their talk. She was happy, my daughter. Clearly, Anne hadn't said anything yet about our fight. Fight? It was more than that. It was a deluge.

■ ■ ■ ■

After dinner, while my mum did the washing up, I sat in the living room with my father on a couch so old, it merited its own page in the family encyclopedia.

Orange Floral Couch, circa 1953: understuffed and sagging, this vintage lime-and-orange couch is nevertheless a persistent source of delight and comfort for the Haddon family household, especially for George Haddon, who smokes cigars in it after victorious Arsenal games. Evidence of this tradition in the form of burn holes is viewable on the northwest arm of the couch, closest to the side table, where Edna Haddon keeps a dish of salted cashews at all times.

"Sherry?" my father asked, standing by the empty bookshelf he used as a bar.

"Sure," I said.

"You want cheese or something, Frenchie?"

I laughed. "No, Dad." He handed me a small glass. "This is great," I said.

"So!" he said, settling down in the recliner near the TV. "What's new? Anne told me you had a lot of success with your last show?"

Ever gracious, Anne was faithful with the Sunday check-in calls. When her parents weren't in Brittany, we followed the French tradition of having long lunches with them each Sunday in the Parisian suburbs, and Anne would use the time between the meal and dessert to call my family, passing the phone from Camille to me. Because it was always Anne who made the phone call, she was usually the one who presented a summary of the past week, and a glimpse of the week ahead. She was astonishingly considerate, my wife.

"Yeah, quite a few of them have sold, actually, for pretty good prices. And then I've got that mess," I said, gesturing to the garage, where my car was now parked.

"I see," went my father, as if that explained everything. "So how long will you be here?"

I reached for my glass. "Well, it depends, actually. I'm supposed to deliver the painting on Tuesday, but I'm hoping that I can move the appointment earlier, as I'm already here."

"I thought you came because they needed it earlier?"

"Right," I said, gulping down the drink.

"But then they, eh, moved the appointment back."

My father frowned. "I see. Well, I can't keep up with you. And how's Anne?"

I scratched the back of my neck. "She's good. Tired, overworked, you know. She's got a new case. These new mums out in Lille who didn't know that you're not supposed to be slogging back wine while you're pregnant, so they're lobbying for a massive logo of sorts, right on the bottle."

"Are they mental?"

I almost spit out my sherry. "What?! No, Dad, they're not *mental,* they're just . . . I don't know what they are, actually. They're just not informed."

We drank our sherry and listened to the clanks and plunks of my mother putting away the dishes.

"So no more kids, then?"

"Jesus," I said, getting up to pour us more sherry.

"You know, I think we might have had another, is all I'm saying," said my dad. "But by the time we felt like it, you were seven. Camille's what now, five?"

"Yeah, five."

"Well, it's now or never, I think. My siblings, we all have a two-year difference, which is no difference, really. But then you

171

look at your mother. Five years between her and Abigail — and they hardly talk."

"So it's already too late for us, is what you're saying."

My dad knitted his brows together. "Possibly."

I sighed and sat back down. The sherry had warmed me, as had the stew that was still settling in my guts. I wanted at that moment to come clean to my father, to ask him for advice. After all, he'd cheated on my mother all those years ago, and although I never really understood how far it went, it had probably gone far enough for him to have an opinion on what I should do. But then my mum appeared in the doorway, wiping down a plate.

"So if you're free tomorrow, love, I was thinking we could show you the new things they've done around Gadebridge? It's really the nicest little park."

Claiming tiredness from the long journey, I kissed my parents good night and said that rain or shine, a trip out to Gadebridge sounded very nice, indeed. And then I shut myself in my small bedroom and sat down under the *Dirty Harry* poster, put my head into my hands, and endured the tight throat and nasal-drip condition that heralded a cry.

It was strange — or at least, among the

people we knew, it was an anomaly — that I, an only child, had married another only child. It was even odder for Anne to be an only child, and French. Proper bourgeois families, especially if religious, get up to as many as five Barbour-jacket-wearing off-spring. But Anne's mother had suffered secondary infertility when she and Alain tried to conceive after Anne's birth. It was a taboo topic, apparently a source of profound guilt and shame, as the two of them always wanted a large family. I'd asked Anne whether her parents had ever thought about adopting, and she said her mother was for it, but her father thought it embarrassing — like parading around a banner communicating to the public what did — and couldn't — happen in your bed.

And it's true that Anne and I had discussed having another child, about three years ago, but Anne's career picked up, then mine did, and we lost time basking in the fact that we were busy and successful, with a child who kept us busier still. Despite the exemplary maternity-leave benefits for women in France, I don't think Anne was ready, or could even envision slowing down. And time passed. And I met Lisa. And even more time was lost. And now, it's true what my dad said, a five-year difference would be a lot. And plus, impregnation seems improbable. You have to have sex for that.

Much later, unable to sleep, I padded into the living room and — against my better instincts — pulled out Anne and my wedding album from the bookshelf. This second wedding, the one the Bourigeauds insisted on, took place about a year after our first one, at their place in Saint-Briac. Although both weddings were by the seashore, that is where the similarity between the two events ends.

Seeing as how we hadn't invited any relatives to the Cape Cod edition, our French wedding was the first time that Anne actually met my parents. My father liked her the minute he saw her, but my mother seemed uncomfortable around her, ill at ease. It happens a lot with Anne — the dark hair, her boyish hips that make her endless legs look even longer, the way she carries herself with a dancer's posture — a lot of people peg her for a cold person before giving her a chance. It's true that she's choosy socially: she's economical with her words. I can see how other people find this haughty, but the truth is that she's shy. And although she's good with bourgeois small talk, when it comes to keeping up with someone awkward like my mum, Anne's at a total loss. I remember after the wedding, when I asked her what she talked about with my mother, she covered her eyes with her hands like a little girl. "Oh my God," she said. "The weather."

Anne was disappointed by her first encounter with my mother, and she didn't know how to carry forth with such an outcome. Being a traditionalist, she'd hoped to get on splendidly with Mum, because that's what daughters-in-laws *did.* She'd filled her head with visions of weekend visits to my parents' and long walks with Edna, the two of them exchanging giddy little intimacies, my mother telling her an indicative story about me when I was younger, and Anne smiling and saying that I hadn't changed at all. Walking arm in arm back into the house, like queens from different countries, teasing their menfolk who would, of course, be chatting around the fire. Lunch would be prepared. We would all break into song.

Anne's debut with my father went a great deal better. He and Anne had already spoken on the phone several times while I was still at RISD, and Anne had even sent some postcards from Cape Cod after our first wedding, sprinkled with phrases like *I can't wait to meet you* and *your almost-*

daughter, Anne. After the reception in France, my father yanked me aside and whispered, "Good God, Richard, she's gorgeous." He let out a faint whistle as he watched my new bride interact with his own wife on the deck. "And you know, she'll stay that way, too. It's in their constitution. Not like the English, God help us." By this time, Anne had come up between the two of us and was standing at my father's side. He threw his arms out and gave her an embrace in the French tradition, kissing her eagerly on both sides of her face, twice.

"I'm so happy for the two of you," he exclaimed, ratcheting things up to a bear hug.

"I know!" she said, slightly crumpled. "So am I!"

It was a lovely dinner, carried out mostly in English, which Alain and Inès spoke with accents made even more attractive by the copious amounts of wine served. My parents, of course, were completely smitten by the house, and also by Anne's family, whom they found just as warm and hospitable as could be. I remember that meal well, much better than the reception, which was a whirl of handshakes and embraces and too much white wine. I remember how happy Anne seemed to have us all together. I remember thinking, At some point, this will be us. We'll have a child and the child will marry, maybe in this very house. And I remember feeling real love for my parents, real love for my mother in her ridiculous turquoise tunic and my father in his favorite silk bow tie, which, I knew from watching him tie it as a child, had a small hole in the back of it, near the tag.

The guests started filtering out around four in the morning, but rather incredibly, my father was still up, gesticulating over a final glass of port with Alain de Bourigeaud. I went up to the two of them, raised my glass to Alain, thanked him for the perfect night. My father suggested a stroll, just a wee walk to get the bad stuff moving through him before he called it a night.

"You two go," said Alain, smiling. "I'm going to do a tour of the border there, make sure no one's fallen off."

My father tossed his arm around me, and we headed for the back of the house, toward the country road. He was heavy-footed, his arm leaden on my shoulder. It had been some time, a decade, maybe, since I'd seen him that lashed. But it was a good drunk, a joyful one, and I was glad to be there with him, glad he liked my wife. Glad that I was entering the type of family that he could be proud of.

"Ah, Richard!" he cried. "What a night. What a party! I'll tell you something, I think she's just great." He chucked me under the chin with his free hand. "A little frosty in the beginning, but that's the French in her! And God, but she is clever! But listen, son," he said, pulling me closer as we stumbled onto the road. "She's most terribly in love with you. You can feel it when you talk to her, it's lovely. But listen, I want to tell you something." He clutched my shoulder. "Listen. Don't forget her."

Somewhere beyond the torchlights that were still burning and the buzz of the alcohol and the music and the gorgeous guests, something inside of me wakened to this comment, wakened in the way you do from a dream that is unsettling, not right.

"What do you mean, forget her?" I asked. Behind us, I could hear cars crunching their way out of the gravel driveway and Anne's parents crying *merci* and *à bientôt* into the dark.

"I don't know, Rich. I've made some mistakes with your mum, you know. And there were times when I wanted to go off and leave, to find something better. But you know what? It doesn't *get* better. If you really love her, if you really, really love her,

178

it won't get any better than this. But just try to remember that you *do* love her, you know, because it gets so easy to forget. I'd like to tell you that it's all a romp in the hay and that you'll never want another girl, but I know you, and of course you will, but just, just try to remember . . . okay?"

"Remember *what,* Dad? Why are you telling me this?"

He stumbled over a sprinkler head and grabbed on to my arm. "Richy, just remember that what you have is *good.* And even though you don't think that matters, it does. Everything else comes after. And like I said, she's French."

"Thanks, Dad," I said, not knowing whether to thank him or fetch him aspirin. I rewired my brain to send his comments to the starboard of my cerebral cortex, where they could be harbored, and forgotten, and not ruin my night.

We made it about halfway up the road before my dad got sick. I rubbed his back as he heaved against the neighbor's bushes.

"Good Lord," he said, pulling a handkerchief from his pocket. "I haven't done that in years!" He turned around with a big smile. "Do we need to do something with it?"

I flinched at the celebratory pile in the

dark. Then I started kicking clumps of pine needles onto it with my dress shoes until the noxious mound was out of sight.

9

I remember the moment I decided I wanted to ask Anne-Laure to be my wife. For some people, the realization probably builds gradually, but for me, I was as sure in a single moment as I was ever going to be in my life.

It was because of a toy-filled chocolate egg. It was a weekend, a warm weekend in Providence, and we were on our fourth date — except the use of the term *date* is anachronistic because with Anne studying in Boston, she had to come down for entire weekends at a time. In the beginning she stayed with her cousin Esther, but once I learned to be a bit handier with the mop and the broom, she started staying at my place.

It was one of those early weekends when simply being in each other's presence could occupy us for hours, when her every gesture seemed contagious and new. Her smile contained multitudes. Her hair held constellations. The mere act of her pointing out something that she found funny struck me as a gesture of extreme import and grace.

I'd pick her up from the train station and she'd be in these *outfits*. Silk camisoles, silk blouses, wide-legged pants. I don't think I saw her with her shirt untucked for months, except, of course, when we made love. And bloody hell, when that happened did the good-girl walls come down.

On that particular Sunday, she'd suggested a bike ride out to Barrington beach and promised me a picnic. We met at India Point Park and biked twelve miles until we reached our destination, an elegant, narrow stretch of rocky beach along the coast. In common Anne fashion, she had everything prepared: a blanket, towels, a small umbrella just in case, and a cooler full of treats.

In tiny jars and Tupperwares, an array of perfect things: peppered herrings, deviled eggs with paprika-spiked mayonnaise, wasabi peas, curried chicken salad, chilled grapes — all things that she had managed, in the time- and space-defying way that Anne has, to prepare in the three hours between our rendezvous at the park and the moment she'd left my bed.

And then she took out a final container of

something gelatinous and yellow, grinning as she set it down.

"Pineapple Jell-O?" she said, slightly embarrassed.

I started to laugh.

"It has real pineapples in it!" she protested, pointing to the jiggling chunks. "Or, okay, canned. But still. You wait and see how well it goes with the chicken salad."

We sat on that lovely beach as the seagulls shit around us, getting progressively sunburned, stuffed, and happy. We got sleepy on the two bottles of rosé I'd brought and fed each other grapes and hypothesized about what would have happened if Manet's famous painting *Le Déjeuner sur l'Herbe* had featured a naked man instead of a woman. And then she told me it was time for the real dessert.

From inside the cooler, she pulled out something wrapped in a cotton napkin and twine.

"Here," she said, handing it over. "Surprise."

I unfolded the napkin to reveal two chocolate eggs in the white-and-orange foil that had been both a reward and a catalyst for many actions in my youth.

Anne started laughing and plucked out the one she wanted. "They're my absolute favorite," she said. "If you get a better toy than me, though, you have to trade."

"How in the world did you get these?" I asked, turning the famed concoction over in my hands. Kinder Surprises were famous across Europe, but in America, they'd been overtaken by the Cadbury egg, which, cream-filled though it was, did not contain the secret assembly-required toy that the Kinder version did.

She squealed when she saw what was inside hers, a tiny raccoon bandit. As for me, I got a knight with an old-time prospector's mustache.

"What the hell," I said. "I've got the down-on-his-luck version of Yosemite Sam, and you've got a raccoon Zorro."

She clutched the raccoon against her chest. "Mine's *perfect,*" she said with a smile so wide I felt drunker just for watching her. Dizzy with joy, I pulled her to the sand.

"I love you," I said. It was the first time that I'd said it. She still had the raccoon bandit clutched between her fingers. "You're ridiculous. You're perfect." I brushed her hair out of her face and stared into her eyes. She got me with her delight over this simple plastic toy. Got me with the care she put into the picnic, the things she'd done to transform a Sunday afternoon into a moment that would make me look at my life and realize that I wanted her with me, in it. Always.

How had I gone from those feelings — all-encompassing and complete — to growing distant from her, even taking her for granted? You love this one person, you love things about her that make her stand out from the rest. And then time passes, and she morphs into other people: warden, marshal, mother, financial partner, friend. And you lose sight of the reasons that you loved each other initially, loved each other as lovers, not as friends. Eventually, you lose sight of the extraordinary happenstances that brought you together, and it's the bad things you start collecting like an army of plastic soldiers, ready to defend yourself against whatever's coming next. But the good things? The finest things? The goddamn magic moments? These things start to flicker. These things, you forget.

The morning after I arrived at my parents', I called Julien at the gallery and bashed my mother's hopes of going out to Gadebridge because I got the green light: the buyers would accommodate an early arrival. I was on my way to London town.

I'd woken up that morning and assured myself it wasn't her, it couldn't be, that there was no way I'd be seeing Lisa at the other side of a door, but still, I paid more attention than usual as I got dressed. I didn't shave, because she didn't like me shaven. And then, as punishment for thinking she liked me better one way or the other, I *did* shave, and did a sorry job of it in my haste.

From the return address on Lisa's letters, I knew that the place I was going to didn't match up, although the postcode district was the same. I spent a considerable amount of time in M1 highway traffic inventing ways that the buyer could still be her — she had a rented office, maybe, she'd used the address of a neighbor — before I brought myself back into reality. It didn't matter. It couldn't matter. It. Wasn't. Her.

I double-parked in front of 5 Wells Rise and resisted the urge to honk. I checked my reflection in the mirror, and pulled up, then pushed down, my socks. I took a slug of lint off of my pant leg, still thinking what if? What if nothing, Richard. Man the hell up.

I got out of the car and went up to the white town house. It was narrow and sleek, the kind of place Lisa wouldn't be happy living in. She liked her buildings dowdy, mossy, old.

I rang the bell and focused on my breathing. It either wasn't, or it was.

"Da-ave!" I heard a man's voice cry out. "Dave!"

I closed my eyes. My heart was speeding. After the turn of many door locks, the door swung partly open.

"Hi, there," said a small man. "Yes?"

"I'm Richard Haddon," I said. "The artist." I nodded to the car behind me. "I've got your bear?"

"You made it!" he exclaimed, clapping his hands together. "Oooh, let's do something about the way you're parked. You'll throw your hazards on?"

A tall man came up behind him and reached out his hand.

"I'm Dave, by the way," said the small one. "And this is Dan!"

Dan and Dave. Dave and Dan. Unless she was involved in a sexually unfulfilling triangle, I wasn't going to see Lisa Bishop today. I used the ten minutes it took us to liberate the painting from the Peugeot to talk my body out of interpreting this information as a blow.

Once the damn thing was off the roof and safely inside, Dan and Dave invited me to take my shoes off and join them for tea.

Their house was antiseptic, and I mean this in both an olfactory and an aesthetic sense. Fragrance-wise, it smelled of lemongrass, and all of the furniture — all of it — was white.

That isn't to say that their apartment wasn't cluttered. All of the available surfaces were occupied by art. Now, "art" is subjective, and at the risk of belittling my own projects, I should probably say that I found their personal taste attractive. But I didn't. It was a mess.

There are any number of collectors. There's the new breed of interior-decorator types who don't care what it is or who painted it, as long as it's the right size and the color scheme goes with the carpet. Then there are the impressives, who care about the opposite: who painted it, and how much it cost. These are the financial fellows who think expensive art will get them laid. More likely, it's the size of the *domicile* itself that's getting them laid, it's the location in Notting Hill, or Tribeca, or what have you, but if it comforts them to think that a Rothko got their dick licked, so be it.

Then there are the obsessives. These are the people who are into one kind of thing. Mexican folk art, African sculpture, steampunk clocks — usually it's ethnic, or originates from a subculture of some kind.

My hosts, Dan and Dave, were none of the above. They were the worst types: the eclectics, the types who buy art because they like it, with no consideration as to how such or such an acquisition would harmonize with another piece. Whether a watercolor of four sheep grazing in a muddy field would look good besides a mixed-media sculpture of an electric guitar with a three-foot penis, for example.

I was standing in front of a velvet bowling ball encased inside of a giant bell jar when Dan brought out a tray of what looked — and I'm being kind here — like phlegmy seltzer, next to a large plate of dried algae.

"Shall we?" asked Dave, moving toward the center of the room, where a polar-bear skin ran underneath a glass table.

"Is that real?" I asked, toeing it with my sock.

"Goodness," said Dan solemnly. "We're vegans."

"It's made out of a synthetic fiber called aramid," Dave explained. "It's heat resistant. It will be the fiber of the future when the atmosphere is boiling and we don't have any skin. So you see, with the polar bear . . ."

They invited me to sit.

Dave and Dan were both sitting lotus-style

with no socks on. There are few things more disconcerting than being in close proximity to a stranger's naked feet, except being asked by these same strangers to hold hands.

"Holy Danh," Dave started, his dry palm in mine, "symbol of unity and wholeness, thank you for bringing Richard Haddon here to complete the circle of creative life. For you, eternal snake god, we put our tails in our mouth and thank you for being able to see things through from start to finish, and for holding together this beautiful world of art and health."

I watched in disbelief as both Dan and Dave stuffed their right hands in their mouths and bit them. They remained that way for some time.

"Gggon!" mumbled Dave, his mouth full of hand flesh. He motioned at me with his free hand to join. "A snake symbolizes unity, eternity, especially when they swallow their own tails!"

What did I have to lose, really? I was in an international state of limbo with my wife, and soon enough, the world was going to overheat to the point at which it would burn off all my skin. I bit my wrist.

Afterward, his forearm glistening with saliva, Dave passed me a glass of fermented tea.

"Dan and I are pagan Continuists," Dave explained. "We're completers of the circle. Like our snake god, we, too, try to be the belt around the world that keeps it from bursting apart. So when it comes to art collecting —"

"We need to meet the artist," finished Dan. "It's very important to our belief system that the artist delivers the work himself."

"Sometimes it's not possible, obviously," said Dave. "Sometimes, the artist is dead."

Daniel sighed. "When that happens, we call in a medium to contact him beyond the grave. We're really committed to this full-circle way of thinking."

"It's the same thing with our diets," said Dave, nodding toward the tray. "We only eat food that is multicellular and photosynthetic. Multicellular food contains cells that can only fulfill their self-identification process by reaching out and attaching themselves to other cells. So it is with algae. Same thing with kombucha."

"Have you always been . . . Continuists?" I asked, peering into my glass.

"Oh, no," said Dave, shaking his head. "I was born Catholic. So was Dan."

"Yes," said Dan, taking his partner's hand in his. "It's been quite a path for us. Are you an angry person, Richard?"

I took my first sip of the beverage. Effectively, yes, it tasted like a perfectly fresh seltzer that someone had used as a receptacle for their nasal drip. "I don't know." I shrugged. "Sometimes?"

"You don't seem very angry from your wonderful *Blue Bear.*"

"Well, I painted that while my wife was pregnant. It was . . . a different time."

"That's very kind of you to share that," said Dan. "That's very intimate."

I smiled. They smiled. I drank more bogey tea. After a while they let go of each other's hand.

"Dan and I have a question for you, Richard. We would like to ask permission to keep in touch."

"Keep in touch?" I said, setting the glass down. "By, eh, how?"

"Energetically," they both answered at the same time. "We work with an energy communicator to make sure that the people we are socializing with, the food that we are eating, and the objects we are surrounding ourselves with are all contributing positively to our vital cycles."

"All we need is your permission for the energy communicator to check in from time to time," continued Dave. "She'll never contact you physically, I mean, by phone or letter, but on a monthly basis or so, she'll tap into your aura."

"From here?" I said.

"That's right, from London. It doesn't matter where you are; luminous radiation has a tremendous range."

"Although you might want to tell us if you travel *very* far away," added Dave. "Or somewhere that is too populated, like China."

"So I need to tell you when I'm going on vacation?"

"You don't *need* to do anything," said Dave, shaking his head. "We just need to know if you feel open to the possibility of being tapped into. You know, from time to time."

"Will I know it's happening?" I asked.

"Some people get headaches." Dan shrugged. "But that's actually a good sign. A higher-order type of thing."

I felt exhausted, depleted, and entirely spaced out. The fact that I couldn't call Anne to laugh about the fact that this emotionally loaded painting had ended up with a couple of triple-level vegans made me feel almost incapable of meeting the world outdoors.

"Would you like a baby as a parting gift?"

I gaped at Dave, confounded. He held up his glass at an angle as a response. "A culture starter? So that you can make your own kombucha?"

"That's very kind of you," I managed, "but I have to take a ferry back. It might, uh, spill."

They mumbled in agreement that a boat would be no good. We all hugged again, and I found my shoes. Before I put them on, I cast a final glance at *The Blue Bear* in the corner.

"Excuse us," Dan said, following my gaze. "You must want to say good-bye."

I was surprised to realize I did. At the threshold between still owning it and never seeing it again, I felt flush with a deep sense of loss and sadness.

I walked across their living room toward the sentimental assembly of light and shade and color that captured an emotion that I didn't know how to get back. I stared at the painting for quite a while, hoping for an answer. But the only thing that came was the numbing disappointment of having nothing happen.

"Thank you for having me," I said, turning toward them. "I hope that you enjoy it."

And with that, I tied my shoes back on, slipped into my coat, and walked out into a world with no snake god holding it together, where everything I'd needed to help me find my place had come suddenly undone.

10

When I got home, my parents were both out. In the kitchen, a hot pot of yellow curry was stinking up the house. I checked my cell phone: nothing. Or nothing that I wanted. I had a text message from Julien asking how the delivery went. It was going to take me a while to come up with an answer.

It was gone. It felt like everything was. With *The Blue Bear* delivered, sitting however many hundred miles from the endangered species of my family, I had to fight not to sink into a despondent bog. If I never came home again — if Anne didn't let me back — what, really, would she miss? She would miss the convenience of me, surely, she'd need to get a nanny, there would be a lot of logistics things like that. She wouldn't miss the comfort of me because I hadn't been comforting for a long time. It had been ages since I'd made her laugh.

And she certainly wouldn't miss the sex. We'd had a great sex life, even after Camille's birth. But after a while I began to feel self-conscious about our acts. At some point, I started making Anne ashamed of her desires, and she, accordingly, started having fewer of them. It began to feel wrong somehow, letting a mouth — one that had asked you to leave the chicken thighs out to thaw an hour earlier — open and close around your dick.

I think there were a lot of times when I turned sexual opportunities into outcomes I could resent. There was this one time at a highway gas station during a little getaway to Cinque Terre — we'd had a fight because I'd tossed Anne's Andrea Bocelli CD out while she'd been asleep and the fight turned into witty banter which turned into something else. I remember her cupping her hands around my face, how I fumbled for the seat belt buckle so that we could get closer. The heat of her palms moving down my pants, her breath warm against my neck, and her twisting in her seat, about to move her right leg over to crouch on top of me. And I remember her expression when I pulled her hand up to my lips, and asked if she wanted anything from inside.

Anne would have had sex with me in that

Italian parking lot, but I didn't let things get there because I assumed she couldn't possibly want to do it in a public place, and I walked into the convenience store with my half-mast erection thinking it was a shame that she wasn't more adventurous. And I think I've kept doing that. Assumed my way through years of similar moments — chosen inertness over spontaneity, and blamed my wife when I was disappointed. I assumed and blamed and displaced my way into another women's arms.

As the curry odor began to overpower the house, I sat there bemoaning the brute physicality that we'd once shared. I mean, Jesus: *kissing.* Kissing with tongue. I literally cannot remember the last time I snogged my beautiful, lost wife. I hate that things have gotten so familiar between us. And yet, five hundred miles away from her, I want familiar back.

My parents came home around 6 p.m., all apologies and red cheeks because they'd gone to Gadebridge.

"Your mum was just so excited when it didn't rain," said my dad. "How did the dropping-off go?"

"It was nuts," I answered, rising from the couch. "They're nuts. They're 'Continuists.'

They complete circles. They have to meet the maker of everything in their house."

"Well, isn't that a nice way of doing things," said my mum, pecking my cheek on her way to the kitchen. "Did you stir this while we were out?"

"No," I replied.

"That's okay," my mum said. "It doesn't need to be stirred."

I shook my head. My dad sat down in front of me on the recliner.

"You okay?" he asked.

"I don't know."

His face darkened. "You want to go to the local?" he asked.

"Oh, Jesus," I said. "Green Acres? That place is the worst."

"Yeah," he said. "But it's close."

"It's okay," I said. "I'm tired. There was a lot of traffic, and these people — they were exhausting."

"I'm sure." He flicked something off his trousers. "You know when you're heading back, then?"

I shook my head. "No . . . I thought I'd spend a bit more time. You know, I'm here so rarely. Alone."

My dad was squinting at me.

"Richy," he said, leaning closer. "You okay?"

"Yeah." I felt my eyes water. "No, Dad. I fucked up."

His eyes didn't move from me. He sat back in his chair.

"Dammit." He sighed. He crossed his arms and remained silent for some time. "Is she going to forgive you?"

I shook my head.

"Was it a friend?"

"No," I said, reddening. "It wasn't anyone we knew, it wasn't —"

"You boys want some crackers?" my mother yelled from the kitchen.

"No, love," my dad called back. "We're fine!"

"I'm actually really hungry," I mumbled.

"Scratch that," he yelled out. "Cheese and crackers would be grand."

He leaned forward in his chair again. "Do you want to talk about this?"

"I don't know," I said. "I can't."

"We can talk about it," he said. "I won't hold it against you."

My brow furrowed. "I didn't think you would."

"Well, we really love her, is the thing," he said. "You kids need to find a way to make it work."

"It's felt like nothing *but* that," I said.

He took a throw pillow from behind his

back and turned it over in his hands, troubling the tassels at each corner with his fingers. "You still don't get it, do you?" he said, frowning. "You know what? I don't think I want to talk about this either. I'm going to help your mother with the snacks." Right before he reached the doorway to the kitchen, he turned around. "If you've already made a mess of it, don't make it worse by being disappointing. She doesn't deserve it."

I watched him disappear into the kitchen. From the couch where I was sitting, I saw him greet the woman who had been away from his side for only three minutes with a kiss.

Before dinner, I called my in-laws' landline again. Inès picked up and told me Anne was out, having a cocktail with a friend.

"A friend?" I said. "In the off-season?"

"Hmm-mm," she said, distractedly. "Pierre."

"Oh," I said, running through the shortlist of our Breton acquaintances for such a name. "And how was your day?"

"My day? My day was fine, Richard. When are you coming back? The Martis are coming over on Tuesday. We're doing paella. I know," she huffed. "It takes all day. But they're just back from Spain, so you know, it's a gesture. I've got a soufflé dropping here, I have to run."

"Wait, can I talk with Camille?"

"She's with Alain," she answered. "On the beach."

"Okay," I said. "Well, if they can call me, after dinner?"

"Of course," she said. And hung up.

I had no way of knowing what was going on in Saint-Briac, whether Anne had come clean about our situation or if Inès was distracted because she was busy in the kitchen and didn't really care to talk to me because there wasn't any question around whether or not I was coming back.

I walked back into the dining room having no more clarification around my new family than the one that I was born into, these parents of mine waiting patiently in front of the same type of supper they'd been sharing for forty years.

At the table, I picked up my fork and slammed it into a potato.

"Darling, let's say something first," she said. "It's nice to have you here."

I put my fork back down. The more time I spent at my parents', the more selfish I became.

"Isn't it a treat for us all to be together?"

began my mother, now holding my hand.

I waited for the rest. There wasn't any.

"That was lovely." My father smiled. "Shall we?" He winked in my direction, thus giving me permission to go at my potatoes again.

Over dinner, I watched their gentle ministrations in a state of disbelief. I'd always seen their kindness toward each other as proof that they hadn't traveled far enough or often enough, that they had uncomplicated brains. But now, as I watched my mother trim off a choice piece of fat from a lamb hunk for my father, when he transferred some of his potatoes to her plate when she ran out, when he got up, unasked, to fill up our glasses with more water, all I saw was love.

"How long have you two been married, again?" I asked, my mouth full of lamb curry.

"Richard." My mother laughed. "Count back!" She patted at her lips with her napkin. "You were born in 1968, and I had you when I was twenty-three, no, twenty-four —"

"Almost forty years," my dad said, putting his hand on hers. "Isn't that something!"

My mum turned to him and beamed.

"In this house the whole time," I said.

"In this house the whole time!"

"Amazing." I raised my glass in their direction.

"Don't be mean," said my dad.

"I'm not being mean," I said. "I'm astounded. Jealous. Or I'm not. I dunno."

"You sound a bit drunk, actually," said my mum. "Are you feeling all right?"

In the living room, the phone rang.

"I'll get it," I said, jumping up. "That'll be the girls."

I skidded into the living room and got it on the third ring.

"Hello?" I panted.

"Oui," said Anne. *"C'est moi."*

"I'm so glad you called me back," I said. "Is everything all right?"

"Of course," she said. "Why not?"

"Anne," I said, trying to still my heart. "I delivered the painting."

"I don't want to hear about it."

"No, listen. It was totally surreal. They made me take my shoes off and . . . we held *hands,* honey. They made me drink fermented tea."

On the other end, silence.

"They're *Continuists.* You ever heard of that? They think everything has a cycle. That was the thing behind it, they have to meet the people that make their art."

Another pause. "I'm just calling to tell you that I'm going to take Camille overnight to Mont Saint-Michel. Pierre and Marie have a house there."

"Who's Pierre?"

She sighed. "You've met them. They're in town. Anyway, it might be one day, it might be two."

"You sure I know them?"

"Richard, I'm just telling you so you don't call the house."

I slumped down on the fold-up chair in the kitchen.

"Anne," I said. "Please. Have you . . . told your parents?"

"Nothing," she said. "No."

"We need to talk. We need to talk in person. I want to come back to Brittany."

"Well, that's not an option right now."

"I can stay in a hotel."

"We'll talk after we get back from the Mont. *Camille?!*" she called. "Wait, here's Cam."

Before I could protest, the phone went to my daughter.

"Hi, Dad!" I could hear the healthy sleepiness pumped into her voice from a day spent by the ocean.

"Hi, pumpkin. Are you guys having fun?"

"Yes, we flew some kites today. Mine was,

like, a turtle?"

"A flying turtle! And what are you all having for dinner?"

I could almost hear her shrug. "Chicken?" I heard someone yell something in the background. "Chicken and soufflé. Oh, and Grandma says she made an apple tart."

My mouth watered. For my family. For our normal. For my mother-in-law's food.

"Well, I hear you're going to Mont Saint-Michel tomorrow, sweetie. You let me know about these Pierre and Marie people, okay? You let me know if they're nice?"

"When're you coming home?"

"You have to ask your mom." I did it. It was cruel. I allowed my little girl to think that the decision was her mother's. But I wasn't about to sit there on shame-induced house arrest while my wife went gallivanting around a tidal island with some tosser named Pierre.

After dinner, my parents and I agreed to watch some telly. I sat on the couch while my mother made chamomile tea and brought out a platter of assorted biscuits on top of a flowered paper towel. My father sat in his recliner. He kept staring at me.

"If you want to take some of these home for Camille, let me know," said my mum, putting down the platter. "It's bake-sale time again."

In short order, she returned with three cups of tea. Handing a saucer to my father, she said, "I put some honey in there for you, love."

"Perfect." He kissed the air in front of him.

"Don't you two ever get annoyed with one another?"

My mum sat beside me on the couch.

"You're certainly in a mood!"

"Well," I said, "*don't* you?"

My mother shrugged, picked up her cup of tea. "Well, I used to hate the way he ate eggs. Remember, love, you had this really specific way of dragging the knife across the plate? And he's not much of a teeth brusher."

Everyone went silent.

"Is that it?"

"Richard," went my father. "Don't."

"Well," said my mum, "you stop noticing it, don't you? You'd go batty if you didn't."

"Let's get on with the television, shall we?" my father said, reaching for the remote.

"Dad, come on. Consider it research. There must be something that drives you mad."

He sighed. Looked at his wife. "Well, sometimes Edna wears too many scarves."

My mother burst out laughing.

"Like, she'll wear a scarf over a scarf. She looks a little . . . homeless."

"He doesn't know the difference between a shawl and a scarf!" said my mum, still giggling. "I like to think I'm like those Indian women who —"

"Mum," I went.

"What? It's true. They always look like they're about to go dancing around the room with a baton or something. I think it's very romantic."

"I should be filming this," I said, taking another biscuit. "This is very good."

"Would you grant us some peace now?" said my dad. "The news is coming on."

We settled into our respective seats and stared at the glowing screen. So my parents were able to supersede the things that annoyed them about each other by turning them into quirky characteristics that they found *endearing*. Anne and I had done this in the beginning, too. Exasperated that I never knew where anything was, she bought a giant golden piggy bank at a Chinese supermarket and made me put a ten-centime piece in it every time I asked her where my phone was, had she seen a certain pair of socks. And when Anne's long-standing interest in the actor Vincent Cassel grew into an obsession that saw us attending all his overbearing, around-the-world-in-ninety-minutes action films, I comforted myself by realizing that I, too, could age into sallow skin and neglected gums and she'd still love me, as long as I could drive a speedboat and do Brazilian martial arts.

What had happened to our ability to take each other lightly? Time. But look at my parents — forty *years.* Maybe there was a high somewhere in marriage, like in running. If you kept going long enough, the endorphins must kick in. Anne and I were at eight years, almost; our marital runner's high was still at least a decade off. How did married people *do it* without cheating? Sweating and grunting and drooling on their pillows nightly side by side, expected at some point to reach over and caress the person who had become as familiar and uninteresting as an extension of their own arm, and fuck?

Lisa used to tell me that I'd hate her if we married. That all the reasons I adored her — her spontaneity, her flightiness, her love of dancing in public to any kind of music, or no music at all — were things that I would criticize her for if we actually moved in together and attempted a real life.

"If you're so down on marriage," I'd said,

"why are you marrying Dave?"

"He can go the distance," she said. "He doesn't overanalyze things like you. He just wants to build something, you know? Start to finish. For us to have a nice life."

I said I wanted that, too.

"But you don't, though," she said. "You get nervous when you're happy. For you, the good things are finite. You wait for them to end."

"But they *do* end," I said. We were on a bench somewhere, eating a sandwich. I remember there was a pigeon that was giving me a hard time. "They do. Look at you. You're leaving."

"But what we have isn't *good*. It's enjoyable. It's hedonistic. You're cheating on your wife."

"You knew I was married before this even started."

"It's true," she said, tossing a mealy tomato to the pigeon. "I did. I won't do this again, you know. The highs are too high. It's not — it's stressful."

"So you'd rather be bored."

"Not bored," she said. "Comfortable. Safe. Yeah, a little bored. I don't want to be exhausted. I want to be sure about things. I want to have a kid."

"You want what I have," I said. "You want

what I *had*."

"You still have it," she said, putting her arm through mine.

"I don't, though. You fucked everything up."

I grabbed an orange pillow off the couch and clutched it to my chest. Nothing would be helped by my thinking back on Lisa.

"It must be tough for Samira to do these reports," interrupted my mother, nodding at the screen.

I turned my attention to the television where the *More4 News* newscaster, Samira Ahmed, was summarizing the current situation in Iraq.

"I'm going to tell you something," my dad said, leaning forward in his chair. "I heard that they cracked into one of these nuke shops, and you know what it was? You know what it was, really?"

I shook my head.

"It was a place that sold hot air. They just filled up balloons! So you had all these soldiers and inspectors with warrants and what have you, with nothing but balloons. I tell you."

"Hot air," I said. "That's good."

"Isn't it?" he said, leaning back.

"Maybe I can steal it. I've, um, been

thinking about going back to some more political stuff, actually. No more paintings for a while."

"An intellectual challenge would be good for you," said my father, giving me a loaded glance. "Especially right now."

I shrank beneath his gaze. "Yeah, well, I don't even have a real idea yet. I've got to get it sorted."

"I think it would be lovely to have an exhibit of hot air," said my mum.

"Exactly," I huffed. "It's obvious. Ugh. I'm going to bed."

"But it's not even nine!"

My dad put his hand out. "Let him be."

I kissed them both and made my way through the dining room to my bedroom. In what she must have thought passed for a whisper, I heard my mother ask my father if he thought I was all right.

That night, I dreamed that Lisa was on the television, on *More4 News.*

"So, do you own *The Blue Bear* now?" Samira asked her.

"Ugh," Lisa responded, "I tried to. But he's doing different things now. He's moved on to Iraq."

"I see," said Samira, shuffling her cue cards into a tight square. "Does that make you feel lonely?"

"Lonely?" Lisa scoffed. "Hell no! He's trying to impress his wife."

Samira swept her hair behind her shoulders with her hand.

I woke up in a fog of 3 a.m. befuddlement, my anger at Lisa and Samira's indifference to my work chastened by the sight of the wet drool spot on my pillow. They were wrong about me, the phantom newsreader and my mistress. I wasn't considering doing something political just to impress my wife; I wanted to be someone worth taking back. I wanted Anne to be proud of me again, wanted to do art worth discussing. I wanted an epitaph if the worst came to pass: *Here lies Richard Haddon, much more than hot air.* And if it was too opportunist or too flashy, frankly, my dreamed-up Lisa, I don't give a damn.

The next morning, I was awakened by a knock on my door.

"Darling," my mum called gently, "you've got a phone call."

I tossed the comforter off and stumbled to the door, hiding my sleepy, boxer-wearing self from my mum.

"Who is it?" I asked, squinting.

"It's a Harold Gadfrey?" she said. "From

the boat?"

I rubbed a fist across my face. "What time is it?"

"I don't know," she said. "Eight?"

I threw on a cardigan and hopped into my trousers. Mum was waiting for me in the hallway to escort me to the phone, gesticulating excitedly that she'd already put the kettle on for tea.

I cleared my throat before grabbing the receiver. "Hello?"

"Richard? Hullo there! It's Harold! Harold Gadfrey. From the boat? I was wondering if you'd like to take up that invitation for a meal? I was thinking breakfast?"

"Breakfast?" I repeated.

"Have you already eaten, then? I had a meeting that was canceled. And now I have this time! And I just thought, well, you know!"

"Breakfast."

"Yep! Can't work without it. My treat!"

I glanced around the kitchen. "Where would you want to go?"

"Maybe one of the outdoor places on the Marlowes, since it's nice? Could you do nine?"

My head ached for caffeination. Was this my life now? Breakfast dates with men?

"Sure," I said, weakly. "Why not."

I found Harold standing outside of an atrocity called the Muffin Break, notorious for its self-serve icing bar. I blinked in the decidedly un-English sunlight glinting off the store windows. Neither of us knew how to greet the other. We went with shaking hands.

I chose an ancient-looking apple cinnamon muffin, and Harold got a tuna-and-cheese toastie. As validation that I was truly on a man-date, he paid for us both.

"So you'll be going to London, yeah?" he asked, chewing, once we were outside. "When's that?"

I was surprised by his memory. All I could remember about Harold was the Xerox connection, and that he loved his wife and kids.

"It got moved up, actually," I said. "I've already been."

I gave him the short version of my visit to the Continuists, how they wanted to keep in touch with me. How they were telepathic spies.

"Well, that certainly sounds like something for a new art project. Telepathy and such?"

"I'm afraid there's not much to spy on, right now, actually," I answered. "I'm still at my parents'."

"I thought you were off to Brittany? Family reunion and all that?"

Again, I was astonished. Did other people pay this much attention to other people's lives?

"Not exactly," I said, picking at a suspect piece of dried apple in my muffin. "I'm a little out of sorts."

Harold had the tact to remain silent.

"I'm . . . you know . . ." I kept picking at my pastry. "Having problems with my wife? Sorry. That makes it sound like she slipped outside a warranty of some sort."

"Do you want to talk about it?"

I met his eyes, amazed to find them wide open and sincere. "Yeah, I don't know, actually. You wouldn't approve. I mean, this would definitely be our last toastie."

"And what a toastie it is!" He knocked his pastry against my muffin in a mock "cheers." "You'll of course correct me if I'm out of line, but I'll take it that you dallied?"

"Dallied? Uh, yeah."

"And this other woman," he continued, adjusting his jacket. "Are you still seeing her on the side?"

I pictured salad dressing in a little plastic cup. "I'm not. It's done."

"Well, that's something," he said approvingly. "That's good. And do you think your wife wants getting back? She's open to wooing and all that?"

"Wooing?" I repeated, trying not to laugh. "Like, what kind, exactly?"

"Well, I can get you a really good rate on aerial banners, for example."

The look on my face redirected the course of his romantic advice. "Is she more of a dinner-and-flowers type, then?"

"Uh, she's more of a wish-you-hadn't-done-it-in-the-first-place type. Mostly, she wants time."

"Yes, well, I doubt that she really means that. Women rarely do. You're an artist! Go large, Richard! Fly something through the sky!"

Harold shrugged and looked around him. I imagined the air filled with sparrows. His own harem of happy birds. And then I imagined a battery-operated toy helicopter cutting through the blueness, dragging a laminate banner behind it: ANNE-LAURE DE BOURIGEAUD! LET ME WOO YOU BACK!

Suddenly Harold's palm was on my shoulder. Massive. Slightly damp. "I'm afraid I've got a ten o'clock on the DocuTech 60. But I want to tell you, and I know it's not the done thing, but, I like you, Richard. And I sincerely wish you the best."

"No, thank *you,*" I said, trying to ignore the panic rising in my belly. Once he left me, I'd have nothing to do all day. "It's been good to admit all this to someone I don't know."

"I feel badly," he said, glancing at his watch. "Leaving you in think."

"You got me out of the house at nine a.m. to have breakfast with a near stranger." I smiled. "It's a start."

He tightened his grip on my shoulder. "What do I know, really? But I think you have to fight. Personally, I'd be a bloody mess without my wife."

As I watched Harold return in the direction of the chain shops, the singsong of his whistle echoing back, I thought how lucky he was to be able to put that statement in a conditional tense.

I returned home to an empty house with a visceral desire to cleanse. To purge. Starting with my childhood closet. Thanks to my mum's inability to sentimentally prioritize, my closet was filled with the remnants of a person I no longer am: yellowed essays, awkward pre-dance photos from sixth form, cross-country running medals, a punctured soccer ball.

In a storage bin underneath a stack of musty clothes, I found a bunch of VHS cassettes labeled *Football Match, School Play.* Beneath these lay the camcorder my mother gave me when I passed my A-levels. I used to love making mock commercials with my friends, but inside my bedroom when I was alone, I got more serious, bellowing voice-overs for atmospheric close-ups of the objects around me, along with Godard-inspired jolting cut-ins of my cat.

Surprisingly, I found the camcorder's

charger beside it in the box. I plugged it in, wondering how long it would take to fuel an electronic device that hadn't been used in twenty years. I watched incredulously as the power light turned red, my spirits lifting as it did. If my Sony Betamovie BMC-100P could power up like a phoenix, dammit, so could I.

With the camera still charging, I popped in one of the generically labeled *School Play* videos. It took several seconds for the aged tape to rev back into life, but when it did, I recognized my old friend Matthew from secondary school, all toffed out in poofy knickers and a velvet cape and tights.

The musical was *Once Upon a Mattress,* in which Matthew played Prince Dauntless, a tit-for-brains whose mother's unpassable character tests prohibit him from finding a wife. In the scene I'd stumbled onto, he was dashing about the stage, hoping to hear good news from Sir Harry, just back from the swamps.

"You have been on a long and arduous journey, sir!" Matthew said. "But say, please tell me! Have you brought me back a bride?"

I fast-forwarded until I found myself in the role of King Sextimus the Silent. Since I was playing a mute, the only stage indications I'd been given were to chase maidens through the halls. It seems that Mrs. Green-blum, the drama teacher, had a handle on my character even then.

I turned the video off so it would charge faster and lay back in my bed. A long and arduous journey, indeed. I'd catapulted off track. What I'd had with Anne had been *good.* My own parents were still married, and by some miracle, so were hers. I re-wound the tape in the camcorder and decided to erase it. I wanted to erase every-thing. Start over. Return.

It was raining by the time my parents came home, the perfect weather for a project I'd dreamed up inside my head.

"I just want to film you," I said, helping my mum put canned beans up in the pantry.

"Film us doing what?"

"Arduous journeys?" I said, brandishing the old camcorder. "About how you two met?"

After assuring them that I just needed to practice in case my next art project had anything to do with film, I had them sit next to each other on the orange couch, but the lighting looked stilted. I moved them into the kitchen and put two chairs back to back so that my mum was facing the stovetop, and my father, the fridge.

"Are you holding us hostage?" asked my mother.

"I just want you to talk."

"But I can't even *see* him."

I got the camera rolling.

"And why do you want to see him?" I asked.

"Well, I don't want to sit here in the kitchen and talk if I can't see him. Are you there, George?"

My dad moved his arm and reached out for her thigh, hitting her in the elbow instead.

"Okay," I said, from my perch in the hallway, the record light blinking red. "Welcome to my parents. Edna. George. When did you two meet?"

My mum burst out laughing.

"We met swimming," my dad said, pulling back his hand. "She had on a red suit."

"A one-piece," said my mother.

"I offered her an ice cream."

"A Mr. Whippy!" said Mum. "You know, from the little lorry that used to pull up outside?"

I moved in for a close-up. My mother twisted sideways to get a better look at my dad.

"Get back in your chair, Mum!" I ordered, zooming out. "Okay. And then? What'd you think of each other's families?"

My father pursed his lips.

My mother laughed. "Is he rolling his eyes back there, Richy, or what? He didn't like my father!"

"I didn't like your *brothers.*"

"Oh, they were just trying to intimidate you. I always liked his mum. She was very beautiful. And young. And she was always wearing yellow. It's a hard color to pull off."

"So did they approve of you as a couple?"

My mother's smile widened.

"Are you kidding?" said my dad. "They approved."

I paused the camera and sat back in a chair. I had no idea what I was doing. But there was something grounding about being with them in the kitchen, filming this place where I'd eaten countless bowls of cereal and not done enough dishes, been bandaged and given biscuits, and had my dirty nails scrubbed with a brush. There was something about them not facing each other that highlighted the disconnect between what the image looked like — two people stuck in chairs — and what they were saying: two people in love still, and happy with their lives.

"What about the first time you kissed her?" I continued.

223

"Richy." My mum blushed. "Please!"

"She kissed *me,*" my dad said, moving his hand back again to try to pat her. "We were on — it was on the Larsens' doorstep, wasn't it? I'd taken her to a party and I was about to walk her home."

"It's always so expected when someone takes you to your doorstep," my mum said. "I didn't want to wait."

"And Dad? Let's see, do you know her favorite color?"

"Purple."

My mum made a clucking noise. *"Violet."*

"And Mum, do you know Dad's?"

"Easy," she said. "Yellow. And his favorite toothpaste is Gleem."

I ignored her non sequitur and charged ahead with my inquest.

"Dad: Mum's favorite gift you ever gave."

"Oooh," he said. "A tough one. You?"

"Quite." She smiled. "Or . . . my fiftieth birthday. *Italy."* She sighed. "Oh! I'll remember that trip all my life."

I stayed silent for a long time, just filming their faces as they passed over their memories, my mum staring wistfully ahead of her as if the rolling Tuscan landscape were reflected in the fridge door. She took a Kleenex from the inside of her shirtsleeve and wiped it under her eye.

"And what do you love most about her?" My father looked up at the camera when I asked this.

"She's kind," he said. "She's silly. She doesn't get wound up."

"And what do you dislike?"

"What?"

"What do you dislike?"

"Oh, come on, Richard," he said, frowning.

"Awww. We're being honest. You're sitting back to back."

"Yes, go on, dear," said my mother, folding her hands in her lap. "This should be interesting."

"Well," he said, adjusting his position. "She's not, you're not — she's not a good driver."

My mother sucked her lip in. "Unfortunately, that's true."

"Okay, Dad. One more."

"No," he said. "That's all."

Mum twisted around in her chair again. "Well, that can't be *all*, George. Personally, I have a lot of them! He's a hummer, but he's only got one tune. And he never puts the top back correctly on the malt bottle. And you squirt dish soap onto the cutlery instead of on the sponge."

"Well, don't hold back now."

"But he's a good dancer. You're a great dancer, Georgie. And he makes the bed in the morning, how many people can say that? And you know, he doesn't disappoint me."

She fell silent.

"He doesn't disappoint me, often."

My dad looked at the floor.

"Can we stop now?" asked my mother, looking at the camera. "I want to get the beef going, for supper."

"Sure," I said, leaving the camera on. "Thanks for playing. Dad, you may kiss the bride."

"Don't be filming this!" he said, turning around to reach for her.

But I did.

Lisa's favorite toothpaste: Tom's of fucking Maine. Her favorite color? Coral. After a notable orgasm, she'd hum a little song while she washed up in the bathroom. She was all lightness and bubbles and pink.

Anne's favorite color is cream, not white. What do I love the most about her? She smiles when she's sleeping. At least, she used to. I like watching her make iced chamomile tea in the summers, with her sleeves rolled up. I like when she prepares picnics. I love the sound of her voice drifting down a hallway as she reads Camille a book. I love the way she brightens when we're in Saint-Briac, when she stares out at the sea with her hand on top of her head so her hair doesn't get tangled in the wind. I love the way she used to kiss me after a party, in the car before we drove away, with a light bite on my lower lip. I love that she listens to classical music at full volume in the house, and I love that she's raised our daughter to swing her arms and dance in circles and enjoy it, enjoy all kinds of music. I love Anne when she's happy. I loved it when she was.

And Lisa? Who is Lisa? Four months since I'd last seen her now and it's starting to feel like she's someone I invented. If it weren't for the fact that I could still conjure up the textures and urgency of our lovemaking, I'd think she didn't exist.

Under different circumstances, it might have proved too tempting to be only an hour's drive away from my ex-lover. Six months ago, I wouldn't have been able to sit still, much less play canasta with my parents, knowing that Lisa Bishop was nearby. But this was my childhood home, and the only woman who had ever slept here and interacted with the cupboards and the closets, who knew where my mother kept the rarely used ground coffee, was my wife. Back in high school, when I had girlfriends, I always went to their houses. But Anne had slept beneath the *Dirty Harry* poster on countless visits, never once suggesting that I take it down, the two of us happily entangled in my too-small bed.

Lisa didn't know my favorite toothpaste, and she didn't know that I had a weakness for strawberry-flavored milk, nor that if I had the time for it, I would have all of our sheets ironed, just like they were at the Bourigeauds'. She'd never seen my mother place a pillbox on the counter, and stand there in the kitchen counting out vitamins in her floral robe and naked feet. She'd never pressed a Band-Aid over an open cut on Camille's kneecap. But she did know that right before coming, I liked a single finger up the bumhole and that I wasn't averse to a roaming tongue inside my ear. She knew I liked a hand cupped around my balls while she sucked me, and that I liked her to narrate what I was doing to her during sex. But so what, actually? Anne knew this, too. My favorite places to fuck were different with Anne, because she was different, she was Anne, but my wife, also, knew about my quirks. The only difference was that I'd allowed Lisa to add things to my sexual glossary while I'd halted all such exploration with Anne.

I want to be a bigger man, a less predictable man than the kind who confuses love with sex. It's something you do in your early twenties. It's disorientating. It's weak. With Lisa out of my life now, I can't identify whether I did or didn't love her. It scares me to think that I didn't. Despite my desire to be forgiven, something in me needs to hold on to her, still.

After dinner that night on the *More4 News* report, more news about Iraq. Samira Ahmed kicked things off:

"More confusion this evening around the meaning of 'regime change' by and to the Americans. We'll be going live with UN weapons inspector Scott Ritter, in Michigan. Can you hear us, Scott?"

"Yes, hi, Samira. Thanks for having me."

"So it's been about six weeks since President Bush outlined the five conditions he deemed necessary for a peaceful resolution of the conflict between the United States and Iraq, is that right?"

"That's right."

"And if I'm not mistaken, that's the first time the phrase *regime change* came up?"

"Well, not exactly," said Scott. "The phrase is being used somewhat haphazardly to mean any number of things. Back in April, Bush was still saying that Saddam had to go. But now that Congress has passed the Iraq Resolution, that's changed. Bush says now that Saddam can stay in power if he complies with the five conditions in the resolution."

"But it's a bit vague, isn't it?" continued Samira.

"The language leaves a lot of room for interpretation. And expansion. Right, I mean, the language itself is actually leaving room for future changes in the administration's policies. Personally, I think it's very naive and misguided to think that Hussein is going to comply with any of this."

"And what does 'regime change' signal for you?"

On the split screen, the inspector fell silent. "Well, I stick by the original definition. Hussein's gotta go."

From my bedroom, I heard my cell phone ring.

"If that's Camille, love," my mum said, her eyes still on the television, "let us say hi?"

I made it into the bedroom just in time to see that I had a missed call from Julien. I shut the door and called him back.

"Haddon, where've you *been*?" he shouted. "I was really starting to think they murdered you! I even called your wife."

"Shit, you shouldn't have done that," I said, sitting on the bed.

"No?"

"She found the letters."

"Oh, Jesus," he breathed into the phone. "You idiot."

"Yeah," I said.

"So?"

"So, she's not talking to me. I'm exiled. But I can't — listen, the painting was no problem. Except that they were nuts."

"So it wasn't Lisa, see? I told you."

"Nope," I mumbled, picking up what looked like a cracker crumb off the bed.

"But did you see her?"

"Yeah, no, Julien," I said quietly, "I didn't *see* her while I was in London. Although I'm the only one who seems to be aware of it, I'm trying to be a decent guy again."

"Then how'd Anne find the letters?"

"You know what?" I said. "I don't really want to go into that right now."

"Okay," he said. "I'm sorry. I just wanted to make sure that the buyers weren't holding you captive."

"Oh, they are, though," I said, leaning against the wall. "Telepathically. They put

231

nodes inside my head."

Julien laughed, but not really. It was one of those uncomfortable laughs. A placeholder. A grunt.

"Listen, Richard. This might not be the time to tell you, but you got another letter."

"You're serious," I said. "From her?"

"Looks like it. Yeah."

I sank my head into my hands. That made five. Americans certainly do have a curious way of signaling that the old regime is over.

"You know what?" I said. "Just read it. Read it, I don't care. Read it to me now."

"You sure?"

"Yeah," I said, "Go on."

I heard him ripping paper.

"Okay," he said. And began.

Dear Richard,

Yesterday, I passed a gallery and there was a photograph in it that made me think of something you might do. Or it made me think of you. I guess that's the same thing. I know you don't care much for photographs, but this was of a battered sailboat in a cornfield. There was a scarecrow in the boat. It didn't look composed either; it looked like the world had grown around this boat. It was in black-and-white. Beautiful. I wish we had seen it together so that I could have heard what you thought of it. So that we could have talked.

I suppose it's inevitable. Here it is: I miss you. Dave and I have set the date for our wedding: July 21. Now that it's set, though, it feels definitive. It makes me miss you. I'm sure you can understand this better than I can, as I've never been married. It feels like a good-bye. I mean, it is a good-bye, obviously, and it has been, it's just, what do I do with the missing part? What do I do with the part of me that does miss you, that falls asleep at night, sometimes dreaming of a parallel life?

"That's enough," I said, my eyes closed. "Stop."

"You sure?" said Julien, rustling a paper. "It goes on over the back page."

"Yeah, no," I said, standing. "This can't go on like this. It isn't right."

"She sounds indecisive."

"That isn't it," I said. "She's selfish. Just throw it out, will you?" I asked. "Don't keep it."

"You're serious?"

"I am. I've had enough. She's still getting me in trouble and we're not even involved

233

anymore." I fumbled in my breast pocket, wishing I still smoked. "I've got to do something. I have to . . . something big."

"Well," he said. "Like what?"

"I can't just apologize. My regime has got to change."

"Well, I don't know what that constitutes in your world, but when I was with Alejandro, I started eating cilantro?"

"Right. Right. That's very helpful. I'll swing by when I get back."

When I hung up, I regretted the phrasing. I should have said "if."

Back in the living room, my parents were still watching the telly. I sat down glumly on the couch and turned the camcorder back on.

"But I wanted to talk to Camille, dear!" said my mum, turning toward me. "My goodness, is that on again?"

"It wasn't Camille," I said, zooming in on her. "And yes."

"It's not going to be a very interesting video you're making," said Dad. "Us watching the tube."

"Excuse me," I said, training the camera on my father. "But how do you make love last?"

"Honey, are you all right, dear?" asked my

mother, reaching for the volume on the remote control.

I panned from my mother's face to my father's, and back again.

"No."

"Sweetheart?" My mum got up from the couch and came and sat down next to me. I filmed her face, her hand. I filmed her moving a pillow out of the way so that she could put her arm around me.

"Would you put that thing down?"

My parents stared at me. The lights from the television flickered in the darkness.

"What do I do?" I asked, my voice strangled. "What have I done?"

My mother leaned her head against me. She didn't ask about what.

"You act before it's too late," my dad said. "You stop just sitting here."

My mother moved her hand in circles around my sweater. Around and around and around. From comforting, to broken, to back.

I turned the camera off.

That night, I couldn't sleep again. I kept going over the ways that Anne and I had wronged each other, and how we'd gotten past it. In the beginning, our missteps were so small. A late arrival at an airport, a vacation cut short because Anne had to return to work. A wrong turn, a phone left in a taxi, a shirt shrunk in the dryer. But chocolates, tulips, weekends in quaint hotels, the old tools in the marital arsenal, none of that could help me now. I can only imagine the amount of time it will take to win back Anne's trust, and time, I just don't have.

All night I thought of options. A themed playlist, a filmed confession, something she couldn't interrupt or stop. I even thought about writing a poem, God help me. Somewhere around three in the morning, I wondered if I couldn't get Lisa to write a deposition confirming that I never replied to her letters, and it was around that point I realized I was getting nowhere, that I had to sleep.

My dreams were quick and scattered — bright moments here and there. The look on Anne's face the first time we peered into our newborn's diaper, so horrified by the tar-like excrement, we laughed. Her seated on the edge of our bed, rolling a stocking over her calf, standing to check her reflection before going to work. Anne nuzzling against my chest at night, telling me I smelled.

I woke early the next morning and sat up straight in bed. No one else was awake yet.

I stared at the opposite wall of my small bedroom, my lack of sleep tempered by the clarity of knowing what needed to be done.

Regime change. Regime change! I finally had a plan. In addition to the myriad of personality and behavioral adjustments I'd have to make to win Anne back, there was one thing in particular I could do to prove that I wished my past mistakes undone. Anne hadn't stopped me when I decided to put *The Blue Bear* up for sale instead of just exhibiting it. And I hadn't stopped myself with Lisa. Lisa had stopped me. But this former error, the loss of that one painting, I could stop. It didn't belong anywhere other than our house.

In the selling of that painting, I'd forgotten Anne-Laure, twice. Once in the arms of another woman, and once in my own mind. I would get that painting and bring it to her, and prove that I could do it: go back to first-love feelings, to comments without agendas, to youthfulness, to laughs. I could do it. I *was* doing it. In Anne's absence, I was falling for her. Falling back.

12

It was 5:30 a.m.: I'd only slept two hours. After a shower, I assessed my sanity level and sent Julien a text.

> I'm going back to get The Blue Bear. I'm sorry. I never should have sold it. I'll reimburse you/them. I'm sorry, but trust me. I need this to work out.

Then I turned off my cell phone so I wouldn't be deterred from my mission by a barrage of furious replies.

I left my sleeping parents a note, steeped some Irish breakfast, and pulled out of their driveway at six, making it to 5 Wells Rise an hour later. From my car, I considered phoning Dave and Dan to apprise them of my intentions, but weren't we supposed to be in cosmic touch? And besides. This was about me. Anne. Us.

I rang their doorbell and tried to focus on

something other than the toxic mix of caffeine and incertitude inside my bowels. It would be all right. If there was anyone who could understand the cycle of mistakes and forgiveness, it was homosexual Continuists.

It was Dave who appeared in the doorway, looking bright-eyed in a pair of white Thai fisherman pants and a wrap sweater with nothing underneath it.

"Oh, my goodness," he said. "Richard. This is a surprise." His brow furrowed. "Da-an!" He called back into the house. "We have a *surprise!*"

Dave smiled with his lips together, but he didn't say anything further until Dan appeared.

"Oh, this *is* surprising," said Dan, from the doorway.

"It's a bit difficult," said Dave. "We haven't done Ashtanga yet."

"I don't think this will take long," I said, shifting my weight. "And again, I'm sorry, it's just —"

"No, no," said Dave. "It's fine. Spontaneity is the cornerstone of creativity. We're just a bit more amenable to the creative forces when we've done our morning standing poses, but no matter, come in."

I took my shoes off and followed them into the living room, and there it was, *The*

Blue Bear, hanging right over a fainting couch on the left side of the room.

"She looks good, doesn't she?" asked Dan, following my gaze.

"Um, yeah," I said. "It's just, that's the thing, actually." I stuffed my hands into my pockets. "I need to buy it back."

Dave gaped at his partner.

"I can explain, obviously. You see, I never meant to sell it."

"Listen," Dave said, shaking his head nervously. "I'm just going to do a quick *chaturanga* to counteract this tension."

I watched as Dave dropped to the ground and went through some belly-downward nonsense before rising to face me with his hands in prayer.

"I need to buy the painting back," I continued, unsure what to do with my own arms and feet. "I know it's not professional, and I'll refund you for the trip over and so forth, but I never should have sold it. It's sentimental, and I really need it back."

"This is so unsettling," said Dave, closing his eyes. "I don't feel safe."

"Guys," I said. "Gentlemen. Can we just — you know, I made it all the way out here with this painting, and I get that you have an unorthodox way of doing things, and I'm fine with that. In fact, that's why I feel like you'll get — you'll respect — that I need it to come . . . home to me." I was searching for "holistic"-sounding language. "That this isn't its right place."

"Well, that isn't true, actually," said Dave, bringing his hands down. "Amira's initial energy reading was very positive."

"You know," I continued, "I have a lot of other paintings. Ones not in the show! I can send on a catalog and photos when I'm back. I'll give you one of them. Any one you want."

Dan and Dave exchanged a glance. "I'm afraid, Richard, that you're going to have to leave us alone for a little while."

"Okay," I replied, glancing toward the door. "But I'm not going to go far."

They sat me down on the couch with a bowl of warm water and lemon juice, a mixture, they explained, meant to calm the personalities of those with too much fire.

The lemon tincture wasn't all that bad. It was having a curiously calming effect on my thoughts. Or maybe it was just the fact that I finally felt confident, felt *right* about something, after so many months. I'd made a mistake in selling the painting, and I was undoing that mistake. I was a man who could make bad things better. I slurped the tepid mixture and stared at my *Blue Bear*

241

and I felt it in my belly. We were going to go home.

After about fifteen minutes, Dan and Dave came back. Dave had put a shirt on under his wrap sweater, and Dan was carrying what looked like a heavy sculpture covered by a weathered Mexican blanket.

"So, we've talked about it," Dave said, lugging the thing over to the couch. "And we respect and honor your sentiments, and your honesty in coming here. But we can't let you buy back your painting. It goes against all the tenets of Continuism."

"We can't go backward," said Dan, sitting down.

"No," Dave said. "We can't."

They fell silent. I tried not to look at whatever it was beside them.

"How about, would you be willing to re-contract it as a gift? As a donation?" I asked, refusing to believe that they could be so stubborn. "I could make a donation myself, to any charity you want."

"Well, that's very thoughtful of you," said Dan. "But the *Bear* needs to stay here, Richard. It's the painting's course. It was just by chance that Dave was in Paris the night of your opening. There were signs. For the *Bear* to go back now, when it's only just arrived . . ." He looked down at his hands.

"Defeatist," said Dave, shaking his head.

"Wrong," added Dan.

I closed my eyes, certain that if I could break through the hippie rubbish to level with them as bipeds, I could get my way.

"What about a print of it, maybe? A photograph? I could even paint a copy."

"Oh no," said Dave. "Replicas don't work. The art has to be *honest.* True to self."

"Speaking of truth," said Dan, pulling the drug rug off of the thing beside him, "we were thinking as a *gesture,* that we'd send you home with her."

I stared in horror at the monstrosity in question. It was some kind of folk-art cross between an African fertility sculpture, license-plate art, and a totem pole. The wooden structure was in the shape of a woman with twelve gigantic breasts, each of which had a nipple ending in a bright burst of blue straw. Her elongated neck finished in a head with eyes that looked like they'd been made from the bottom of a green glass beer bottle, and she was wearing a crown made out of license plates from states in the American Midwest.

"This is *Ngendo,*" Dan continued. "A mother goddess."

Dave nodded. "She will carry you home."

"Right," I said, putting down my lemon water. "She's not carrying me anywhere. I'm not going home with that. I need the painting." I pointed to it. "*That* one. I'll pay you double for it. Or not, okay, not double, but listen. I'll do anything to get it back. I painted it for my wife and I was an idiot to sell it, and I need it back."

The men stared at me with their moisturized lips pursed, their hands upon their knees.

"Um," said Dan, at a loss for words. "I don't think you understand the symbolism of this gesture. Ngendo is a protector. She's a very powerful life force to have inside the house."

"I'm not bringing my wife a fucking fertility sculpture," I shouted. Then, quieter, "I'm sorry." I looked down at my feet, trying to drive away the overtiredness and the helplessness and the scary feeling that I was going to fail.

"I painted this when my wife was pregnant with our first child. Our *only* child. Which is one of the reasons why a fertility sculpture —" I exhaled. "Please," I said. "I'm begging you. I need to have it back."

They continued to sit in silence. Dan reached for Dave's hand. They looked at each other, sharing some secret sentiment.

"It is so generous of you to share that with us," began Dave. "So vulnerable, and honest. But we've worked very hard to overcome our own demons, and the only way we've been able to do that is by charging forward in transparency with our truest selves, so to go back on something we feel strongly about because you've made a mistake . . ." He shook his head. While saying this, he reached out and rubbed Ngendo's head.

I felt my chin start to tremble.

"Guys," I said. "Please."

I looked wearily at the monstrous, wooden sculpture. Good God, if only Anne were with me, we'd be healed by the absurdity of it all. But without the painting I had nothing: no proof of my intentions, no proof that I'd even done it, made up my mind, decided to come back.

"Oh!" said Dan, jumping up. He ran into the kitchen and returned with a tiny plastic baggie filled with bright pink powder. "Kumkum! Just crush some on her head."

"It's made from turmeric," said Dan. "Do you have any food sensitivities?"

"I can't take this," I said. "I can't take this thing home."

"But you must."

"Please." I could hear the echo of my voice

— high-pitched, whining — reverberating in my head. They didn't budge.

When thirty seconds passed without a word from either one of them, I realized that it was time to hoist the white flag. Even if I tried to rip it off the wall, I couldn't get *The Blue Bear* out of the house without their tackling me. They were clearheaded, they had low cholesterol, and they seemed really awake.

I stood up. I looked at my painting. And then I looked at The Thing.

"So she's really supposed to heal things?" I asked, flicking one of my fingers against a license plate.

"Indeed!" said Dave, rising. "We'll help you get her to the car."

While I got my shoes back on, they dragged Ngendo to the mudroom. Dan opened the door to help Dave out with her, and I saw I had a fresh yellow parking ticket on my car.

"Don't worry, Richard," Dave said, putting his arm around me. "Things will get much better now that you have her."

Tarnation. Corrosion. Failure. Hell. What kind of people were they to botch my plan? It didn't mean a thing to them, that painting, whereas for me, it was the past proof of my goodness. The year I did the *Bear.*

I was not done yet with my mission. And this time, I wouldn't fail. With the four-foot-high Ngendo strapped under three seat belts in the backseat, I headed to number 17 Chalcot Road, the address that had accompanied all of Lisa's letters.

It was just a short drive to cross the park on Prince Albert Road. *Do you have Prince Albert in a can?* we used to torment the fellow who worked at the corner shop when we were little. *You better let him out!*

My heart was racing and my hands stuck to the wheel with sweat. It wasn't over. If I could accomplish this next endeavor without breaking down entirely, I would be able to come up with a way out of this mess. Find my way back to sensibility. Write Dan and Dave a letter. There had to be some way that I could get the painting back.

In front of 17 Chalcot, I opened up the glove compartment and took out Lisa's letters. My hand was trembling. I hadn't called ahead here, either. I'd erased all traces of her number so that I never could.

I stared out of the windshield at their house. Or *his.* It was a town house, the bottom level painted teal. The other two floors were brick. There was a fucking flower box in the downstairs window. With actual flowers. Just keep thinking this way, I told myself, grabbing the letters. She now grows things in dirt.

I caught a glimpse of the time before I shut off my car. Just after 8 a.m. She probably wasn't even up yet, the hedonist. I didn't care. I'd come to do something and I was going to go through with it. Like a Continuist, by God.

I swallowed. I felt nauseous. I forced myself out of the car. *You're doing this for Anne, you dicknut. You're doing this for your life.* I shut the door and straightened out my blazer, my wrinkled, rumpled shirt. I forced myself into walking. Forced myself not to care about my sweaty hands and shirt.

I punched my finger into the doorbell. I stared at the door, trying to ignore the pot of purple pansies by the steps. I hated purple pansies. Always had. I mean, in terms of mood, whose standard operating mode is neon purple? How could she come home to that each day?

I waited several moments, then rang the bell again. Finally, I heard footsteps. They were light. They were girlish. They were hers. I closed my eyes and steeled myself in place. If I could have disappeared right then into the pavement, I would have.

I watched as the peephole flicked open.

Stayed open. Finally closed. My heart slammed against my rib cage. She was right behind the door. But the door didn't open. I rang the bell again. Again, the peephole opened. And again, it closed.

And then the door opened, and there she was: Lisa looking trip-over-yourself gorgeous even though she was clearly just out of bed. She had one of those waffled white robes on over something fussy and pink, and her hair was long and messy, and she still had those freckles. She looked stupidly adorable. She was wearing leopard-print slippers with two pom-poms hanging off the side.

She put her hand over her mouth. I watched her cheeks turn red.

"Richard," she whispered, shaking her head slowly. "What are you doing here?"

I just stood there, her letters in my hand. "You can't . . ." she continued, looking behind her. "Why didn't you call?"

"What, I can't be here?" I asked, standing up on tiptoe to see behind her myself. "Is that it? But you can just keep sending all these shitty letters to my house?"

She looked at what I was holding. "I didn't send them to your house."

"You're getting *married*," I said, flapping the letters at her. "Why are you writing me?"

"I don't know," she said, taking a step closer. "I was worried about you. I wanted to stay in touch."

"But I never wrote you back!" I must have spoken too loudly. She looked over her shoulder again.

"Maybe we can go somewhere?" she asked, tightening her robe.

"Yeah," I said. "No." I reached out and stuffed the letters in the pocket of her robe. The pocket was not as deep as it looked. I really had to jam them in there. I could feel the warmth of her, the nearness of her breast.

"Richard," she said, touching my hand.

"You don't get to do this," I said, stepping back. "Does *he* know that you've been writing me?" I looked up toward the second floor. "*Dave*. Does he think I'm some great friend?"

"If you give me just two minutes," she said, "there's a place on the corner. Or we could go to the park?"

"Yeah, what, so we can reminisce? So we can walk around and be all shy and shit until you finally say, oh, I wish that I could kiss you, but I just *can't*?" I glared at her. "I have been trying to be done with you. Which is what you said you wanted. And just as I get closer, you needle your way back into

250

my life."

"They're just letters," she said softly. "I didn't think you'd —"

"You didn't think I'd what? You don't want me to forget you! You want to live in this fucking town house with these bloody awful pansies, and from time to time send a bomb into my life? Well, let me tell you something, I *want* to forget you. I don't *like* you anymore."

"But I didn't *do* anything!"

"You said you missed me!"

"Well," she said, clutching her robe around her neck. "I thought you'd be happy to hear that."

"I risk my marriage for you, and you leave me, and *then* you have doubts?"

"I didn't say I had *doubts,* Richard," she said, raising her voice. "I said I missed you. Which I'm allowed to do. And I'm going to call bullshit if you try to tell me you haven't missed me back."

"Oh, I've missed you, all right. I've missed you all the way into the ruin of my life. My wife isn't speaking to me. I'm holed up at my parents. I'm playing . . . we've been playing *cards.* Missing you has potentially left me with a lot more to miss than you. So you take those things." I pointed at the letters. "And you stop it. *Really* this time. We

251

were never friends, and we're not going to be. I don't want to hear from you ever again. I don't want to have any idea what you're doing with your life. And I don't want you to know what's happening in mine."

She shifted her weight in the doorway. She clutched at her robe. Her expression was sad but also — she was doing that *thing* with her lips. Tilting her head. "Did your wife find out?" she asked.

I stared at her incredulously. "Fuck you," I said. "You see how long you can stay faithful to that toff, and then I'll ask you if your precious Dave found out."

"I never pretended to be anything I'm not!" she said, her eyes flashing. "I never pretended to want you to leave your wife. This isn't my fault! You can't come here and make me feel like your problems are mine!"

I shook my head. "It's amazing," I said. "I think I actually might regret it. I haven't felt that yet, but being here . . . It was a mistake, wasn't it? Us?"

Her eyes watered. "I don't think it was. And you don't mean that."

"You're a carousel," I said. "It's just one pretty ride. No responsibility. Up and down, and down."

Her chin started to tremble. "There's no

reason for you to be like this. We could have actually talked. You could have told me what was going on. I was always kind to you, I never lied."

"What, now you want to give me advice about my *wife*?"

Her lips pursed. In the background, I heard the sound of someone coming down the stairs. Lisa reddened.

"Is that him?" I asked. "Shall we?"

She put her hand on the door.

"Nervous?" I asked. "You feeling nervous? You just wait. Maybe I'll start writing *you*. Fuck things up in *your* life."

"I'm so sad you did this," she said, moving back behind the door. "But it's done. You won't hear from me again." She looked behind her. "Please take care of yourself, Richard." She shook her head. "You make me sad."

And then she shut the door on me. I watched as she passed into the living room, drawing the shades that gave out on the street. I strained to hear their voices, but I couldn't make out their words. I kicked the pot of pansies. A little dirt flew up and onto the brick path. Then I bent down, picked up the whole damn pot, and shook it up and down until the guts fell out into a heap of dirt and fertilizer and uprooted purple flowers.

I made her sad! Ha! I wanted her *angry*. There was nothing more despicable than making someone *sad*.

I stood there as my belly started to tremble and my hands started to shake. Unless she was hell-bent on using the international postal service, I'd gotten what I wanted: I wasn't going to hear from her again.

But I needed something else from our interaction. I wanted permission, or assurance, really, that I would be okay. I wanted the ache in my knees from bending down beside Camille to push her floating plastic penguin alongside her in the bath. I wanted to watch Anne across the room at a party, her head cocked in discussion. I wanted to watch her undress in front of the closet, see the little indents like the parallel curves of a cello on her back. I wanted to feel her naked against me, hold her to my chest, smell her hair around me, feel her breath against my neck. I didn't have my painting, and I didn't have a plan, but what I did have standing on my ex-mistress's doorstep was the unwavering conviction that I wanted Anne-Laure back.

13

I drove back to Hemel Hempstead grateful
to have the steering wheel to still my shaking hands. It hadn't gone like I'd planned,
none of it. Lisa — I'd gotten in and out of
there quickly enough to preserve her image
as some kind of hallucinatory vision, but
the residue of seeing her was wreaking
havoc on my nervous system. But I'd done
it: I'd behaved in such a way that she
wouldn't want to see or talk to me again.

But I didn't have the painting. In my
mind, I'd seen myself valiantly crossing the
Channel with *The Blue Bear,* surprising
Anne not only with the fact that I'd had the
chutzpah to pull the gesture off, but with
the gesture itself.

I was back to zero. But dammit, I couldn't
stay at my parents' place forever. Anne-
Laure was an intellectual. A *lawyer,* for
God's sake. I couldn't give her too much
time alone to think.

I pulled in front of the house and jumped out of the car. I dashed into the living room, where my mum was Windexing the coffee table in her robe.

"Goodness, where's the fire?" she asked, accepting a quick kiss.

My dad was in the kitchen, halfway through a bowl of Weetabix. I grabbed a square and popped it in my mouth. My mother came to the doorway and leaned against the frame.

"I'm going home," I said, chewing with my mouth open.

My father put his spoon down. "So, did you two talk?"

I got a carton of orange juice out of the fridge, ignoring his question. My mother, sensing tension, went off to Windex something else.

"What, are you just . . . going?"

"She's my wife."

My father rolled his eyes. "I hope you have a plan." He folded his arms on the table, and watched my face for signs. "Oh, Jesus," he said. "You don't. Well, Richy. I hope she can forgive you."

On my way out, I stopped in front of my mother's "craft closet" next to the guest bathroom, a narrow lair of wrapping paper, streamers, sequins, and other party goods. I grabbed several sheets of blue construction paper, a glue jar, and a pair of children's scissors, and stuffed them in my tote. I also grabbed the videos I'd started making of my parents, and the camcorder, too. It was the equivalent of me leaving with their portrait: something old, with scalloped edges. It was me, grasping for faith.

My mum saw me to the car with a weathered ziplock full of biscuits and a turkey sandwich.

"I put extra mayo on it," she said. "Oh, and I found this." She shrugged a camera bag off of her shoulder. "I don't think it's the same make, but I think the video camera will fit, if you want to take it?"

I pulled her to me. "Thanks."

My dad walked out and gave me a knowing look.

"Go get 'em," he said, putting his arm around my mother. It was 10:17 in the morning. Things were looking grim for me. I got in the car quickly so they wouldn't see me cry.

The ferry ride was interminable. With it being midweek, the boat was emptier than it had been on the way over. I bought a trashy tabloid and a proper newspaper, and in each, I felt the tidal undercurrents of war,

war, war.

Three hours in, once I was apprised of the latest idiocies taking place under Bush's direction, I pulled out my pilfered craft supplies and started making my runner-up apology: an origami blue bear.

What I wanted was to create a bear of the teddy-bear variety, but the only version I'd learned with Cam was the grizzly bear, and unless there was a resident origamist on the boat, I didn't have the resources to learn a new form now.

Of course, origami purists don't use glue, but Camille and I do. The chubby pink elephants hanging from a mobile string in her bedroom, the surprised-looking panda Camille gave me for Father's Day, the conical turtles she left scattered around our potted plants, each of these was held together by a glitter glue stick, and God knows I needed help holding things together right now.

Six hours, two teas, and one foot-long hot dog later, we neared the port of Saint-Malo. In the smoggy gray of the late afternoon, the fortress city looked foreboding, its stone houses and steep rooftops standing shoulder to shoulder, angry and judgmental. I imagined men with arrows positioned in the turrets. Men with sacks of cow manure, awaiting my arrival, my doomed attempt to get back home.

Once I got my car out into the serpentine lot outside the ferry, my nervousness had amplified to dysentery levels. One of the things I was risking was exposure to the in-laws. If Anne went ballistic, if we fought in front of Camille or Anne's parents, there wasn't any going back.

Although Anne had never come out and said so directly, she'd always made it sound like her father had engaged in the cherished French tradition of the *cinq à sept.* You work until five at the office, enjoy a bit of rumpy-pumpy with the mistress, then nip home for veal chops at seven with the wife and fam. And it wasn't just the Frenchmen who kept this schedule; Frenchwomen, especially exquisite-smelling, meticulously turned-out women like Inès, enjoyed these extramarital activities, too.

But that didn't mean that we could have a row in front of the Bourigeauds. That would only make it worse. I decided that I'd call Anne from the golf course, when I was just around the corner, and let her make the decision to come out. If she wouldn't, I would huff and puff and blow the damn house down.

I did a drive-by before calling. Anne's

259

parents' ancient Land Rover was parked right outside the front entrance. Seeing that I was driving our only other car, this had to mean that they were in.

I reversed down the lane and parked right next to a stand of laurel trees in front of the neighbor's property. I touched my temple, my breastbone, the left and then the right of my heart, trying to remember the proper order for the sign of the cross from my last appearance in church.

I picked up my phone. I crossed myself again. *Anne,* I typed. *I have to talk to you. I'm outside.*

I put the phone down on the passenger seat and waited. Right away it began to beep.

WHAT!?

I'm outside. I'm parked in front of the neighbors'. We have to talk.

Digital silence. If this were a decade earlier, I would have initiated this conversation outside her bedroom with a handful of rocks.

You're serious. You're here?

I went for factuality. Wrote: *Yeah.*

I could almost feel her fuming from the house.

This is not okay. Give me five.

I breathed out deeply, breathed in deeply, shut one nostril with my finger like we'd learned back in Lamaze. The breathing wasn't helping. The hot dog I had on the ferry wasn't helping. My head, my heart, my intestines — it was all a mess.

After several minutes, I heard crunching on the gravel. Fearfully, I slunk out of the car. And there she was in a flowery tunic over tapered trousers, and the pair of brown pumps she usually wore to work, coming down the road. She looked beautiful and elegant and extremely put out.

"What are you *doing* here? You couldn't call?"

I remained quiet until she got closer. "If I called, you would have said not to come."

"Damn right! Richard, Jesus! We're about to sit down to lunch! What am I supposed to do, be like, *Surprise!*"

"I had to come. I had to tell you something. I tried to get *The Blue Bear* back."

"You what?"

"I went all the way to London to try and buy it back. I wanted you to know that . . .

261

I wanted us to have it. I never should have —"

"You tried to get it *back*?"

"Yeah," I said, shoving my fist into my coat pocket, rooting around for my replacement bear. "I went all the way back there, but . . . These guys, you've never met people like this in your life. They're, they've got this like, religion, and —"

"Well, did you get it back?"

My shoulders raised. "No, but I, uh, I made you this."

I pulled out my paper offering and held it in my hand. With his downward-facing nose and his stubby little tail, the bear looked like he was seeking forgiveness in the ridges of my palm.

Anne gaped at my creation wordlessly before taking it into her own hands. She stared at its intricately glued muzzle, its chubby little ears. She turned it upside down. And then she shoved it into the depths of her own pocket.

"What are you doing here? I mean, really? Did you give any thought at all as to how I was going to explain this?"

"Yes."

"And?"

"I don't know," I said. "I was thinking . . . maybe we could go away together, just a day or two to talk?"

"Oh, please," she said, kicking at a stone. "This is just like you. You're so selfish. You're so selfish, even now! We're going to have to make up something, you're passing through, your phone's dead. You had to go to Paris. I don't know. But you're going back."

"Anne," I said, "I miss you. I swear to God I did everything I could to get that painting back."

"And what, you thought that was going to make everything all better? That I was going to forgive you because of *that*?"

Coming out of her mouth, my rationalization sounded ludicrous. But shit, yes.

"Oh, God, I'm so angry," she said, looking it. "Now we're going to have to go in there, and thanks to you, I'm going to have to pretend . . . I can't believe this! You're like a child. And Jesus, what the *fuck* is that?"

She was peering into the backseat of the Peugeot.

"The buyers gave me that instead of *The Blue Bear*," I said. "It's . . . an exchange."

"What the hell is it?"

"An African fertility sculpture."

Her face turned vermilion red.

"Listen to me," she said, her arms crossed.

263

"I'm giving you a three-hour time-out. Whatever I say in there, you follow my lead. But after lunch, you're going back to Paris. No, don't even — you are going back. So you just shape up and we'll play nice in front of my parents and then get the fuck out. And don't —" She shook her head. "This is the last time, Richard. You can't pull stuff like this. It isn't fair."

"I'm sorry," I said, my body temperature plummeting. "I just thought."

"Right," she said. "Exactly. You didn't *think* at all."

She spun on her heels and started walking up the road. Leaving the car there with Ngendo, I followed her toward the house.

Anne thrust the front door open, and yelled out, "Surprise!" Her voice was all sunshine. The ozone-burning kind.

Camille came running around the corner, her favorite wooden spoon in hand.

"Daddy!" she said, falling into my arms. I avoided Anne's gaze and hugged my daughter, inhaled the fruity perfume of her hair, rubbed my chin against the freckles that had been coaxed out from the sun. "You're back!"

"It's just a surprise, Cam," Anne said, stroking her back. "He's just here for lunch.

He's got more business, with the paintings? I know," she said, frowning. "I know, honey. But it's okay. We're going to have such a nice lunch!"

"Mais, dis donc!" exclaimed Inès, coming in from the kitchen, wiping her hands on a dishcloth. *"Quelle surprise!* But, Anne, you didn't say!"

"It was one big surprise, Mom, even for me."

I kissed Inès on both cheeks and handed her a metal tin of rosehip tea I'd purchased on the ferry.

"Oooh," she cooed. "My favorite! So you're back! You're lucky," she said, wagging her finger. "I made quite a lunch. Alain was supposed to have one of his golf friends over. But they've got a problem with their dog."

"I'm sorry to hear that."

"Well, it's an awful dog. Okay!" she said, clapping her hands together. "Alain should be back any minute. He's just having a coffee at the club. Do you need to bring your bags in? Take a shower?"

"The thing is, *maman,* he's only here for lunch," said Anne, feigning a frown. "He has to go back to Paris. It's a whole thing with the gallery. There's been a . . . there's been a problem with one of the paintings.

265

The one he had to deliver. The people . . . they didn't pay."

"And they stole my cell phone, actually," I added.

Anne snapped her head in my direction, her eyes narrowed. She took a deep breath in. "That's right. That's why he couldn't call."

"These people stole your cell phone? My God, are you all right?"

"No, I'm fine. It happened in the Tube."

"It didn't!" Inès gasped. "That's terrible! Surely your gallery can take care of this for you? Why ruin your vacation when —"

"Let's go in and set the table, *non?*" suggested Anne, her hand on Camille's back. "We can talk about this later. Mom, I'll make a salad."

"I'll make it," I said.

Anne's eyes flashed. "Well, that'd be *great.*"

Camille helped me make a dressing with her wooden spoon, and Inès asked me about my mother and my father as she cut and dressed the roast chicken she'd prepared. As Anne navigated around me, filling a water pitcher, uncorking a white wine, I found myself feeling that if we could just surrender to the normalcy of these actions, enjoy the food and wine, then maybe Anne

266

would reconsider and let me stay. Not stay indefinitely, but long enough to take a walk with her along the beach. Long enough to explain.

Alain came in with his cheeks as pink as a crawfish, raving about his day out on the course.

"Glad to see you, son," he said, administering a back clap. "I didn't know you were back! Just got to wash up — I'll be down in a bit."

Because even when she was acting out she remained useful and productive, Anne went into the yard and cut some lilacs for our lunch, arranged with wild laurel leaves in a crystal vase. Camille showed me the drawings she had laid out in the sunroom: sea horses, dolphins, giant sunfish, each one surrounded by a makeshift frame of sandy shells. I picked up a seashell and held it to the light. My heart felt like it was breaking. I took my daughter's hand and put the shell back down. "I'm so glad you're having fun here," I whispered.

Camille held up her favorite drawing, a purple starfish. "I am!"

The meal started out civilly enough, with my in-laws inquiring after my parents' health, apprising me of the beaches where they'd gone for walks, pass the bread, the wine, the water.

It wasn't until the conversation turned to the exact reasons why I had to get back to Paris that things took a downturn.

"I'm not really understanding this," said Alain, wiping at his mouth with a cloth napkin. "So you go all the way to London to deliver this painting yourself, but they hadn't already paid?"

"Eh, it was a wire transfer, Papa," said Anne, passing the chicken.

"Very well, but if it's a simple question of a transfer, one would think that —"

"White or dark meat, Daddy?" asked Anne, holding the platter in front of him with two hands.

He chose dark.

At that point, Anne steered the conversation to her own work, updating the table on the charges the pregnant drinkers had officially filed: placing the lives of others at risk, attempting to mislead the consumer, manipulation of terms. We chatted about the potential factors behind fetal alcohol syndrome — a happy lunchtime topic if ever there was one — before Inès asked about my current projects, mentioning that Anne said I'd had great success with my last show.

"It's surprising," I said, stress-eating French bread. "I mean, I always thought

268

the genre was a bit prosaic, but apparently, narrative stuff sells."

"Well, I don't see the harm in doing commercial work in public, and experimental work behind the scenes," said Alain.

"Right," I answered, clearing my throat. "It's just —" And then I mumbled something about Iraq.

Anne put down Camille's knife and quickly reached for the bowl next to her. "Potatoes? Richard? They're delicious, Mother. I love the sauce."

"It's capers. Capers is the trick. And then with the lemon, you want to —"

"What's that about Iraq?" asked Alain, cutting into his chicken.

"Let's not get into this now, maybe?" begged Anne.

"What about Iraq?"

I took some potatoes as a conciliatory gesture, adding them to the silo of roasted fingerlings already on my plate. "It's interesting to me, being English," I said, "that we're historically so rational, but with this — with Bush — Blair's full-speed-ahead on something so unfounded."

"Well, I wouldn't say that the ethnic cleansing of hundreds and thousands of people by a dictator —"

"Right," I interrupted, briefly meeting my

wife's eyes before pursuing the conversation. "But the charge is that there are nuclear weapons. And none have been found."

"I don't think," said Anne, glancing at Camille, who was staring wide-eyed back at her. "Can we get into this later?"

"Well, I'm just interested to hear what Richard proposes," said Alain.

"I don't have anything concrete yet," I continued. "But there's the absurdity of searching for something that probably doesn't exist, and — of course — there's such symbolism around petrol."

"Petrol's a necessity," said Alain. "Nothing absurd about that."

"More wine?" said Inès, holding the empty bottle at an angle.

"I'll get it," I offered, grateful for a break. "White?"

"Might as well stay consistent," said Alain, who hated white wine.

In the kitchen, I leaned against the counter and closed my eyes. When I opened them, I looked out the window, where a small, gray rabbit was making his way across the lawn. His tail was almost perversely cute: a veritable pom-pom on his bum. A haiku from a Japanese poet I liked in college popped into my mind, something about walking on the roof of hell while gazing at the flowers.

I opened the fridge and took out a bottle of white wine, taking in the colorful snapshot of the time I'd missed. There was a fruit salad swimming in its own liquid in a giant Tupperware; half an avocado tightly wrapped in plastic; three bottles of cider; and all the fixings for savory crêpes: *sarasin* pancakes, Emmental cheese, eggs, tomatoes, ham, crème fraîche. I loved eating crêpes in Brittany — cutting into their buttery, eggy center with a cold bowl of cider, the way it was traditionally served in the northwest.

As I stood in front of something as familiar as this fridge, it truly seemed impossible that the worst would come to pass. How many times had I carried grocery bags into this kitchen? Swept the beach sand up from the tiles? Changed the litter for the sociopathic British shorthair that Inès used to have before it took off for fairer pastures? You didn't just throw out a near decade of togetherness. We had a goddamn *life.* I felt a rising confidence being around the physical things that Anne and I and Camille had enjoyed over the years. It was good for me to be here. It was good for me to be seen.

The upturn in my outlook was dashed by the changed atmosphere on my return. Camille was on the carpet, forming a battalion out of candlesticks, and Anne had moved her chair back from the table and pushed her plate away. Inès had a pinched look to her face. Alain's cheeks were reddened, as if he'd just fallen silent on my behalf.

"Everything all right, then?" I asked, walking around the table to fill up empty wine-glasses with feigned cheerfulness.

When I got to my own glass, Anne watched me pour with narrowed eyes. "You probably shouldn't be drinking before such a long drive."

"It's Thursday," said Alain. "It's preposterous to go back so close to the weekend. And as to what you said, Anne —"

"Alain," said Inès, "leave it."

"Suit your damn selves," said Alain, draining his glass. "I'll just go back out on the green if you're going to be impossible."

I looked from Alain to Inès, whose face was pained. All of the sudden I knew why. I followed her gaze to Anne, who had two tears streaming down her face.

"Chérie," said her mother, reaching for her arm.

"Anne," I said quietly. It came out like a plea.

"Honey, can you . . ." She swiped at her eyes and turned around to face Camille. "Sweetheart, can you go and play upstairs for a little while? The grown-ups need to talk."

Every synapse in my body readied itself for flight. I felt like my very pores were begging her, *Anne, don't.*

Camille looked up at her mother, her expression changing from preoccupied to concerned when she saw her mother's tears.

"It's okay, love," Anne said, reaching for her. "You go on and be a big girl? I'll be up in just a minute and we'll read that new book *grand-maman* bought, okay? And you can take a cookie on the way up, love. *D'accord?*"

She kissed Camille's temple. Camille looked at me. Anne kissed her again.

"Go on, *mon coeur.*"

We all watched Camille walk away, which took a while, because she kept turning around to see if one of us was going to get up and come with her.

When Camille was out of sight, the room fell quiet. No one dared cut into their food or reach for a glass of wine. I tried to meet Anne's eyes to beg her not to betray me, to betray *us,* but she kept her gaze on the table. She started tracing the grain of the wood with her right hand.

"He cheated on me," she said, almost inaudibly.

273

My insides went molten hot with the realization that she'd done it. My entire body was paralyzed. My legs felt like they were stuck in moon boots, magnetized to the floor.

Alain and Inès both looked at me, waiting for an explanation, for some kind of defense, but I just kept standing there, completely dumbstruck. As the silence lingered, I watched color fill Alain's cheeks.

He crossed his arms in front of him. "*What is going on?*"

Anne looked up at me, her eyes flashing. "Do you want to explain, or should I?"

This was foreign territory: I didn't know whether I should be honest, or try to save my reputation. But the energy coming off the three of them made me feel like there was nothing left to save.

"Richard's been having an affair," said Anne. "With an *American.*"

There was an audible inhale of breath from the other end of the table. Inès got up and moved over to where Anne was sitting. She tried to put her arm around her, but Anne pushed her away.

"All right," Inès said calmly, folding Anne's napkin into a perfect square. "All right." She looked at me for some kind of assistance, but was apparently disappointed by whatever she saw in my face.

"Goddammit, Richard," said Alain, standing up. *"Qu'est-ce que tu peux être maladroit!"* He began pacing around the room. With each footstep, my throat tightened. I was having a hard time getting air. My nasal passages felt like they were on fire.

He had called me clumsy. *Maladroit* is worse than clumsy: it's inept, it's bumbling, it's unfit to be dealt with. It's all of Alain's initial hesitations about me, confirmed.

"Oh, for fuck's sake," said Alain. "I'm getting something stronger." He walked out of the dining room and left the three of us alone. Anne wiped fiercely at her cheeks with the napkin her mother had folded for her, and Inès rubbed Anne's back. I tried to push past the sludge of humiliation in my brain to find a way out of having these people despise me, but my mind was throbbing black.

Alain returned with a bottle of whiskey and four glasses, which he filled and passed around.

"So, are you going to say something, you shithead?" he asked, knocking his glass back.

"Alain." Inès scowled.

"Well, I'd like to know what the plan is!" he said, starting to pace. "Why are you telling us this? Why drag us into it? This is the kind of stuff you have to figure out on your own!"

"Va te faire foutre," Anne mumbled.

"What?!" shouted her dad.

"You're my parents!"

"I *never* would have embarrassed my family like this," he protested. "This is private!"

"Oh, come off it," said Inès. "Would you sit the hell back down?" She glared at her husband before turning her attention back to Anne. "Listen. Both of you. It's difficult. I'd never say the opposite. In thirty-five years, you can bet that Alain and I have had our troubles, too."

"Inès," he said, "don't."

She shook her head. "Now, your father has had his *dalliances —*"

"Dammit," said Alain, swiping at his whiskey glass. "I'm leaving."

Anne grumbled, "Good."

"No, you're *not,*" said Inès, slamming her hand down on the table. "You sit back down, Alain de Bourigeaud, or I am going to show you what a problem really is. Now listen. It's unfortunate, but it happens. But the important thing is looking toward the future. You have to be able to forgive." She looked across the table at me. "Honestly, the very best thing would be if you enlarged your little family."

My legs flooded with a rush of circulation. I made use of this new development to exile myself to the window at the end of the long room.

"I know you two don't like to hear this," Inès continued, "but you're still young. It's the best thing, really."

"He has an affair, so we have another baby?" said Anne. "This is great fucking advice."

"What elegant language," said her father, glaring at Anne. Then he nodded over at me. "And that one. Is he even going to say anything?"

I spun around. "What am I supposed to say here?" I said, visibly shaking. "I had no idea this was coming! What do you want me to say?"

"I agree," he said. "Say nothing."

I pressed my head against the window. The glass stung cold.

"Alain, I think you *should* leave," said Inès. "You're not helping."

"Fine by me," he said, standing once again. "I'm keen to see where this is going to leave us in the morning. Quite a vacation, if you ask me."

"Just go," Inès repeated. "Go golf. Get out."

Alain bid us good afternoon with vitriolic

cordiality and left the room with his whiskey glass and the whiskey bottle.

"Sit back down here," Inès called after me. "Listen, this is going to be all right."

When I did sit, Inès reached her hand across the table to cover mine. I still hadn't made eye contact with my wife.

"I'm going to ask you a question," she said, moving her other hand over Anne's. "And just be honest! I've been married almost four decades. I've been through this, too. When is the last time you made love?"

"Mom!" cried Anne, flushing red.

"Well?"

"My God. It's none of your business!"

"In a way, it is," said Inès. "You brought it up."

Anne pulled her hand out from under her mother's and put it against her forehead. At this point, any shred of pride I had had slipped under the table, dissolved into the carpet, and seeped into the ancient cracks along with decades' worth of crumbs.

"Who are you going to talk to about this?" Inès continued. "Probably not each other! But it's the most important part. It's like falling off a horse, you know. You have to get back on."

"I literally can't handle this," said Anne.

"Yeah, Inès," I said. "Although we appreciate —"

"Oh, don't you start also," Inès said. "It's just the three of us, that blockhead isn't here. Listen to me." She grabbed Anne's hand again. "Your father was discreet about it, but he saw elsewhere, also. And for the first two times, I wouldn't let him touch me, but —"

"He cheated on you *twice*?" said Anne, aghast.

"For certain, yes. There might have been — Listen. The important thing is that I was suffering, too. You don't get anywhere by being withholding."

"You can't be serious," said Anne, her eyes blazing. For a second, her gaze met mine. She was outraged, indignant. I wanted to take her side.

"The thing is," her mom continued. "What I want to say is that it's when you let others disrupt your intimacy that those other people become important. They take on a dimension that they might not otherwise have if —"

"Please stop it, *maman*," Anne said. "Just stop." She got up from her chair and walked over to the window, where she traced her finger slowly along the sill.

I swallowed hard, caught between my urge to go to Anne and the feeling that I should

279

remain there in the doghouse, prisoner to her mother's reactionary talk.

"I'm not saying this to hurt you," continued Inès. "It's from experience. I want to help."

"By what, implying that I don't give it enough to my husband? That if I just made him happier in —"

"Anne," I said weakly.

"That's not what I'm saying," said Inès, frowning. "What I'm saying is that even though it seems like the hardest bridge to cross, you have to cross it. Otherwise, you're just friends."

"No shit," said Anne.

Inès closed her eyes and put her hands on the table.

"You two," she said. "You two have to make it. You have a daughter. You've always been fine! And just the fact that you shared this with us makes me think that —"

"Well, I regret that," snapped Anne. "He's not even supposed to be here! He just . . . he just showed up! I don't know," she said, gazing out the window. "I'm drunk."

"You're not drunk," I said quietly. I know Anne-Laure. The little girl in her needed her parents to know.

"I know it's none of my business," Inès said, putting Anne's half-touched plate on top of her own. "But I think you should stay, Richard. I think the two of you should go away. One day. Two days. I'm imagining this story with the gallery, it's all rubbish?"

I nodded. She continued: "We'll watch Camille, we'll give you all the time you need." She looked across the table at me kindly. Her eyes seemed to say, *Go to her, comfort her, get the damn girl back.* But I was frightened. Incompetent. I felt rushed through with despair.

"I'll go up with Camille now," her mom said softly. "See if I can read to her, get her to nap. And I'll send that fool out golfing. Take all the time you want. Darling, whatever you need, we're here."

Anne wrapped her arms around herself. She was still staring out the window, but I could see from her profile that her cheeks were wet with new tears.

"Thank you," I mouthed to Inès. I had a strong urge to put my hand over my heart.

Inès tilted her head and looked at me with both gentleness and pity.

"Please, Richard," she said, nearly whispering. "Please work it out."

When Inès left, I got up and went to my wife. I looked at the curve of her small shoulders beneath the flowered fabric of her tunic, her fingers wrapped around her

281

elbows. I put my hand on her shoulder. She started to cry.

"Chérie," I said.

"I'm sorry." She wiped roughly at her face with her shirtsleeve. "It just came out. Not that they fucking *care.*"

"It's out now," I said. "It's okay."

She cocked her head to look at me with disbelieving eyes.

"Right," I countered. "It's not *okay,* but I understand why you told them. It's —" I couldn't summarize the what-next of my in-laws knowing that I'd cheated.

"My fucking father," she said, swallowing. "He's probably *proud* of you, I swear it."

"I'm sure he wants me dead."

"Non! He's up there in his stupid club chair like, That guy's a real man! And my mother! Who talks like that? They're robots. They're just . . . my mom treats it like math!"

"Did you know?" I asked. "About your dad?"

She pulled away from me so that my hand fell to my side. "I don't know. Maybe? But to have her come out and just say it like that, like it was nothing, I just . . ." Her eyes welled up again. She turned back toward the window.

"It's okay," I said, wishing I could hold

her. "It's all right."

"No, it's fucking *not,* and you know it. As if I didn't have enough to —" She fell silent. "I don't know why I did that. Fuck."

I looked out the window at the turquoise sea, wishing that she hadn't said it, certainly, but nothing was her fault. Regardless of what she'd said or hadn't said, this was all on me.

She turned around again. "You still have to go, Richard. You still have to. Things are even worse now. But I can handle them by myself. With you here, and my father . . ." She shook her head.

It took a certain amount of courage to manage my suggestion. "And what if," I attempted, "we both went back?"

"Don't shift things," she said, shaking her head sadly. "Don't. Maybe I'll leave Camille with them and go somewhere myself."

"I still feel that if we could go somewhere, if we had the time to —"

"What, so like my mom says, we get back on that horse? Some romantic inn somewhere? With a complimentary breakfast?" She walked back to the table.

"That's not what I'm saying. To talk through things. To . . . talk."

"I don't want to talk to anyone right now," she said, starting to stack plates. "I want to disappear."

"We're not going to get through this if we're not together."

She looked at me, incredulous. "Together," she replied. "Right. You were in London, I haven't even dealt with that yet. London. It's too much."

"If we could just get out of this house together. Even for a walk?"

"A walk? And what, a decaf? Will that make everything all better? Excuse *me* if I actually have feelings, if I can't just chinny-chin up. Excuse me for being fucking heartbroken. I'm sure that makes things tough."

"I don't want to leave you," I said, moving close to her again.

Her pupils darkened before my eyes. I knew her answer before she said it.

"You already did."

14

And so I left. Left with a four-foot piece of subpar folk art as my only companion, no declaration of love professed, no chance to explain what I'd intended to communicate by trying to get *The Blue Bear* back. Left. Right. Left.

It seemed impossible to find a happy ending. With her parents knowing about my affair now, all of the worst-case scenarios I played in my head ended in divorce. Regardless of what Anne wanted to do in her heart, the knowledge that her beloved parents' opinion of me had shifted would compel her to bring things to an end.

Would things have been different if I'd managed to get back the painting? Anne was a sentimentalist at heart — if she'd come down that gravel path and found me with *The Blue Bear* strapped to the Peugeot, would she have run to me, called me a scoundrel, and kissed my aching lips? Would

I have picked her up and twirled her around in the midafternoon sunshine and maybe one of her high heels would have fallen off and we would have laughed about it and everything would have been all tickety-boo, like in the films?

Probably not. But at the same time, *yes*. During the four-hour drive back to Paris, I needed a punching bag, and Dave and Dan were it. If they'd let me have my stupid painting back, maybe instead of being on the A13 back to Paris, I'd be at my in-laws', still.

I had another problem, and it resided in my phone. Between the time that I'd texted Julien that I was setting out to retrieve *The Blue Bear* and the current hour, I had eight missed phone calls from him and a cascade of text messages that started off concerned and quickly escalated into capitalized tirades: *U BETTER FUCKING CALL ME!*

When I finally made it back to Paris, our house loomed dark before me like another person I had wronged. Once inside, I turned some lights on and checked under the sink. Even though I remembered taking out the rubbish and recycling before we left for Brittany, the house was filled with the sickening odor of old trash.

Right when I was moving Ngendo from

one corner of the living room to another, trying to figure out where she looked "best," my cell phone started ringing. It was most likely Julien, but it could also be Anne. Anne reconsidering. Saying she, too, was coming back.

Instead, it was my father. Having worried enough people that day, I picked up the phone.

"Richard," he said. "It's Dad."

He wasn't hip to the soothsaying abilities of modern telecommunications. "Dad," I said. "I know."

"We were just wondering . . . where are you?"

"I'm home," I said, sinking to the couch. "In Paris."

"Oh," said my father, his voice descending into disappointment. "I see."

"Yeah, no, it didn't go as I had planned. We had lunch, and then she told her parents. Right at the table. You know, about . . ."

"Oh. My."

"Right, so. I'm in Paris, and she's there." I pulled open my duffel bag and turned the camcorder over in my hands.

"There's nothing I can do, probably?"

"Thanks. But, yeah. No."

"Well, the important thing, if you'll permit me . . . is making sure she realizes that the other person, whoever she was, was a mistake. Was just a . . . Or maybe that won't work. I guess it's different with everyone."

"Yeah," I said. "I'm fucked."

"Well, I guess you just call us, if there's anything we can do, Rich. Your mum's upset."

"You told her?"

Silence. "Yes?"

I leaned back and stared at the ceiling. This was giving a whole new meaning to the term *family affair.*

"Thanks, Dad. I think I'm just going to knock off. It's been a long day."

"You call us, whenever. We're thinking of you both."

A siren cut through the line somewhere in the background near my father's house. I hung up and stared at the ceiling again, where there was a crack developing to the right of the light fixture, so small it was nearly imperceptible. I'd never noticed it before. But it was there.

After snacking on some mushy crackers from the pantry, I started watching the interview I'd done with my parents, but it made me too sad. I was gut-punched by their ease with each other. That was what struck me, watching the footage now that I was back in Paris. Their sense of humor.

That was the downturn, I think. The dark place on the time line. The point at which Anne and I stopped making each other laugh.

I drifted off to sleep that night with memories of Anne-Laure and me that summer on the Cape when she was pregnant, when we didn't know where we were going, and we didn't care. When it was a luxury to simply wake up together and burn toast in the toaster, to cram our toes into the sand. To talk about the maybes. All those million, jillion flecks of sand. And now? Beneath those possibilities, eyeless, hairless creatures with throbbing pink insides. Everything rotting and rising up beneath us. To drown, to drown seemed best.

The next morning, I was woken up by the ringing landline. I rolled over and fumbled for the telephone, my eyes still shut.

"Hello?"

"Richard! Jesus, finally! Where are you?"

"What?" I said, my mind working in small movements. Julien. Calling me. Here.

"I mean, what the hell took you so long? I've been calling you nonstop."

I rubbed my face. "Yeah?"

" *'Yeah'?* You fucker! You can't just go barging into people's houses because you've had a change of heart! I could get *sued,* Richard. What were you thinking?"

"First of all," I said, sitting up, "you have to understand that these two guys aren't like us. I thought they'd understand."

Julien made an exasperated sound into the phone. "Can you just tell me — what happened?"

"They wouldn't give it back."

"Please tell me you didn't do anything stupid. You didn't, I don't know, fight, or break anything?"

"Jesus. No."

"So everything was all right?"

"Lovely. They gave me an African fertility sculpture instead. Oh, and my marriage is fucked."

"A what? Wait, what?"

"Her name is Ngendo. She's got blue breasts."

"I don't understand. Did you buy it? And I'm sorry about your —"

"No, it was a gift, actually."

"So, no money exchanged hands."

"No. Unfortunately."

"And you didn't threaten them."

"No, I'd say it was the opposite, actually. I was given some kind of a tea with a small baby inside."

"What? No, you know, don't answer. You

need to come by so we can sort this all out. I'm going to have to send out some kind of notarized letter of apology. I just can't — I just don't understand what you were thinking."

"I needed it back. I needed it for Anne. I thought that it might help us."

He let out a trough's worth of disbelieving clucks. "For a man that's had little to no experience with women, I sure understand a lot more about them than you."

"I *am* sorry," I said, pulling the comforter up. "Really."

"Just don't *do* anything else, Richard. Without running it by me."

"I thought I'd have a morning poo now, J, is that all right?"

In lieu of a reply, he hung up.

I got out of bed and stretched my arms. My back was in pretzel knots from the previous day's drives. I went into the bathroom and splashed water on my face and had a mouth full of Winterfresh when the phone rang again.

"I'm brushing my teeth now, do you need to know that also?"

On the other end, silence.

"Julien?"

"No. It's Anne."

My stomach clenched. "Oh, hey! Hi there!

I literally just hung up with Julien, that's why . . . he was very . . . I'm in hot water with him about trying to get the painting, because I hadn't told him."

"Richard," she said. "I have a problem. I'm coming back."

Winterfresh, how you carry me on your minted arms of grace! She was coming back to me, my little donkey. Love lift me up on high!

"That's great!"

"I said I had a *problem,*" she huffed into the phone. "It's my case. Things have exploded."

I willed myself to take some time before I spoke. I needed to be the one she turned to. A confidant, again.

"What happened? What's going on?"

She remained quiet for a while. "Well, to start with, the president of the Auchan supermarket chain was caught with all this correspondence saying that the Lille women were a bunch of dimwits. He called them sluts."

"Oh, shit."

"In writing. I mean, in a *fax*! In a company correspondence to the wine departments of all the different chains. It's . . ." She composed herself. "And then, over the weekend it appears like Guigou has taken their side."

"Wait, what? The Minister of Health?"

"Apparently, she's got some communiqué ready saying that lack of information is a disservice to consumers and that she will do everything necessary to secure the future of women's health because our future relies on women, *et patati et patata.*"

"Shit," I repeated.

"Right. Deep, deep shit. So I've been called back to Paris. We have to beef up the defense."

Don't be excited about this, Richard, I coached myself. She's distressed.

"I'm sorry to hear that," I said. "I know how much you need this vacation."

"No," she said. "You're delighted. I can hear it."

I swallowed. "Is there anything I can do?"

"Yes," she said. "Actually. My parents are going to look after Camille and drive her back at the end of vacation so that she can stay and have a nice time. But our offices are being painted. They planned to do it over the vacation break. So I'll have to work from the house."

"I'll stay out of your way. Whatever you need."

"No, listen, there will be people with me. We need to — this is going to be like a round-the-clock thing. So I need . . ." She faltered. "We have — we have a lot to fucking *talk* about, Richard. But this week, this needs to be my focus. I need you to give me peace."

I grabbed a fistful of comforter and twisted it in my hand. "Are you saying . . . do you want me to go to a hotel?"

"I don't know," she said. "I mean, yes, obviously, but the thing is, I don't want my colleagues thinking anything is . . . wrong, you know? I just want —" She fell silent. "Listen, I'm going to leave right after breakfast. So we'll see when I get home."

I released my grip on the comforter. "Okay," I said. "Can I make us lunch?"

Silence. Again.

"I don't know," she said finally. "No. I'll grab a sandwich. Just . . . I'm going to need to pretend like you're not there, Richard. Otherwise I won't get through this."

I told her to drive safely, and she said she'd see me soon. "Soon" I could work with. "Soon" got me out of bed.

15

When I was living in Providence, I was friends with a group of graffiti artists who called themselves the Danger Five. Esoteric more than dangerous, they specialized in re-creating scenes from children's books that possessed some undercurrent of horror. One of the scenes they painted the most often was from Richard Adams's *Watership Down* showing the runt rabbit, Fiver, on his hind legs in front of a barbed-wire fence, preparing to run across the field to warn his family that the warren was in danger from the humans moving in.

Being more or less respectful of those that carry badges, I've never dabbled in graffiti myself, but that would change this morning. I wanted to have a clear message waiting for Anne's return.

With most people still on holiday, including many cops, I felt relatively confident that I could execute my plan without being arrested. On my way home from the paint shop, I bought all of the fixings necessary for a champion duck confit along with a veritable buffet of Anne's favorite cheeses and this obscenely priced pear juice that she liked. And flowers: three bunches of delphiniums and two of freesia. Our house would look and smell like new beginnings. Our house would smell like spring.

My plan was to adopt an air of entitlement. I figured if I just started graffiti-ing the middle of the sidewalk outside our house, any passerby would think I had the right to do what I was doing. That's the way things go. If you do things in plain sight, people don't interfere. It's when you get all surreptitious that the trouble starts.

Cautious under pressure, I outlined my design first in chalk. It wasn't very complicated: the word *I* plus a heart symbol plus a drawing of a donkey: I LOVE *ÂNE*. I'd decided to do the entire thing in hot pink. If you're going to go large, go the full monty.

I was just adding the bow the donkey always had around its tail in Anne's zine when I felt someone behind me. Instead of finding some bourgeois old lady with a snappy little dog, I was face-to-face with the billed cap and navy sweater of a French gendarme.

"Good afternoon, sir," he began.

I gulped. *"Bonjour."*

"May I ask you what you're doing?"

"Yes," I said, putting the lid on the spray paint. "This is my house."

"This is your house?" he asked, pointing. "Do you have identification?"

I fumbled through my wallet.

"Mm-hmm," he said, looking at my permanent resident card. "I see. And do you own the sidewalk, too?"

I looked down at the article in question.

"Um, no."

"Then may I ask why you're defacing it?"

"It's . . . it's for my wife. Our anniversary. Her name is Anne? You see, the donkey, *âne*?"

"Do you paint a lot of donkeys?"

"I'm sorry, what?"

"Do you often paint this animal?"

"Well, not really. I mean, sometimes, with my wife. I'm an artist."

"I see," he said, writing something down. "And is your wife an artist as well?"

"No," I said. And then, not wanting to disparage her, I said, "Well, she does cartoons?"

He wrote something down again. "Sir, if you'd be kind enough to come with me."

"Come with you?" I repeated. "Where?"

"To the commissariat. I have a few questions I'd like to ask."

"Don't you just . . . I imagine you just fine me?"

"Oh, don't worry," he said, smiling. "You'll get fined. But I have a few questions about your recent activity in this area."

"Activity?"

"Yes," he repeated. "Your other work."

"I'm sorry, you can't just force me to come in for questioning."

"You're defacing public property, actually, so I can."

"Will it take long?" I asked, looking at the house.

"Will it take long?" He laughed. "You might have asked yourself that before you did this to the street."

And that is how I found myself in the local branch of the French police station in a dusty office with a guard — an actual guard — on a folding chair outside.

As it turned out, they wanted to investigate my involvement with a new group of graffiti artists called the Jackasses that had been painting wounded donkeys in visible places throughout Paris.

"We think they're English-speaking," said Paul, the cop who brought me in. "Because donkeys? Democrats? They're painted with gun wounds, except they're dripping oil. You know anything about this?"

I know that I felt suddenly envious of these upstarts, and not a little embarrassed about my hot-pink donkey half finished on the street. Someone had jumped on the Iraq art bandwagon first.

"The Jackasses have defaced a *lot* of public property," he continued. "We'd be very inclined to be lenient with anyone who could help us find out more about them."

"I wish I could help you," I said. "But this is a mistake. A ridiculous coincidence. My wife, whose name is Anne, used to do these drawings of donkeys because back in college, you know, *âne,* Anne?"

"You've mentioned that, yes."

"So I was just . . . we were in a fight, sir. I was just trying to set things right. She's coming home from a trip today, and I wanted to surprise her."

"And where was this trip?"

"Brittany. To her parents'?"

He nodded. He wrote something down.

"I'm sorry," I said, shifting my weight in the chair. "Am I actually in trouble?"

He looked over the stack of papers on his desk. He'd photocopied my passport, my ID card; he'd printed out the home page of

Julien's gallery, which currently featured the glossy, noir-styled photograph of a latex-covered Catwoman being sodomized by a glowing Jedi saber.

"Do you know a lawyer?" He folded his hands on top of his desk.

"Oh, man," I said. "Yes."

He pushed a heavy black phone across the desk to me. He picked at something in between his teeth. And then he said, "I'd call."

Anne arrived two hours later in a business suit she couldn't have been wearing when she left her parents'. It was what I called her "va-va-voom" look: a rather low-cut cream blouse with an attached tie, a navy blazer, and a matching pencil skirt with four-inch, open-toed snakeskin heels. I actually watched the officer blush when he caught sight of her walking toward us.

"Hello, Officer," she said, putting out her hand. *"Chéri,"* she said turning to me, all light and sweetness. *"Ça va?"* She kissed me to the side of my lips.

"Yes," I said, trying to wipe the happy shock off my face. "I'm fine."

"Is this your *lawyer?*" asked the cop.

"Yes," I said. "And wife."

"Anne-Laure de Bourigeaud, Esquire,"

she announced, handing him a card. "And I brought you these, sir." Out of her briefcase, she removed a stack of magazines: the zines she'd self-published back in college. "As you can see, it's been a private joke between us for some time."

The man flipped through the first copy.

"Wow," he said. "You're really good at drawing."

"With all due respect, Officer, what exactly is the charge?"

He closed one book and picked up another.

"Defacing public property, organized misconduct. But the second one would be dropped if it turns out you're not part of this group."

"Well, I can assure you, sir, we're not," she said, pointing to the books. "This was just a little misstep on my husband's part. It's my understanding, however, that he used water-based paint. As soon as we get home, we'll wipe the whole thing off. It won't happen again."

The officer bit his lip. "I'm sure you can understand," Anne continued, looking toward a framed photograph of a woman and a child on his desk. "The things we do when we fall out of grace with our wives?"

"Lord, yes," he mumbled.

"And I'd be sure to follow up with the minister of health to let her know what a good job you, personally, are doing looking after the external sanitation of our city."

His eyes lit up.

"If you have a card?"

"Oh, sure," he said, patting his pocket. "Here!"

Anne slipped it into her briefcase and treated him to a magnetic smile. Like magic, he softened; his posture relaxed, he even had the gall to put both hands behind his head before realizing how inappropriate this position was.

"Well, I suppose Madame de Bourigeaud, if you could *assure* us that it won't happen again —"

"You have my word."

"We could let him off with just a fine. But the minute you get home, you have to clean it up."

"Consider it done," she said, reaching out her hand. "And thank you again for your hard work."

"And you for yours."

Anne shifted her winning smile to me. On cue, I stood. We walked out of that office like we were heading into the sunset, but once we hit the paved courtyard, she promptly dropped my arm.

"I have to return the rental car," she said, her voice devoid of emotion.

I bit my lip. "So, you went home first? To get the books?"

"Obviously," she said, smoothing out her skirt. "I needed evidence."

"So did you see it?"

She stopped in her tracks. "You know that this isn't what I meant by needing to focus, right? Me picking you up in *jail*?"

I nodded. "But . . . you saw it?"

She looked into my eyes. She looked more tired than angry.

"One thing at a time, Richard. One thing at a time."

When we got home, Anne made me kill the donkey. Telling me to wait in the kitchen, she came back from the laundry room with a scrub brush, a small towel, a pail, and an ultratoxic, all-purpose French elixir called white spirit.

"I appreciated the gesture," she said. "I did."

And then she handed me the pail.

While the hot-pink paint bled into the pavement crevices, I let myself imagine that Anne had been pleased by what she found. A donkey signifier, a graffiti wink. More original than a box of chocolates, even if it had almost landed me in jail.

But by the time I got my scrub brush onto the donkey's unfinished tail, my thoughts turned to the Jackasses, these anonymous miscreants who had gotten on the political art train before me. For weeks, I'd been searching for a personal way into an Iraq project, but for the life of me, I couldn't come up with anything that wasn't either carcinogenic — like boiling British and American food items in petrol — or Matthew Barney–level ambitious, like restaging the swimming portion of the Olympics in a pool of blood. But I wasn't Matthew Barney. I was a sorry, soppy wanker washing a pink donkey off the street, no closer to a killer art project or winning my wife back than I had been that morning.

After I was done scrubbing away my unfinished valentine, I went back into the house and found the duck I'd made earlier reheating in the oven and a fresh salad laid out. I put away the cleaning supplies and stood at the foot of the staircase, where Anne had left me a note.

R — I need to eat in my study. Too much work to do. I put sheets in the guest room. Friday, we can talk.

"DINNER?" I shouted up the stairs in the direction of her office. "Friday? Anywhere you want?"

A minute later I received a text message from her.

No, Richard. Just talk.

The guest room in our house, like many guest rooms in other houses, I suspect, is hardly used by guests. On rainy days, Camille likes to play with the random assembly of knickknacks we keep in a trunk at the foot of the bed, but it's otherwise used as a neutral, time-out space when either Anne or I have a reason (insomnia, rancor, sickness) not to share the marital bed.

Against the far wall, there was an ancient television that only played VHS cassette tapes propped up on a credenza, inside of which lay a veritable treasure trove of bad taste: *Crocodile Dundee, Mannequin, Adventures in Babysitting,* and of course, the film that laid the ground rules for all French romantic comedies with sound tracks featuring a synthesized guitar, Sophie Marceau's big breakthrough, *La Boum.*

When Camille was still a baby, on the nights when the umpteenth bottle warming and the rocking and the relentless lullabies emanating from her wind-up teddy bear had left us past the possibility of going back to bed, we would come into this room together and climb under a down blanket and watch the beginning of an old film. Anne finds cinematic schlock calming. After fifteen minutes of Andrew McCarthy (the sensitive sculptor whose work the world just doesn't understand) and Kim Cattrall as a reincarnated ancient Egyptian running around a suburban mall together, I'd feel Anne's weight increase against me, purring, fast asleep.

Looking through those movies we'd watched so many times almost made me capitulate to the magnetic force I felt, pulling me out the door, across the hallway into Anne's study, where I could hear her working still. I wanted to get up and go to her, insist that we get into the hard stuff, except that I knew her working style. I had seen her compartmentalize her relationship with her father and other emotional distractions so that she could get work done. If I interrupted her now, if I forced her into a discussion that would only hurt her further, she wouldn't be able to sleep that night, and would be even angrier at me in the days to come.

Without Anne's alarm to push me into

consciousness and with Camille still away, I slept later than I'd planned to. When I woke up, I could hear people in the house. After making the bed and getting rid of any evidence that I was sleeping in the guest room, I showered and put effort into dressing like a man incapable of infidelity, which in my case meant: khakis pants.

I came down the stairs slowly, assessing the smells and sounds permeating the house. Someone had made coffee, and I heard women's voices — cheerful — coming from the living room. Certain that no one could sound that perky unless they were already caffeinated, I felt confident that I could get into the kitchen and back upstairs with a cup of coffee without coming into contact with any legal eagles.

But when I hit the bottom step, I saw a tall man at my sink. Tall is an understatement; he was a fucking redwood. He had a mug of coffee in his right hand and he was staring out my window.

Apparently endowed with supersonic hearing as well as supersonic height, he turned around before my foot hit the kitchen tiles.

"Oh!" he said, putting his mug down. *"Bonjour!"*

There were no real blonds in France; this

chap had to be Belgian. With distinctly un-
French enthusiasm, he came up and
pumped my hand.

"I'm Thomas," he said. "It's nice to finally
meet you."

I scratched my head, easing into the connection of synapses and neurons that were
sending messages to my brain that I wasn't
awake enough to deal with. Green eyes, full
lips, a boyish flop of hair. This fellow wasn't
only taller and younger than me, he was
perversely attractive.

"It's nice to meet you, too," I said, staring
at the mug he had been drinking out of. It
was one of my favorites, a red one with the
slogan *Jacobsen does what you wish your
mower would do* written in white script. I
asked, "Are you new?"

"Relatively. I transferred from the Luxembourg office a few months ago."

"Hmm," I said, piecing together why my
wife, usually a broadcaster of interoffice
movements, had not mentioned the arrival
of young Thomas at Savda & Dern. "Are
you a Luxembourger, then?"

He nodded and made a gesture toward
my coffee machine. "Can I get you some?"
he inquired, reaching for a mug. I nodded,
and watched the Ken doll serve me coffee.

"I'm from Antwerp," he continued.

"Milk?"

"It's fine," I said, reaching for it. It seemed strategic at that moment that I take my coffee black.

"Oh!" said Anne, appearing in the doorway with two empty glasses and a mug. "We were going to get some more, also. Thomas, Richard, you've met? Thomas just transferred to Paris . . ."

She said other things, I'm sure of it, but I was concentrating on her outfit, a slim-fitting rose-petal-pink cashmere dress that I'd never seen before, and on the fact that she wasn't — in a breach with her normal sartorial policy — wearing it with a blazer. She also had on high heels, which, I was happy to note, were not new, but were still a trifle high for 9 a.m.

Anne kissed me on the cheek and wished me good morning, thus kicking off the opening act of our happily married show. I responded in kind by offering to make more coffee (no need to wait for it, I'd just bring the whole pot out), and after doing this and meeting an equally attractive paralegal named Selena, I retreated to the kitchen to eat the croissants that Thomas had been *such a dear* to buy.

The appearance of the Belgian shocked me into the realization of how rarely we interacted with fresh blood in gray Paris. In London, and certainly in the States, your circle of friends is an evolving, pulsating entity that can forever expand to incorporate people of all sexes and sizes because meeting new people is exciting, and it's good to have replacements for your old friends in case you grow bored.

But in Paris, we're around the same people all the time. And none of them are single. In fact, if they aren't related to us by blood, they are by lifestyle: married with one or two children, both spouses employed, most of their furniture from IKEA except that love seat there which they found during a weekend trip to . . . and onward.

Convinced that lurking around the second floor like some kind of recluse would only worsen my anxiety, I checked with Anne to see if there was anything I could bring them back for lunch, accepted her response that they were intending to take a break at noon and go out, and — exhausted, fearful, itchy — I took off the fucking khakis and put on a pair of jeans and neon sneakers and ran the hell away from my house.

16

I half walked, half ran all the way to the sixth to the Premier Regard, where I was surprised to find Julien, an hour before the gallery opened, already inside.

"You're not much for the telephone recently, are you?" he asked, unlocking the front door for me.

"Did they call you?" I asked, out of breath.

"What, the people you tried to *rob*?" I followed him to his desk. "No," he continued. "Which is why I've drafted an official letter of apology. But I was hoping you could write a side letter. Something heartfelt. If these people are such collectors, I'd like them to collect again from me."

He passed me his laptop so I could see what he'd written.

Dear Sirs,
    On behalf of the team here at the Premier Regard gallery, we'd like to of-

fer our heartfelt apologies for the mix-up that occurred last week.

After over a decade in business, we pride ourselves on working with some of the most renowned names in contemporary painting along with a cutting-edge selection of up-and-comers from all four corners of the world. As you can imagine, being art lovers yourselves, some of the artists whom we work with also come with an artistic temperament that manifests itself in a variety of ways, sometimes not appropriate, sometimes off the canvas. We hope that you will excuse Richard Haddon's recent and unscheduled visit to your home as proof of his unbridled creativity, that you will also excuse us for the many inconveniences this may have caused you, and continue to think of the Premier Regard gallery as a creative home away from home during any trips you might have to France.

"What can I possibly add to that? You want me to write 'I'm sorry' fifty times?"

"I don't know, Richard," he said, exasperated. "Just write something. I want a personal touch."

I gave the computer back, grabbed a sheet

of paper, and copied out my favorite section from Kerouac's *On the Road,* which I often use in birthday cards and wedding cards when I don't know what to say.

"The only people for me are the ones who never yawn or say a commonplace thing, but burn, burn, burn like fabulous yellow roman candles exploding like spiders across the stars."

I'm sorry. Thank you for your hospitality, for Ngendo, and the tea.

Sincerely,
Richard Haddon

"Who's Ngendo?" Julien asked, reading it over.

"I told you! The sculpture . . . ? Anyway, Julien, I've got problems. There's a Belgian in my house."

Julien narrowed his eyes. "Oh?"

"Anne's come back to Paris. She had a work emergency. She's got this team of ridiculously good-looking paralegals in our kitchen."

"So you're both there together?"

"Yes," I said. "And no. She's too busy with a case to get into anything."

"Your wife doesn't want to talk about the fact you cheated on her and you want to press the subject? Sorry, am I missing something here? Aren't you British? Aren't you supposed to be all, carry on and turn the other cheek and sweep things under the carpet?"

"I'm trying to save my marriage."

"By bringing up your affair?"

"If we don't have a proper confrontation about it, we're never going to heal."

"Heal?" he said, wincing. "My God, are you all right?"

"No," I said, exasperated. "I need something to . . . I want you to reconsider letting me do something about Iraq."

I watched him close his eyes. "You've got the clientele for it," I insisted. "British, American, French . . ."

"We talked about this," he said. "I thought I made myself clear."

"You said you didn't think me capable of doing political work again."

"No, I said you couldn't sell it *here.* I signed you for the oils, Richard!" he protested. "We've sold almost every one! Do your political stuff publicly. Do it in a squat. I can't represent it."

"So you're actually telling me to go to another gallery?"

"For your installation? Yes. But you keep your oils here. Don't fuck me."

314

"You're fucking *me."*

"Don't bust my balls because I'm being pragmatic. You're not well known enough to run around doing whatever project you feel like. You're going to look crazy."

"Well, thanks for the vote of confidence," I said, standing. "Shit. You're supposed to be my friend."

"Richard —"

"I'll show you. I'll go to Sabounjian."

"To Azar?" He laughed. "Oh, go ahead. He hates me. You think I'm tough? Good fucking luck with him."

"I can do this," I said. "I need to."

"So fucking do it! That's the thing about you, Richard. You spend so much time complaining and analyzing, but no one's standing in your way! Go to Sabounjian! Go to Saatchi! Go to Gagosian, for all I care! I've been watching out for you, and you want to fuck me. You're the one who's a shitty friend."

I had my jaw closed so tight, I could feel my shoulders shake. A dozen things went rocketing through my mind, but the more seconds that passed in which I didn't say them, the more I realized I was screaming, and being screamed at, by my closest friend.

And so I left Julien at his cluttered desk with his acidic coffee and his belief in brand legacy and predictability and his new haircut which I hadn't commented on.

The real reason I was angry was that I was worried that he wasn't wrong. That I didn't have it in me to do something daring, that I maybe never did, and that I was heading down a path that would lead to my being ridiculed and made to feel superfluous, and that the world, my wife, the critics — no one would be wrong.

In order to give Anne-Laure space and get some distance from my interaction with Julien, I spent the rest of the day roaming around Paris trying to think. I saw a romantic "comedy" that focused on the burgeoning love affair between a young Romain Duris and an older, married woman. He broke the heart of his sweetheart back home and the older woman decided not to leave her husband, and all the uselessly expelled energy made me feel quite grim.

After that, I trudged up to the command post of the aging glitterati, a gilded seafood slash cocktail palace called the Dôme. I ordered a severely overpriced dish of shrimp and a half carafe of rosé, an unfashionable wine choice for the time of year, a fact my judicious waiter had the tact not to point out. Some people self-soothe in retail outlets; I bask in pink wine. I raised my glass to the dowdy baronesses with their eggplant-colored hair, I saluted the right-wing horrifics in their pink pressed shirts. To each their fucking own.

I headed back to the house around five, a wee tipsy but in most ways feeling a good deal more upbeat about the world. Knowing Anne's work ethic, I doubted that her colleagues were gone yet, but I also knew that Anne and I had to be nice to each other for those same colleagues' sakes, so I found myself hoping that they were still there.

What I hadn't counted on finding was a shoeless Thomas recumbent on my couch. And in front of a platter of cheese sticks and Chablis, no less. *Certes,* the coffee table was covered in papers and files and Thomas was curled up with what appeared to be the largest, perfect bound manuscript in the world, but still, the man might have had the decency to keep on his damn shoes.

As I was standing in the doorframe gaping at this leviathan of a man, Anne came out of the kitchen. I might say that she *pranced.* Her face was bright and her eyes were brighter, but everything went all category-two hurricane when she saw me standing there.

"Oh," she said, clutching the packet of

crackers and salmon *tarama* in her hands. "You're back."

"I tried to stay out as long as possible." Thomas had finally noted my arrival and — hark! — was hurrying to put back on his loafers. "But I got cold."

"Of course," she said. "We were just — we're still working, but, you know. It's been a long day."

"Making headway?" I asked, walking into the living room to accept the outstretched hand of Thomas, who was now standing.

"We're definitely getting there," he said, not a little flushed. "You would think it would be easy, but . . ." He shook his head.

"I know," said Anne, reaching for a wine-glass. "It's just wine!" She put the glass to her lips and drained it. "You want some?"

"Sure."

Anne left to get another glass. I stared down at the table, noticing the conspicuous absence of a third plate, a third glass.

"Where's Selena?" I asked.

"She had to pick her daughter up from day care," Thomas offered.

"Oh," I said. "And — no kids yourself?"

He sat back down and reached for his own glass, which seemed discourteous of him as I did not yet have mine. "Not yet."

"Do you have a wife?"

Again, the smile. "Not yet."

I watched him take a sip. Those lips! I bit the lower flap of fatty tissue that constituted my own sorry pair, their plushness compromised by too many cigarettes and poor decision making and a chronic lack of sleep.

"A girlfriend?"

"Well, I *did* have . . ." he said. "But she didn't want to move."

"Here we go," said Anne, arriving with more wine.

"Well, that's too bad," I said, reaching for the bottle.

"What's too bad?" asked Anne.

"About Thomas's girlfriend," I replied.

"Oh," said Anne. "Well, it's tough, isn't it? If you don't want to relocate."

"She's very close to her family," Thomas said.

Like a bunch of Robotrons, Anne and I hummed and hawed our agreement that yes, it sure was hard. Relocation. Yes.

Uncomfortably, we bandied on until I could no longer identify whether the rising tension had to do with the fact that Anne and I were going out of our way to pretend that everything was hunky-dory for this fellow, or whether they actually had work to do and I was in their way.

"Well," I said, standing. "I've got some

319

stuff to do in the studio. Um, dinner plans?"

I watched my wife look at Thomas and it cut me like a knife.

"We were going to maybe get some take-out, actually, or pizza, because" — she motioned to the paperwork on the table — "we're not yet out of the dark."

I saw Thomas swallow. *Courage, Richard. Class.*

"Do you want us to order something for you?" Anne asked.

"That's okay," I said, trying to sound cheerful. "I'll probably go out."

Which I did a half-hour later, making quite a show of pretending that I was late for something, even though we all knew I'd only just gotten in.

So what if my wife was downing Chablis with a Robert Redford lookalike during a work obligation that looked like it wasn't any work at all? So what if my closest friend in Paris didn't believe in me, didn't want to support me, actually *preferred* when I was a hack? So what if I had no idea whatsoever how to approach what had happened between Lisa and me with my wife? I was an artist. Suffering was my oyster. If I couldn't talk things out, at least I could draw.

After slogging my way through two unneeded pints of Stella at a nearby pub where I penned potential sketches for an Iraq project accompanied by existential scribbles like *What does it all mean?* I slumped back home two hours later to find the house deserted. The lights were off, the glasses put away, the papers on the coffee table, vanished. I searched in the living room and on the kitchen counter for a note, but I found none. The absence of a hint about Anne's whereabouts hurt me more than her absence. You left *notes* for people, dammit. Even if you were angry. Now I had no idea where to put myself, strategically. I didn't want to start a movie downstairs if they were coming back. I'd fed myself and was dehydrated and fuzzy from alcoholic drink, and short of going at the pint of butter pecan ice cream in the freezer, there didn't seem like there was much else for me to do. So I went up to the guest room, to mourn out of sight.

I had only to open the door a crack to spot her garish, neon glory: Ngendo, the fertility goddess, assaulting me with all twelve of her blue tits, a note attached to her head.

I forgot this was in the living room, it scared Selena half to death. Can you arrange for something to be done with this? I don't want it here! We've gone out to dinner.

Thanks. — Anne

The "thanks" threw me. Thanks for what? Thanks for making myself scarce? But I knew that the "thanks" was just a placeholder for other words and phrases that she might normally have written. *I hope you had a good night? I hope you had a good dinner. Sorry for all the people in the house. Sorry we're not talking. I'm sorry that it's like this. I'm sorry about what you did.*

Swallowing through the sudden tightness in my throat, I taped the note back and gave old Ngendo a pat on her horrid head. I walked over to the television set and opened up the credenza, pulling out the well-worn copy of *Crocodile Dundee*. I stripped down to my boxers and got under the covers while Paul Hogan slunk through the outback in a butchy, leather vest. I watched the lovely Linda Kozlowski filling up her water bottle in the iconic black one-piece with a G-string back. I listened for the front door. I listened for footsteps. I listened for the sound of Anne putting down her keys.

Nothing came. Nothing happened. Groups of minutes passed. By the time the American journalist and her crocodile

322

hunter were on the plane for his first trip to New York City, I was fast asleep.

17

Anne and I spent the next day avoiding each other completely. The legal task force had returned: Thomas and Selena and an older gentleman named Jacques whom I'd met at the company's holiday parties. They picked up where they'd left off, camped out in the living room amid a shantytown of documents and books. On my trips down to the kitchen, I gleaned tidbits of their conversation. Legal jargon that gave me no indication if they were making any headway against the pregnant winos: *admissible evidence, failure of consideration, declaratory judgment.*

I spent the day holed up in my studio, sketching. At some point in the middle of the night, I'd finally had a solid idea for an Iraq project — a personal way in. Startled from a bad dream, or perhaps still in one, I'd been stewing over the donkey graffiti artists, which made me think of an old friend of mine, a burly fellow who went by the street name Didactic, who had recently become something of a celebrity in England for fathering the concept of reverse graffiti. I remembered going on a mission with him through the Greenwich foot tunnel that runs under the Thames and leads (rather appropriately, given the tunnel's filthy state) to an area called Isle of Dogs. He'd brought along his power washer, a regular bottle of dish soap, and a shoe brush. Once we'd taped his plexiglass cutout to the wall, we set about washing the area around it so that when we were finished, and the cutout was removed, we had reverse-graffiti'd one of the psychedelic eyeballs that Didactic was known for at the time.

Even though it was after five in the morning, we went back to his place for breakfast, and I remembered that he changed out of his dirty clothes and threw them, along with the shoe brush, into the clothes washer. I remembered asking him if the shoe brush didn't melt, and didn't all of the street guck get all over his clothes? While he fried us eggs and rashers, he shrugged and said that all the nasty stuff just went out with the water.

Which is where I got the idea to wash symbolic articles in gas. Petrol was more carcinogenic, more toxic surely than street grime, but then again, so was war. Before dawn, I started scribbling ideas out in the guest room, and it was these excited thinkings I spent the morning working on in my studio while my wife toiled one floor below me with her legal eagles.

The trick, I thought, was to wash *things* in oil, not clothing. The absurdity of such an endeavor echoed the ever-mounting irrationality of the search for nonexistent WMDs in Iraq. Both a purging and a cleansing, the objects I would wash would have a link to both my British and American pasts.

What I'd do, I thought, was set up two machines: one of an American make, and one British — if I could still manage to find one now that Thatcher had all but abolished British manufacturing. The articles that went into each machine would have some tie to that respective country. As for the oil? The oil would be foreign.

To the public, it would read as a commentary on fruitless endeavors and wasted energy, energy as both physical and combustible matter, a pillaging of resources, a costly waste of time. To me, it would be a sentimental inventory of my past mistakes.

I could call it *WarWash*. Sardonic and

polemical, with a nostalgic bent thrown in. Certainly, there was a lot left to figure out, and it would be a battle to find a gallery willing to show work using hazardous materials, but having stumbled on something on which I could apply my passion, I felt some life in me return. I was certain I was on the right track. Certain this was worth trying.

With my confidence bolstered, I put the rest of my energy into creating an itinerary for the next night: the night Anne said we could be together, when she'd have time after her case. Even though she said she didn't want to do dinner, in the private confines of my studio, I allowed myself to think of it as a date.

Arranging an evening with your wife dedicated to a discussion of your extramarital affair is not an easy task. I ran the gamut of our special places: Aux Lyonnais, a wonderland of oak and beveled glass where they were such fans of aspic, I wouldn't be surprised to see the cutlery served *en gelée;* Nani-waya, a Japanese cantine where the shared tables would prohibit intimate conversation; La Régalade, for which I needed to reserve two months ago, and had not.

After combing through my memories, magazines, and outdated restaurant guides, I decided that stilted and formal wasn't what we needed. I needed to make Anne *laugh.* I picked out three places — appetizer, entrée, dessert — and then I called my dad.

"Do I bring it up or does she?" I asked, after explaining my plan.

"Well, she's already brought it up by finding out," he said. "So you do."

We stayed silent a long time.

"Good luck," he said. "Do good."

Before the legal team broke for lunch on Friday, I caught Anne in the kitchen.

"We can still go out tonight, right?" I said, touching her lightly on the arm. "I've made . . . arrangements?"

She swallowed, placed her hands on the counter. I was worried she had forgotten about the note she'd left me when we returned from the police station, or was going to back out. But instead — mildly, weakly — she said, "Okay."

I sequestered myself in my studio for the rest of the afternoon, determining how to approach things. Around five, while the legal session was wrapping up, I showered and chose a semiotic outfit to change into in the guest room. Signs and signifiers: a gray cotton dress shirt that Anne said she loved my eyes in, a navy wool blazer she'd bought me on a trip to Burgundy one winter, the

328

white Stan Smiths that she called "boyish."

I sat down on the guest bed and listened to the shower go on in the next room. The team had departed, I'd heard them say good-bye. My guts were clenched. My left knee was bobbing up and down, a nervous tick I'd never been able to shake. I was as anxious as if I were being called to trial myself. Which I was.

Fifteen minutes after I heard her shower end, there was a knock on the guest room door. Anne had always been a fast dresser, much faster than me. To look at her, people assumed she spent hours preparing, pampering herself with different creams and potions in front of a vanity table, but she wasn't like that at all. She was an expert dresser. Like a musician, she had different registers: power outfit, seduction, family gatherings, leisure. When I opened the door, I caught my breath. She'd gone with "Look what you risk losing, you fucking wanker": navy Dries Van Noten cigarette kimono pants with a cream-and-rust-colored dragon slinking up the side, a pale pink double-paneled tank top made out of cashmere and silk with a vertiginous V-neck; black steel-toe and calf-hair booties that she'd gifted herself with after winning her first case. Over this, a thick felt coat the color of wet moss. Her eyes were lined with kohl, her hair was tousled, up.

"You look incredible," I whispered.

She clutched her coat around her cleavage. "Should we go?"

In an effort to make the night feel different, I'd called us a cab. The car, sporting the logo of the only Parisian company that reliably showed up when called, was idling by the sidewalk when we locked the house. I gave him the address, the Pont de l'Alma, a stone bridge that connects the seventh arrondissement to the eighth. Anne looked at me knowingly before folding her hands in her lap.

"So?" I asked as the taxi edged us onto the Boulevard Raspail. "How's it going with the case?"

She contemplated me before answering. "You look nice," she said.

Shocked, I managed a thank-you.

"The case is going," she continued, taking a lipstick out of her purse. "Jacques is holding us back a little, he's very methodical. He doesn't trust our energy, I think."

I wanted to suggest that maybe he was just too old, but I held my tongue.

"The problem with a case like this is that your common sense keeps kicking in and saying it's ridiculous — it's ridiculous to not know *not* to drink, it's ridiculous to not have *some* kind of role model around you, if not your family, at least the TV. I mean, it's not like these women were living in a hut somewhere. Lille's a major city. So we have to dig pretty deep to come up with a counterargument that isn't rooted in, well, scorn."

"When's the trial?" I asked.

She sighed. "The Monday after next week."

"Wow."

"Yeah. So, do I get to know where we're going, or is it a surprise?"

"You seem to have guessed the first place."

I watched her face darken.

"Don't worry," I said as her gaze strained out the window. "We won't be eating there."

The Bateaux Mouches is a relatively old company that operates a fleet of tour boats around the Seine. They offer lunch cruises and dinner cruises with previously frozen, three-course dinners that are notoriously substandard, along with daytime and night-time scenic trips. Whenever Anne and I take Camille for a walk along the river, at one point or another, the flat, white boats float by — the top level completely open, filled with happy tourists waving from their orange seats. At night, it's thrilling to see them pass under the city's most famous monuments, illuminating the stonework and the turrets with their dazzling web of lights, passing through Paris's watery spleen like a massive flashlight.

Every time we pass one of these boats, Anne says the same thing: "Isn't it funny that I've never been." It makes sense, of course. The Bateaux Mouches are something you do as a tourist, much like the double-decker bus tours in London or New York. But I felt sure that deep inside her, she was dying to go. So that night we would.

When we arrived at the small port by the bridge, I rushed around to open the door for her before paying the cab. Then I offered my arm to assist her down the steep boat ramp that was decidedly not made for women in high heels.

"Top level or the bottom?"

It was the first week in November, and at 6 p.m., the evening air had a biting chill. But still, she answered, "Top."

I gave the attendant the tickets I'd bought online and we went up the short staircase to the upper deck, where it became clear relatively quickly that all the other tourists had opted to stay warm in the glass-enclosed level below.

Once the boat churned into action, kicking up the dirty green water into modest waves, Anne sat down on a bench and took a pack of cigarettes out of her purse.

"What?" she said, with a defensive shrug when she saw me staring at her.

Anne and I had both been smokers when we met, but she gave it up when she was pregnant, and I, out of sympathy, did my damnedest to give it up, too. Later, when Camille was three or so, we started smoking again only at parties, pinching other people's cigarettes because buying our own would signal that we were back to our bad ways. About two years ago, we gave it up for good. Which made the unopened pack of Davidoff's on Anne's lap even more surprising.

"I've been really stressed," she said, taking one out. Gesturing to the space between us, she said, "This is stressful. You want?"

Fuck it, I thought, we might as well be on the same psychosomatic page.

And so we smoked as the boat chugged its way toward the monuments both historical and recent: the Palais de Chaillot, the tunnel where Princess Diana died, the Champs de Mars, the Eiffel Tower.

"Do you think, though," I asked, pulling my scarf tighter around my neck, "that you'll win?"

I watched her pull elegantly on the cigarette. "I don't know. I felt sure we would. But now?"

"And who's this Thomas fellow? Is he good?"

She narrowed her eyes at me.

"What?" I said. "I can't help it."

She exhaled a halo of gray smoke. "Try."

And so I tried. We talked more about her case, both the sureties and the chances, before I told her about my ideas for *War-Wash:* that I was going to ritually cleanse both my country and my own mistakes. In gas.

She ran her hand over the railing, stretched her fingers toward the water.

"So you'll be washing what, like old letters? The British flag?"

I decided to take the sting of her comment without commenting on it myself. "Yeah, basically. Some things that allude to the future, a lot of things from the past."

She started fiddling with her wedding ring. Dark tendrils of hair danced around her neck, shaken by the wind. I longed to touch her face.

"The thing about this project, though, is that Julien won't take it," I continued, stubbing the cigarette out under my shoe. "We had a fight about it, actually." Anne raised her eyebrows, which encouraged me to go on.

"You know, he wants me to keep doing the same old, same old. But the oils — they were a fluke, really. An intermission."

"So find someone who will, then," she said. "Find another gallery."

I stared at her, amazed. Where art thou, my pragmatist?

"The thing is, Richard," she said, tossing her Davidoff into the Seine. "It's his business. He has the right to choose what he does and doesn't want to sell. And it would be good for you to have extra representation."

"Oh no," I said. "It would be incredible. But it's not going to be easy, pitching something made with gas."

"It's the content that matters," she said, shrugging. "People display noxious things — used tampons, dead animals — all the time. Most of the time, it's laughable. You just have to make it good."

"So you think it's worth doing?" I held my breath.

She pulled her coat around her. "Of course."

I wanted to ask her so many other questions. *Do you really think so? Would you love me more?* But instead, we both fell silent as we approached the majestic white-and-gold bridge that graced the entrance to the Invalides.

"Tell me," she said quietly. "*The Blue Bear.* Did you really try and get it back?"

I nodded. "I kind of barged in. I begged."

"But why?"

"Because I *do* care about that painting. When I painted it, the way I was when I painted it." I looked down at my sneakers. "The way *we* were."

Her attention strayed to the bridge, where a fleet of winged horses presided over the passing cars and pedestrians above us.

"You remember how that bathroom always smelled like french fries?" she asked.

I laughed. The people we'd been housesitting for in Cape Cod that summer had two children, and whether it was a proclivity for fast food so entrenched that it had literally become part of the walls, or if it had been some cleaning product with a high percentage of canola oil, it was true, the bathroom had smelled like fries.

"I wonder what they're up to," I said, thinking of Charles and Donna. Back then, we'd been such good friends. "We should get in touch."

Anne looked away from me, and I felt the numbness that comes from having said the wrong thing. On both sides of us, the flesh- and beige-colored buildings of Paris passed us by.

"I want you to tell me one thing," she said finally, pulling her coat tighter around her throat. "You didn't sell it to her? She really didn't buy it? That's not why you wanted it back?"

I felt pinpricks through my body. "I promise you, it wasn't. It went to two men, a couple."

She looked unconvinced. "You promise?"

"I swear."

"But she's in London?"

I swallowed. "Yes."

"Was she when this started?"

I shook my head.

"She was in Paris."

"Yes."

She bit her lip and looked away from me. She reached for a tissue from her purse, but just sat with it, wringing it between her hands.

"In Paris," she said. "How long?"

My heart was caged. "How long was she in Paris?"

"How long did it last?"

I looked away from her toward the water again, the slope of the embankments, the weathered houseboats lined up against the Seine.

"Richard?"

"Seven months."

Her face lost color. I thought I might be sick.

"But it wasn't —"

She held her hand up. She closed her eyes. "Don't."

An older couple mounted the staircase and nodded hello before moving to the front of the boat to take their seats. The man took a camera out of his knapsack. The woman fluffed her hair.

"What did I do to you?" Anne asked. "What did we do?"

The wind made my eyes smart. I was already close to tears. "It wasn't your fault. It wasn't anything you did —"

"Of course it wasn't something *I* did. You did this. You."

I looked down at the orange vinyl floor, cracked here and there and coated in grime. At the bow of the boat, the older woman changed positions, insisting that her husband take a photo of her in profile against the Seine.

"If you could have any idea how sorry I am to have hurt you."

Anne closed her eyes. "Don't. *Don't.*

There's nothing you can say." She brought the tissue she'd been clutching up to her face. "It fucking makes me sick, Richard. Seven months." She put her hand against her stomach. She actually looked ill.

"I'll get you something," I said, rising because she, too, had taken to her feet.

"I need to be alone awhile," she said, pushing me away. "I'm going downstairs."

She walked quickly to the staircase, but I didn't go after her. Seven months. It was too long.

I sat down, trembling from the falling temperature and regret. Probably, when we docked, Anne would ask to go home. And she would have every right to. I was a fool to think we could solve this on a fucking *date*. I was a fool to think I could solve any of the problems that I'd started. We were just digging deeper now, down through the silt loam, into the worms.

I had scheduled the next part of the itinerary for comic relief, but when we docked at the Maison de la Radio, a circular gray structure that looked like it was inspired by a Cold War diaphragm, I was mortified by my naïveté. If by some miracle, Anne hadn't already hailed a taxi, the least that I could reward her with was a confession that we were going to one of the city's top restaurants: something stupefyingly expensive and atmospheric, Le Tour d'Argent, or Jules Verne. Instead, I'd picked a twenty-four-hour steak house chain named Hippopotamus, a red, black, and gray temple of bad taste where the dishes were bottomless: you could eat as much steak and creamed spinach and roasted potatoes as you wanted.

When we'd first moved to Paris, when Inès's greatest joy was babysitting her new grandchild, we'd arranged decadent weekly date nights, pushing ourselves to make our evening as riotous and splendid as possible so that the happy fuel would last us through the gummy take-away dinners and predawn risings that characterized our life as new parents.

We went dancing, drinking — we've always loved to dance. When we got bored with one club, we went to another, knowing that inevitably we'd end up at Le Pulp, a gritty lesbian-run establishment in the Grands Boulevards district around the opera house. Here, we'd slug ourselves silly with tepid beer and dance to indie pop music until we were famished and dehydrated, ready to eat.

The Hippo chain by the opera was just a short walk from the Pulp, and even though the quality of meat was far from exemplary and the place was full of bloated men in metallic blazers who had pilgrimaged there from the nearby strip clubs, we loved the contagious charm of the provincial waiters and the endless cuts of steak that would appear alongside a bowl of *frites* and sizzling vegetables as soon as we had ordered.

It was our little secret — our cheesy place. Now, with Camille older (and eating solid foods), Anne paid more attention to our diet. She was always reading labels, tracking down the provenance of our culinary choices. Our late-night trips to the Hippopotamus had become a ritual of the past.

But when I found her waiting for me at the bottom of the boat ramp, I decided not to lie. It was clear that she'd been crying, but she also had a look of pride back in her face. Her lips were freshly touched with lipstick, her posture was straight.

"So," she said, her arms crossed. "What now?"

"If I said 'Hippo Malin' . . . ?" My heart was beating wildly.

She shook her head, the faintest glimmer of a smile passing ephemerally across her lips.

"I'd say you're an asshole," she said, shifting her purse on her shoulder. "But yes."

The Hippopotamus was packed — a good thing, as it allowed us a distraction while we sat at our table and waited for the menus to arrive. I felt completely anchorless. On one hand, the rhythms and habits of our last decade together were literally within reach, but on the other, there was this fucking iceberg between us and it was my fault that it was there, and both of us knew there was no way around the crash.

"So, are you thinking Hippo Malin?" I asked cheerfully once the menus arrived.

Under the heading *For the love of meat,* the Hippopotamus had a variety of prix fixe menu options, and our favorite, the preposterously named Clever Hippo, consisted of either an appetizer and an entrée or an entrée and a dessert for nineteen euros.

"I don't know," she said, turning a plastic-coated menu page. "I'm not very hungry."

I looked at her, and longed for her, and wished that I could simply reach out and take her hand and make everything all right.

"Please, Anne," I said softly. "Please order the Clever Hippo."

She looked up, clearly astonished to see that my earnestness was genuine, but said nothing else until the waiter arrived.

"Welcome to Hippopotamus!" Our young attendant had lightly spiked hair and reeked of Drakkar Noir. "My name is Antoine. Can I get you two started with one of our signature cocktails?"

"I think we're ready to order, actually," said Anne.

"Wonderful. What can I get you?"

"I'll have the Hippo Malin menu," said Anne, keeping her eyes on the table. "With the tomato tartare and the Hippo steak."

"Excellent choice. And you, monsieur?"

"I'll have exactly the same. Rare?" I looked at Anne for confirmation. "Both rare."

"Faultless! And are you aware of our new Beef Effects?"

"I'm sorry?" said Anne.

Antoine opened up her menu to a page near the back. "On our new list of Beef Effects are highly favorable options for guests of all persuasions. Have you just been to the cinema?"

"Uh, no," I said.

He turned the page. "Well, you might appreciate the Beef Effect *Gourmand*. You can have unlimited sauces for your steak."

"But isn't that always the case?" asked Anne.

Antoine shut the menu. "And will you be drinking wine?"

"Please," said Anne. "The Côtes du Rhône."

"Very good!" he said, gathering our menus. "I'll get your carpaccios right out."

"A for effort," I said, when he was gone.

"You get five euros off if you've just seen a movie," she remarked, raising her eyebrows at the Beef Effect Cinema option. "Not bad."

We sat in silence and drank from the carafe of water on the table, waiting rather conspicuously for our bottle of wine. When it arrived, we waited until Antoine had left again to pour ourselves much larger portions than he'd originally served.

We raised our glasses but did not clink them together. The service at Hippopotamus was excessively efficient. We didn't have a lot of time.

"Can I ask you if they said anything?" I asked, tracing the outline of the French map on the paper tablecloth. "Your parents, when I left?"

Anne shifted in her seat. And then she shifted again. "Well, my father said nothing, obviously. Or rather, he sort of pounded me on the shoulder the next morning and said, 'Oh! You'll work this out!' You know, soldier

344

through." She put her napkin on her lap. "As for my mother, well, we talked about it."

I waited expectantly.

"We talked about it. That's it."

"And Camille?" I asked, clenching my hand into a fist.

"We have to talk about that," she said, leaning back to make way for our tomato tartares, which consisted of fine tomato slices covered in chopped tuna and parsley, with an unsightly dollop of what looked like canned salsa sitting on top. Anne pushed her plate away and reached for her wine.

"I don't know what to tell her," she continued, "but we have to tell her something. My parents never said anything to me, but I'd listen to them fight at night, and it was bad."

"But we don't fight."

Her face went tight. "What do you mean, we don't *yell* in front of her? I'm going to tell you something. The silence is worse."

"I told my father," I said, not knowing what else to say.

She snapped her head up. "You did?"

I nodded. "I mean, not in so many words, but . . ."

"And what'd *he* say?"

I dethroned the mound of salsa with my

fork. "That I'm a fucking idiot. He loves you."

If this had been a movie, I would have said that I loved her, too, but it wasn't a movie, it was a chain steak-house restaurant, so instead of a romantic declaration, we got Antoine.

"Everything A-OK?" he chirped.

"You can take this," said Anne, motioning to her plate.

"Was it not satisfactory?"

"I'm just not very hungry."

"The wine is very good!" I said, tapping my finger against my glass. I felt bad for the poor bloke.

When he left, Anne slumped back in the booth.

"I see no way out of this, Richard. I really don't. I have thought about this and thought about this, and when I'm not thinking about it, I'm thinking about the fact that I'm not thinking about it. It's driving me insane. I'm sick from it. I can't eat. The only thing I have is work, and even there I'm losing focus."

"But don't you think, is there no way that we can just, I don't know." I realized there was no way to say what I wanted to say without sounding like an ass.

"What?" she said. "Just forget it? Pretend

it didn't happen?"

I pushed my fork around my plate.

"Let me tell you something," she said, leaning in. "And you look at me when I say this. You think I think monogamy is a walk in the fucking park? It's not great, Richard, and I'm not even sure that it's natural. You think I don't have nights where I feel like I'm getting into bed with my brother? You think I don't *get* what you did? Because I fucking do, let me tell you. I get it. The difference here —" Her eyes welled up, she balled up her napkin. "The difference is that you *lied*. And you *loved* her. You didn't just get your rocks off, you fell —"

"I didn't —"

"Don't bullshit me," she yelled, slamming her hand on the table. "I read the letters," she hissed, talking quieter now. "And you were going to *leave* us. And I can tell you that if it wasn't for Camille and the fact that I'm so fucking crazed with work, we wouldn't be here. You'd already be out. There is *no* reason for me to forgive you. Nada. You haven't given me a reason, and I don't see you giving me one now. You know what you could have done, Richard? You could have told me when you met her. I don't know when it happened and I don't know where it was, but I'm guessing there

347

was some kind of buildup, some moment when you could have said, 'Anne, I've met someone, and I'm attracted to her. And I have doubts. And I'm bored. And I need a fucking break.' "

"What are you saying?" I asked, pushing my plate away. "That it would have been all right?"

"I'm saying that we could have *talked* about it. I'm not as sheltered as you think. I don't know what I would have felt at that moment, but I know that we could have talked about it, and that hearing about it then, when it was an interest instead of after the fact, it would have left us with a chance. Because I would have understood you. Because I've felt that way myself."

She patted her eyes with her humongous red paper napkin while Antoine came up hastily to swoop my plate away.

Anne waited with her lips pursed until he was out of sight. "But what have you left me with instead?" she said, her voice cracking. "I mean, really? Have you thought about it? You had a love affair. You had . . ." She faltered. "You had a fucking *life* with someone else. And I'm supposed to forgive you? What do I get out of it? What do I get out of forgiving you? If I was someone else, *anyone* else, we'd already be divorced."

"I know," I said, quaking. "I know we would."

"And sometimes I even want to do it! I want to just say, 'Fuck it,' and move on. But you've changed everything. You've changed *us*. We were lucky, Richard. What we had was really, really good. And you fucked it."

Antoine reappeared with two plates heaped with steak and all the fixings steaming on a plastic tray.

"Good God," Anne muttered.

"Antoine, I'm sorry. Could we, ah, get those to go?"

The good man didn't bat an eye.

"But of course. Would you like a sauce sampler to go as well?"

"What the hell," I said, throwing my napkin on the table. "Sure."

We left the restaurant with our resolutely un-French doggie bags with an even less French hippo on the front. Anne was marching quickly and I had to work to keep up with her. When we reached the taxi stand at the corner of Rue Montmartre and the Boulevard Poissonnière, I slowed. But she kept going.

"You don't . . . ?" I called out, gesturing toward the taxis.

"Walk."

We cut through the Grands Boulevards past the imposing structure of the Paris stock exchange and spilled out onto the Boulevard de l'Opéra, all gussied up with lanterns for the night.

"Walk," she said again, crossing the street even faster.

We passed the Hôtel du Louvre, where we'd sometimes started our erstwhile evenings out with a glass of champagne, and then crossed through the palace gates to the museum.

Everyone who has been or lived in Paris has their favorite place, and Anne-Laure's was the square court of the Louvre. Beyond the polemic pyramid addition, through a nondescript passageway, lay a much smaller, more intimate courtyard with a fountain that never worked. At night, the stone sculptures of the former kings and ministers who inhabited the palace are lit up from below, and the roofline glows with a fearsome troupe of gargoyles, caught forever in midscream.

The edge of the fountain was cold beneath our legs — freezing, actually — when we sat. I reached into our doggie bags and produced a sheaf of paper napkins, offering them to Anne to sit on, but she declined.

We stayed without speaking for a while,

taking in the stonework that looked pink here and ochre there from the lights. Without the throng of tourists ant-farming their way through the palace's exterior corridors, the courtyard was romantic, ludicrously so. A year ago, we would have held each other, we would have kissed and laughed about the city's self-conscious beauty. No woman possessed more confidence in her appearance than Paris. But that night we just sat there, hoping for the interruption of a sight or sound to break up the loveliness that we couldn't share.

"If I could take it back, Anne," I said finally. "If I could have not done it —"

"But you did."

I stared down at my hands. "I really miss you," I said quietly. "I miss us."

She crossed her legs and rubbed her upper thighs with her hands, trying to warm them. "You haven't *been* here for months, now. It's been half a year. Just going through the motions."

"I don't want it to be like that," I said. "It's my fault. But I'm back. I promise you, it's over. It's been over a long time."

"Because she left," Anne said. "Because she left you. Otherwise, it would still be going on. Or you would have left with her."

I stared through the passageway toward

the glass pyramid that was lit up like a yellow Rubik's cube, dropped from some far-off galaxy into the night. I tried not to let it cut me, the fact that even Anne knew that Lisa hadn't loved me back.

"It's true, isn't it?" Out of the corner of my eye, I saw her looking at me. "You would have left."

"I wouldn't have," I snapped. "No. And I know what the letters say. What they make it sound like. And it's true that there was a point when my real life didn't seem real. There was a moment when I did think," I said, glancing up, but she was looking away from me, her face tight, her fists curled, "I did think, like an idiot, that I would go. But I know now that it isn't true. If it had actually come to that, I wouldn't have done it. I didn't actually want to. It was like I was possessed."

"What am I supposed to do with that?" she asked, her eyes flashing. "Thank her? Should I be grateful to this person who didn't want you back? She must have been pretty fucking special."

"She wasn't," I said, twisting my pants between my fingers. "She just, at the end of the day, she just wasn't you."

Then, the guttural sounds of Anne crying. The kind of weeping that comes from an

unopened place within where comfort cannot reach.

"Even now my mind is going. I can't get
it to stop," she managed. "Where? Why?
What did she look like? Was she gorgeous?
How did she . . . kiss? And the fact that you
made love to her, imagining you, and I don't
even know what to imagine." She held her
breath. "I can't get it to stop. To forgive you,
I'd have to have no love left for you at all.
Which would make it . . ." She put her hand
to her head. "You've . . . you've ruined us.
You've totally ruined us," she said, crying
harder. "For nothing."

"Anne, I *love* you," I said, grabbing her
hand and pulling her to face me. "I love
you more than anything in my whole stupid
life and I'm sorry that I made such an awful, painful, incredible mistake and that I
kept on making it. I am going to be sorry
about this for the rest of my life. But I have
never, *never* been so sure about us. *For* us.
I can't . . . I can't be me without you.
Please."

I took her other hand. "I knew it the
fucking minute I saw you in that stupid bar
with your cousin. You are . . . a more-than
person, Anne. Goddammit. You are more
than a best friend and a wife, you're more
than beautiful, and if I hurt you it's maybe

because I've always known and been ashamed of the fact that I am less than you, and always have been."

Her chin trembled. In my hands, her skin was cold. "I will do whatever it takes to prove to you that it will never happen again."

She bit her lip hard as a tear fell down her cheek. For the first time since I'd reached for her, she squeezed my hand back. "But what do you do about the fact that it happened? What do you do about that?"

I started to cry. "What do I do?" I said, dropping her hands. "What do I do? I don't know what to do. I did it. I can't make you love me back."

"But I *do* love you," she cried. "But I can't get past it! I can't! I'm so angry and I'm so sad and I'm embarrassed and ashamed and I'm furious at you. I hate you, and at the same time I just want to go back. And I don't know what to do either," she said. "I just don't."

I looked up at the sky and the buildings and the gargoyles and the sculptures. I looked out at the pyramid and the stupid, spinning carousel in the park beyond. And beyond that, beauty. More beauty everywhere. Lights and boulevards and thoroughfares and people going places and people coming back. And it was sitting there in a place that had been a safe place for us, a place that had always been calming and right, that I realized that if I really loved her, I had to let the decision to stay with me be hers.

"Anne," I whispered, touching her hand again. "I'm going to go."

"You're going to *go?*" she repeated, wrapping her arms around herself.

"I mean I'm going to *go,* go. I'm going to leave."

She turned to me, her eyes bright in the darkness.

"Really leave?"

I tried to keep my chin from trembling. I nodded yes.

"I don't want to force you, or make it harder for you with my presence, or with Camille, I don't want you to decide we stay together because of her. I want it to be you, Anne. I want this to be about us."

"But we can't —" She caught herself. "So, we're separating?"

My throat felt full of shards. "I don't know. Maybe?"

She smoothed her hair back and rubbed her legs again. I put my arms around her to warm her, and she didn't pull away.

"I don't know what else to do," I said, my

face against the dried-flower smell of her hair.

"I know," she whispered. "I know."

"I really fucking love you," I said, holding her tighter. "I do."

She pressed her face against my shoulder. I could feel her tears through my shirt. We sat that way for minutes, absorbing the silence of the present, the last hours of darkness before our unknown future would begin.

18

I moved in with Julien for a while until I could find my own place. Into an old duffel bag went an assembly of sentimental things: the never-ending Australian novel that previously held court by my bed, the videos of my parents, the camcorder, photos of Anne and Camille, slipped out of pewter frames. I purposely left a lot of necessities in the house, seeding reasons for me to get back inside it.

When I told Julien what had happened, our previous quarrel was forgiven. After ten days of sleeping on his couch and washing the dishes from the limited variety of pasta recipes that I made us every night, I was able to discuss *WarWash* with him without feeling like he was being condescending, or going out of his way to knock me down. I could see where he was coming from — his gallery was an ongoing dinner party, and I wanted to show up with an unpredictable, drunk guest who was probably going to break things. After reiterating that he and Azar Sabounjian had "history," he told me that it still might be worth my trying there. That I had his blessing if I did.

We didn't talk much about Anne-Laure. Those first weeks I kept my thoughts and fears inside my head, where they could shapeshift to suit that day's particular outlook. The truth was, talking to other people about our separation made it feel too real. Safely harbored in my memory, the things that she and I had said to each other could be analyzed any number of ways, and positively, even. If I talked too much about it, it would become clear how bad things were.

After days of unreturned phone calls and e-mails sent to addresses which turned out to be spam, I finally found a small apartment through the classifieds, that French stalwart of shabby real estate, *De Particulier à Particulier.* A widower was temporarily letting out his writing office while he took a cathartic cruise on the houseboat he and his wife used to live in, on the Seine. He was traveling to Amsterdam, and then he'd see. He said he had another friend interested so if I got back together with my wife, to simply call him. He told me he hoped I would.

The apartment was an architectural impossibility: a fourteen-meter-square duplex on the sixth story of a narrow building in the tenth arrondissement. The first floor consisted solely of a table that was built into the wall, two benches, a sink, and a stovetop with two burners. The staircase had been designed to maximize space, with each step imitating the shape of a single foot. The only closet space was built beneath this staircase with a curtain to hide your mess. Upstairs, there was a triangular-shaped slab of wood in the corner of the room and a stool: this had functioned as the fellow's writing desk. To the left, a futon, and in front of this, a double window that opened out onto the roofs. The bathroom was only a little larger than your standard airplane loo, and it was designed Swedish style with no separation between the shower and the shitter. When you showered, the water went everywhere, and then — eventually — it went down the drain. The owner had kindly left a squeegee for me to use after each shower, and he reminded me not to leave any electronic appliances out while I had the water running.

There was a shelf above the bed where I put some books and photos, and a free-standing hanging rack to the side of the window with just enough room for a couple of pants and shirts. I had to keep my coat on the back of the front door. There wasn't room anywhere else for something bulky. It was a rickety building, and my next-door neighbors were forever sautéing things in fish sauce, a condiment that managed to permeate each of the apartment's cracks, but there was good, creative energy in the space, and I was grateful to be there. It was reassuring somehow, to live somewhere so small. I felt enveloped, bolstered. And terribly alone.

It was already the new year — January 15. The holidays had come and gone without my taking part in them. In the week after I left our house on Rue de la Tombe-Issoire, Anne and I had had painful, silence-filled discussions about Christmas and New Year's. Even though we'd agreed to talk to Camille, to tell her that her mom and dad were taking that most vague and disconcerting of relational options, the infamous "break," Anne thought it might be too much for her to spend Christmas without her father. We agreed that I could go out to Brittany for the twenty-fourth and twenty-fifth and stay in a hotel, but then the Bourigeaud seniors overturned our plans:

they'd decided on a destination Christmas in Marrakesh for everyone except me. "They thought a change of scenery would be good for us," said Anne over the phone. "I'm sorry."

And so I'd spent the holidays with my parents back in dear old Hemel Hempstead. When you're crashing your parents' friends' annual pre-Christmas Christmas rasher party without your wife and daughter, you can't get a lot past people. The dinner party was at Tabatha Adsit's house, a neighbor down the road, and in between courses of bacon-wrapped cabbage and bacon-wrapped goose and bacon-wrapped everything, I had to repeat over and over again that I wasn't divorced.

"We're taking a break," I explained, passing along a spinach salad covered in imitation bacon bits. "We're taking some time off."

"Oh, it never works, Richie," said Rufus, Tabatha's husband. "You remember back at uni?" He looked around the table. "We used to do that all the time. I mean, basically you're saying you want to sleep with other people, and then maybe you do, and then you've screwed the pooch."

"Rufus," whispered Tabatha. "Leave it."

"Well, I hope you two work it out," he

said, dumping salad on his plate. "She was a lovely girl."

It didn't help that people were conjugating everything in the past tense. Every time someone had something nice to say about my wife, they spoke as if she were dead. *We always liked her. She was so beautiful. You two seemed so happy.*

And then, of course, there was public concern about Camille. People wanted to know what we were telling her, wanted to explain how damaging a situation like this could be for a child if we weren't clear about it. I replied that it was impossible to be clear about something that we weren't clear about ourselves. Most often, this response got me a reminder not to be selfish. That this wasn't about us.

The truth was that Camille *was* confused. Terribly so. It was heartbreaking to see. Upon their return from Brittany, I got to the house before Inès dropped her off, and Anne and I made sure to have all the emotional buffers on hand: her favorite kind of sparkling cider, two napoleon pastries, and a surprise school-night sleepover with her best friend, Marie, arranged later that week. Since she'd spent the last part of her vacation alone with her grandparents, I was anticipating a big-girl version of my little daughter: an energized bunny filled with stories of the things she'd seen and done without us. This led me to wrongly assume that Camille would be too distracted to make much of our announcement that Daddy was going to be leaving for a while. But vacation was one thing, home was another. And home was a house with both Mommy and Daddy inside.

Neither Anne nor I knew how far we should go to make our five-year-old "get" it. Anne's opinion was that if we told her the real truth, she'd grow up resenting me, and might not trust other men. And though this line of thinking was more generous than I deserved, I was none too eager to one day have a spiteful adolescent writing angsty poems about me, so I agreed to reiterate the vague message that we were "spending time apart."

Having told some people — most importantly, Anne-Laure — that I was moving forward with *WarWash,* I should have spent the holiday week at my parents working hard on sketches and a pitch. But once there, I was pulled back into an incubator of nostalgia and self-centeredness. Everything was starting to overlap and I was worried that the project was going to become too much about me and my marital problems when, shit, in order to be credible and timely, it needed to allude to the actual, horrid things taking place in Iraq.

Accordingly, to offer myself an outlet for my overflowing sap, I started up with the camcorder again. With it being the holidays, the Haddon house was filled with the comings and goings of couples of all shapes and sizes, except for the divorced. The desire to document these well-enough-adjusted people came from a perverse place, but it made me feel better to get out of my own head and into the lives of others. Somewhere in between their stories of financial hardship and shared memories, their advice on navigating flatulence and bad breath, was a deeper message about making love last. They were happy to sit across from each other at dinner every night, comforted by their shared bed; these clockwork rituals hadn't made them run screaming into another person's arms, and I thought if I recorded them, some answer would rise up through the footage to help me learn why not.

I decided to call this side project *Witness,* and by inflating my own case a little — a lot — I was able to convince some of my parents' friends to participate in my documentary about married love "for a gallery in the States."

The first couple to rise to the occasion was the Adsits, our rasher-dinner hosts. I filmed them back-to-back in their living room, as I had done with my own parents, and afterward, Tabatha admitted that she hadn't had such a good time in years. Apparently, she'd had a laundry list of irritations molding away inside of her, just waiting for someone to come along and ask her what drove her nuts about her mate.

Despite his garrulousness on the subject of my own marital troubles, Rufus Adsit stayed recalcitrant during his filmed portion, the clever man. He said he loved Tabatha's cooking and that she made a good bed with perfect hospital corners. When I asked when he first realized that he loved her, he blushed scarlet red. "She was very nice to my parents," he managed. "She was very natural in the home."

In addition to my parents' other closest friends, the Bainbridges, I also called up Harold. It was harder to lie to him about the purpose of the film; we'd shared a man stroll, after all. Right away, he knew that this had something to do with my wife.

My interview with Harold and Rosalyn Gadfrey lasted aeons — I had to do it over two sittings. Despite having two children with Rosalyn, and sharing nearly twenty years of marriage, Harold was still besotted with her, and her with him. It was difficult for me to get them to share what bugged them about each other.

Rosalyn: "He leaves his socks balled up in the dirty hamper."

Harold: (hands up) "Guilty as charged!"

Rosalyn: "Well, he does snore a bit, but you get used to it, don't you? It's sort of like the ocean."

Harold: "My Rosie loves the beach!"

I got hours of film. Tapes and tapes. I had four interviews so far, all happy couples, all from Hemel Hempstead, all heterosexual, all white. Not exactly a sociological slice of life. I could have turned it into something bigger, traveled into London, interviewed other people there, but when I finished with the Gadfreys, I felt like I had enough. In the beginning, listening to other people's gripes kept me sane. But as I rewound the tapes and watched the marital confessions from the privacy of my too-short childhood bed, I saw that they weren't complaints as much as confessions of how much these people loved each other. Confessions about the sacrifices they'd made and continued to make in order to live the life they'd decided on, to make each other happy. By the end of the sessions, I wasn't inspired or comforted, I was jealous. And very, very sad.

When I returned to Paris after the holidays to my Tiny Tim–sized abode, horrid January was upon us with its holiday markdowns and its tattered storefronts. I couldn't sit about sniffling at other people's recollections forever. I had to move forward with *WarWash.* Make something of myself by making stuff again.

My first choice for new representation remained Azar Sabounjian — one of the most intimidating gallerists in Paris. Elegant and frank, he was a major force behind the revitalization of contemporary art in the capital, repping heavy hitters like the British photographer Martin Parr and the controversial American photographer Larry Clark. With my C-level status, it would be a long shot for me to even get a meeting with Azar, much less a private show. But for the long-term health of my self-confidence, I had to try. I also had to test out my idea in a Laundromat that was far enough out of the way that I wouldn't be recognized if I blew anything up.

My destination was a crumbling building called the Lavo-Magick! on a long street that ran along the border between the twentieth arrondissement and the Bagnolet suburbs, referred to in French as *la banlieue,* and commonly followed by the modifier *chaude,* meaning dangerous, meaning (in racially charged code speak) that its residents are neither affluent nor white.

I'd come equipped with bits and bobs to sacrifice: Goodwill T-shirts, a Rod Stewart cassette tape, inconsequential photographs, an old IKEA catalog, and a quart of oil.

When I arrived at the Lavo-Magick!, I saw that I had competition — deviant customers had passed this way before. The storefront was covered in tags and graffiti, and there were iron bars across the two windows facing the street. A puddle of urine lay fermenting on top of the pavement, and a plastic bag of clothing lay next to that. On the other side of the cement steps leading into the Laundromat was an old — as in petrifying — pile of dog shit.

The inside wasn't as bad as the exterior led me to expect. Except for a couple of tags and intersected initials on the walls, the Laundromat was clean of both graffiti and piss. There were four fold-up orange chairs in the corner, and four corresponding washers and dryers, which was kind of sweet. One chair per machine.

Fearful that someone might come in soon,

I stuffed my objects and clothing into a washer and shut the door. For the first time, it occurred to me that my little experiment might do irreparable damage to an actual person's store. Or, at the very least, the person who used washer *numero quatro* after my dark passage was probably going to find their textiles covered in hot sludge. I checked my wallet — thirty-five euros in cash and a two-euro coin. I had a permanent marker in my bag and a scratchpad. I'd leave an out-of-service notice. And some cash. No, not cash, no way of knowing who would pick it up. I'd look up the contact info of the Lavo-Magick! once I was home. Make a donation of some sort. With a good-luck glance to the ceiling, I opened up the detergent compartment and poured in a couple lugs of gas.

As I sat there watching my discarded goods whirl away into oblivion, I wished that I could get in touch with Anne. I longed to have her beside me to witness forty-two minutes of Rod Stewart ballads being washed away in oil. But you lose the opportunity to share the good things when you do something bad. That was the worst of it maybe, or it was at that moment. Wanting to reach out and make my wife laugh and not having the right to. Not being able to make her smile anymore.

After twenty minutes, a tired-sounding beep signaled that my "clothes" were ready. I opened the door and peered inside. The steel container wasn't as gloopy as I thought it would be — I'd imagined that a mixture of gas and water would have caused the concoction to congeal in oleaginous globs on my belongings, but this wasn't the case.

The cassette was in bad shape — sorry, Rod. The shirts looked like they'd been used to slough off an afterbirth, but strangely, the smell was not unpleasant, a mixture of car exhaust and prune juice. The catalog had gotten the worst of it — it was a battered, pulpy mess, and when I saw the little balls of magazine paper wadded up inside the steel drum's grid, I felt pretty certain that between this and the addition of a hazardous material into the otherwise sanitary space, the poor washer might never work again.

I scribbled the out-of-service message I'd planned on and tried to suppress the guilt inside my heart. It hadn't been *that* much oil. It might, quite literally, come out in the wash. I could put the Lavo-Magick! in the acknowledgments page of the exhibition booklet, if there was one. I could give them some art.

Feeling moderately better once my hand-scrawled sign was on the washer, I took out my mess and transferred it to a dryer, thus preparing to demolish yet another machine.

Or blow up a whole neighborhood. Only about a minute into the dryer cycle, my wife-free (and thus severely compromised) brain kicked back into business, suggesting that it probably wasn't a great idea to combine dry heat and gas. A burning smell confirmed this and I shut the whole thing off, anxious that any moment a neighborhood watch group was going to come in and accost the idiotic foreigner concocting lab tests in their Laundromat.

I shoved the gooey lumps of stuff back into the bag I'd brought everything in, left a twenty-euro bill on top of the ailing washer as penance, and got the hell out of the Lavo-Magick! The fact that I hadn't burned the place to its foundations seemed like magic indeed.

It took me four more days of preparation before I had the courage to call the Azar Sabounjian gallery. By that time, I had desperation more than courage. Camille had been invited on a weekend to Bordeaux with her best friend, Marie, which meant that I had three days ahead of me in which I'd be unexpectedly alone. I figured the time would pass less torturously if I had something to think about. If Azar turned me down, I could spend my weekend wallowing. If he accepted my ludicrous proposition, I could gloat.

I dialed the gallery, and when the phone started ringing, I missed not having a landline. What if there was one of those echoes you sometimes get with cell phones? What would I do then? After five rings, however, a receptionist picked up. I detected a British accent, although she was speaking in French, but I didn't want to be overfamiliar with a person I didn't know yet, so I asked her, in French, if I might speak to Azar.

"May I ask who's speaking?" she said flatly.

An awkward question, as Azar had no idea who I was.

"A dissatisfied client of the Premier Regard gallery?" It was the first thing that came to mind, but it was a lousy thing to do to Julien. Reputation was everything in the Parisian art world — word would get around. But then again, by his own admission, Julien had a bone to pick with Azar. If I acted aware of their past history, it might help my case.

"May I ask what this is about?" the voice

continued, apparently unfazed by whether I was dissatisfied or not.

"I'm an artist," I fumbled. "I've had quite a few shows in the area, and I have an idea for an installation I'd like to talk to him about."

"But you've never shown here?"

"No," I said, swallowing, "But I've shown at the Atelier Buci and the Premier Regard —"

"I understand that," she continued. "But we don't just take artists on references."

"I don't have any references." Too late, it was out. "I mean, I'm not intending to use these galleries as references. I just wanted to . . . pitch an idea?"

"I'm afraid that —" There was a long pause, and the sound of the phone being put down on a hard surface. I heard muffled voices in the background.

"Could you hold on, please, Mr. —"

"Haddon," I supplied.

And so I held. After a modest eternity, a man picked up.

"This is Azar Sabounjian," said a polished voice on the other line. "What can I do for you?"

It was all very well and fine to have a written proposition sitting on the table beside me; I'd forgotten to prepare something conversational to say.

"My name is Richard Haddon, and I've done several shows in the area —"

"Alice explained that to me, yes?"

"I have an idea for an installation that would be perfect for your gallery."

"You're familiar with my gallery?" I thought I heard him typing.

"Of course."

"I see," he said distractedly. "And where'd you say you've shown before?"

"Well, I'm from London originally," I mustered. "So I've had some shows over there, and also in the United States and in Paris."

"Where in Paris?"

"The Premier Regard, Espace 66, Atelier Buci —"

"Aha," he replied, coughing. "So you know Julien?"

"Yes," I replied, careful not to insinuate whether I considered knowing Julien a good thing or a bad.

"Has he sold your work?"

"Yes," I said. "A lot."

"So why don't you do your installation there?"

"He doesn't do installations," I replied.

He snorted, which I took as a good sign.

"And what's the installation about, exactly?"

"The situation between America and England in Iraq."

"And you said you're British."

I admitted I was.

After a pause that seemed longer than it needed to be, he said, "I'll tell you what, Richard. I like installations. I like international art. I like young art . . ."

I quivered. I was in my midthirties. Was I young, or was I old?

"I'm not a fan of unsolicited phone calls, but I fucking *hate* George Bush." His words were crisp and clipped. "Look, why don't you pop by the gallery, let's see . . . *Alice?*" he hollered. "Friday the twenty-eighth?"

My response took all of two seconds to conjure. Thanks to the demolition of my marriage, I didn't have a single Friday in my future with anything planned.

"I'll give you ten minutes," he offered.

"Ten minutes is good."

"Come after lunch, then. Let's say three?"

"Three o'clock," I repeated. "Perfect."

"Very good, then," he said. "I'll see you tomorrow."

The dial tone blared its taunting singsong in my ear. Sweet fuck all, I thought, putting the phone down. The twenty-eighth was *tomorrow?*

19

The next day I set out for the sixth arrondissement with my portfolio and my sketches and a gastric ulcer. In the last decade, I hadn't embarked on any type of professional endeavor with an uncertain outcome without a pep talk from my wife. But instead of sitting at my kitchen counter listening to Anne's wisdom while the coffee hissed and the butter softened and Camille got raspberry jam on her school shirt, I'd taken my breakfast upright at a café next to a bunch of inebriates who made fun of my briefcase, a telling reaction for a country with a 9.7 percent rate of unemployment.

Too restless to faff about at home, I spent the morning walking back and forth across the Seine until the gallery district opened. It seemed like it would be a good idea for me to be aware of the work of my contemporaries, which I presently wasn't, and hadn't been for quite some time. After two hours of wandering, I felt doomed to failure. My proposition contained neither images of topless women in printed cotton under-pants, nor neon signs spelling out ironic words like HAPPY, nor copious amounts of dirt. It was all right. I could always move back in with my parents and work at the Muffin Break.

When 2:45 arrived, I made my way toward the Rue Saint André-des-Arts where the Azar Sabounjian gallery was located next to an Isabel Marant shop — the hand-drawn star accompanying her logo on the window a signifier that one had entered the kingdom of the hip.

When I entered the gallery, the reception-ist was on the phone — it was the same woman I'd spoken to the day before, still placing too much emphasis on the wrong syllables, the way we English are wont to do in French. She had endless legs and high-waisted pants, which even on a girl of her attractiveness drew an unnecessary amount of attention to her pelvic floor.

When she hung up, irrevocably convinced from her phone call that she was English, I introduced myself in my native tongue and told her that I had an appointment with Azar. This was strike one for me — I hated when people defaulted to English when I'd been speaking French, so I don't know why I did it with her. I'd meant to be intimate, but I'd been offensive. With a little checkmark in her agenda and a perfected shrug of nonchalance, she informed me (in French) that Monsieur Sabounjian wasn't back from lunch yet, would I like to wait for him in that highly uncomfortable chair?

Still not back from lunch at 3 p.m., he was a Frenchman indeed. The receptionist — Alice, if I remembered from my conversation yesterday — sauntered back and forth making photocopies and pushing things about on her desk and huffing and puffing while she typed out what was meant to look like, but did not appear to actually be, work-related business.

At 3:20 I began wondering whether or not I should go to the loo. This was a hard call to make. If I waited, I might end up waiting so long that I'd have to go while we were talking. If I went now, I might be in the toilet when he arrived, which would be worse. Tossing the magazine I'd been pretending to peruse to the far side of the bench, I stood up and casually asked where the bathrooms were. Without taking her eyes off the computer screen, Alice pointed down the hallway, informing me that it was just to the left in her insistent French.

I walked down the hallway past a series of bondage photographs that appeared to be executed with Fruit Roll-Ups and string cheese until I found the bathroom, which was completely papered in aluminum foil. When I made it back to the reception area, I was greeted with the unfortunate sight of a handsome man in a three-piece suit sitting on the edge of Alice's desk.

"Richard, I presume?" he asked, tilting his head to one side. Bloody hell, I thought, reaching out to shake his hand. My hands weren't even dry yet.

"Shall we chat in my office, then?" He indicated the way.

"Yes," I stuttered. "I just need to fetch that . . ." I reached for the briefcase that I'd left beneath my chair and followed the man who held my destiny down the hall.

Azar's office was just what I'd expected: organized and meticulous, with two shelves showcasing a tightly curated selection of books. His desk was a massive mahogany structure with a leather top, underneath of which ran the pelt of what I hoped was an imitation panda.

Azar walked behind his desk to a see-through swivel chair and gestured toward a stool for me to sit on. Danish in design and certainly expensive, it was nonetheless a stool, and I wondered if he also had a dunce cap for me to put on.

"So," he began, folding his arms on the table. "I don't have a lot of time."

"Right," I said, snapping open my briefcase to remove my portfolio and sketches. "These are some photographs of my recent work, along with press clips." I slid the portfolio to him.

"I'll look at that later," he said, pushing it to the side. "Let's talk about Iraq."

"Brilliant," I said, trying not to redden. "So I've got a proposition here, you could read it, or . . . ?"

"Why don't you just summarize?" he asked, leaning back in his chair.

"Very good," I said, trying to sit as straight as possible on my stool. "So the idea is, it would be called *WarWash,* and although I know there's not a war yet —"

"Oh, there will be."

"Right, so I'm English, but I spent a lot of time in America, and the fact that they're teaming up around something so unfounded is, you know, absurd. So the idea would be to make the installation an interactive one based upon mistakes. I'd have two washing machines, one British and one American, and I'd have certain objects that remind me of errors made in each country, both, uh,

381

personal and governmental, that I'd wash in each respective machine, and the public would be invited to bring in objects as well. But everything would be washed in oil."

"Oil," said Azar, his eyebrows lifting. "As in petroleum?"

"Right. And behind all this, behind the platforms, there would be a hanging line where we'd dry the objects, after. I'd identify the object and the person who donated the object with hand-stamped dog tags."

"I see," he said, drumming his fingers on his desk. "So they'd look like corpses?"

"It would depend on the size of the object, of course," I offered, "but seeing that they'd be covered in sludge, they might. Either that or, uh, fetuses."

"Fetuses." He nodded, writing something down. "I see."

I fell silent. You couldn't really say much after the word *fetus*.

Flipping through my portfolio, he said, "I'm assuming you've already tried this?"

Relieved, I said I had.

"And nothing blew up?"

"No," I said, trying to sound convincing. "But you can't dry anything. And paper makes a mess."

He nodded. "Do you have a materials list in there?" he asked, looking at the sheaf of papers on my lap.

I handed him my proposal. To my horror, he began reading it out loud.

" 'Needed: 2 washing machines, one a Whirlpool (cost: 400 €), one a Tricity Bendix (cost: 350 €). Anticipate 1 converter and 1 surge control (cost: 25 €). 2 large wicker laundry baskets (IKEA: cost p.p 9 €). 6 containers of gasoline (cost per container: 18 €). 3 packets of latex gloves (cost: 10 €). 2 large stockpots (cost p.p: 15 €). 2 wooden platforms of 10m2 (supplies from Castorama estimated at 100 €). 50 "dog" ID tags: (200 €); metal engraver (75 €); laundry line (15 €); laundry pins (5 €); nylon to create permutated version of the American and British flag (25 €); paints to create flag (40 €); black tarp (20 €).' "

He rubbed his chin, reached for a pen and marked something on a piece of paper. Then, without glancing up at me again, he continued.

" 'Setup: The installation requires approximately 40m2. The two washing machines are to be placed side by side, the American one on the left, the British one on the right. There should be a distance of one and a half feet between the two machines. One laundry basket should be placed on the left side of the American machine and one on the right side of the British machine, with a canister of petrol beside it. Behind the two machines will hang a fused oil-painted version of the British and American flags to be created by the artist (see drawing attached). This flag will be painted in such a way that the fact that there are two flags will become evident the farther the visitor steps *away* from the machines. The washing machines, laundry baskets, and oil containers will be mounted on a wooden platform. The setup should call to mind a political debate. The laundry lines will be hung to the right of the machines. Black tarp will be used underneath the drying objects, and will be cut in such a way as to recall body bags.' "

Again, he jotted something down on his infuriating piece of paper. He was probably making out a grocery list. *Could you tell my wife I'm thinking wild mushrooms and farfalle? And we're out of double-ply toilet tissue. Thanks, Alice, you're a doll.*

He leaned back and ran his fingers through his luxurious head of hair before picking up the last page of the proposal.

" 'Artist's statement,' " he continued reading. " 'This installation, tentatively entitled *WarWash,* is designed to highlight the senselessness of the American and British government's WMD pursuits in Iraq by engaging the public in an absurd domestic act: the washing of things in oil. By selecting objects that remind the artist and the public participants of their past mistakes, the exhibit will be engaging on an intellectual, visual, and olfactory level, and should appeal to fans of artists such as Sophie Calle and Maurizio Cattelan.' "

That was it. There was nothing else to read. Only my drawings were left, which he'd hardly glanced at.

Azar swiveled once to the right, and then he swiveled to the left in his fancy swivel chair. Then he pushed all of my papers into a neat little pile and placed a silver paperweight in the form of a pinecone on top of the stack.

"Very well," he announced, nodding. He jotted down a final line, which apparently ended in an exclamation point.

"Come with me," he said.

On our way out of his office, instead of turning right to take me back to my high-waisted compatriot wasting time online, he walked me around the corner to where an archway was covered with drop sheets attached to the ceiling with blue electrical tape. He unzipped a plastic makeshift door and gestured for me to walk through it. I understood what Julien meant when he'd said that Azar was "tough." He had a back door for rejects.

Once he'd made it through the plastic door himself, Azar reached into his blazer and pulled out a pocket flashlight.

"We're still working on the electric," he said, twisting the flashlight on. "And obviously, the paint."

I stared around the space and said nothing. He'd examined my skill set. He'd seen my way with a brush. It was possible that he was going to ask me to touch up his decorative molding.

"Right, so, that's that," he said, pulling aside the plastic and motioning for me to walk through. Back in the hallway, he brushed off some dust that had collected on his suit.

"This space," he said, "will be ready by the end of March." He shook a piece of dried paint off his elbow. "Will you?"

Without waiting for my RPM level to descend back to a normal rhythm, he continued: "Because we've never worked together, you'll have to front the installation costs yourself. If it sells, though, we'll reimburse you. That work?"

I found myself mesmerized by his perfect

teeth. I was flabbergasted. I simply couldn't speak.

"Fantastic," he said, smiling. "I think this will be grand." He reached for a card from the inside of his jacket. "Call me next week — set up a time with Alice."

Making a concerted effort to mask my excitement, I mentioned that my phone number and address were written on my proposal, that I didn't have a card. He looked at me with a certain compassion and extended his hand.

"Ah, and if you ruin my gallery, you pay for it. We'll come up with a rider."

"A rider," I repeated. "Of course."

Azar saw me to the door, and on the way properly introduced me to Alice, who *was* British, the little minx. They both told me to call if I needed any help getting supplies and wished me *"Bon weekend."*

In a daze, I stumbled out into the pre-cocktail-hour bustle of the neighborhood, bumping into old ladies with shopping caddies and women carrying cut flowers. It had happened. He said yes. After months of feeling like I'd been cut off from an essential source of energy, I had a tiny percentage of my old self back. I felt electric. Proud and nervous. I wanted to tell Anne.

I walked up the steep hill past one of the branches of La Sorbonne, in the direction of the Luxembourg Gardens. I was swinging my briefcase. I had bounce in my step: my afternoon was a musical, and Paris was my stage. I made it all the way to the fountains at the entrance before I realized that I simply could not contain my enthusiasm, I had to tell my wife. I took my cell phone out of my jacket and found that it was dead. I'd been using it so little recently, I hadn't thought to charge it before I left the apartment, and now I had no way of sharing my good news with the one person who mattered. I sat down on a bench and weighed the pros and cons of stopping by our house. On one hand, I was right by it; on the other, since it wasn't even five o'clock yet, it was doubtful that Anne would be home, especially because Camille would have already left for Bordeaux. If Anne were there, she'd be upset that I hadn't rung before coming by. But then again, maybe she'd be moved to know how much I wanted to see her. I decided to try it. I was only a fifteen-minute walk away, and I could always leave a note. Maybe she'd agree to go to dinner with me? Maybe there was a small chance — just a tiny one — that she didn't yet have plans?

When I made it to our street, I stopped just outside the gate, surprised to see lights on in the kitchen. And then I saw my wife. She passed in front of the window. She was talking on the phone. Even though I had our keys on me, I still felt like the only right I had was to stand there and to observe her from outside. She was filling something up with water in the sink, nestling her cheek against her phone while she did so. Probably a vase for flowers. Unlike the slothlike state of my apartment, Anne would still be keeping an impeccable house.

I walked up the front path, rehearsing a speech — *I just got wonderful news, my cell phone has no batteries, I wanted to come by and share it* — when I saw another figure pass before the window. He said something to her and she nodded, pointing somewhere in the kitchen, still talking on the phone. When the person turned around, I saw that it was Thomas. Thomas in my kitchen. On a Friday night.

My heart started thumping wildly and my head felt squeezed. They could be working; it was entirely possible that they were working. At the court hearing, the jury had voted for the pregnant women but the winemakers had asked for a retrial, which the judge had granted. Anne had more work than ever, she'd told me that herself. But it was also one hour away from officially being Friday night, my daughter was out of town, and the man she'd made that daughter with was living elsewhere. I watched Anne walk away from the window and I felt my knees buckle. I couldn't move. One time, when I was a child, I'd swung too high in a playground swing and fallen from a good distance onto my stomach. I remembered being facedown in the sandy dirt mix, staring at the ants there, the inside of my stomach aching and completely devoid of air.

With the same hollowness inside me, I turned to go, certain that nothing good was going to come from my surprise visit, when I heard the door unlock behind me. "Richard?" Anne's voice said.

I had to force myself to turn around.

"What are you doing?"

"I . . ." Empty-handed, empty-headed. What a fool I was.

"Are you okay?"

"Sure!" I said, shrugging. "I was just in the area and had news, and —" I shoved my hand in my pocket, retrieving the evidence. "My phone died, so I couldn't call, but I see that I, um, should have, so."

I let my gaze fall down her body and was mildly comforted to see that she was wearing flats.

"I'm sorry to bother," I repeated.

"No," she said, shifting her weight. "It's just . . . a surprise. I saw Camille off, she was thrilled, as you can imagine. We have to . . . we'll have to come up with something. This is the second time the Merciers have taken her somewhere."

I nodded, bobbing my whole body in time with my stupid head. "Right."

"Um, you can come in if you want to? We're . . . Thomas is here."

"Right," I said, still bobbing. "I noticed."

"We're . . . working. Or just wrapping up, I —"

I wasn't listening to her. There was a ringing sound inside my head. All I could think of was that at any moment he was going to appear behind my wife, in my fucking doorway with his Big and Tall apparel and those lips and no shoes.

"Yeah, no, I have to go, it was just that I was right by here, so, if you're working?"

"You said that you had news?" she asked. I watched her glance behind her.

"Oh! Um, yeah. I got . . . I pitched *War-Wash* to a new gallery. Azar Sabounjian?"

She raised her eyes, impressed.

"And he took it, actually. I mean, he's taking it. For April."

"Oh my God, that's wonderful!" she said, coming down the steps. She put her arms around me and enfolded me in the smell of her, an intoxicating blend of lime and cedar that wasn't her normal scent.

I must have looked shell-shocked from her touch because she stepped away.

"I'm really happy for you," she said. "That's marvelous."

"Yeah, I was kind of hoping that —" I looked down at the walkway. "It was stupid. Obviously, you had plans. I just wanted to tell you. I wanted you to know."

"Yeah." She looked behind her. "With the retrial, we've been working such long hours, you know. We try to make it fun."

Don't ask about Selena, Richard. Don't ask about Jacques. Don't let on that your guts are all in slipknots because you don't know what the fuck Thomas is doing there alone.

"You could come in, though?" she said. "We could have a glass to celebrate?"

"No," I said. "I've interrupted you. Another time."

"We will," she said. "This is a big one."

I tried to smile. "It is."

She smiled back at me, and I crumpled further. In the way she was holding herself, the strain of the smile on her lips, I saw that what I'd first taken for sadness was actually pity.

I stuffed my hands in my pockets. "I like your new perfume, by the way."

"Oh," she said, reddening. "Thanks."

I stared at her and felt my humiliation start to shift toward anger. I wanted my wife back. I wanted to go into my own house. I wanted to know what that guy was *doing* there. Instead, I made a pathetic salute and let myself out onto the street where not so long ago, I'd painted I LOVE *ÂNE.*

Fragile and tidal are the bonds of those in a détente. Only ten minutes ago, I was hopeful, buoyed by good news. And now, walking toward home again, a home that wasn't home really, I felt crushed by disappointment and, worse yet, ignorance. I'd been assuming that this separation was as hard for Anne as it was for me. But now I realized that my wife might be experiencing this period in a completely different manner. That instead of feeling confined, she might at last feel free.

20

Although I admire T. S. Eliot, I don't agree with his socio-meteorological views. April is not the cruelest month; February is. Interminable and joyless, I spent most of the month searching for the materials I needed for *WarWash* and ruminating about the objects I was going to wash myself. It was a real challenge to find articles that reflected my own personal errors and the national experience at large.

For the British machine, I had to throw in my mother's recipe for beef tongue and lentils, a calamity she'd forced upon us every fortnight of my young life because she'd read somewhere that growing boys need folate. I had my dad ship me a pea coat I'd pinched from Alistair Parnell in primary school that was still wadded up in the bottom of my closet in a garbage bag. I'd gotten everyone to call him "Pansington Bear" for wearing it, and when I found out that the coat had belonged to his older brother who died from a brain aneurysm the past winter on a ski lift, I combated the horror of my shame by continuing to make fun of him. That coat, that memory, I definitely wanted drowned in gas.

I had a tea towel featuring a portrait of Margaret Thatcher and reproduced the winning Euromillions ticket an Englishwoman had purchased for the £113m lottery, a sum she couldn't collect on because her elderly husband had thrown the ticket away. And I had to — *had* to — include a glossy of David Beckham being sent off in the 1998 World Cup match against Argentina, a kiss-of-death red card that gave the Argentines the win. And finally, a visitor pass from the Charing Hempstead Hospital from seven years earlier when my father had a supraventricular tachycardia: a kind of minor stroke. For the American machine, I had a couple of random items from the box of stuff I'd taken from our house on Rue de la Tombe-Issoire that I wanted to include: a copy of *The Atkins Diet* and a postcard of the World Trade Center that I'd bought during a pre-9/11 trip, addressed to my parents but never sent. A lot of the other stuff I wanted I had to find on treasure sites like eBay and Craigslist: a George Bush "American Heroes" action figure; a presinkage poster of the *Exxon Valdez;* a Florida voting ballot. But the other things I needed were still inside our house, under the bed where I kept a shoe box of souvenirs and photographs, artifacts from my first years with Anne. Things that had always made me smile. Things that now, if I were confronted with them, would break my heart.

I arranged my reconnaissance mission for a Saturday so that Camille would be home. By that point, it had been two months since I'd moved out. We should have had a visitation schedule, we should have had a *plan,* but every time I tried to ask Anne-Laure what she was thinking long term, she said she needed time.

And so my moments with my daughter were stolen and haphazard, spontaneous invitations to the movies, hot-chocolate excursions, sleepovers on school nights, when Anne had to work late. And although a proper schedule would have guaranteed me more time with Cam, it also would have made me feel like I was already divorced.

When I rang the doorbell to our house, my little girl opened the door in fairy wings, a tiara, and a poofy princess dress.

"Enter, enter!" she cried, waving at me with her wand. *"Daddy's here!"*

I swept her up, taking care not to knock the plastic tiara from her hair.

"How's my little princess?"

"I'm a fairy *godmother*," she said, absorbing my kisses. "Jeez!"

Anne was in the kitchen, her hair pushed back with the moth-eaten silk scarf she wore on weekends to signify the kick-off of an epic bout of cleaning.

She rose from her crouching position in front of the sink and snapped off her yellow plastic gloves. She leaned in to kiss me once on each cheek, a gesture so unnatural, it stung more than if we hadn't kissed at all.

"Ugh. My hands smell like plastic," she said, avoiding my eyes. "Camille wants to help you, if that's okay? Do you need a bag?"

I nodded toward the giant tote on my shoulder. "I brought one," I said. "Thanks."

"And if she . . . if she seems up for it —" Anne flinched. "Do you think you could put her down for a nap?"

"Of course," I said, feeling every inch the babysitter and not at all the dad.

"Right," she said, standing straighter. "Do you want . . . a coffee?"

I did, but I couldn't take the awkwardness between us a single minute more. "I'm good," I answered. "Thanks."

"Cam, you want more juice?"

"I drink *ambrosia*!" she said, twirling her wand around her head. "Daddy, come *on*!"

I followed Camille up to the second-story landing, taking in the smell of the rug pads on the staircase, the baked-bread odor of my house.

"Where do we start?"

"In the bedroom," I answered, my stomach clenching as I said the word out loud. I hadn't been inside our bedroom in a month.

"Okay!" She trotted down the hallway, full of pony energy.

I was relieved to see that Anne had left the bedroom in hotel-like shape. The bed was made impeccably and the air smelled freshly scented, tinged with the slightly burned fragrance of a room recently vacuumed.

I avoided looking around too much. I didn't want Camille to sense my discomfort at being home again. This was just a regular, totally normal day, with Daddy looking through his time capsule while his daughter jumped on the bed.

I pulled the white Stan Smith shoe box from its hiding place. Camille tucked the layers of tulle underneath her and sat down on the mattress, swinging her stockinged feet within inches of my face.

"Are you making a painting?" she asked,

folding her arms.

"No, honey," I answered, taking the lid off the box. "More like a huge collage."

The first thing that greeted me was a copy of the contract for *The Blue Bear.* This I'd have to photocopy, but then it was definitely going in the wash. Underneath that, proofs of purchase for paint supplies that should have been in our downstairs file cabinet in a file marked "Tax."

"Mom said you were going to put things in the wash," said Camille, catapulting herself off the bed and toward the closet. "So do you want a T-shirt?"

"Well," I said, leaning back on my elbows, "it depends. See, the thing is, you know when you started out with the origami animals? And sometimes you made mistakes? Like, maybe sometimes a rhinoceros ended up looking more like a unicorn, and so you started again until you got it right?"

She tilted her head at me, unsure where I was going.

"Well, see, I'm looking for the equivalent of that first rhinoceros. The one I didn't get right."

She scrunched her face up in a frown.

"Okay," I said, relenting. "Find me a T-shirt. A really dirty one."

Cam disappeared for the laundry room,

and I continued my hunt. The fact that I remembered the box being in better order made me realize how long it had been since I'd put something meaningful inside. Three years ago, I'd been adding something regularly: one of Anne's emblematic grocery lists (*To buy: yogurt [Whole fat, please?], [Do you want??]*), a business card from a memorably bad restaurant, the hokey champion dog stamps my mother used each time she sent a card.

But underneath a wretched photo of my twenty-two-year-old self at a Phish concert in New Hampshire (a very American error that was *absolutely* being washed), I finally found one of the items on my agenda: the proof copy of the *Providence Phoenix* ad I'd taken out with my wedding proposal. I didn't want to wash it, I just wanted to see it. To hold it in my hands. *Anne-Laure: Will you marry me? Richard H.*

Camille returned with something from the laundry, an exercise shirt of Anne's, one of those double-layer waffle-mesh numbers in watch-out shades of neon that probably had three figures on the price tag.

Thanking her, but knowing I'd never wash it, I put it aside and kept pawing through the box. Underneath a Popsicle stick from the first frozen ice cream bar Camille had ever eaten in Brittany, I found item three on my need list: my entrance ticket to the Nan Goldin exhibit at the Pompidou on Saturday, January 12, 2002, the day that I met Lisa.

Surreptitiously, I slid the cursed bit of paper into my bag. Camille, meanwhile, having tired of my archaeological dig, was scooching her way back up the bed and underneath the covers.

"Here, Daddy," she said. "Do you want?"

I looked up and saw her holding out the chartreuse glass bowl that Anne used to house bookmarks, Camille's latest origami animals, and other sweet-dream knick-knacks by the bed.

"Look!"

And in her small fingers was my paper blue bear. Slowly, I got to my feet and joined her on the bed, casting a cautious glance down the empty hallway.

"Let's see there," I said, accepting the bowl and the bear. I turned the creature in my hands.

"Did Mommy tell you I made this?"

Camille shrugged. "No."

This was an even better sign than her having kept it in the first place. When something was extra important or difficult, Anne kept it to herself.

With an imitation growl, I set the blue bear on the comforter and poked through the other things in the bowl. There was a frequent buyer card for a new coffee place in the neighborhood (customer appreciation and take-out cups both new concepts in Paris), a weathered bookmark from the Shakespeare & Company bookstore, a drawing of a heart with a smiley face in it (*signé* Camille), and a miniature card with a gold-leaf *Thank You* written on the front.

I picked up the card. It was the tiny kind with a hole through it, the type that florists put into hand-delivered bouquets. I looked through the bedroom door toward the hallway, but it was still just Cam and me.

"So, what's this?" I asked aloud, somehow feeling that my snooping would be condoned if I made Camille a part of it.

Dear Anne-Laure,
   I can't thank you enough for going out of your way to show me the ropes. You're an inspiration and a real example for me, and I wish you only the best.

Yours,
Thomas

"Well," I humphed, sliding the card into my pocket. Since when were subordinates at Savda & Dern using informal object pronouns with their bosses? *Yours?* He wasn't *hers*. Anne was *mine*. That was our bed she was sleeping in, our life, our house. This life was still mine.

"Okay!" I said, rubbing Camille on her back. "I think that'll do it!"

"But you don't have a lot, Daddy," she said, pulling up the covers.

I kissed her on her forehead and told her it was fine. I took off her tiara and placed it in the bowl, careful to put everything right back where it had been next to the lamp.

"When you wake up, you have Mommy call me if you want to pop out and see a movie? It's no problem. I'll come back."

Her eyes rolled back with sleepiness.

"Okay?"

"Okay," she said. "I lurv you."

I pried the wand out of her hand and placed it on the side table.

"I lurv you back."

I left the house somewhat unceremoniously, beelining through the kitchen with a "Camille's napping!" and a "thanks for everything!" to Anne, none too eager to let on how jealous I was of the note I'd found. Focus on the good stuff, Richard, I told myself. Your bear was in there, too.

I headed for the gallery, in pursuit of one last article for the American machine, along with some figurative distribution of an olive branch or two. The last time I'd been by the gallery, Julien hadn't been able to hide his consternation that Sabounjian was actually doing my show, and I hadn't been able to hide the fact that his envy made me pleased. It had been an awkward interaction, and we hadn't spent real time together since. He was long overdue for a visit, and a request.

I found Julien sitting alone at his desk, staring at the wall in front of him. The desk across from him where Bérénice used to sit had been removed. I tapped on the glass and he waved me in.

"Hey!" To my astonishment, he got up and hugged me. "Look," he said, pointing to the empty table. "She's gone."

"I noticed," I said, hands in my pockets. "Good thing or bad?"

"She eloped. I wouldn't have pegged her for the type, you know? But she took up with a motocrosser. Turned out she had a really wild streak running through her. Anyway, what's the pleasure? On the way to see Azar?"

"No-o." I pulled a seat up. "I just came from my house. My real one."

Julien cocked an eyebrow. "And?"

I pulled the note card out of my pocket. "This dude's been sending flowers to my wife."

Julien made a show of putting on his eyeglasses. "Hmm," he said, flipping it over. "Well, well. It's pretty PG, honestly."

"I found it by her bed."

Julien took his glasses off. "So you one-up the bastard. I've got a friend who makes the most *incredible* terrariums, if you wanted to send flowers —"

I grabbed the note back. "It's a tough case they've been working on," I said, shoving it back in my pocket. "He's just a colleague. Friend."

"Sure he is. Of course." He put back on his glasses. "Oh. Hey — you got more mail."

"Can you be more explicit?"

"Gah, sorry. Right. From your mother. And the nutters. They wrote us back. It's a postcard, look." He started flapping it in front of me. "Stonehenge. I mean, really."

And he began to read.

Dear Mr. Lagrange,

Thank you for getting in touch with us by mail. Although Mr. Haddon's visit was certainly surprising, we ourselves are staunch supporters of the creative impetus, even when these instincts might be judged (by judgmental types) as "inappropriate." This being said, we have had some issues with the painting, the energy is off. But we've recently acquired a very powerful piece of ironwork from Canada, so this might have something to do with it. Please ask after Ngendo the next time you see Mr. Haddon. We trust she is doing well in the next chapter of her life!

What Ngendo was doing was sitting under an old towel in our basement, leading our mismatched Tupperware and rusting tennis rackets and storage bags of old clothing toward a higher plane of life.

Julien tossed the card over. "It doesn't sound like they're going to sue us, so that's something. And here's whatever from your mom."

"Speaking of letters," I said, taking my mum's envelope from him, "I know I asked you to toss it, but I was wondering if, by any chance, you might've not listened and —"

"You think that I don't know you?" Julien asked, rising. "Know you by now?"

He singsonged his way into the back room and emerged with a manila envelope marked *Miscellaneous.*

"Lisa's last letter?" he asked, proudly pulling out a yellow envelope.

"I'm getting rid of it. It's going in the wash."

He nodded, unconvinced.

"I'm serious. That's why."

"Good," he said, handing it to me and folding his arms. "Tar it."

"And, Julien?" I said, putting the letter in my bag. "Thank you for Azar. I mean, you recommended me, and —"

He cluck-clucked his way through the end of my sentence as the French are wont to do when a conversation gets too cuddly.

"Just do some more oil paintings for me somewhere down the road? Before you become famous?

"Okay," I said, smiling. "I'll have my people get in touch with yours."

We embraced, and I left feeling caffeinated with pleasure that our friendship seemed intact. My life didn't feel right without him.

With it going on eleven o'clock, the filth had cleared from the Parisian sky, the birds were back, and the weather was almost balmy — I decided that there was no use in turning the reading of Lisa's last letter into an occasion. I could very well incriminate myself on any pigeon-shit-coated bench.

Although I couldn't help picturing Lisa seated as she wrote out my address, with just the right amount of flourish at the *R* and the *H,* seeing her handwriting on the front of the envelope no longer moved me into paroxysms of torrid daydreams as it once did. Usually, I was ritualistic with these readings, touching the outside of the envelope as if searching for braille, thumbing it, sniffing it, opening it carefully with the cap of a Bic pen. But this letter, this last one, wasn't sticking to my heart. It registered with me elsewhere, aggravating the tension in my shoulders, registering as a dull thud just beneath my forehead. For the first time, it didn't feel exciting, it just felt wrong.

The beginning of the letter was as I remembered it when Julien read it to me over the phone.

Dear Richard,

Yesterday, I passed a gallery and there was a photograph in it that made me think of something you might do. Or it made me think of you. I guess that's the same thing. I know you don't care much for photographs, but this was of a battered sailboat in a cornfield. There was a scarecrow in the boat. It didn't look composed either, it looked like the world had grown around this boat. It was in black-and-white. Beautiful. I wish we had seen it together so that I could have heard what you thought of it. So that we could have talked.

So, scarecrows were a thing now. I'd seen quite a lot of them popping up in installation videos and short films. This was probably because they were fucking creepy. I'm glad we never got to have the conversation Lisa desired. I have absolutely nothing to say about a scarecrow in a boat.

I suppose it's inevitable. Here it is: I miss you. Dave and I have set the date for our wedding: July 21. Now that it's set, though, it feels definitive. It makes me miss you. I'm sure you can understand this better than I can, as I've never been married. It feels like a good-bye. I mean, it is a good-bye, obviously, and it has been, it's just, what do I do with the missing part? What do I do with the part of me that does miss you, that falls asleep at night sometimes dreaming of a parallel life?

As I contemplate this next adventure, I have to say that I feel grateful to have had an experience that will keep me warm. Something illicit, you know? Something naughty? All this being said, I hope that you are able to rehabilitate things with your wife. I wonder, I can't help but wonder, do you think we'll ever see each other again? I want to. I already want to. I am going to make a terrible wife.

And the letter ended there, signed *love*. But I felt no tingling. No heat. At that moment, I felt nothing but disappointment for my predictable ex-lover. A game player. A manipulator. She wasn't what she was.

No. I felt it in the pit of me. I was never, ever going to see Lisa Bishop again. Not even by accident. I felt it in my soul. There was a part of me that wouldn't be surprised if she called off the wedding — if my imperviousness made her try to get me back. But I knew it, I really *knew* it — even if Anne wouldn't forgive me — I wasn't ever going back.

I stuffed the letter into the tote with the things I'd taken from my house and ripped open the white envelope from my quirky mum. I was surprised to feel my throat clench when I pulled out a magazine image of a lemon tart with a purple Post-it note attached.

Darling,

Daddy told me what happened with Anne-Laure. Please, I hope that you don't mind. I know you'll think this is silly but there is something about the bitters and the tartness and the sweet — most people opt for apple, but there is something special about this one. The meringue isn't half as difficult as you'd think to make. I just thought you might have a go at it for her. Anyway. Pie.

Love,
Mum

You love people. They disappoint you. But sometimes, they don't. They just keep loving you, right through it all, waiting for you to wake up and appreciate them. To say, "I love you. I've always loved you back."

21

March. A month to get through. Marching. Marching on.

By the beginning of the month, I had all the materials I needed for my exhibit along with a real crisis of space. I hadn't thought of this when I was putting my pitch together, but constructing two separate 10m2 platforms in a 14m2 apartment was a mathematical impossibility. Not to mention that I had to hand-paint a 6 × 9-foot flag.

With Anne and Camille on yet another state-sanctioned vacation until the end of March, my studio at the Rue de la Tombe-Issoire was sitting empty, but Anne didn't offer up the use of it and I didn't ask. It wasn't my finest moment, but I finally had to apprise Azar of my situation at home. He was glad to hear about it — thought it added pathos to my brand — and said I could use the still-unfinished back room of his gallery as my studio and build the installation there. Airing my domestic laundry in public proved to be well worth it — it did me good to leave the house.

Several weeks before the opening, Azar sent out a press release to his contacts and to current clients of mine at the Premier Regard gallery — a generous gesture of Julien's, seeing as I finally found out why they didn't get along. It turns out it had nothing to do with any poncy art-world bollocks; no one poached an artist from the other person, or anything like that. Rather, they'd both studied art history at the Sorbonne, where they were pitted against each other for the highest marks, but partly because Azar's family was stricter, and partly because France maintains a barely concealed enmity toward men of Middle Eastern descent, Julien had a lot of success at parties, and Azar had more success in school.

It was a silly rivalry, and it should have been behind them, and Julien's sharing of his contact list went a long way to make this so. The press release was sent out with an open call for mistake-themed objects, and accordingly, once I'd built the platforms and made headway with the fused British and American flags, most of my time was spent weeding through donations.

People certainly do respond energetically when asked about regrets. Each morning, Alice would greet me with a trash bag full of "walk-bys," things people had left during the evening on the gallery steps. Most people seemed to view the show as an occasion to roast ex-lovers: we got heaps of love letters, hate letters, real estate listings for homes that went up for sale after a divorce, happy photographs that clearly didn't make the proprietor happy anymore; lots of photos of half-clothed couples, sleepy-eyed in bed.

I tried to find things that skewed toward the political, but they were few and far between. But all this started changing by mid-March, when the political shit truly hit the fan. After failing to convince Blair's government that an Iraq invasion had no sound mandate in international law, and therefore wasn't legal, our deputy legal adviser of the British foreign office, Elizabeth Wilmshurst, resigned. And then, only a handful of days later, despite the fact that WMDs were never found and that neither the United States nor the United Kingdom had the United Nations' support, the U.S. led a surprise invasion of Ba'athist Iraq. The war had officially started in an unofficial way. War.

The protests that had been under way in cities around the world tripled in fervor, with massive marches, strikes, and walkouts in Paris, London, Tokyo, Moscow, America, and Canada, with over three million people gathering in Rome. The fervor and the sheer number of protests — over 2,500 demonstrations by March — led the *New York Times* to write "there may still be two superpowers on the planet: the United States and world public opinion."

In the largely Arabic neighborhood around my apartment, American flags were routinely burned. Most Europeans were familiar with the stereotype that Americans are naive, stubborn, and immensely patriotic, but except for those of us who have dined with them in restaurants and tolerated their requests to have everything but the main protein on the side, we hadn't witnessed it firsthand. But America's backlash against France's position on Iraq was illogical and vitriolic. College friends from RISD started sending me snapshots of dinner menus, circling replacements of the word *French* with *Freedom:* Freedom fries, freedom toast. Gourmet supermarkets caved to public opinion and stopped selling conspicuously Gallic products such as foie gras and certain cheeses. Many wine shops took

French bottles off the racks. Tourism declined, with Paris slipping from the second-most-popular destination for American tourists to the seventeenth.

It was a frightening time, a noisy time — I lived only two blocks from the Place de la République, the center of the protests — and yet I'd never felt more proud of my adopted home. Pompous and grouchy though they might be, I had always found the French to be resolutely fair. Their refusal to participate in a war they considered unfounded moved me. They'd stuck to, but chosen not to use, their guns.

But that didn't mean that it was an empowering time to be alone. I thought constantly about Anne and Camille, but it wasn't about their being safe: I knew they were, they were in Brittany, a region literally furrowed with bunkers in which, if things got *really* real, they could squirrel away with a month's supply of pastries and Anne's favorite board games. It just seemed inconceivable that we weren't together. It had been so long now, the unanswered questions made my mind spin.

Anne was a pragmatist, but she wasn't cold. There were certain roles I'd played in our relationship that could be carried out by others, paid for in the form of babysitters, plumbers, or take-away food, but there was no stand-in for love. I mean, yes, she could be throwing herself into the raising of our daughter, or she could have got a cat, but there was no replacement for a warm body on the other side of the pillow unless there was a new body in our bed.

Ever since I'd seen Thomas at our house that Friday and found proof of his flower delivery, I'd vowed that I wouldn't act territorially, like a dog peeing on a hedge. He'd been at our house for work several times before and I'd seen him there again. On paper, there wasn't anything unusual or troublesome about it. But off the paper, when you realized that Anne-Laure and I were deciding between marital remission or abatement, this young man's presence agonized me. In the mornings, I imagined them interacting at work, agreeing — why not? — they could step out for a quick lunch. I saw the way Anne smiled over her glass of white wine, and I saw him sitting back, his arm stretched out across the booth, his posture a little too comfortable, a little too relaxed.

But Anne wouldn't do it. Would she? It had never been her way before, tit for tat. Especially with a colleague. She was too professional, too ethical, too ambitious for that. Or so I kept telling myself when I woke up in the middle of the night, having dreamed another dream in which I came around a corner in my own house to find them kissing hungrily, her unbuttoned blouse falling off her shoulders, his hands on her pale breasts.

The only tranquilizer for my doubts and anxieties was my exhibition. Any television viewer who had seen the we're-coming-for-ya glimmer of blood thirst in Bush's eyes could have guessed that an invasion would take place, but we had no way of knowing that it would happen ten days before the opening. Azar called me regularly to let me know that it was horrible — the coming sacrifices, the untimely deaths — and also that it looked like we were going to get a *lot* of press: everyone on his who's who list of Parisian media had RSVP'd yes.

Despite the good news about the guest list and the political timing that nearly guaranteed that the VIPs would come, I was plagued by the feeling that things could still unravel, that this incredible opportunity could come undone. All alone in the political hotbed that was Paris, I felt like my immediate future hinged upon the success of the *WarWash* exhibition. I knew better than to think like that — it wasn't as if Anne-

Laure was going to take me back just because I scored a show in a cool gallery, but at this point, it couldn't hurt. I wanted to surprise her with the breadth of the exhibit. I wanted to show her that I was capable of re-becoming the artist — and the husband — I once was. I wanted to show her that not only had my regime changed, but that my regime was desperate.

Happily, the day of the show corresponded with the general theme of April in Paris: rejuvenation and rebirth. The streets were ripe with the smell of vendors selling lily of the valley, and handsome couples walked side by side with half-eaten baguettes poking out of cloth bags. It would be a beautiful evening, warm and pleasant, the first day in a long time with no rain.

At my apartment, I spent a long time picking out my outfit. I'd never prepared for a show without Anne: it was my first time rallying solo in ten years. I settled on the beat-up denim shirt I'd been wearing all day, fitted navy trousers, white sneakers. I added a blazer for good measure. The look, when finished, was one part schoolboy and two parts I'm-going-to-celebrate-Brett-Easton-Ellis's-birthday-on-a-yacht.

The gallery was a hub of activity when I

arrived. Outside, two bartenders were smoking while a third wheeled several carts of sparkling water in on a cart. Azar was pacing around the reception area on his phone, and Alice was dealing with a paper jam in the printer.

"Do you think we need a release form?" she asked, waving with the hand that wasn't inserted in the traitorous machine. "I think we need release forms, but Azar doesn't."

"They already signed one when they sent in their objects," said Azar, his hand over the bottom half of his phone. "It was in the open call — by sending something in, you agree to . . . blah blah blah and such."

Alice made a final pull at the jammed piece of paper before giving up.

"Everything's ready to go in the back," she said, nodding toward the hallway. "It looks great."

And blinking hell, it did. Although lighting hadn't been in my original proposition, Azar insisted that we theatrically stage the installation. Accordingly, an electrician had outfitted the ceiling with two giant spots illuminating the platforms along with uplighting around the baseboards in order to heighten the effect of a political debate.

And the flag looked fantastic. It was maybe my best work to date. It had been so long since I'd painted anything abstract, I was worried that I wouldn't be able to pull it off. But by applying the paint in scrims and using a squeegee, I was able to create a cross between a Jackson Pollock and a Gerhard Richter. I was really proud of it. If the installation didn't sell, Azar was planning on selling the fused-flag painting for fifteen thousand euros.

I looked through the American basket first. Next to my *Atkins Diet* book and the postcard of the Twin Towers was a gold-leaf, 1974 yearbook from Sharonville High in Cincinnati that a retired teacher had sent me with a note that read, *I always thought I'd be a writer. But you know what they say about those that can't . . .* Another teacher, also from America but now living in France, sent in a weathered blue T-shirt marked COLUMBINE HIGH. Shelly Hampl, the American fan with a proclivity for inflatable sneakers, handed over her son's collection of baseball cards with a note that only said, *He's gay now.* Other things that I'd selected from all the donations: a photograph of a toddler howling on a Santa's lap, surrounded by poinsettias and a banner that read CHRISTMAS!; a poster of George Bush holding a shovel; an expired U.S. passport; a blank SAT test form (which I probably could have sold on eBay for a fortune, but, you know, *art*); a mix cassette tape covered in rainbow stickers with a declaration in permanent green marker (*I love you, Cassie! 1999!!!*); a graduation cap with an orange tassel and an engagement ring with a small hole where the stone had been.

A tisket, a tasket, in the British basket along with my mum's recipe for beef tongue and Alistair Parnell's stolen pea coat, I'd selected a beat-up copy of *The Wasteland* (not only is the title apropos, but T.S. was born in America and was later naturalized as a British subject, so well done, sender); a place mat with a screen print of Tony Blair on it; the Cadbury chocolate bar "Snowflake" that was launched at TV presenter Anthea Turner's garish wedding in 2000, ushering in a new decade of corporate-sponsored marriages; and an advertisement for the "Squidgygate Phone Line" that allowed the public to hear the entire thirty-minute, bugged conversation between Diana, Princess of Wales, and her close friend James Gibey about her possible dalliances for thirty-six pence a minute.

By the time I'd checked the power on both machines, rearranged some of the clothespins, and fiddled with the lights, the guests had started arriving. I could hear bottles popping and glasses clinking in the other room. When I joined them in the reception area, I recognized a well-known culture critic for the French newspaper *Libération*. He was engaged in conversation with a man in jodhpurs. And there was Shelly Hampl, who had already cornered Azar. I was just about to make my way toward her for a hearty session of glad-handing when a couple at the door caught my attention. Both were dressed in white with different-colored blazers, and one of them was carrying a small box. I couldn't believe it: it was Dave and Dan.

After a cursory *bise* with Shelly that of course turned into a hug, I greeted my Continuists.

"Gentlemen," I said, grasping their hands. "This is a surprise."

"I know," said Dave. "And we don't do surprises!"

"We're in town for the spring openings," said Dan.

I clapped him on the shoulder. " 'Tis the season!"

Dave adjusted his grip on the white box. He looked around warily at the crowd. "There's actually something we wanted to talk to you about," he said. "Might you have a minute?"

"Sure," I said, gesturing down the hallway. "We can go back there."

As we walked, I allowed myself to imagine various scenarios as to why they were here. Maybe this was about Ngendo; perhaps they wanted her back? That would be a godsend, as her repatriation would score me points with Anne.

"Well, this is certainly ambitious," said Dave, taking in the installation. "It's so different from your paintings."

"But that's what we wanted to talk to you about," said Dave hastily, handing me the box. "I'm not sure if Julien shared our recent news with you, about the energy in our home? Amira did another reading of *The Blue Bear.* And it came back —"

"Awful," said Dan, nodding sadly.

"It was full of red and purple energy. There was even some black. It's really bad news for us. This has never happened with any of our art."

"Well, I'm sorry to hear that," I said, surprised by the box's weightlessness. "Should I open this?" I asked. "Or save it for later?"

Dan placed his hand over his heart. "Open it," he said.

I took off the lid and removed a single piece of tissue paper. Underneath this was a photograph of *The Blue Bear* in their house.

"Oh," I said, holding it up to the light. "Thank you?"

"We're so sorry," said Dave, "but we have to give it back."

"Sorry if I'm a tad slow here," I said, staring at the picture. "You want to send the painting *back*?"

Dan didn't give me time to react. "Once a negative reading is actualized," he explained, "it can create waves of bad energy throughout the house. If they linger long enough, the black energy particles can actually be activated in the body. It's terribly unfortunate, but the bear just didn't gel within our personal space."

"I had black energy in my organism once," said Dave quietly. "From my college roommate. It took me six months to get my system back."

Dan reached for Dave's hand. "We spoke to your gallerist," he continued. "Everything's arranged."

"You spoke to Julien about this?" I asked, looking down the hall to see if I could catch sight of the man who had withheld such vital information from me.

"We did. It's very unfortunate news, actually. I hope everything's all right."

"Jesus, well, that depends." What I wanted

to ask them was what the hell was going to happen to the money I got from the sale? And who performs energy readings on paintings? And why the hell didn't they give me back *The Blue Bear* when I *wanted* it in November?

But in terms of energy, it felt pretty important that I not get upset. This was my big opening, and dammit if I was going to let two crackpots dressed like they were just off the set of *Miami Vice* ruin it for me.

"Well, I'd prefer to sort the details out with Julien, if you don't mind," I said.

"Right," said Dan. "Of course. In the meantime, Amira said it would be very cathartic if you washed it." He pointed at the photo.

"Like an anointment," said Dave. "It will create the mental space necessary for you to welcome the painting back."

Well, I'd had it with professionalism. I cracked. "I wanted this painting back *months* ago. I actually *needed* it, and you guys wouldn't give it back to me. And now you're telling me that —" I stopped to try to calm myself and failed. "I'd like you to take that fucking *sculpture* out of my house."

"Oh, you'll need to keep Ngendo," said Dan. "Clearly, she still has work to do within your life."

They left — taking their holier-than-thou eye rolls and their Kombucha breath with them. I was about to toss the photo of *The Blue Bear* into the American machine when I felt a hand on my shoulder.

"Julien," I said, turning. "Jesus! Why didn't you tell me about the *Bear*?"

My well-prepared ex-gallerist handed me some wine. "What do you want? They only called me yesterday. I didn't want to upset you. Plus," he said, raising his glass, "there's absolutely nothing to worry about. They don't even want a refund."

"You're not serious."

He smiled broadly. "I didn't believe it, either. I even called my lawyer. They're going to sign a donation form. So the only thing is, we can't resell it. But we can donate it or, I don't know, do you want it back?"

"Yeah, I fucking wanted it back! Months ago. But what good is it now?"

"Speaking of," Julien said, putting his arm around me. "Your wife just arrived."

After giving the photograph to Julien for his gallery files, I headed through the body-choked hallway to find Anne and Camille looking at something behind Alice's desk. I stood there for a while, watching them. Anne had put Camille in a pink-and-wine-colored dress with a butterfly collar and a little pair of black boots. Beside her, Anne was in a camel-colored tunic I'd never seen over a pair of slim pink jeans. Close-fitting and cashmere knit, it hugged her every curve. Through the open space in Alice's desk, I could see that Anne was wearing my favorite pair of heels: round-toe stilettos in electric blue with an embellished heel of gold and silver chains. She'd put her hair up into a chignon that, owing to her French-ness, wasn't strict, but tousled, and she had a simple gold bracelet around her wrist, which danced down her arm as she pointed at something in the book she was looking at with Camille.

Keeping my eyes on my family in order to avoid locking my gaze with some well-wisher who might try to interrupt me, I made my way to them, bending down to hug my beautiful daughter first.

"Daddy," she cried, letting me sweep her up. "You're back!"

"No, *you're* back, sweetheart."

"Mommy said you're gonna do something really smelly."

"That's right, love," I said, kissing her again. "Very."

With my hand still clasping Camille's, I stood up and greeted Anne. Her skin smelled like gardenias. I wanted to nuzzle my face against the soft place just above her cheekbone, wanted to let my mouth graze her ear, wanted the din of chitchat and drinking around us to fade away.

"You'll never believe what happened," I said, eschewing how-was-your-vacation questions to tell Anne the big news. "The Continuists were here, the ones who bought *The Blue Bear*? The guys who wouldn't let me have it back?"

"Really?" she said, looking around us. "They're gone?"

I nodded at the door. "You know why they came? To bring me a photo of it to throw in the wash. They're sending it *back*."

"The painting?!"

"And not because I asked for it. Because it has *bad energy*."

Behind her desk, I saw Alice, who had been pretending she wasn't listening, raise her eyes.

"Don't worry, Alice love, it's not a business thing. It's just a bunch of nutters who do energy readings on their art."

She waved her hand through the air, pretending she hadn't been eavesdropping.

"Bad energy?" Anne repeated, looking

nervous. "Do you have to pay for it?"

I shook my head no. "But I can't sell it. They've drawn up some contract: donation only. So we can keep it . . . if we want?" I flinched.

I wanted terribly, acutely, to take her hand. I didn't. We stood there staring at each other, until she took a deep breath. "Why don't we just focus on tonight? And then we'll see."

"Richard!" said Azar, coming over. "Twenty minutes good? And you must be Anne-Laure," he said, kissing her. "It's lovely to finally meet you. And hello there, princess."

During the several times I'd brought her by the gallery, Camille had developed something of a crush on Azar, the proof of which was evident in her immediately flushed cheeks.

"In the meantime . . ." He made an apologetic smile before turning back to me. "Can I steal you? There's some people — press — I'd like you to meet. If you two want to run in the back there to see the installation, by all means, you should."

Azar whisked me away to speak to this person and that one, but my mind was in the back room with Anne. I wished I'd been beside her when she saw the finished installation under the lights, the ominous empty clotheslines with their waiting pegs, and the flag glowing in the background, like something stuck and bled.

I spoke with a couple of journalists and bloggers while the crowd around us swelled. People were pushed out into the street, drinking and smoking. The reception area was too small to accommodate all of them, but Azar was firm about not letting the "laypeople" into the back space until we were ready to start the washers. Then the party would continue there until the wash was done, and I hung and tagged the items.

After I'd made the rounds, making progress with my sound bites, Azar made eye contact with me and tapped a knife against his glass.

"*Tout le monde, bonsoir! Merci d'être venus!* Now, if you'll just follow us into the back room, we're going to start the show!"

Like any event mixing food and humans, the exodus occurred in fits and starts of people getting refills on their beverages and loading up their plates with extra cheese and grapes. It took a good ten minutes to get even half of the attendees to the back, by which point Azar said he thought that was as good a time as any to start.

I took my place by the machines and

scanned the room for Anne. She was standing in the corner with Camille, looking around at all the people. And then she looked at me. I couldn't read her face.

"Thank you again for coming," shouted Azar above the noise. "I'd like to say a few words about this installation, mostly that we're very proud to have Richard Haddon here. Richard is a British citizen who spent a great deal of time living in America, and now the poor sod lives here." People laughed. "And when we agreed to work on this together, the war in Iraq had not yet started. And now it has. What you see before you is a living representation of the absurdity and senselessness that has informed this conflict from the get-go, absurdity that will be replicated by the act that Richard is about to undertake, a kind of sacrificial washing of regretted items in oil.

"Some of you who donated things are actually in this room," he continued, looking around. "Others mailed them in. And many of the objects were chosen by the artist himself, but each one has a certain relationship to the country it represents, and most call to mind mistakes. On the left, we have America. On the right, the United Kingdom. Richard is going to begin the washes on both machines, calling out each item, and when he's done, he'll hang the articles on the clothing lines back there and identify them with dog tags. We invite you to enjoy this space while the machines are running, but when the drying starts, we'll be putting up a guardrail around it because of the hazardous material. We have masks in the reception area for any of you troubled by the smell, and I'd also like to point out the various exits: one there to the right, and one down the hallway behind you. Again, thank you for being here. Let the wash begin!"

The swell of the crowd gave me courage, but not quite enough to get rid of the uneasy feeling in my stomach. I would be starting with the American machine and washing Lisa's last letter. I was going to have to push myself into a dissociative state in order to maintain the nerve to call it out in my wife's presence.

Positioning myself in front of the American washing machine, I picked up the first article, and yelled, "Expired U.S. passport; Colin Peterson." And then I tossed it in. I picked up another item: "Used T-shirt from Columbine, Colorado; Julia Mavis." I went on like this until people had started chitchatting again, by which point, I wasn't hollering so much as passionately mumbling.

Then there was only one item left to cite. I looked nervously around the room and saw that Anne and Camille were still there in the corner, watching my every move. I swallowed hard and said, "A final letter; Lisa Bishop," and then I tossed it in, my heart pumping so quickly, my vision became blurred.

Trying to convince myself that I hadn't played out of bounds — that the intersection of the personal and the public wasn't disrespectful when it was art — I poured a full quart of oil into the machine, set it to cold/cold, light spin, and then, after a second's hesitation, I pressed start. I moved quickly to the British machine, calling out the items with as much confidence as I could muster while I sent out a silent prayer to please not let anything explode while I was standing in front of the Tricity Bendix.

When I finally turned around, I wasn't surprised to find the room half emptied, with pockets of people paying only a cursory amount of attention to what was happening in the spinners. I scanned the room of fickle art lovers for my wife. In the corner where she had been, Julien stood now, entertaining Camille. And then I realized why. Anne was coming toward me, an agenda on her face.

"So," she said, with a look that squashed any hopes I'd had that my installation might have impressed her.

"This is quite a crowd."

"Anne," I said, "it wasn't, it was just that I —"

She held up her hand. "Just one thing, I don't want to ruin this — but you still have her letters?!"

"I got rid of all of them," I managed. "Except one."

Anne's gaze followed mine to the Whirlpool machine. Her lip twitched. "You destroyed it."

I nodded. I watched her expression turn from hurt to hurt less to bemused.

"Well." She sighed, walking away from me to trail her finger along the washing machine's glass window. "You think the stuff in there is going to make it? Did you sign an insurance rider in case it blows?"

I assured her that I had, and joined her by the machine, close enough to touch her. A groom and bride in front of a toxic cake.

"Oh," she said, pointing at my cuff. "You've got tapenade on your shirt. Or, um, gas?"

I scratched my nail against the stain while I struggled for something to say.

"Anyway," she continued, "I have to tell

you something." I watched her swallow. "I don't know how long I'll stay with Camille tonight. I mean, we'll stay for the drying portion. But I, uh, have to tell you something else."

Her tone gave me goose bumps. It wasn't like Anne-Laure de Bourigeaud to use colloquial interjections. "What?"

"Well, I went on a date, Richard. Or, two dates, actually. I guess."

My limbs were noodles. The din around me swirled.

"We didn't say anything about *dating*," I gasped. "I thought we were just giving each other space!"

"Well, nothing's *happened* yet. I mean, you know."

"You went on two dates!"

"I was just trying." She looked nervously around us, and when she spoke again, it was a whisper. "I feel like I have to know."

"Anne," I said, reaching for her. "Please. It's Thomas, isn't it. It's that guy."

To my horror, she blushed.

"It's not important who it is. But I felt like I should tell you."

"But did you have to tell me *here*? Christ on crutches," I said, faltering. "I'm going to be sick."

"I'm not *doing* anything. I just needed a

nice time."

"How many nice times?"

She swallowed. "I shouldn't have said anything."

"No!" I said. "Yes. No! We need rules about this! I literally had no idea that . . ." I noticed a man watching us. I glared and he fell back into conversation with the people he was with. "I just didn't think that we were at this point," I whispered back. "I wished that you had said something earlier. I don't know what this means."

"I'm not sure you get any input on what I do or don't say. Or when. Listen," she said, flustered. "It was wrong for me to tell you here, but it's also not a big deal. Yet. I just wanted you to know that I'm not sitting around making pros and cons lists. To really work through this, I have to know . . . I have to know my options."

"I can't hear this," I said. "I can't take this right now."

"I know," she said, taking my hand. "I'm sorry. I guess I just felt, when I heard you call out that letter . . ." Her fingers were cool. My palms were sweaty. I wanted to collapse.

"Let's pretend I didn't say anything," she said, giving my hand a tepid squeeze. "You can throw my little confession in the wash."

"Please don't sleep with him," I begged. "Please."

She could have countered by saying that I had no right to ask her such a thing, but instead, she pulled away from me — crossing the room to gather up Camille and disappear out of sight.

The extent to which I'd misjudged our progress astounded me. With the positive energy and buzz around the opening, I thought we'd have a talk that night, that maybe she'd say she missed me, that we could do dinner alone soon. And when she'd said she couldn't stay long at the show with Camille, I'd been so far gone in positivity that I thought she might suggest that I stop by the house after the opening, and that maybe — sweetest maybe — things would progress in such a way that I'd never make it back to my apartment. In a state of profound disbelief and disappointment, I started transferring the slick mess out of each machine to the body bags.

Azar made a second announcement, this one for the drying portion, which drew a larger crowd. Humans are always keen to gape at devastation.

Alice was on hand to help me operate the engraver. As I hung each item, she punched a description and the donator's name onto a dog tag, which I draped around the peg to hang over the corresponding thing. Most everything had survived, curiously, although the photographs and posters had become barely recognizable surfaces of gasoline and ink. The stuffed animals were horrifying, which meant they looked like art, and Lisa's letter had been reincarnated into a ball of greasy pulp. If I had a pair of fake teeth to add to it, her final missive would have looked like a teratoma.

The drying portion was a protracted process involving latex gloves and the careful transfer of the ruined articles into giant bins. As soon as something was hung, it started to drip. A boon I hadn't thought of before was that all of the soiled articles looked like they were dripping blood. Even before I was finished, the cameras started going off behind me. One person even hooted. I thanked the faceless cheerleader for restoring a small fraction of my pride.

Several people in the audience had donned protective face masks, spurring the photographers to take pictures of the crowd. While I was answering some questions for a Finnish journalist, Anne came up and announced that they were heading home. Camille was at her side with her nose pinched.

"I know. It's like a gas station," I said, going to ruffle Camille's hair and then stopping myself when I realized that my gloved fingers were covered in gunk. "But what'd you think?"

Camille was too distracted by the Finnish journalist's conspicuous lack of eyebrows to compliment her dad.

"I'm sorry for interrupting," said Anne to the journalist, "but we really have to go. Congratulations, Richard." It came out sweet and sad.

"Jesus, will you call me?"

Anne looked embarrassed that I'd asked this out loud. "Honey, say congratulations to your papa?"

The minute Anne and Camille pushed their way out of earshot, the journalist was on me. "Is that your wife?"

I watched Anne kiss the people she knew in the crowd good-bye.

"Well," I said, peeling my ruined gloves off. "She was."

22

By all the benchmarks that the art world possessed, the show was a success. I got great press in *Text zur Kunst, BOMB* magazine, and *Art Forum,* along with a lengthy write-up from Lisa's former employer, the *Herald Tribune.* I was even contacted for an interview with *The New York Times,* for which I had to have a professional head shot taken for the first time in my life.

By mid-April, the situation in Iraq had become an absurdist, ghastly mess. When the bronze statue of Hussein fell, massive looting started and continued unhindered by the foreign forces there. In a crystalline revelation of its international priorities, the United States sent troops to guard the Oil Ministry and nothing else, leaving Iraq's National Museum to be stripped bare of its "cultural inheritance" — the inheritance of something foreign and thus unimportant, belonging as it did to the great dark realm of the "other."

According to the news reports, it was mayhem in the streets: looters running barefoot with used office chairs and desks, ceiling fans and smashed computers piled on top of donkeys. A reporter from the Associated Press claimed he saw a group of men wheeling a hotel's grand piano down the street. The news reports seemed almost giddy with the magical realism of it: *just look at what they're taking!* Everything laced with visual contradictions between "there" and "here."

There: car bombs; dusty basements stockpiled with foreign-purchased weapons; journalists dying in hotel bars three minutes after ordering a Schweppes; terror and confusion only worsened by long periods of silence.

And Paris? My Paris? Phone calls from Azar that my installation was going to sell. Three different potential buyers, possibly a fourth. Articles and sound bites that I was some kind of soothsayer. Overexcited, underexposed bloggers claiming that a little-known Englishman was "the new face of French art." I should have been happy, proud of myself, even. But in those first weeks of too-warm, overpollinated April, I felt like the new face of despair.

Anne had rebuffed all my attempts to discuss the trajectory of our marriage, along with my passive-aggressive inquiries into her "dates." *Time,* she kept telling me. She needed more *time.* But with my installation over, I had nothing but time, and even though I knew that forcing her to talk through things when she wasn't ready would backfire, it was getting harder and harder to stay quiet.

And then, as if things weren't glum enough, *The Blue Bear* returned. Claiming it would be bad for his business karma to store a painting that had already sold, Julien asked me if I wouldn't take it. I wanted to call Anne to talk about it, to see if she didn't want it — or at least, would store it — in our much larger house. *Her* larger house.

But I didn't want the painting to arrive at la Rue de la Tombe-Issoire in defeat, a pitiful reminder, a deflated balloon. I had visions of her instructing deliverymen to carry it down to the basement. I saw her head cock as she watched them maneuver it down the stairs, I saw her going down there later and covering it up with a sheet, her face filled not with regret, but resignation. And what if *he* was there? The faceless dater? The man who was wining and dining and romancing my wife? What if they had a drink after the delivery van left, and he asked her about the painting: why was the bear blue? She would pour wine for both of them and laugh, or shrug her shoulders. She would say it didn't matter. That she couldn't remember. That it was just this thing she had to store in the house.

And so I told Julien to deliver the damn thing to my flat. It arrived in a white van one morning, driven by a surly Greek who equated "art handling" with the literal dumping of the article onto the street, followed by an über-succinct text message: *HERE.*

Getting a 117 × 140 cm painting up one of the narrowest staircases in Paris was no small feat, but fitting it into my 14m2 apartment was a tour de force of space management.

I tried hanging it behind my bed, but it only fit if I tilted it ninety degrees so that it was in the shape of a diamond. It almost fit behind my clothes rack except for a delinquent curve where the right side of the wall folded into the back wall of the bathroom. I even attempted to hang it on the ceiling of my dining room slash kitchen, but there was something discomforting about having it above my head. Finally, I decided to hang it on the wall just to the right of the stovetop.

This wall also curved, causing the painting to wobble back and forth each time the front door was opened or closed.

It didn't look good there. It looked awful in my flat. It dominated what little space there was, and plus, it was absorbing all of the malodorous cooking fumes from my fish-sauce-loving neighbors. And yet I felt comforted to have my old friend back. It seemed appropriately pathetic that it had made so many useless journeys only to end up in a glorified hovel with tired, old me. With two more weeks of exposure to the neighbors' abuse of condiments, the fissures of the canvas would take on the odor of an unwashed sexual organ, an olfactory essence that would stay with the painting for the duration of its life. This, too, felt appropriate. After all, I felt like I was emanating something putrid myself. The damp heat of aimlessness. The soured odor of defeat.

The time passed. And passed, and passed. Young men whizzed about on scooters in collarless jackets and the lilies bloomed. I found a café to have coffee in the morning where I could stand at the counter and listen to the regulars discuss the scores from the previous night's games. I'd listen to the waiters complain about the things that had or hadn't arrived from the Rungis Market for the midday lunch service, complain about the fact that even the Americans were no longer leaving tips.

And I started pity-watching the *Witness* videos again. My parents, the Gadfreys, the Adsits, their recorded happiness, in loops. After my morning coffee, I'd lope around the Canal Saint-Martin area where the neighborhood's graffiti artists sprayed their tags underneath the street artist Invader's famous ceramic space aliens, looking for another direction in which to take my filming, something that had nothing to do with romance.

But I couldn't help it. Morning after morning, I found myself stealing images from lives that weren't mine. I didn't actually film people — I'd become too depressed to find the energy to use my camera again — but mentally, I cataloged their joys, storing them like cathartic shots of serotonin for the times I felt the worst. In the evenings, especially, when I had nowhere left to roam, when I literally *longed* to watch Cam's nose crinkle with concentration as she squeezed toothpaste onto her alligator toothbrush — it soothed me to think back on the random moments of contentment I'd witnessed that day, to know that there were people out there having so much fun.

On these walks, I sought out fleeting moments. Intimate little poems. A pair of women's sandals left by the canal. The cork to a champagne bottle rolled beneath a bench. A child sleeping against her father's shoulder. A woman's finger pressing the wet spot on his T-shirt where their child had drooled. A balloon in the shape of a dog discarded in the grass. An older woman breaking off baguette pieces for family members on a blanket. A passed bag of dark figs. A young couple leaving a movie theater, their hands going up to shield their eyes from the daylight at exactly the same time. All of these walk-by-and-you-miss-them moments that constituted other people's lives.

It wasn't healthy to back up this sentimental voyeurism against the videos I'd filmed in England, but that's exactly what I found myself doing, night after night. In between the words spoken and the false complaints lobbed — deep sighs about wet towels, too much baking soda put into homemade crusts — in these films, there was the omnipresent palpability of these couples' hard-won love. The irrefutable proof that other people were happy, and I was very sad.

In effect, what I had done with these

videos was to film a giant absence — the more I watched the footage, the more I realized that Anne and I weren't there. If someone asked us questions about our relationship, Anne would turn away. We were losing each other. I had lost her. I have lost my wife.

Near the end of April, I finally got my daughter to myself due not to the fact that she missed me, but rather to canceled sleepovers: most of her girlfriends had the flu that preys on tiny citizens at the change of each season.

I'd planned a parade of activities for us that weekend, each one designed to fill up my emotional Camille bank so that I missed her less viscerally during the week, as well as provide her with happy memories she could overshare with her mother when she got back. In this way, my innocent daughter unknowingly fulfilled two roles: therapist and public relations specialist.

I took her to the zoo nestled in the center of the Jardin des Plantes, which would have been depressing had I not had a five-year-old in hand. While staring at the monkey cage, all Camille saw was furry, alert beings who used their hands and feet in the same way that she did, who hugged their little ones the way that Anne and I hugged her. She didn't see the unkempt cages, the unraked piles of hay soiled with urine; she didn't see how the baboon had lost too much of his fur from stress, or how the mother kept rubbing her back repeatedly — unnaturally — against the bars.

I took her for a lemon butter crepe at Le Train Bleu, the most beautiful restaurant in Paris, if not France. Perched on the second story of the titanic Lyon train station, the space was a gilded celebration of arched ceilings, frenetic molding, champagne buckets, and glitz. Surrounded by elderly couples, businessmen, and Eastern European eye candy, I couldn't have been happier to be there with my little girl. Well, I might have been happier if her single fold of wheat flour hadn't set me back fourteen euros, but I was pretty happy, still.

We went to the movies: *Finding Nemo.* I took her to McDonald's and made her promise not to tell her mom. I bought her a pair of green-and-white ballerina flats with ladybugs on the toe tips. I caught myself staring at her while she was eating, asking questions. She looked so much like her mom.

On Sunday afternoon, my final act as wonder dad was a pony ride through the

Jardin de Luxembourg on the miniature Shetland horses Indian men kept lined up near the tennis courts. There was a sharp wind cutting through the imported palm trees in the park, and when we got back, Camille was exhausted. Anne was coming for her at six, and as it was only four o'clock, I set her up in the bedroom for a nap, promising myself I'd wake her after an hour so that she wouldn't throw a tantrum when her mother tried to put her down at her regular bedtime that night.

I went downstairs to the small table that had been doubling as my dining area and editing room, although I wasn't actually getting any editing done. Over the past weeks, I'd been toying with the idea of turning the interviews into some actual form of art, editing them in a way where I wove them in and out with unrelated content, but I hadn't had the heart to cut anything yet. I just kept watching the films in their entirety. It was embarrassing. A sappy drug.

I sat down and cut to the first film I'd done of my parents and chose one of my favorite parts, seventeen minutes in.

"What's your favorite memory of Dad, Mum?" went my voice.

She was chewing on her finger. "I don't know," she said. "Just one?"

"It's difficult, isn't it?" said my father, beaming. "I'm such a lively man!"

"Let me see now," she said, still biting. "When I told him I was pregnant, he wore a pillow to work. Under his jumper. You remember that?"

My dad laughed. She continued: "And then there was a, remember, we were coming back from our honeymoon in Italy? We were in this small plane, just a ten-seater, really, and there was all this turbulence. It was awful."

My father was nodding in agreement.

"And it just got worse and worse. And your father, whenever we've taken a plane together, when it gets bumpy, he holds my hand. So it was getting terrible, we had two seats next to each other, and there was this narrow aisle and just one seat to our right with this young girl in it, remember? She was sixteen or seventeen maybe, and she was terrified. I think it was her first time flying. She kept rocking back and forth. And your dad just reached across the aisle for her hand. He didn't ask or anything, he just took it. You remember? And we sat like that, the three of us, until the turbulence passed."

"That was a tough plane ride." My dad coughed.

"That's it?" My voice again. "That's your

favorite memory?"

"It was a very kind moment, Richard," said my mother. "When I get angry with him, I like to remember how he made that girl feel safe."

There was a long period of them not speaking. My mother drummed her fingers on the table. My father watched her hand. I felt suffocated by the anaconda crush of it: silence. Silence. Silence.

All of a sudden there was a knock on the door. The Jesuits again. I put the film on pause but I didn't get up; I decided to see how long it would take them to give up and go away.

The knock became more insistent. I switched the video on-screen to the one of Harold and Rosie. I didn't need a bunch of adolescents from the Society of Jesus catching me red-eyed, viddying my own parents.

Another knock. "Richard?" went a woman's voice. "It's me." Warmth flooded through my body when I realized it was Anne.

I jumped up and undid the flimsy latch that masqueraded as a lock.

"Hey!" I said, surprised.

"Hey."

"Did you want to come in?"

She cocked her head. "It's five."

"Come in?" I swung the door open.

"It's five, Richard. I was supposed to get her at five." She was still standing in the hallway.

I lowered my voice to a whisper. "She's sleeping. I thought that we said six?"

Anne bit her lip. "Did we?" She exhaled. "Shit. Well, I have some errands to do, so —" She rifled through her purse.

"No, no," I said again. "Come in! I can wake her, or we can just —" She stepped into the flat. I put my hand on her collar, insinuating that I wanted to take her coat.

"Oh," she said, loosening one arm out. "Thanks."

When I turned to hang her coat up, I heard her gasp.

"Oh. Shit!"

"Yeah," I said, frowning. "I told you."

"Look at that," she said quietly, reaching out to touch *The Blue Bear.* "You could have . . . we could have stored it for you."

"Yeah. I don't know, I didn't want to . . . I kind of wanted it back."

She turned to me and smiled. My girl-friend. My wife. I remembered back in Cape Cod how she'd fall asleep with a book below her stomach while I was painting, the curtains lifting and falling in the breeze, the rhythm of her breath. The swell of her small

453

stomach harboring our first and only child.

"Well, it's good . . . it's nice to see it," she said, folding her arms. She stared at it awhile longer before taking in the cassettes and wires and the black pads of my headset.

"What is all this?" she asked, picking up a cassette tape.

"Oh," I said, moving to the table, wishing I had a tablecloth to throw over my sentimental mess. "It's nothing."

"And who's that?" She pointed to the frozen frame of Harold and Rosie that I'd hastily thrown up on the screen instead of my parents. They were caught in an embrace. Rosie still had her apron on. It was climbing up her bust.

"That's a guy I became friendly with on the ferry, actually."

She raised her eyes.

"He's — that's Harold. And his wife."

"But what is it?"

"It's nothing, it's just a project I started a long time ago that I was messing about with."

There was a noise upstairs.

"She's sleeping?" said Anne, looking toward the staircase.

I nodded. She picked up another tape.

"You don't want to talk about it? When did you start it?"

I sat down on the seat under the staircase. "It's nothing — nothing official. I was just faffing about the first time I was back at my parents', you know, this fall." I felt like I was stuttering. The words came out all wrong. "I found this old video camera, and I started filming them. Interviewing them, really. And then I started interviewing other people. Not a lot."

"Other couples?"

I shrugged. "Yeah."

"So it's a documentary?"

"No," I said. "I don't know."

She turned an empty cassette case over in her hands.

"You never mentioned it."

"Well, there's not much to mention. It isn't very serious."

Anne looked at all the crap spread on the table. "It doesn't look that way to me."

"I don't know what it is."

"Can I watch some?" she asked, her hand hovering over the keyboard.

I swallowed. "I don't know."

"Is it pornographic?"

"Jesus!" I said. "No! It's my parents, and their neighbors, and then the guy I met on the ferry, and his wife of like a zillion years."

She looked contemplative. "So, can I watch some?"

I looked up the staircase, hoping Camille might choose that moment to wake up.

"It's not fully edited. It's not even close. But . . ." I reached for the mouse. "I can show you Harold. He sells copy machines."

I unclicked the pause button. Harold was rubbing his wife's back, and she had her head against his shoulder. Light streamed through the window behind their sink, illuminating the oven.

"Where is this?" Anne whispered.

"That's at Harold's," I said. "In Great Gaddesden. Not far from my parents'."

Anne nodded and continued watching. Harold and Rosie were embracing because Rosie had admitted something that made her sad. Their hug lasted a long time. Finally, after kissing his wife on the cheek, Harold sat back down. Rosie rubbed at her eyes with the dish towel and sat down as well.

"You want to keep going?" said my voice. "Because we could stop."

"No, please," said Rosie. "I'm embarrassed. It's such a silly thing." Harold reached out for her hand. "Ask us anything. Something funny."

"Okay," I went. "Can Harold cook?"

Rosie burst out laughing. "Can he cook?! Well, he can grill things? He can cook an egg. For a lot of men, that's cooking. Yes, I'd say he cooks."

"I make a very good ham sandwich."

Rosie nodded vigorously. "That's true. Very generous with the mayonnaise, though, isn't he?"

"See?" I said to Anne, reaching for the keyboard. "It's not exactly deep stuff."

She swatted at my hand. "Shh," she said. "They're sweet."

"And Rosie," went my voice again. "Can she cook?"

"Does a bat have wings?" said Harold. "Oh, she can cook, all right. Rosie used to make a blood pudding that would have you —"

An alarm started going off on my phone. I turned it off and put the video on pause.

"What's that?" asked Anne.

"I was going to wake Camille up so she'd sleep tonight, you know?"

Anne nodded.

"Should I wake her?"

Her eyes widened. "I don't know." She looked at the computer screen. Harold was twisting the dish towel around his fist, and Rosie was frozen in midlaugh. "I guess so," Anne said. "She's got a big week."

"Right," I said, standing. "Are her friends better?"

Anne shrugged. "Not really. Everyone's still got the flu. Do you want me to get her?" she said, half standing as I walked toward the stairs.

"No, no," I said. "Stay comfortable. Hopefully she's not too deep asleep."

"Can I watch more of this?" she asked.

My face reddened from surprise. "Well, sure," I said. "If you want to."

"Is that all right?"

I stood there like an idiot, staring at the screen. The heat from Anne's presence carried over me in waves. There was something in the air that was making me feel both nauseous and excited, like the artificial hunger you get from eating foods cooked with MSG.

"Is that all right?" she repeated.

"Sure," I said, leaning over to switch to another video clip. "But it's really nothing. You just — this is the beginning of Harold's bit, so you just hit play."

A few seconds later, at the top of the staircase, instead of Harold's baritone I heard my own voice ring out:

"Okay. Welcome to my parents. Edna. George. When did you two meet?"

"We met swimming. She had on a red suit."

"A one-piece."

"I offered her an ice cream."

"A Mr. Whippy! You know, from the little lorry that used to pull up outside?"

I put my hand against the wall to steady myself. The clever girl had figured out how to watch the video of my parents. I felt flushed with shame for both the fact that she was seeing it and the fact that I'd tried to hide that I'd been watching it before she arrived. In the bedroom, I sat down on the edge of the mattress and listened to the breathing of our sleeping child. My parents' voices filled the kitchen below. I was overtaken with the need to cry.

I moved closer to the top of the bed and bent my head toward Camille's. I put my hand to her forehead — it was clammy, but not too hot. The poor thing was caught in the snarled web of sleep. It felt cruel to wake her up, but something dark was building inside of my small flat. An undeniable sadness was seeping up into this room and I was worried that if I didn't get Anne and Camille out, I would never be able to feel safe in this place again. They were too near to me. I loved them too much. And the love overtaking me combined with the fact that I was going to spend another evening alone, doing nothing with it, being weighted down to motionlessness by my own actions, made me want to get it over with, and fucking be alone.

"Sweetheart," I said, my hand on her shoulder. *"Mon lapin."* I shook her gently. "Mommy's here, darling. It's time to go home."

I watched one eye open. And glare.

"Mmmmggghh," she went, pulling the blanket over her.

I pulled it back down. "I know, love," I said. "It's no fun, is it, but you have to wake up. You'll have school tomorrow, and —"

"I want to keep sleeping!" she said, turning the other way. "I want to stay here!"

I tried tickling her back.

"You'll be back soon, love. But Mom's waiting downstairs."

"It's so *stupid*!" she said into her pillow. "I don't want to!"

My chest burned. Again, I felt an aching need to cry. I would wait until they were gone, though. I would wait, and I'd shut down that bloody computer, and then I'd sit inside the bathroom that was the size of most people's sinks and I would do it. I would cry.

"Camille," I said, "let's go now. Your mom needs you to go."

Camille tossed off the blanket.

"You're *mean,*" she said. "I don't want to."

"I know, sweetheart. But haven't we had fun?"

I brushed hair out of her sticky, sleepy face and saw that she had tears smarting in her eyes.

"Oh, love," I said, holding her. "Don't you feel well?"

"I'm tired," she said, her face hot against my jumper. "I want to stay here."

"Darling," I said, kissing her head. "Trust me, I know. But your mum's made a great dinner and, here you go, let's get your shoes. Can you put your shoes on?"

Camille kicked and frowned.

"There you go, love. Let's try to be smiley for your mom, yeah? She'll want to hear about the zoo, I think. And the horses?"

Camille shrugged her little shoulders.

"Okay," she said, "Fine."

I had to help her to her feet, as she was still wobbly with sleep. I tossed the duvet back into place and thumped at the pillows so that I wouldn't be totally depressed when I came back up and saw the imprint of a body that was no longer there.

"Let's go, then, pumpkin," I said, reaching for her hand. "Careful with the stairs? You got your jacket?"

461

"It's downstairs."

"Tickety-boo, then," I said. "Down the hatch we go!"

I started down the stairs with Camille behind me, turning now and then to make sure she put the right foot on each step. Anne had had a fit when she'd seen this staircase, dubbing it the architectural personification of an accident waiting to happen.

At the foot of the stairs, I turned and reached for my daughter, and swung her down the rest of the way so we were both facing the kitchen table. Anne closed the computer abruptly, wiping at her eyes.

"Hey there, Camille bird!" she said, bending down to take Cam in her arms. Watching the two of them together made my heart drop all the way down to the soles of my damn shoes.

"You've got everything, sweetheart? You've got everything, yes?" Anne stood up and nervously ran her hands through her hair. A little bit of mascara had smudged beneath her right eyelash.

"That was great." She nodded in the direction of the computer. "That was something. Really."

Before I could respond, she reached to the right of *The Blue Bear* for Camille's coat.

462

"You were having a great nap, weren't you?" she said, helping Camille into it. "A lovely little rest?" She helped Camille get her other arm into her jacket and then she came to me. She kissed me once on each cheek, letting her lips linger there just long enough that when she pulled away, I could feel dampness on my skin.

"It's very good," she said. "It is."

My throat caught. I just nodded. I couldn't say anything else.

She swallowed hard. "Okay, sweetie, kiss your daddy."

And Camille did.

Anne cast another look at *The Blue Bear* and then stared down at the floor. It seemed like she was about to say something, but she didn't. After thanking me for the weekend, she pulled the door open for Camille and followed our daughter through my traitorous door.

As poorly insulated as the building was, I could hear their every footstep. Little feet and big feet making their way down the wooden hallway, then stepping carefully onto the first turn of the winding staircase, which was wooden, and slippery, and also classified as an accident waiting to happen in Anne's architectural book.

I waited until I couldn't hear footsteps in

the stairwell anymore. Then I sat down and opened the computer. The film was paused on an image of the TV in my parents' house. I rewound the video several seconds to confirm what I knew Anne had seen.

"Oh, I wanted to talk to Camille, dear!" said my mother, turning toward the camera. "My goodness, is that on again?"

"It wasn't Camille." My voice. The camera zoomed in on my mum's face. "And yes."

"It's not going to be a very interesting video you're making," went my father. "Us watching the tube."

"Excuse me. But how do you make love last?" My voice — the lens focused on my father's aging face.

"Honey, are you all right, dear?" My mother picked up the remote control from the coffee table.

The camera panned from my mother, who looked worried, to my father, who looked confused, and then back again.

My voice: "No."

"Sweetheart?" My lovely mum got up from the couch. The camera jiggled as she sat down beside me. I had filmed her face first, then her hand. I had filmed her moving a throw pillow onto the floor so she could put her arm around me.

"Would you put that thing down?" My

mother again.

And then my voice came out strangled, almost choked.

"What do I do?" A pause in which my mother's eyes well up. "What have I done?"

More images of the television. An attractive woman was holding up a roll of toilet paper, demonstrating how thick and sturdy each individual ply was. And then the film salt-and-peppered into nonexistence.

I sat there staring at the computer, stunned that Anne had seen this. Seen me falter, seen me blabber, seen me with my parents, my voice broken in half. And I ached to realize how much I missed them all at that moment, how alone I felt without my parents, daughter, wife. How safe it had made me feel when my mother had come over to me, had sat by me on the couch. I was remembering the feel of her hand moving in circles on my back when I heard footsteps on the stairs outside my door. My heart sped up when I recognized two pairs of feet.

There was a kerfuffle in the hallway, and then a knock again. I opened the door and found Anne standing in the hallway, holding Camille's hand.

"Sorry," she said, "Can I come in?"

"Did you forget —" I stopped myself. "Sure."

"Camille, love," she said, turning. "Mommy's just going to be a second, all right? Here." She punched the switch that started the timer for the hallway light. "Just one sec."

I opened up the door wider and whispered, "You're just going to leave her there?"

"Leave the door open a crack," she said. Then she pulled me behind the door, near *The Blue Bear,* where our daughter couldn't see us. "Just a second, sweetie!" she called again.

"Richard, listen," she said, her face turning grim. "It's about . . . the dates."

I closed my eyes. "Don't do this," I said. "Not again. I can't."

"No, listen, it's —" Her voice was trembling. "I *did* go out a couple times. I got a babysitter, the whole thing. I got —" She turned around nervously. "You all right, little rabbit?" she called out.

Camille yelled back, "No!"

Anne started to whisper. "And it just felt like — I tried. I really tried to. But you have to tell all these *stories,* you know? You have to explain everything and everybody, you can't just drop names, and it was just so — it was just so easy to make this buffoon fall for me, but it was also so depressing."

"I am telling you that I can't take this," I said, my legs going numb. "Not now. Not here."

She took my stupid face into her hands.

"I want you to come back. Richard. I think you should come back."

"Mommy!" Camille cried. "The lights went off! I'm scared!"

Anne turned and yanked open the door, slammed her hand against the light switch again.

"Put your arm through the door, Camille," she said. "I'll hold your hand. But stick your finger into your other ear, though. Mom and Daddy need to talk."

"Jesus," I whispered. But Camille did it. Anne stayed firmly planted behind the partly opened door holding on to our daughter's tiny hand. Outside in the hall, Camille started humming.

"It's not going to be easy," she said. "I know it. But I want you to come back."

"You're serious," I said, feeling my chin start to tremble. "Please tell me that you're serious."

"I am serious," she said. "I'm serious. But I won't be your second choice."

I couldn't help it. I started crying. "You're

not my second choice," I choked. "You're not."

"I don't know what will happen," she said, looking down at the small white arm poking through the door. "But I miss you. And I miss our fucking life."

"*Mom!*" cried Camille. "The lights went off again!"

"*Goddammit,*" Anne hissed, squeezing Camille's hand. "Just a second!" With her free hand, she smoothed her hair back. "I think that this should happen tonight. Like, now."

"Now?!" I balked. "What will we tell her?"

"I don't know. I just don't —"

"Mo-om!"

"Jesus, Cam, all right!" Anne yanked the door open. "Camille, I swear to God, I just need one more minute. Hit that switch there. I promise. Then we'll all go home."

"I don't want to hit the light."

"*Je te jure,* Camille, *si tu ne —*"

I dashed out into the hallway and hit the light for her, promising her that we needed just one more minute inside.

Then Anne closed the door behind us and pulled me toward her and kissed me, kissed me deep and right.

"There's no going back on this," she said, her breath hot against my skin. "Forward is forward."

"Cam's gonna need therapy for this hall-way shit," I said, kissing her above her eyebrow, on the corner of her lips. Deep inside my pants, I felt my seigneur start to rise.

"I've already got her seeing someone," she said, prohibiting my retort with another kiss. "We'll talk about it. We've got time."

23

The widower who owned my small apartment was delighted to hear that I was moving out. Instead of letting it out to the friend he had first mentioned, he was thinking of using it himself when he came back from his cruise.

"You use so much less space when you're alone," he said over the phone. "And the bathroom! I can't believe it. A bar of soap, a tube of toothpaste. I'm like a bachelor again."

After deciding whether or not we should pursue some kind of couples therapy (we decided not to), Anne and I tackled the question of how to announce to our families that we were staying together. Finally, we decided that if we started showing up places together, they'd figure it out. It wasn't their business, really, as long as we knew what we were doing. We were back together again. Living in the same house. Quarreling over the fact that I'd brought back unsalted butter from the store instead of salted. What other ending could they want?

Explaining things to Camille was another matter altogether. We admitted to her that we'd been having some problems, but that we'd worked them out together, that that's what grown-ups did. I still worry that my departure and reappearance will lead her to think that marriage is expandable — that it ebbs and flows over time, with the principal characters coming and going as they please. But how can you tell the truth, the real truth, to a five-year-old? Expandable is exactly what a marriage is. If you refuse the possibility that bad things might happen, a marriage cannot survive.

It isn't easy. Neither of us is joyful every day, but there is an equilibrium and a rightness that has returned to our lives — the sense that we are doing exactly what we are supposed to be doing, and together. And though it would be a lie to say that we've had an about-face in the bedroom, there is an openness between us now that makes our coming togethers feel like the truest version of love — love in all its tenderness, its frustration, and the realization that despite its shortcomings, this place, with this person, is the place we're meant to be.

I never found out if Anne actually slept with the person she'd been seeing, nor if it had been Thomas, and it's possible that I never will. Sometime after I moved back into the house, she admitted that he'd been transferred back to Luxembourg, but that's all that she will say about it, and over time, I've realized that that has to be enough.

Composed and faultless from the outside, Anne-Laure has a reserve of lust and strength and anger that I rarely see, but it is there, and it makes her capable of hiding things from me. When we've made love lately, I've noticed a lack of self-consciousness in her that I haven't seen in a long while, and it makes me think that something *did* happen with that person, whoever he may be. Little things — the way she'll touch her breasts when she's on top of me, the veil of sweat she no longer wipes from her brow. She acts noticed and beautiful, and it makes me think they fucked. It makes me think that she spent time — or maybe just a moment — with someone who took time to appreciate her body, who truly found her beautiful, who made her feel powerful and feminine and mysterious again.

And I can't let it matter. Because in the end, it doesn't. If I let it matter, we'll fall back into a cycle of resentment and claustrophobia again. I love her. I love her deeply. We are in this for the long haul. It isn't always going to be pretty, and we will fall again — somewhere down the road, one of us is going to mess up. It might not be with another person — it might not be an affair — but there will be a hurdle. A reckoning. And a making up.

Because in the end, that's why some of us stupid humans get married. Because we know that we can lose each other, and find each other again. Because we're capable of forgiveness. Or at least, we *think* we are. I wouldn't have been able to forgive myself if I had been in Anne's position. And the fact that she had the courage to bring us back together makes me love her, and our small family, and our future even more.

At the end of May, *WarWash* sold to a German publishing magnate who spent a lot of time in Paris. Anne went to retrial with her winemakers, and they lost. In two years' time, all our favorite bottles would have swollen lady bellies on them.

We'd resumed our Sunday lunches with the Bourigeauds, but only once a month. Although it appeared to be true that Alain's opinion of me hadn't shifted much either way, I'd lost face with Inès. I was in a sentimental meritocracy. I had to prove myself worthy before she was ready to have me back.

As for *The Blue Bear,* it spent most of the early summer propped up against our dining room wall. It was both a comfort and a hindrance, but every time we started to talk about where we could put it, no place seemed right. It carried history with it now, and not all of it was good. It was much too loaded an object to put in our bedroom, and Camille had long ago abandoned any desire to have it back in her room, which was currently covered with glow-in-the-dark posters of constellations, her latest obsession. The living room didn't feel like the right place for it, and we agreed that if it were in the dining room, every time we had people over, it would invite their questions. *The Blue Bear* had reverted to what it originally had been, a private link between Anne and me, difficult to explain but completely comprehensible to us both.

But it couldn't very well sit against the wall forever, and it seemed like a step in the wrong direction to store it in the basement once again. On our eighth wedding anniversary, Anne told me she had a solution. She also told me that it would require quite a bit of trust.

"It's ours now, right?" she asked. "To do with as we please? You have papers to prove that?"

I said yes, excited. She was on the fringe of lawyer-speak, which meant that she was planning something potentially unlawful. She'd hired a babysitter for Camille and told me that we were going out to lunch, but that first she needed — we needed — to drop something off. And that I should wear sneakers, be prepared for a long walk.

By 11 a.m., we were on the sidewalk with *The Blue Bear* strapped haphazardly to a luggage dolly. Somewhat bluntly, Anne announced that we had to push it toward the Seine.

"This is our anniversary present? You're throwing it in the river?"

She shook her head. "Come on."

We pushed our way up the Rue de la Tombe-Issoire, which was harder than I thought, what with the dolly wheels spinning out every which way on the bumpy sidewalk. We went by the grim medical buildings around the Port Royal RER station where the scenery eventually gave way to smaller buildings and shops with roasted chickens in the windows and wicker baskets of fruit.

We passed parks where tiny children pushed plastic objects through playgrounds, watched by grandparents shooing pigeons from their charges. Young people on bicycles rolled merrily through puddles and a public bus pulled up to a corner and yawned, its passengers descending in a small parade of tweed. We walked on through the fourteenth into the sixth, pushing for a while, pausing to talk, with me more amused than nervous as to where our walk would take us. I was glad to just be near my wife, to be taking in various sights and happenings that we could discuss over lunch. As for the painting, I trusted her. Whatever destination she had picked for it, whatever kind of celebration, would be right.

After nearly an hour, we reached the Seine. Without speaking, Anne indicated that we should cross in front of the Institut de France, where they decided which words would enter the French lexicon each year, and push across the Quai de Conti to the Pont des Arts. The metal footbridge that led directly to the Louvre had chain-link guard-rails that were covered — garroted, really — by thousands of padlocks. Lovers, tourists mainly, came to this spot to commemorate their devotion by writing their names on a padlock and locking it to the bridge. This tradition, which had gained popularity in recent years, had offered much-needed diversification to the illegal immigrants selling miniature Eiffel Towers along the river. Now the entrance to the bridge was lined with men selling various-size padlocks, some as small as the lock on a child's diary, others as big as one's hand.

"Okay," said Anne, wiping a little bit of sweat from her forehead. "We're here."

I looked at the tourists taking photos, at the young people bent down in front of the cavalcade of locks to inspect the messages written on them.

"I'm okay if you want to be rid of it, but I don't think I can handle throwing it into the river," I said.

She gestured for me to help her get it over the steps. "We're not."

Once we got the thing to the middle of the bridge, Anne pushed it to the side and leaned against the railing, taking time to admire the domino view of bridges beyond bridges, white arcs across the Seine.

A man in a brightly patterned tunic approached and asked if we wanted to buy a lock.

"No thanks," Anne said, grinning. "We've got one."

I waited until he approached the couple

477

next to us to speak. "You crazy little donkey," I said. "You just want to leave it?"

She nodded, grinning wide.

"That's the plan?" I asked. "This is our lock?"

She smirked. "Too sentimental?"

"No," I said, basking in our closeness. "It's right."

I looked around at all the people on the Pont des Arts. There had to be at least fifty, maybe more.

"Won't someone chase after us or something?"

"I've put some thought into that," she said, pulling a sheet of paper from her bag. She held it up for me. In typed letters, it read *GRATUIT, VRAIMENT*.

"Free. Really," I repeated.

She reached for my hand. "Are you okay with this?"

"I absolutely am."

We stood there in silence for a while, watching the couples holding out their cameras with one hand to take a photo of themselves on the bridge, the tourists running their fingers along the different locks. Blue ones, gold ones, plastic-coated, plated, initials scrawled in permanent marker, in white correction fluid, some bearing no names at all. In the pink light reflecting off the sprawling Louvre, with the play of the river and the sun, the locks looked like a massive school of fish, happy to be exactly where they were, planning to swim nowhere. All their traveling done.

"Do you know what people do with the keys after they've locked their locks?" Anne asked, trailing her fingers along the painting's edge.

"They keep them," I said, turning my face into the sun.

"Nope," she said. "They throw them in the Seine."

I had a sudden vision of hundreds of keys, covered with algae and plankton, anchored there by whatever wish had been whispered before they had been tossed. "So, artist," Anne said, her head tilted. "Should we see the dear boy off?"

Together, we undid the security cord and lifted the painting off the dolly.

"Jesus," I said. "I'm nervous."

"I know." She giggled. "I am, too."

"Do we run away after, or what? Will someone call the cops?"

"I don't think so," she said. "We'll just go. Although I want to keep the dolly. I use it all the time when —"

"Hey, Esquire," I said "Let's keep it romantic."

She laughed and agreed that I was right, and then I admitted that it *had* been kind of useful for moving large things in the past, and so yes, why not, we'd extricate the dolly.

This bit of business settled, we reached for each other's hand and stared at our big painting.

"Okay," she said solemnly. "Good-bye."

Just behind us, near the steps where the lock sellers gathered, we saw a gendarme giving the illegal vendors a hard time.

"Uh-oh," Anne whispered. "Let's make a break for it. You'll push?"

I nodded, too happy to speak.

"Okay," she said. "On the count of three. One."

I took my position right behind the empty cart.

"Two!"

I put my hands onto the push pads, and watched her bend her knees.

"Three! *Go!*"

Deliriously, ridiculously, we pushed our way forward, past the tourists, past the teen-age lovers, past the vendors hurriedly gathering up their forbidden wares. We scurried down the steps on the right bank and dashed across the street with our unruly dolly, causing cars to honk and drivers to curse. At the perimeter of the Louvre, we crossed the street again, moving quickly toward a square just outside a church.

"Down there," said Anne, pointing toward a small street that ran perpendicular to the park. "Come on!"

Before I turned to run again, I checked to see if there was anyone chasing after us to say that we didn't have the right to do what we had done. There wasn't anyone behind us. There wasn't anyone. On that blue day, that perfect day, our new day in Paris, we were free to carry on.

ACKNOWLEDGMENTS

Rebecca Gradinger: This book would still be in my desk drawer if it weren't for you. You worked almost as hard as I did to make this happen. I'll be forever thankful that it did.

Sally Kim and the fantastic team at Touchstone: Since our first encounter, I've been waiting for the other shoe to drop, but apparently, it isn't going to. Not only did I find the kindest, most even-keeled, and enthusiastic of editors, but she came backed by a delightful and talented team. Susan Moldow, David Falk, Meredith Vilarello, Brian Belfiglio, Jessica Roth, Wendy Sheanin, Christine Foye, John Muse, Paul O'Halloran, Elisabeth Watson, Cherlynne Li, Linda Sawicki, Carolyn Reidy, Melissa Vipperman-Cohen, and Sylvie Greenburg at Fletcher & Company: Thank you all for believing in this book.

To my family: From the red tent with

interior pockets for my journals that fit around my mattress to the electric typewriter on which I wrote my first stories, as a little girl you gave me the means and space to dream. By not questioning my decisions, you gave me the confidence to keep making the right ones. Thank you for all you do.

Gabby: I still reach for my phone sometimes to call you. I know you're somewhere reading this with our New Year's Eve noisemakers and a cheap bottle of champagne. I did it! You're always in my heart.

Annie: Thank you for understanding me. Gianni: Thank you for your generosity and your bon vivance.

My friends! You have danced with me, cooked with me, and survived my circuitous storytelling after too much Côtes du Rhône. Thank you for the decadence and beauty you've brought into my life.

Thank you to the teachers at Greenwich Academy who showed me so much support at a young age, and especially to the late Candace Barackman, who, when I started crying during a particularly grueling SAT math tutoring session, made me cry even harder by saying, "You just need to take this dumb test and you'll be done with it! Everyone knows you're going to be a writer."

Thank you to the literary magazines who have supported my work and to the literary cheerleaders who have let me read it out loud. Thanks especially to Halimah Marcus, Benjamin Samuel, and Josh Milberg at *Electric Literature,* the good folks at *Tin House, Slice Magazine, The Cupboard,* and Penina Roth. Thank you Jim Shepard, Maggie Shipstead, Kevin Wilson, and Ned Beauman for saying such nice things out loud. Matt Bialer, thanks for being there first.

Mylo: Thank you for keeping my chair warm. And my heart.

Gabriela: My unexpected comet, my lucky loaf of bread — you were with me for each word of this. Thank you for letting me be a better version of myself.

And finally, Diego: You saw me through the beginning, the almost-end, and the transformation of this Blue Bear. There's no one else I would have shared this journey with. Thank you for our life.

Grateful acknowledgment is made to the following for permission to reprint the selected excerpts:

Excerpt from "Everything Good Between Men and Women" from *Tremble* appears courtesy of C. D. Wright.

Excerpt from *Fear and Trembling/Repetition* (Kierkegaard's Writings, Volume VI) by Søren Kierkegaard, edited and translated by Howard V. Hong and Edna H. Hong, copyright © 1983 by Howard V. Hong, appears courtesy of Princeton University Press.

Excerpt from *Søren Kierkegaard's Journals and Papers, Vol. 6: Autobiographical, Part 2: 1848–1855* by Søren Kierkegaard, edited by Howard V. Hong and Edna H. Hong, appears courtesy of Indiana University Press.

Excerpt from "Brits 45 Mins from Doom"

ABOUT THE AUTHOR

Courtney Maum graduated from Brown University with a degree in comparative literature and French translation. She then lived in France for five years where she worked as a party promoter for Corona Extra, which had everything to do with getting a visa and nothing to do with her degree. Today, Maum splits her time among the Berkshires, New York City, and Paris, working as a creative brand strategist, corporate namer, and humor columnist. She's also the author of the chapbook *Notes from Mexico.*

courtneymaum.tumblr.com